SHALLOW ROCK

B.E. SMITH

Copyright © 2024 by B.E. Smith

Layout design and Copyright © 2024 by Next Chapter

Published 2024 by Next Chapter

Cover art by Jaylord Bonnit

Large Print Edition

This book is a work of fiction. Names, characters, places, and incidents are the product of the author's imagination or are used fictitiously. Any resemblance to actual events, locales, or persons, living or dead, is purely coincidental.

All rights reserved. No part of this book may be reproduced or transmitted in any form or by any means, electronic or mechanical, including photocopying, recording, or by any information storage and retrieval system, without the author's permission.

CHAPTER ONE

Lost Lake, New York: June 15th, 1973.
SATURDAY

Deputy Kelly Mackinaw brought her Plymouth Duster to a slow, rolling stop. There was something up ahead in the fog. She'd been watching for wildlife, but this looked human.

"What is that?" she asked, leaning over the steering wheel.

Mitch Herkemer uncurled from his slouch in the passenger seat. "Where?"

The eyes had caught her attention. The figure was absolutely still, like any animal caught in the headlights, but there was no shine to its eyes; they were empty black holes.

"Just up ahead, on the shoulder."

It looked like a girl—long hair hanging down past her waist, a faded gray dress, pale skin the color of mist. Kelly frowned. "It's a little girl."

Mitch leaned forward. The windshield wipers on slow automatic swept away the condensation that formed instantly after each pass.

He let out a slow sigh. "That's Sarah Punk," he said.

"What the hell is she doing out here in the middle of the night?"

The wipers made two full passes. "She's a ghost."

The girl appeared to be fading, the fog seeping into her body. Kelly looked at Mitch. She'd only met him a few hours ago, so it was hard to tell if he was pulling her leg. He had to be.

"Fuck off. Who is she? A friend of yours?"

"I wouldn't call her a friend. She's been dead for fifty years."

Kelly had been hearing bullshit ghost stories about Lost Lake ever since she was a girl. She honked the horn.

"Jesus," Mitch said, shocked.

The girl didn't flinch. She stood, shoulders hunched forward, arms at her sides, staring at them with lifeless, hollow eyes while long fingers of murky vapor crawled up her skinny legs.

Kelly flicked on the four-ways and opened the door. "Okay, let's see what she wants."

"She doesn't talk," Mitch said.

Kelly slammed her door shut. Dank, heavy air

wrapped itself around her neck, sending chills creeping down her spine. She'd called their bluff, but the girl still wasn't moving. As she came around the front of the car, the girl's body drifted away from her—thinning, dissolving into the surrounding haze.

"Hey!" Kelly shouted. "What are you doing?"

A hole opened up beneath her eyes. A high-pitched scream sliced through the sluggish air.

Kelly dropped into a crouch. "Son of a bitch!" she shouted.

"She screams," Mitch said from the other side of the car.

"No fucking way." Lightheaded, Kelly stood up.

"Told you," Mitch said.

"That was a bird."

"You think so, man?" Mitch was standing too. His voice was shaky.

Kelly walked towards where the girl had been standing, thinking maybe there was a stump or a rock there in the shape of a human. Nothing but fog and the stink of decay. She crouched down, looking for footprints. Nothing.

"I try to deal with her on a righteous level, you know," Mitch said. "But she still scares the shit out of me."

Kelly scuffed the gravel with her boot. "I don't believe in ghosts," she said.

Mitch sat up straight. "Okay, we're here," he said.

A single, naked bulb cast a blurry, bluish circle over a door to their right. Kelly brought the Duster to a halt on a patch of sloping, hard-packed dirt. She looked around. Besides the light, nothing but fog.

"Never go past the light," Mitch said. "Another twenty yards and you're in the lake."

Kelly put the car in park, set the handbrake for good measure, and got out. She could hear water lapping against rock.

"I see why they call it Lost Lake," she said.

"Yeah, it's not always this bad." Mitch was crouched down with his face close to the doorknob, key in hand.

Kelly held her watch up to her face. Nine o'clock; the drive from Trapper Lake had taken almost an hour and a half. It hadn't been too bad. Except for the bit of weirdness near the end, Mitch had been good company.

"It's got something to do with the shape of the hills, thermal layers, pressure," Mitch said with a shrug. He stood up, opened the door, then turned and nervously scanned the enveloping fog.

"That ghost of yours hang around here?" she asked.

Mitch reached inside the door and flicked on the lights.

"Not just here, but yeah, this is part of her stomping grounds. I guess my dad didn't tell you that."

"Doesn't matter."

"That's cool. I just didn't want you to think we were hiding anything from you," he said.

"Beggars can't be choosers," she replied.

Kelly had been hired on short notice when a Wanakena Sheriff's Department deputy had been abruptly dismissed. Looking to hire the department's first female deputy, Gail Harmon, the Chair of the Board of County Supervisors, had done a thorough search for a suitable candidate. Kelly, an ex-Airforce MP, graduate of the first female course at the New York State Police Academy and granddaughter of a past sheriff of nearby Essex County, was at the top of a very short list.

Kelly had jumped at the chance to get back to the Adirondacks where she grew up. The Buffalo PD, where she had been serving for the past two years, hadn't given her any hassles about her contract. The biggest problem turned out to be finding a place to live. Wanakena was the most sparsely populated county in the United States east of the Mississippi. There were no apartment buildings or rooming houses, and with summer starting, all of the motels and cottages were completely booked up.

Sheriff Herkemer had suggested that she stay at the old lumber camp on Lost Lake, which he was in the process of converting into a year-round residence. It was a work in progress, but it had electricity and indoor plumbing. His son Mitch was up there working on it. There was plenty of room.

They brought in bags of groceries and a cooler from Kelly's car. While Mitch put the stuff away, she had a look around.

The cookhouse was a long rectangular space with a kitchen area at the end of a dining table that ran the entire length of the room. The walls bore the legacy of fifty years of hunters and family campers overlaid on the rough décor of nineteenth-century woodsmen. There were whitened antlers over the door, cryptic markings carved into the beams recording opening dates, weather reports, and the tally of yearly hunts. Ashtrays bearing the logos of forgotten companies lay on the white vinyl table cover.

On one wall, a faded wooden sign proclaiming The Moose River Cooperage Company hung in the middle of a cluster of dusty, black-and-white photographs of lumberjacks and log riders. On the other wall, beer bottle caps of a hundred different brands were nailed side by side in long, orderly rows.

There was an unshaded bulb over the door and another over the kitchen area, where a wood stove co-existed with a new electric range, and a faucet sat next to a cast iron pump.

When he was finished, Mitch took two bottles of Black Label from the old, lever-handled Admiral fridge and handed one to Kelly. "So, what do you think?" he asked.

She nodded. "We had a hunting cabin on Whitefish Lake when I was a kid. A lot smaller than this, but pretty much the same."

"You hunt?"

"Sure. I've got an older sister and two brothers. My sister hated the bush, but it didn't take me long to figure out that I'd rather be out in the woods shooting guns and getting dirty, than staying at home getting supper ready. My mom wasn't crazy about me going out, but my dad was cool with it. What about you?"

"Sure, used to." Mitch paused to consider the question. "It's been a while."

He was a good-looking guy; a solid, six-footer with broad shoulders and big hands. She could imagine how he must have looked in high school, with his blond brush cut, clear blue eyes, and square jaw; he would have been the perfect, All-American North Country Boy. Now, with his hair down to his shoulders and a solid tan, he looked more like one of the Beach Boys. He was around her age; late-twenties, a little spacey, but not a freak. Definitely a whiff of weed coming off of him, but no threatening, macho vibes.

"Come on, I'll show you the best part of this place," he said.

At the far end of the cookhouse there was a screened-in porch with a mismatched assortment of chairs and a comfortably battered-looking couch.

Mitch settled into an Adirondack chair with a sigh. Kelly hooked her patrol belt over a nail by the door and stood looking out at the lake.

Fog lay on the surface of the water under a moon-bright, cloudless sky. She breathed deeply, taking in the cool night air, listening to the throbbing voices of bullfrogs and the whine of mosquitoes fretting against the screen. It felt like home. If she and Mitch could be cool, it would be a great place to stay.

"How many people up here?" she asked.

"Not a lot. Over on your right, is Mrs. Ratsmueller and beyond that, the Margin shack. But nobody's up there this summer. On the left is Mrs. Anderson. Around the other side of the bay, there's the three new cottages. Then, way the hell at the other end of the lake is the Parker place."

"And how many ghosts?"

"Just the one," Mitch replied, looking up at her with an easy smile. "But she gets around."

"Sarah Punk...she's the one who lures kids into swamps and drowns them?"

"There's more to it than that, but yeah, that's her."

Kelly shrugged. Mitch believed in ghosts; most people did. To her, ghost stories, superstitions, religion, were all just bullshit reasons not to face hard truths. She wondered what hard truth the Sarah Punk story was covering up.

It had been a big day for her; the culmination of two weeks of paperwork and interviews, running back and forth between Trapper Lake and Buffalo. She had been sworn in at the station by Gail Harmon. The sheriff had been there with a few members of the police committee and four of the other six deputies. They had ranged in attitude from curious to just shy of openly hostile.

She was dog-tired, but too keyed up to sleep. "Go

ahead, I know you're dying to tell me," she said, resting her rump on the low ledge of the window frame.

She figured that the story would tell her more about Mitch Herkemer than Sarah Punk, which was what she wanted. If there was anyone she needed to be worried about up here, it would be the strange man sleeping in the next room, not some little girl ghost.

CHAPTER
TWO

"According to the people of Shallow Rock, Sarah Punk was a web-footed night crawler who ate frogs and snakes and other slimy things. A pale, skinny creature who was never seen except at dusk or in the early dawn when the mists shrouded the swamp," Mitch began.

"She lived alone in a crooked, half-submerged old shack in Shaker's Bog with her baby boy, Moses. How she came to be in that condition is not clear. Obviously, there was a man involved at some point, but he's never mentioned. The locals claimed she was crazy, but I always thought there might be more to it than that.

"Late one afternoon, two hunters from this lumber camp, Jim and Baron Margin, were out duck hunting in Shaker's Bog. They weren't having any luck, probably drunk. Sarah was out there gathering punk with baby Moses strapped to her back. One of these guys figures she's a duck and takes a shot at her. Wounds her, kills Moses."

"Fuck," Kelly said.

"Yeah. Sarah freaks out, starts wailing and screaming at them. These dicks throw some money at her and get out of there. The townspeople buried Moses in the old cemetery in Shallow Rock. First chance she got, Sarah dug him up and buried him in the muck underneath her shack. Sarah Punk was fourteen years old."

Kelly looked away. "The hunters were never prosecuted," she said.

"No record of anyone even making a complaint."

"How do you know that?"

"I was kinda obsessed with Sarah Punk when I was a kid. She scared me, and I had this feeling that if I could learn the facts about her, it would somehow transform her from a ghost into a real person."

"That makes a lot of sense."

"When I got older, I researched her as best I could. I talked to some of the old loggers that'd worked here. Looked through old police files, newspapers, memoirs, even census data."

"But her name wasn't really Sarah Punk, right? It's a nickname," Kelly said. "Like Polk Salad Annie."

Mitch gave her an appreciative nod. "I never met anyone from outside Wanakena County who knew what punk was."

"So, what did you find out?"

"I found out that Shallow Rock didn't officially

exist until 1936, even though people had been living there since Indian times. It was off the map, beyond the pale, a hole in the wall. A last refuge for French Army deserters, British Army deserters, renegade Indians, runaway servants, escaped slaves, escaped prisoners; anybody who needed a place to hide and was willing to fend for themselves. There never was a church there, so there were no church records."

"So, no record of any Sarah; Punk or otherwise," Kelly said.

"They say that after Moses died, she wandered around Shaker's Bog calling out for her baby, and sometimes sobbing, letting out a terrible, piercing scream, like the one we heard tonight."

"That was a crow," Kelly said. "Came right out of the fog at me, almost took my head off."

"That's why you hit the deck so fast?"

"Natural instinct. All those noises—screaming, sobbing, moaning—they're just night sounds. It's easy to get spooked in the dark," Kelly replied, looking back out over the lake.

Mitch went on. "The next fall, Jim and Baron Margin, along with a third hunter, Joe Stilwell, went back to the exact same place. They didn't give a shit about what they'd done, right? But maybe it *was* on their minds. Anyway, they'd been drinking and jerking around for hours when suddenly they realize... it's getting late..."

He paused until Kelly turned to look at him.

"The sun's going down, and the mist's starting to rise..."

Somewhere out in the fog, a loon called to its mate. Kelly didn't flinch. Mitch was getting into it; he picked up the tempo.

"They hear a mournful Mowwwwsusss... Mowwwwsusss. They see Sarah Punk coming through the mist. Then they don't. One minute she's over here, then she's over there. They start shooting their guns off in the air to scare her, but she keeps coming and she won't stop that terrible moaning. Mowwwwsusss... Mowwwwsusss."

Mitch stood up.

"Suddenly, she rises up out of the murky water right between the two brothers. They freak out and blast away at her." Hunched over, he fired an imaginary shotgun from the hip. "Bam! Bam! They shoot right through her and blow each other away..."

Kelly grinned as she felt the willies crawling up her neck.

Mitch turned slowly towards her, straightening, hands falling to his sides. His voice took on a more normal tone.

"Joe, he got the hell out of there. He went back to the camp, told his story, and then took off. They say he *ran* all the way to San Francisco, jumped on a tramp steamer, and sailed to Shanghai."

"The eyewitness disappeared," Kelly said.

"There's a police report from September 21, 1921.

Hunting accident, two brothers killed by shotgun blasts, Jim and Baron Margin."

"Hard to imagine two guys blowing each other away like that," Kelly said.

"The police never caught up with Stilwell, so all they had was his account—second-hand—from the other lumberjacks, and the bodies which had been out in the swamp for days," Mitch said.

"Then almost anything could have happened."

Mitch sat down and took a swig of beer. "The sheriff was suspicious, of course, but the lumberjacks stuck to their story. He went out to Shallow Rock a week or so after it happened and talked to the locals. Nobody knew anything 'cept that Sarah Punk hadn't been seen for months. They all figured she was dead; drowned herself in the swamp."

"I saw that coming." Kelly finished her beer and wondered if she wanted another one. "Her suicide wasn't reported, right?"

"Shallow Rock people don't go to the police about trivial matters like suicide. They figured she was lying there under her shack with baby Moses. Nobody had the inclination to take a look, not even the sheriff."

"There was no investigation into the death of Sarah Punk," Kelly said.

"Not even a mention of her in the police report about the hunters. The sheriff never speculated on what caused the hunting accident. I guess he didn't want to say that they'd been killed by a ghost."

"Good call."

"After that, there were lots of sightings of the ghost of Sarah Punk wandering around Shaker's Bog and Lost Lake, crying and screaming and calling out for Moses. They said she liked to sneak up on kids who were by themselves and try to lure them into the water."

Kelly shrugged. "It's a cautionary tale. Don't go wandering off by yourself, kid, or Sarah Punk will drag you into the swamp and make you sleep next to her dead baby."

Mitch nodded. "Basic ghost story stuff. But there's more."

"Of course there is."

"Those two hunters, Jim and Baron Margin, were part of a family that has lived in Wanakena County for generations. Several of them worked here as lumberjacks at one time or another. After the war, when operations at the camp were closed down, they built a squatter's shack just down the lake. Some of them lived there for a while, and after that, they used it as a hunting cabin. You had this bizarre situation where Sarah Punk was haunting them, but these hard-assed bastards just ignored her."

"Sounds to me like they didn't believe in her," Kelly said.

Mitch sat back in the chair and clasped his hands behind his head. "Well, maybe they should have."

Kelly waggled her empty beer bottle, but Mitch, looking up at the ceiling, didn't notice.

"In fifty-two," he went on. "A couple of Margin

men, cousins Joe and Frank, were guiding a hunting party they'd flown in from Jersey. The weather was lousy and getting worse; the hunters wanted to go home. There was an argument out on the lake. Frank was put ashore."

Mitch turned towards her. Using his right hand as an airplane, he went on. "Something went wrong right at takeoff. As they were struggling to get aloft, the plane tilted violently to the right, a wingtip caught a wave, and it went cartwheeling into the far end of the lake."

"Into the swamp," Kelly said, playing along.

"*Sarah Punk's* swamp," Mitch added with a profound nod.

Kelly smiled and wondered if he put on this kind of a show for everybody.

"All four men on board were killed. One of them was Joe Margin, son of Jim Margin, who got blown away in the swamp in twenty-one."

"So, a bush plane crashed in bad weather," Kelly said, lifting her beer bottle to her lips and tilting it very high to show that it was empty.

Mitch gave his head a shake. "Sorry, you want another?"

They went back into the cookhouse together.

"Everybody who was up at the lake that day said that they saw something clinging to the right pontoon of the plane as it rose up out of the waves. A white, ragged, ghostly thing. They heard Sarah Punk screaming as the plane went down."

Mitch took a beer from the fridge, popped it open, and handed it to her. He watched her, waiting for her comeback.

"That's easy," she said. "They saw fog and spray, whitecaps. The engine was straining, trying to get up to speed into the wind. *It* was screaming."

She could see him better in here. He had on a collarless, short-sleeve shirt with three buttons at the neck, frayed but clean. Faded jeans, beat-up runners, no socks. Very casual, very cool. Nothing around his neck, no chains or love beads. No rings on his fingers. No rings in his ears.

"It is interesting that three members of the same family have died violently on this nearly deserted lake," she said as they headed back out to the porch.

The fog was clearing. The surface of the water was visible about eight feet below her on the other side of a narrow path. The mosquitoes were more active now, hungrily trying to get at her through the screen. Mitch didn't smoke, at least not cigarettes. Kelly didn't smoke either, and she was glad that he wasn't fouling up the air. She also appreciated that he didn't feel the need to fiddle with a radio and disturb the natural sounds of the night.

From what she'd seen so far, she loved the place. The rough, mismatched furniture; the casual, essentially male disregard for tidiness; the smell of pine, bacon grease, and bug juice. A lake almost to herself; this could really work.

On the way from Trapper Lake, Mitch had talked

a lot about Zen and other spiritual shit, giving her the impression that he was a bit of a freak. She knew he'd done about twenty months in Vietnam, back-to-back, in '68 and '69. A grunt, a volunteer. When his enlistment was up, he'd lived out on the West Coast, went to UCLA for a while. It wasn't clear what he'd been doing for the last few years. He'd only been back in Wanakena for two weeks. He'd kept the long hair and the West Coast bullshit talk, but he didn't appear to be a serious stoner or any kind of an addict.

He was comfortable in the woods. It was strange that he didn't own a car, especially living way the hell out here in the middle of nowhere. But besides that, and the whole ghost thing, he seemed like a pretty straight guy.

Kelly took a seat beside him.

"We used to rent this place for about a month each summer when I was a kid," Mitch said. "There were always a bunch of Margins at their shack. They had a whole pack of kids that came and went. I mostly hung around with Merle and Bobby who were there all the time.

"The Margins loved telling that Sarah Punk story. It was part of their family history. Weird, right? Their great-uncle and grandfather had been real dicks. You'd think they'd want to keep it quiet, but they promoted it, thought it was cool that their family was being haunted. It was really hard on the younger boy, Bobby, but nobody seemed to notice.

"I've never been to Shallow Rock. My dad

wouldn't let me near the place. The Margin kids used to go all the time. They said you could see Sarah's shack, the locals call it the Hell Hole, out in the swamp. They said that Shallow Rock people saw her ghost all the time, like it was no big deal."

Mitch's quiet voice was making her drowsy. She took a long haul on her beer. "And you've seen Sarah, before tonight, I mean?"

"Lots of times. Never as close as tonight. She was always off in the woods. If I thought I saw her, I ran like hell. Mostly, I felt her, you know… watching me, waiting to get me alone."

Kelly sighed. "So, the story worked, right? It kept you from wandering off on your own, kept you away from a dangerous swamp and a town full of banjo players." She had seen *Deliverance* last summer, and it had made an impression on her like it had on everyone else.

"I get that, but Sarah is still around. In fact, from what I've been told, she's more active than ever…"

Kelly cut him off with a weary groan. She rose slowly from the chair, placed her empty on the table, and buckled on her patrol belt. "Tomorrow's my first day on the job, and I haven't even unloaded my stuff yet."

"Right, sorry. Come on, we'll light a couple of lamps in the bunkhouse first." Mitch picked up a flashlight from the ledge near the door and led Kelly outside.

CHAPTER
THREE

The mosquitoes homed in on them as they moved briskly along the short flagstone path between the cookhouse and the bunkhouse. Halfway there, the path branched off to the right, heading uphill.

"If the plumbing craps out, that's the way to the outhouse," Mitch said. "And there's a thunder mug under your bed."

They went up the wooden stairs and in, the screen door banging behind them.

"We've got the electric hooked up to a water pump for the toilet and the shower. There's no lights in here yet. I'm working on it, but it could still be a couple of weeks."

Mitch flicked on his flashlight. "There's just three rooms. This is my room and where my dad sleeps when he's up, which isn't very often at this time of year."

Kelly took her flashlight from her belt and swept it around the big, shadowy space. There were two single beds, one on each side of the room, with simple end tables and dressers. Not a lot of stuff at all. At the foot of one bed were an OD green footlocker and an army-issue duffel bag.

"There would have been ten bunk beds in each room back in the day," Mitch said.

"Yeah, you could hold a square dance in here," Kelly replied. The room had to be forty by sixty. There were six windows along each wall.

In the center of the room stood a tall, square, cast-iron wood stove with a thick pipe leading up through the high ceiling. The stove was cold, a pile of split wood and newspaper in a holder to one side.

Mitch crossed the room to a plain white door set in the middle of the dividing wall. It had a brass plate with a knob and an old-fashioned, almost comically large keyhole.

Mitch opened the door and went into the next room. There was a big cannonball bed with elaborate headboards and footboards of dark wood. It was made up with clean sheets and covered with a big quilt.

Kelly chuckled. "I brought my sleeping bag," she said.

A massive wardrobe on one side of the bed, and a chest-high dresser and a vanity on the other, gave some sense of coziness to this part of the big room. The furniture was all of the same dark wood as the bed. There was a large rug on the hardwood floor.

Mitch set his flashlight down on her dresser and lifted the glass chimney of a kerosene lamp. It had a thick, glass stand, and a wide bowl filled with yellowish-brown liquid.

"You know how to work one of these?"

"Sure, my grandparents had them at their farm. And the Johnny." She shone her light on the white chamber pot beneath the bed. "Never heard it called a thunder mug before. Must be a Wanakena thing."

Mitch struck a wooden match. It hissed and crackled loudly in the stillness of the room, releasing a whiff of sulfur which mingled with the tang of kerosene. He placed the fluted chimney on the base and turned down the wick with the brass knob.

Kelly pointed her flashlight at the wood stove in the middle of the room. It was the same as the one in Mitch's room; on the front plate above the door, a satyr's face overlooked a garland of grapes. At each corner, a maiden, barefoot and lightly draped in transparent flowing robes, perched on a large scroll.

"I laid a fire in there. It's pretty warm tonight, but it can get nippy around here because of the damp," Mitch said.

He opened the door on the opposite wall. "The bathroom is through here."

Kelly came and stood beside him.

With his flashlight, Mitch pointed out the bathroom in the back corner. Shower curtains, pulled back at the moment, formed two of the walls. There was a roughed-in sink, shower, and toilet. There was a large wood stove in here as well. The rest of the room was a jumble of furniture, boxes, and building materials.

"So, you can see, there's no hallway or anything. To get from one end of the building to the other you go right down the middle, through the other rooms."

Mitch shone his flashlight on the back door. "The back door locks. There's keys to the middle doors somewhere," he rapped the door from Kelly's room with his knuckles. "I'll dig them up tomorrow so you can lock yourself in on both sides. You can keep your doors locked all the time if you want. I'll go around outside and come in the back if I need to use the can."

They walked back through to Mitch's room, where he lit another lamp and put it on top of the wood stove.

It didn't take long to unload her stuff: a footlocker, a duffel bag, two suitcases, an overnight bag, and a couple of boxes. The last things to come out were her four new uniforms on hangers, with the Wanakena County Sheriff's Department badges freshly sewn on both shoulders.

On her shirt for tomorrow, a black name tag with DEPUTY MACKINAW in white letters was pinned over her right breast. Over the left breast was a six-pointed silver star almost as big as the palm of her hand. She was embarrassed at how good it made her feel. In Buffalo, she'd worn a silver shield, and that hadn't felt right. The shield said that you were police, but the star—the star said you were the *law*.

Mitch handed her the carefully shaped campaign hat with another big, silver star on it. "I should tell you, there was one more Sarah Punk-related death. This was just a year ago, right across the lake from here."

"Yeah, Gail told me about that. Look, I'm really beat, Mitch. And I have to get up early."

"Sorry, man. I'm going back to the cookhouse for a while, stay out of your way. I'll be quiet when I come in. But if you need anything, just knock on my door, okay?"

"Great, thanks. Good night, Mitch," she said.

Mitch closed the door to his room, and a moment later, she heard the outside door and the screen door shut.

Kelly hooked her patrol belt over a bedpost. Resisting the temptation to collapse on the bed, she took a towel and a man's shaving kit containing her toiletries and went into the bathroom.

Brushing her teeth by the wavering light of the coal oil lamp in her bedroom, she had no sense of fear, only satisfaction. It was too bad that her family hadn't been there today for the swearing-in, but she wasn't surprised. Her father's hardware and sporting goods stores kept them all busy at this time of year.

Back in her room, she changed into a fresh t-shirt and underwear. She made sure that all of the windows were closed and locked. She put the flashlight on the end table next to her bed and her revolver under her pillow.

From the moment she'd seen it, Kelly knew she was going to have a problem with the big mirror on the vanity. Stories about seeing ghosts by looking into mirrors by candlelight lingered from her childhood, and despite herself, she was afraid that Sarah Punk would be waiting for her in the smoky darkness of that curved antique frame.

She didn't believe in ghosts, but she knew that ghosts didn't have to be real in order for someone to be haunted. In that sense, Lost Lake was haunted as long as the people who lived on it believed it was. They would try to draw her into their illusion. Hell, for a few moments back on the road she *had* believed; Mitch's words giving *his* shape to the misty images poking into her weary brain.

It was all bullshit. But fear, like bullshit, was contagious. That's why she made a point of facing it head-on. She took the lamp from the stove and brought it with her to stand squarely in front of the vanity. The middle section of the vanity was low, the mirror, a good five feet tall, rose up from there, held by two slender, curving arms of wood.

Her image bloomed and flickered in the glass, caught in the strange, restless light. Her blond hair became white, her eyes, deeply shadowed pockets. Behind her back, long, sinister shadows swayed in the air. She felt her heart beginning to race as she stared the image down. Biting her lip, she forced herself to look carefully into the shadows behind her back. She had to hold onto the base of the lamp with both hands to keep it steady.

There was a knock on the door. She started and almost dropped the lamp.

"Kelly?"

She took a deep breath. "What, Mitch?"

She hadn't heard him come back in. She wondered how long he'd been standing at her door.

"All that talk about Sarah Punk. It's just a thing, you know. I didn't mean to, like, scare you or anything, man."

Kelly closed her eyes and took another deep breath. "That's okay, Mitch."

"So, we're cool?"

"We're cool. Good night, Mitch," she said, raising her voice a little.

"Night, Kelly." Again, she heard the screen door slap shut.

She looked directly into the hollow eyes of the creature in the mirror and turned down the brass knob, snuffing out the oily flame.

"Enough of this shit," she said.

CHAPTER **FOUR**

SUNDAY

Mitch sat in his father's wide-bellied, aluminum canoe. Back straight, head up, he dipped the pale wooden paddle into the water, pulled slowly, then lifted it to rest across his knees.

He felt the glide, man, and felt, rather than heard, the sound of each individual drop as it left the blade and fell through space to be reunited with the lake. After the last drop had fallen, there was still the faint whisper of water against the hull.

It was Sunday, which was a busy day for the local police riding herd on the cottagers heading back to the city, but quiet on the lake. Kelly would be working hard her first day on the job.

Mitch smiled, remembering yesterday, the first time they'd met. Kelly standing on the steps of the station, impatient to get on the road to Lost Lake. Blond hair in a tight ponytail, blouse tucked into tight jeans, wide patrol belt around her waist. She was wound so tightly he'd imagined that unhooking that belt would be like flipping the lever on an M-67 grenade.

He'd had breakfast ready for her early this morning. She was a steak and eggs kind of girl, just like he'd figured. A meat eater, a fast eater. Great teeth. Very clear blue eyes, even if there were shadows underneath them. She'd wolfed down the food, sucked down the coffee, very grateful, and then been on her way, disappearing down the road into the fog, driving way too fast.

Mitch was in Back Bay at the far end of Lost Lake, cruising the edge of Shaker's Bog, looking for the entrance to Bitch Creek. It was mid-afternoon on an unusually clear day. It was hot, but even at this hour, Shaker's Bog was murky with low-lying mist. He didn't know this part of the lake at all. Kelly had been right about that. The Sarah Punk story had kept him away.

Spotting a possible opening in the vegetation, he worked his way in amongst the deadheads and reeds, snaking past slippery islands of lily pads, only to run up against a wall of tightly packed reeds. In every direction, a stubborn phalanx of sharp-bladed leaves rose up out of the brackish, bug-infested water to block his way. Sweating in the cold humidity, he was assaulted by swarms of bugs.

He thought about the people who had died in this bog. At least eight; Moses and Sarah, the Margin brothers, the four passengers on the plane. The place stank of bad karma, and he wondered what the hell he was doing poking around in it. Carefully, he backed out to the open water, got himself turned around and paddled hard until the fresh air had cooled the sweat on his face and stripped away the bugs.

He rested, letting his breathing return to normal. Looking towards the shore, he realized that he was just off the Parker cottage.

Mr. Parker had built the place in the early fifties; back in the day when people built their own cottages. He had hacked out a path through the dense bush following an old logging trail. A hard, stubborn man, he'd died of a heart attack only a few years after the cottage was built, leaving behind his wife, Rae, and a son, Brian.

Mitch had been to the Parker Place a couple of times with his dad, bumping in on the improvised road. Mr. Parker had been dead even way back then, but Mrs. Parker and Brian had seemed happy. There were always lots of kids hanging around; boys and girls from Shallow Rock who knew the secret of Bitch Creek.

Mitch hadn't known Brian Parker. He heard he'd died of a heroin overdose in Philly a couple of years ago. The Widow Parker, from what his dad said, still came up to the lake by herself and stayed for the whole summer. Staying up here, right at the edge of Shaker's Bog all alone; Mitch thought that was pretty strange.

As he approached, the wind ended its whispering conversation with the trees. Shadows lay thick from the afternoon sun as he came up against the dock with a slight bump. He could hear a transistor radio turned so low that it made no sense at all, insect voices inside a tin can.

"Hello. Hello, Mrs. Parker?"

No answer. He couldn't see past the screen that ran along three-quarters of the length of the cottage. The air had the ashy smell of a dead wood stove.

"Mrs. Parker?"

He went around to the end of the cottage. Leaning on his cupped hands, he pressed his face against the screen door. There was a dark, cluttered kitchen inside. It took him a second to realize that Mrs. Parker was in there, slumped over the table.

He knocked on the door frame. "Mrs. Parker?"

She jerked her head up, grabbed a pistol that lay near her hand, and fired at him.

Mitch had dropped straight down as soon as she'd started to move. Two rounds slammed through the screen door over his head.

"Whoa! Whoa! Whoa!" he shouted, as he crawled back down the dock. "Friendly! Friendly!"

"Stop moving. Get flat on your belly and put your

hands over your head." Mrs. Parker was right behind him.

He pressed his face against the hot wood of the deck. "Who the hell are you?" she demanded.

"Mitch Herkemer, the sheriff's son. I came here a few times when I was a kid. I've been away, in the army."

"Your hair's too long for the army. You look like a fuckin' hippie."

"I got out."

"Get up and turn around. Let me get a look at you."

Mitch stood up and turned around slowly, his hands raised to shoulder height, his most winning smile on his face.

Rae Parker stood barefoot, hip cocked. The pistol, an old Colt .45, was limp in her hand, but still pointing in his general direction. She wore a halter-top dress that might have been red or orange before it had faded into a kind of soft rust. She had to be well into her forties. Thick, dark-brown hair fell down past her shoulders. She had a straight nose and nice high cheekbones above slightly hollowed cheeks. Her pale-green eyes were hatched all around with crow's feet, but her skin was clear and tanned.

"I don't recognize you," she said.

"It's the hair; I always had a brush cut when I was a kid."

She squinted at him. "What's your dad's name?"

"Archie Herkimer."

She lowered the gun to her side. "Well, you're not who I thought you were. I guess you better come on in and have a drink."

Mitch wondered if anyone would react to the pistol shots. Not likely; it was possible that they were the only people on the entire lake right now.

Mrs. Parker said she wanted some water. He rummaged around until he found a fairly clean glass, rinsed it and pumped it full of lake water, then rinsed a tumbler for himself while she sat back in her kitchen chair and lit up a Marlboro.

He sat down across from her; the pistol was back on the table along with all the other litter there. She poured Jack Daniels into his tumbler.

He asked the obvious question. "Who did you think I was?"

"Hack Weechum, or maybe Mulvane. I didn't mean to shoot right off, you just startled me. Shouldn't sneak up on a person like that."

"I'm really sorry about that, Mrs. Parker. It must get freaky out here all by yourself."

"Freaky?" Hostility flickered across her face.

Mitch spoke quickly. "Uh, Mulvane, the new people from down the lake?"

"Big ladies' man. Thinks he can rip off a piece whenever he feels like it. Jesus, I ain't that lonely. Bullet between the eyes is all he'll get from me."

There was a droop and darkness below her eyes. Mitch wasn't sure how she looked. Not lonely, sad maybe, and haunted.

She had a shy smile on her face. She lowered her eyes, then lifted them up, but not to look at him. She was looking over his shoulder at the door. Mitch felt a hollowness running up his spine from between his shoulder blades to the back of his head.

Somebody was behind him.

CHAPTER FIVE

"Are you okay, Mrs. Parker? I heard a shot."

Mitch stood up, turned, and took a couple of steps back so he could see who was coming through the door.

A teenager. He wasn't very tall, maybe five seven, five eight. Pencil thin, not much to show for hips or shoulders or chest. Slouched, loose, walking lightly. He wore faded, wide-legged jeans, and a dark blue football jersey with no name or number on it.

Limp, blond hair draped the sides of his head to his shoulders and stuck out from under the wide, floppy brim of a bush hat. He wore a hunting knife on his right side, a classic Jim Bowie, the leather sheath running halfway down his thigh and tied in place with a leather thong. His jersey was tucked behind the antler handle so it wouldn't interfere with a quick grab. He kept moving slowly, flowing around towards Mrs. Parker.

"It's okay, Bobby, Mitch just startled me when I was taking a nap. You remember Mitch?"

"Bobby?" Mitch said with a big grin. "Hey, it's been a while. Didn't recognize you with all the hair." He stuck out his hand.

Bobby was Merle Margin's little brother. He'd always been around the bigger boys, not underfoot, but always there. Didn't talk much, wasn't annoying the way some little brothers were.

Bobby shook his hand, not a lot of pumping, but a very hard squeeze. "Hi, Mitch," he said. "I heard you were up."

"Yeah, couple of weeks now."

Everybody thought Bobby was strange. It was a little spooky how he would stay off at the edge of any group; there, but not there. You always wanted him to be on your side when you played Guns, because he could hide so well. He was always popping out and taking somebody by surprise. He could lay an ambush, man, just like old Victor Charles.

Bobby smiled; a small, quick movement. His lower lip looked like it had been cut in two and then sewn back together not quite even, a rush job. The gash was just to the right of center, a dark line faintly outlined in white, the lip puffed up on that side. It was an old wound from when he was just a toddler, but it had a fresh look to it. It gave him a battered appearance, like he was forever just coming out of a fight.

Mitch could see his mouth, but even at close range, he couldn't make out Bobby's eyes under the shadow of his hat. From the tilt of his head, he had to be looking at Mrs. Parker. Giving her that little smile. "What are you now, Bobby. Sixteen?" Mitch asked.

"Seventeen this month."

Bobby stopped moving to outflank him, drifted back towards the door and rested his butt on the narrow, two-by-four ledge of the window. When he extended his legs, he revealed worn, blue, Bauer running shoes and white socks so dirty they were gray.

"Finished school?" Mitch asked.

"One more year this September."

"What you gonna do after?"

"Don't know. Maybe join the army."

"I remember you were always good at Guns."

It was at this point that people usually asked Mitch, "How was Nam?" to be polite. They wouldn't listen long, especially if he didn't tell it the way they wanted to hear it.

Everybody back in *The World* figured they knew all about Nam from watching Walter Cronkite on the seven o'clock news. They didn't. But the funny thing was, even the guys who'd been there couldn't agree on what it was like.

Bobby didn't ask, he just sat there looking at him from under the brim of his hat. His coolness was a challenge, but Mitch wasn't into responding to challenges these days.

Mrs. Parker lit another Marlboro. Her chair

creaked as she settled back. "Mitch just dropped by to say hello, making the rounds like polite people do," she said.

"That's right," Mitch agreed, nodding.

This was interesting. They were miles away from the Margin shack. Bobby must have been very close to get here so quickly. Mitch sat down again, scraping his chair back so he could include both of them in his field of vision. "You up all summer?" he asked. "I haven't seen you around."

"No, just got here yesterday. Bin working at Camp Orion."

"Sure, the rich kid camp. You a counsellor?"

"Dishwasher."

"Right, so the place is closed down already?"

"No, I quit. Felt like spending some time at the lake."

Mrs. Parker raised her glass. "You want a drink, Bobby?"

"No thanks, Mrs. Parker, I gotta go. See you around, Mitch."

Mitch stood up quickly, surprised he was leaving so soon. He intercepted him so he could shake his hand. "Good to see you again, Bobby. Stop by any time, I'm up all summer."

"Yeah, I heard. Somebody up there with you?"

"New deputy, Kelly Mackinaw. She's staying there until she finds a place. We're not living together or anything like that."

Another unreadable look passed between Mrs.

Parker and Bobby, then he slipped out as quietly as he'd come in. Mitch turned his attention back to Mrs. Parker. She was leaning on the table now, leaning heavily on her arms, cigarette straight up between her fingers. She didn't offer any explanation about the comings and goings of Bobby Margin. Maybe she wasn't as lonely as he'd thought; Bobby's name wasn't on the short list of people she was prepared to shoot on sight.

Back to that, back to the men he'd almost taken a bullet for. "Who is Hack Weechum?" he asked. "Name sounds familiar."

"He'd be a few years younger than you, I guess. Rough little bastard. Shallow Rock kids are all wild, but not mean by nature. Mostly too lazy to cause any real trouble, but there's always one mean little fucker that takes over and runs the rest of them till he gets sent to prison. That's Hack."

"He been bothering you?"

"Since he was about ten years old."

"I guess he'll wind up in jail soon enough."

"Has already. Picked up for dealing and assault. But he got out. Some fancy-ass lawyer showed up, got him out on parole. Don't know what the hell that was about. He got out about a week ago, back in Shallow Rock by now."

"You expect him to come here?"

"Sooner or later."

"What's he got against you?"

Mrs. Parker put her head down on her arms, her

voice muffled and blurry. "Ain't got nothing against me, Mitch. He wants me. He wants to move in with me and take this place for his own."

"Oh."

Mrs. Parker had nothing more to say on the subject. She stood up, picked up her revolver and held it at her side. "I'm gonna lie down now. Thanks for visiting."

Mitch stood up. "Thanks for the drink, you sure you're okay, Mrs. Parker?" He wanted to shake her hand or give her a hug, but she didn't look receptive.

"Been taking care of myself for a long time, Mitch," she said as she ushered him out the door. "Tell your dad to put Hack away for good next time," she said through the screen.

"What about Mulvane?"

"I can take care of him." She hooked the door closed, yawned, and turned away into the smoky darkness of her cottage.

Mitch paddled slowly away from the Parker place, moving out from the shore at a steep angle, watching to see if Hack Weechum or Bobby Margin were sneaking around.

He came out of Back Bay heading west, back to his end of the lake. When he rounded Birch Point, the three new cottages came into view. They had been built while he was away, and it still took him by surprise every time he saw them. Each one was different, but they were all shiny and sharp-edged, with steeply pitched roofs and way too much glass. Three in a row on triple-sized lots, screened from each other by stands of maple and pine. Elaborate paths and stairways snaked down the steep shoreline connecting them with their long docks and brightly painted boathouses.

Mulvane, Cross, and Dee heading down the lake.

The Mulvane cottage was quiet. Nobody down at the dock, nobody moving around outside. The Cross cottage was quiet too. According to his dad, Mr. Mulvane was a corporate lawyer from Albany; a lobbyist, very well connected. Mr. Cross was also a lawyer who lived in Albany. He did something in finance and spent a lot of time in New York City.

He hadn't met any of the new people, hadn't even seen them. If it wasn't for the light pouring out of the big windows of their cottages at night and the sound of partying on the weekend, he would have doubted that they existed at all.

The last cottage belonged to Mr. Dee. Daniel Dee was the owner of a big GM dealership in Syracuse that had car lots all over the North Country. You couldn't turn on the local TV anywhere without seeing one of his flamboyant, "Dandy Dan Dee," commercials.

He spotted a woman he figured was Mrs. Dee, tottering up the irregular stone stairs to the cottage, in high heels. She had incredibly pale skin, sunburned pink across the back of her neck and shoulders. She was wearing a skimpy bikini, flaming red like the color of her hair. When she reached the top of the steps she turned around and raised a hand to shade her eyes as she looked out at him.

He waved. She waved back, although he was sure she didn't know who he was. Then she stood with her hands on her hips, watching him. It was a bold stance, an unmistakable invitation.

He sat with his paddle across his knees and stared back at her. She looked brassy and fun, but evening shadows were already on the lake and the sun was starting to go down. He waved again and continued on his way, keeping his pace slow and steady. He didn't want to offend the lady.

Beyond the Dee cottage was Steep Rock, a sheer wall of limestone rising forty feet straight up out of the water. It was a good hundred yards long, the summit crowded with trees except for a clear patch near the center where they used to hang out as kids.

It took a lot of nerve to jump off of there. It was always a jump—none of them were skilled enough to dive. If you hit the right spot, which was pretty big, the water was deep. But if you went off the top too far to the left or right, you would hit the rocks. There were a lot of rocks. Some of them stuck up out of the water, but most of them were hidden just below the surface where you couldn't see them unless the light was right.

A clear day was a rare thing on Lost Lake, so you had to have been around for a while to know where the shallow rocks were. Most of the time you couldn't even see the water. They'd called it cloud jumping.

There were cheats prepared. Lichen scraped where you wanted to plant your foot, small rocks placed giving you left and right of arc. Nobody messed with the markers; that was a solid rule. Still, the drop always seemed to take forever. Time enough, while plummeting through the fog, to seriously doubt your aim.

He remembered the last time he'd been up there, just before he went off to boot camp. Merle Margin must have been thirteen and Bobby only eight. No Shallow Rock kids around that day, it was just the three of them. Little Bobby had gone first. He ran from way back in the trees, and without a sound, leapt high in the air and cannonballed it. Merle said Bobby was afraid of the dark. He sure as hell wasn't afraid of heights or hidden rocks.

Time to get home. Mitch pointed his canoe at the lumber camp dock, directly across the narrow bay, and dug deep.

CHAPTER SIX

MONDAY

"There's been a complaint made against Bobby Margin," Sheriff Herkemer said when Kelly reported to work on Monday morning. "We'll go out to the lake this afternoon. It'll give you a chance to meet some of your neighbors."

The sheriff's office, with its living quarters in the back, was on the main street of Trapper Lake, pretty much smack in the middle of the county. It was just under an hour's drive from there to Lost Lake in daylight, if there was no traffic and the fog wasn't too bad.

They drove for twenty minutes on Route Three, then turned off onto Cooperage Road, a single, twisting lane of old asphalt that dropped steeply into the narrow valley that held Lost Lake. In most places, there was no shoulder at all, the thick bush growing right up to the edge of the road. The only sign of civilization was a single line of poles that ran alongside the road carrying one line for Con Ed and one for Ma Bell. After fifteen minutes of this, Shallow Rock Road forked off to the left, a single lane of oiled dirt, leading down to the village of Shallow Rock.

After that, Cooperage became even worse, dipping sharply up and down into small pockets of marsh wrapped in perpetual fog. Over the last few miles, there were several narrow wooden bridges built by the Moose River Cooperage Company in the last century.

Just before the lake, Cooperage veered sharply to the right and was magically transformed into a wide, two-lane, freshly paved promenade. A large, light blue sign proclaimed Shangri-La Lane in white, oriental-style lettering.

Sheriff Herkemer waved towards the sign. "Ignore that," he said. "The new folks had their contractors put it up after they paved this section. Nobody uses that name except them and their friends."

A white sign in the shape of a cross on its side pointed them into a broad driveway. "Mrs. Cross called me this morning. She told me that she didn't want to make a fuss. She just wanted me to have a little talk with Bobby Margin about him hanging around her place."

"But that's not what you're doing," Kelly said.

"Denise Cross was nervous on the phone, sounded embarrassed. I've known Bobby since he was a baby. He's a good kid who's had a lot of shit dumped on him in his life. I just want to make sure I know what's going on before I add any more to the pile."

From what the sheriff had told her, this Margin kid was some kind of lake orphan—no mother, and a father who left him up at the lake every summer with his older brother, sometimes all alone. He hung around the cottages, mooched off people. He sounded pathetic; a textbook example of a sociopath in the making.

Mitch said that he'd met Bobby over at the Parker Place yesterday, said he was kind of looking out for Mrs. Parker. It sounded to her more like a horny teenager taking advantage of a lonely old drunk.

It was past one in the afternoon when they parked the patrol car and walked around to the front of the cottage. Two women in one-piece bathing suits reclined on lawn chairs with bright plastic glasses in their hands and big sunglasses with bright plastic frames on their faces.

Mrs. Cross and Mrs. Mulvane put their drinks on a little white table and stood up. They took off their sunglasses and pointedly gave Kelly the once over—Mrs. Cross quickly, Mrs. Mulvane taking her time. Female cops were a rare sight, especially out in the sticks. Kelly kept her dark aviators on.

The women didn't invite them to sit down, didn't offer to shake their hands. They stood demurely with their soft, manicured hands clasped in front of themselves. Sheriff Herkemer took off his sunglasses, hooked them into his breast pocket, and started in on the polite chit-chat. Kelly took a good look at the women.

Mrs. Cross definitely had a cutesy thing going on: short, brown hair in tight curls around her face, big brown eyes, full lips looking bitten top and bottom, and an overbite showing the tips of two perfect front teeth. She wore a dark blue silk scarf around her neck that matched her high-cut bathing suit and high heels.

Mrs. Mulvane had opted for a white suit of a similar cut; she had dispensed with the scarf, but still had the heels. Her brown hair was straight and bobbed to shoulder length. She was also cute, with an upturned, button nose and high cheekbones, but there were deep shadows beneath her eyes, her lips were thinner than her neighbor's, and tighter at the corners.

Mrs. Cross was subdued and nervous; Mrs. Mulvane was more on the quiet, watchful side. Cross was younger than Mulvane, Kelly figured them for late-twenties, and she was willing to bet that their husbands were at least ten years older.

"So, what's the problem with Bobby?" Sheriff Herkemer asked.

"He's always hanging around. It was cute when he was a kid, but now that he's getting older, it's just not right," Mrs. Cross said.

"I didn't think he was up this year. I haven't seen him at all," Sheriff Herkemer replied in a pleasant tone.

Mrs. Mulvane spoke up. "Oh, he's been around, Sheriff. Since the start of the season."

"What's he doing that bothers you, Mrs. Cross?"

"Well, he comes and hangs around uninvited. He's as friendly as ever, but he *stares* and he just won't leave, no matter how many hints I give him," Mrs. Cross replied.

"Does he go inside your cottage?"

"When you're not around?"

"Sure," Mrs. Mulvane interrupted.

"Do you have a complaint against Bobby Margin too?" Sheriff Herkemer asked her.

"Yes, I do."

"Okay, I'll get to you. One at a time. Have you caught him in your cottage, Mrs. Cross?"

"No, not like that. It's just, if I get up to go inside, he'll follow me in and make himself at home, ask if he can do anything for me. Ask if I need anything fixed," she replied, brushing at her curls.

"Do you ask him to leave?"

"Not in so many words."

"Has Bobby ever threatened you?"

"No, but I *feel* threatened. He's what, seventeen now?" Mrs. Cross had begun to bite the thick arm of her glasses.

"Sixteen, I think."

"That makes him a man, and I can't have a man coming into my cottage when my husband's not around."

"Have you talked to your husband about this?"

"No, I didn't want him to get mad at Bobby, didn't want him to get the wrong idea." Mrs. Cross noticed she was biting her glasses and forced her hands down to her side.

"How does Bobby behave when your husband's around?"

"Well, that's the thing. Bobby never comes around anymore when Hal is here, only when I'm alone. He always seems to know when I'm alone."

"Does this ever happen at night?"

"No, oh no, I don't see him at night," Mrs. Cross said, giving her head a shake.

"But he's out there," Mrs. Mulvane said.

The sheriff ignored her. "Mrs. Cross, you want me to talk to Bobby, but you don't want to make a formal complaint against him, is that correct?"

"Yes, if you tell him not to come around, I'm sure he'll listen."

Sheriff Herkemer nodded. "I can do that." He turned and looked at Mrs. Mulvane. "Is that okay with you, ma'am?"

"Sometimes I get a glimpse of him through the trees, or I can just barely make him out in the shadows. I know he's out there, watching," she replied, her voice dropping to a hiss.

Kelly watched the sheriff digest that without comment or any change of expression. "Does he come into your cottage?"

"I think he does. I'll come out of the bathroom or the bedroom, and the patio door will be open when I know it was closed. Or, you know how it is when you get the feeling that someone is watching you. It's very scary."

"Anything stolen?"

"Nothing important. Little things," she said.

It was like a cloud had passed over the sun. Kelly felt it immediately, a sudden change in all three of them. Tension, a presence. Mrs. Cross shivered openly. They exchanged furtive looks, no one looked at Kelly.

Mrs. Mulvane went on, hesitant. "Little things... missing...or moved, but that's been going on around here for years."

"Okay, okay," Sheriff Herkemer said with a deep sigh.

Mrs. Mulvane pressed on. "I saw Bobby last night after Mick had gone back to the city. I went out to get something from the car. I heard movement out in the bush, so I flicked the headlights on. He was there, he looked startled, but he waved and then went off."

"The path is back there," the sheriff said.

"He wasn't on the path. He was too close to my cottage to be on the path. He was in the bush."

"Okay," Sheriff Herkemer said. He held up a hand as if he knew what she was going to say.

"*She* was with him, or I should say... *following* him."

CHAPTER SEVEN

"Don't *say* that," Mrs. Cross said, her voice hushed and small.

"I saw her. A white shape floating twenty or thirty yards behind Bobby. I was going to shout out to him, to warn him, but then she stopped and looked in my direction. I ran into the cottage, didn't even turn off the car. Now my battery's dead," Mrs. Mulvane said.

Where the hell did that come from? The whole conversation had shifted from the mundane to the unreal in a split second.

After a pause, the sheriff said, "So, you don't want to make any kind of formal complaint. You just want me to talk to Bobby?"

Now they were right back to normal, talking like Mrs. Mulvane hadn't just reported her firm conviction that she'd seen a ghost.

"Tell Bobby he is not welcome here anymore, not anywhere on our property," Mrs. Mulvane said.

Mrs. Cross nodded, her eyes downcast.

"I'll have a word with him," Sheriff Herkemer said.

A nod of the head, no handshake, and then Kelly and the sheriff headed back around the cottage to the patrol car.

"He's not a kid anymore, Sheriff, there's no telling what he might do. I tell you it's strange the way he hangs around the Parker Place, it's like a cult or something," Mrs. Mulvane shouted after them.

Some of the Manson Family had recently gone on trial in California, and cults were on everybody's minds again.

"Where are their kids?" Kelly asked.

"Camp, I guess. None of them came back after the first summer. The Margin boys scared the hell out of them with their Sarah Punk stories. The parents too."

"Why do they stay up here? The women, I mean?"

Sheriff Herkemer shrugged his shoulders. "People want to get back to nature these days."

Kelly looked up at the tall A-frame as she got into the passenger seat of the cruiser. "Yeah, they're regular backwoodsmen," she said.

Sheriff Herkemer chuckled. "Let's go see what Lucy Dee has to say. I think you'll find her a little more down to earth."

They came to the Dee sign, a country gentleman with a top hat and cane, the logo of Dan Dee Motors. The laneway was extra wide, went in about thirty yards and then turned into a circular driveway with a broad parking space off to the side. The sheriff pulled up, got out and gave the patrol car door a good, chunky slam. Broad steps flanked by lawn jockeys led to a big oak door.

"We'll try around front first," he said.

Flagstone steps set into the hillside led down and around to the front of the cottage. As they came around the corner, they caught a whiff of marijuana.

Mrs. Dee was stretched out in a lawn chair in the shade, wearing a skimpy, dark-blue bikini that emphasized her white, freckled skin. Propped up in a chair next to her was Mitch.

Mrs. Dee didn't move. Mitch slowly opened his eyes, took a moment to focus, and then smiled a big smile. "Hey, man," he said without getting up.

"Is she okay?" the sheriff asked.

"Yeah, she's pretty cool now. She was wired when I got here. Really pissed off. She needed to mellow out..."

"I don't need to hear the details, Mitch. Is she breathing? Can you wake her up?"

Mrs. Dee started to stir. Mitch got up and helped her get into a sitting position. Her bikini was tied around the neck but not at the sides. Mitch deftly gathered up the strings and tied it as she sat sagging against him, looking straight ahead, bleary-eyed and oblivious. Mitch whispered something to her, and her head wobbled in their direction. She squinted at each of them in turn, but didn't speak.

"What was she upset about?" The sheriff's voice was low and tight.

"I guess they had a real blowout here Saturday night. She's still recovering. Her husband took off back to the city, Sunday, didn't even wake her to say goodbye."

Kelly looked in through the screened patio doors; the place looked like it had been trashed by a rock band. She looked back down at Mrs. Dee. She had nearly translucent skin, the kind of skin that shows every mark. She had raw, scuffed-up knees, bruises on her arms and thighs, maybe a bit of a shiner. Some party.

"She was going to drive back to Syracuse, so I took her keys. I came over to borrow some ginger. She needed the company, so I stayed."

And smoked a joint. Your dope or hers? Kelly wondered. She was glad she was wearing her sunglasses because she didn't want Mitch to see the look in her eyes.

"She say anything about Bobby Margin?" the sheriff asked.

"She wasn't making sense—cursing everybody, you know, her husband, the Crosses, the Mulvanes. She really let loose on them, man..."

"What did she say about Bobby?"

"I don't know, man, his name came up..."

"Was she mad at Bobby?"

"Don't think so."

"Well, she can't tell us anything right now. We'll have to come back and talk to her in the morning."

"Better not make it too early, Dad," Mitch said.

Sheriff Herkemer sighed. "Well, don't leave her until you know she's okay. Maybe get her to eat something. You should be trying to sober her up, not getting her stoned."

"She needed to slow down, man, she was on uppers, speed."

Mrs. Dee was leaning against Mitch's broad shoulder, body limp, eyes closed.

"You've seen more of this than I have. Do we need to call an ambulance, Mitch? Do we need to take her into town?" the sheriff asked, impatiently.

"No, not now. Look, Dad, they've got a phone here, if she needs anything, I'll call. I won't hesitate."

"Okay, all right."

The sheriff walked over, took a look into the cottage, shook his head, and then waved for Kelly to follow him back around to the car. As they rounded the corner, he took one look back.

"Fucking Vietnam," he said.

Kelly didn't know what the hell Vietnam had to do with it.

CHAPTER EIGHT

Kelly spotted the hitchhikers as she pulled up to the pumps at the Keystone station outside of Trapper Lake; two girls and a guy in the parking lot of the boarded-up diner next door. They were talking to a solid, clean-cut-looking guy standing at the back end of a black pickup truck. The wind, coming in gusts, lifted sand from the gravel and hurled it in drifts around their ankles and onto their backpacks.

Nodding absently at the attendant, she moved away from the pumps to get a better look at what was going on. Other than height, the girls looked about the same; skinny, with long hair down past their shoulders. Hard to tell their age exactly. The male hitchhiker had a beard and looked older. He had his arm around the waist of the taller of the two girls; the shorter one was standing a couple of steps back and to the side.

The clean-cut guy was wearing a dress shirt, half unbuttoned, and blue jeans that looked like they'd just come out of the store. His hair was bushy on top but not long. He was talking; they were listening. The couple were nodding, then shaking their heads at whatever he was saying.

The short girl wore a blue hat with the broad brim turned up. She lit a cigarette and looked casually over at Kelly, checking out the uniform.

"Enjoying the show?"

Kelly turned sharply. There was a man behind her.

"Oh," she said, and moved to the side.

"What you figure's gonna happen?" he asked.

Kelly moved to the side to get a better look at him. Early twenties. Faded blue jeans held up by a wide, big-buckled belt. White T-shirt, damp with sweat, but clean. Loose mullet running down the back of his neck, the rest of his ragged, dirty-blond hair sticking out from under a faded baseball cap. Scuffed, pointy-toed cowboy boots. Very cool, leaning on the hood of an older model Mustang, smoking a hand-rolled cigarette.

"I don't know," Kelly said, and turned back to the action.

"I figure both girls are gonna ride up front, and the bearded guy winds up in the back," he said.

Out by the highway, the bearded guy let go of the tall girl, and they started arguing. The clean-cut guy moved away from the truck, crowding them. The short girl took a couple of steps back and stood next to her backpack.

"I say nobody gets a ride," Kelly said.

"I don't know. Maybe buddy gets the spare wheel," the guy said. "The cute little one."

Kelly looked at the speaker again, taking in new details. He was in good shape; lean all over, flat stomach, thin muscled forearms, strong chest. Prison fit, she realized, noticing the lousy, unreadable tattoos on his forearms. On his bicep, there was a better one, a heart with an arrow through it, and *MAW* in the middle.

"You from around here?" she asked.

"Born and bred." Cocky, smiling at her as he flicked the butt of his smoke onto the pavement.

He had the washed-out, light-blue eyes of a wolf. Modest sideburns, a couple of days' growth on his chin. Scraped knuckles. Scratches, maybe, in the stubble on his cheek.

"All set here, Deputy," the attendant called out. Kelly looked over and saw that he'd been waiting. There was a car on the other side of the pump.

The gas came to eight-ten. Raised voices from the hitchhikers drew Kelly's attention as she pulled out her wallet. The bearded guy had picked up his pack and was stomping off across the highway. She gave the attendant a ten. "Keep the change," she said.

She got in her car and drove slowly towards the hitchhikers.

"I guess he didn't want to ride in the back," the

con said as she rolled past him. He thought it was hilarious.

Kelly pulled up close to the two remaining backpacks. They all turned and watched as she got out of her car and put on her hat; the clean-cut guy staring at her with a frown and narrowed eyes, sweat on his forehead and beefy neck.

"How we all doing this evening?" Kelly asked. Her neck was sweating too. Everybody was sweating in the hot wind.

The tall girl was the only one to answer. "We're cool," she said.

"I'm Deputy Mackinaw. Who have we got here?"

"Sylvia," the tall girl replied. Kelly kept looking at her until she added, "Winslow."

Sylvia's hair was parted in the middle and brushed back over her ears. She had large breasts and slouched. The other girl was definitely younger, with brown eyes and almost no cheekbones. Hands resting on the frame of her backpack, she looked Kelly in the eye, curious.

"Debbie Ruggles," she said. Her hair was parted in the middle too; it came down from under her hat and lay over her flat chest.

"*You're* the new deputy?" the clean-cut guy said in a loud voice. "You gotta be kidding me."

Kelly put her hands on her hips and wondered if she should get into it with him. She was pretty sure she could smell alcohol on his breath. She wanted to, but it was only her second day on the job, not the time to be rousting some local yahoo just because she couldn't take a little shit.

She turned her back on him. "I need to see some ID, girls," she said.

"We're allowed to hitchhike," Debbie said.

"Not if you're under sixteen."

Even at sixteen, the police could send a kid home if they thought she was in danger. As far as Kelly was concerned, they were all in danger, all of the time, but the county didn't want the trouble and expense of getting involved, not with hundreds of kids passing through each summer.

"Do I look sixteen?" Sylvia asked. Bit smart-assed, but not coming on too strong.

"You look fourteen," Kelly said to Sylvia. She pointed at Debbie. "And *you* look about twelve."

A laugh came out of Debbie like a bark. Shaking her head, she knelt next to her pack. "If I am, then I've been hitchhiking since I was about eight years old," she said.

Kelly checked out their gear. Debbie had a lightweight sleeping bag neatly rolled up under a groundsheet on a solid P65 frame. All the pouches were secured. Sylvia had a sporting-goods-store pack with stuff hanging out the pockets and a fat sleeping bag tilted to one side, ready to fall off.

"See! Just like I told you. Harassment! This county fucks with hitchhikers," Clean-Cut Guy didn't like being ignored.

"Yeah, everybody knows that," Sylvia said.

Kelly was well aware of the county's reputation. "Get your ID," she said.

"Fucking Wanakena County, man," Clean-Cut Guy said.

Kelly looked him over again. She didn't know what his problem was. Just showing off for the girls?

"What if I don't have any ID? Where are we, Russia?" Sylvia asked, getting bolder.

"Then I'll take you to the station and fingerprint you, make a few calls. You could be there a while."

"See!" Clean-Cut Guy threw up his hands. "Fucking bullshit."

"And get fucked in some back cell, right?" Sylvia said. It didn't sound like something she would normally say. She was more nervous than angry. While she was bitching, she was digging out her wallet.

"And now they got their very own dyke. Fucking equal opportunity laws, man." Clean-Cut Guy just wouldn't give it a rest.

Kelly rolled her shoulders. He was much bigger than her, and he'd probably put up a fight, which meant she'd have to go in very hard. She could take him, but it wouldn't be easy. She was aware that people were watching: the con, the attendant, and the customer over at the pumps.

The wind kept kicking up and blowing Clean-Cut Guy's hair forward into his face; he had to keep brushing it back.

Debbie handed Kelly a New Jersey driver's license. It looked genuine. Debbie Eva Ruggles of Newark was sixteen and a half. Kelly handed it back to her. "Legal now, but I'll bet you've been through here before."

Debbie shrugged, letting slip a little smile, being cool.

The girls hadn't showered for a few days. Their hair was dull and lank. Sylvia handed Kelly a Maryland driver's license. Sylvia Mary Winslow, eighteen, was from Baltimore.

Kelly handed it back. "What happened to your friend?" she asked, nodding across the highway at the bearded guy who was staring back at them.

Sylvia shrugged. Debbie spoke up. "He's getting out of the county. Doesn't want to get fucked in some back cell," she said.

Kelly chuckled and turned her attention to Debbie. "Where you headed?"

"Canada. Gonna cross at Ogdensburg or Thousand Islands."

"I got some time," Kelly said. "There's a truck stop in Gouverneur. Lots of traffic heading north on Eleven. I could give you a lift, be there in a couple of hours."

"I know the place," Debbie said. "You gonna try to talk me into going home?"

"Nope."

"You gonna try and fuck me?"

Kelly smiled. "That's a chance you're just gonna have to take."

"You're not going with her, are you? Jesus, Debbie, don't do it," Sylvia exclaimed.

"I ain't really with these people," Debbie said, picking up her pack.

"That's what I figured." Kelly walked to her trunk and opened it. She turned to Sylvia. "I can take you too," she said.

Sylvia backed away from her, edging closer to the truck. "No way," she said.

That's how bad the Wanakena rep was, this kid would rather go with some dick than a female sheriff's deputy. "You don't even know this guy," she said.

Sylvia hesitated. Debbie put her pack in the trunk and stood next to the passenger door. Kelly walked past Clean-Cut Guy, moving along the side of his truck, getting a whiff of Hai Karate as she went by.

He watched her, looked over at the people around the pump, then looked at Sylvia. The guy didn't know what to do. Kelly went to the front of his truck, took out her notepad, and wrote down the license plate number.

"Bitch," he said.

"Last chance," Kelly said, as she passed Sylvia.

"No way."

Kelly looked at Clean-Cut Guy. "What's your name?" she asked.

"Fuck you."

"I'm busy right now. Next time we meet, we're gonna have a longer conversation," she said.

She pulled out onto Route Three and headed west. They drove past the bearded guy, hitchhiking in the other direction. "What got into him, anyway?" she asked.

"Gerry? Steve, the truck guy, told him that the police around here like to beat up any guy hitchhiking with girls, get them out of the picture. Fuck 'em up for laughs. Ram a nightstick up their ass."

"Jesus, we don't even carry nightsticks," Kelly said.

"He's chicken shit, anyway. Gave up, goin home to Georgetown or wherever the fuck he came from."

"What was Steve's deal?"

"He wanted us to go to a party at a cottage."

"Gerry didn't want to go?"

"Gerry wasn't invited."

"What about you?"

"I ain't goin' nowhere with a creep like that. I said no."

"What did Steve say?"

"He said I was a little pussy. I told him, 'Yeah, man, but I ain't *your* little pussy.' "

"One time, me and this girl, Cindy Lane, we were in Pennsylvania around Lock Haven, and we got stopped by this guy who said he was a cop. He showed us his badge and told us to get into his car. We told him to fuck off."

"What'd he do?"

"He wimped out and took off."

"Just like that. What were you guys carrying?"

"Some girls carry a knife. I got a small one just for camping and shit, but mostly you just gotta be smart," Debbie said.

"So, this guy, he wasn't in a police car, and he told you he was a cop?"

"Yeah, you know, there's a lotta stupid chicks out there, believe anything, give in way too easily. He said he was undercover. *Man*, they *all* say that."

They'd stopped off at Garnett's in Woodbine for coffee and pie before cruising through the dark to Gouverneur. Debbie was loose and talkative.

She'd been around, had hitchhiked the Great Lakes area and up into Canada. She loved the freedom of the road, of not knowing what was going to happen each day when she woke up. Sure, it was dangerous; there were creeps and killers on the road, men who thought hitchhikers all fucked for a ride. Kids were disappearing all the time, but she was a pro. Normally, she travelled with someone else, a guy or a girl, and she figured she'd hook up with somebody new pretty soon. Somebody better than the inexperienced Sylvia and her lame boyfriend.

You just had to keep your shit together; you needed your own set of rules. Like, there were always guys who would try to get you to go to their cottage or house, offering grass or booze. She had a rule never to do that. She'd sleep in a ditch before she'd accept a stranger's offer of a place to stay for the night.

Some counties had reputations, good and bad. Wanakena's was about as bad as it got. Lots of stories about girls getting raped by the cops. Lots of talk about the Adirondack Triangle; kids going in and never coming out again. Lots of bullshit. She hadn't been hassled the couple of times she'd passed through. Still, she avoided the place if she could. Didn't travel alone even if it meant joining up with a couple of rookies.

Kelly pressed her on the stories. From what Debbie remembered, it was always supposed to happen at night. Cops in uniform, they said. A shag shack with a freaky old bed that squeaked like hell.

"But if you ask me, it's not the cops you got to worry about in Wanakena, man, it's the ghosts," Debbie said.

"Ghosts?"

The Adirondacks had a lot of ghosts, and Kelly knew about most of them. Besides Sarah Punk at Lost Lake, there was Grace Brown haunting Moose Lake, and Mabel Douglas haunting Lake Placid, both murdered by men who were supposed to be their lovers.

There was also some nameless little girl who sat at the window of an old house at Cook's Corners where she'd been killed by her father. There was Grace and Little Ginny Hoffmeister, headless mother and daughter, hanging out by the old railroad tracks near the town of Faust where they had been ambushed by a crazed lumberjack. But she hadn't known that the hitchhikers had their own ghost stories as well. Debbie told her a few. All about ghost drivers, ghost hitchhikers, and ghost towns. She reeled them off one after another for an hour.

"I used to think it was all bullshit, right?" she said. "But, man, the first time I got dropped off near a cemetery at night, I got the creeps. I started walking away, next thing I knew I was *truckin'*, man. I just *knew* something was behind me, ran until I was out of breath. Happens to everybody.

"Swamps are the worst, the fucking mist, you just *know* it's full of ghosts. You get dropped off in a place like that, you hustle your butt up to higher ground. I mean, you can feel them in the air, you can smell them."

They had gotten way off the topic; Kelly had had enough of ghost stories, but Debbie was just getting warmed up.

"There's a story you keep hearing. Hitchhiker, alone on an empty stretch of road. The moon comes up, and all these kids rise up out of the ditches, all dead and shit, and start thumbing a ride. And man, they don't even try to eat you or anything. They just, like, nod at you, like you're one of them. And man, you start to wonder, oh shit, how *long* have I been here? You know, like, maybe I died here. Fuck, maybe I'm dead and don't even know it."

"But you don't really believe in that shit, right?" Kelly said.

"Lotta times people are just fucking with you, making up stories, trying to freak you out. But I tell you, some certifiably weird shit happens on the road, man."

CHAPTER
NINE

Mitch was sitting at the table on the porch, looking out at the lake.

Heavy cloud cover tonight, so dark he couldn't see the other shore. A strong wind hissed in the trees and rattled the rain-speckled screen. It was after ten o'clock and Kelly hadn't shown up. He was worried about her. She'd seemed upset when she and his dad had left him at Lucy's cottage. On a night like this you could easily smack into a downed tree on Cooperage, driving the way she did.

A Creedence, Bad Moon kind of night, after a strange day.

He'd been shifting furniture around in the back room to clear a spot for an outlet, when he'd remembered the stash of magazines he'd hidden away years ago. Lifting the false bottom of one of the wardrobes, he'd found them; four fat Playboys from the summer of 1960. They were just the way he'd left them, except now there was something laying on top of them—something that he hadn't put there.

It was a scribbler with a shiny black cover, the kind you see at general stores. It looked clean and new. He thumbed through it. The pages were empty, untouched, but there was something between them.

Polaroids. Seven dirty pictures starring Mrs. Dee, Mrs. Cross, and Mrs. Mulvane.

In the first one they were all standing together—topless, arm in arm, smiling at the camera. The next picture was of Mrs. Cross, completely naked, sitting on the arm of an Adirondack chair with her legs spread. Then there was a picture of Mrs. Cross hugging Lucy, playfully pinching one of her nipples.

They got dirtier. Lucy and Mrs. Mulvane both down on their knees looking at the camera with a cock in each hand. One with Lucy, looking wasted, lying on the floor while Mrs. Mulvane did shit to her that didn't look like fun at all. The last two were the worst. Lucy taking on three men at the same time while two more waited impatiently in the wings. Lucy all by herself, no sign of the other ladies.

The women were clearly visible in all of the pictures, but none of the men's faces could be seen—only their round bellies, their cocks, and their hairy, white asses. Seven dirty pictures. He looked at them carefully. Cottage pictures. Not all taken at the same place.

And there were seven more pictures which seemed completely unrelated.

Black and white pictures of darkness and harsh light. Tree branches jumping out towards the camera where the flash hit them. Pictures that didn't make any sense. Pictures of nothing at all, mistaken shots, rejects. Mitch looked at them again. There was no subject, at least not centered in the frame.

There *was* something, usually at the edge and off in the middle distance. Pictures like that, you could see what you wanted to see; he saw faces. In one snapshot, something was clearly looking back over its shoulder at the camera. Black circles for eyes and just the faintest suggestion of long hair flying. Sarah Punk.

Mitch figured the stash belonged to Bobby. Bobby had been hiding things in the lumber camp since he was a kid. Anything he wanted to keep away from his cousins. He'd come and go as he pleased, day or night. It didn't matter who was renting the place or how carefully they locked it up. When it came to the lumber camp, it was like little Bobby could walk through walls.

Mitch smoked some of his excellent Northern Lights shit and then sat for a while thinking about actions and responsibilities. He thought about the Zen injunction never to start anything. He reminded himself that everything he did sent karmic ripples out into the universe for eternity. All those ripples would eventually come back to him with all the shit they'd accumulated over the years. And he would have to answer for all of it, good and bad.

Mitch figured he'd fucked up his karma enough for one lifetime. He put the pictures back in the book and put the book back where he'd found it. He didn't know if Bobby had been given the pictures or if he had stolen them. Anyway, that was Bobby's karma to work out, not his.

Then he'd packed up his tools and went to see Lucy.

The moon passed back into the clouds. A fresh drum roll of rain started beating on the roof. The wind caught hold of the screen door at the far end of the cookhouse, opened it a foot, and slammed it shut.

Mitch jumped up, turned and scanned the dimly lit cookhouse. It was empty. He took a moment to catch his breath before going into the other room. As he was hooking the screen door, he saw the headlights of Kelly's Duster poking through the slanting curtain of rain.

"Son of a bitch," she exclaimed, as she hustled through the door.

"Rough day?" Mitch asked.

"That road, Jesus. That last bridge creaks like hell. The wind was screaming through the truss. I thought the whole thing was going to come apart."

Mitch smiled at the way her energy filled the room. "Maybe it was Sarah you heard screaming?" he said.

"Is that meat I smell?"

"Steak. I thought you'd be back earlier." Mitch took a plate covered in tinfoil out of the oven. "You want to eat here or on the porch?"

"Right here, I'm starving." She took off her belt and sat down at the end of the long table.

Mitch got her a beer.

"Thanks, thanks for the supper," Kelly said, between quick mouthfuls. "I thought you'd be spending the night with your rich friend across the lake. Surprised you'd leave her fucked up like that."

"I didn't want to, but Mrs. Mulvane showed up and threw me out. Paranoid, like I was trying to take advantage of Lucy or something. Man, who thinks like that?"

"Yeah, a guy ought to get the benefit of the doubt," Kelly said, looking up at him while she carved up more steak.

"Right on, I was just there to help."

"Did you get Mrs. Dee to talk before you got kicked out?" Kelly asked.

"Get her to talk?"

"Maybe she had more to say about her bitchy neighbors."

Before Mitch could reply, the lights went out. The Admiral refrigerator clunked loudly and went silent. "Oh, shit," he said.

"Were you working on the electrical today?" Kelly sounded amused. All he could see was her eyes shining as she looked at him across the table.

He thought for a moment. "I didn't do anything." He grabbed the big flashlight from the window ledge. "I'll check the fuses."

The rain had let up, now it was just big, random

drops flung at him by the agitated trees. The fuses were fine. No lights across the lake, none on this side either, even though Mrs. Anderson usually left a lot of lights on all night.

"It's the whole lake. Wind probably dropped a branch onto the power line somewhere back along Cooperage," Mitch said as he came back into the cookhouse.

Kelly had put her flashlight on the table and resumed eating. "So now what?"

"All the new cottages have phones. The thing is, the lines run on top of each other, so if a branch takes out the power, it takes the phones too. Somebody has to drive into Woodbine and use the pay phone outside Garnett's."

"Will anybody go?"

"Mrs. Ratsmueller doesn't give a damn; neither does Mrs. Parker. Mrs. Anderson's probably passed out by now. This happened a few days after I got here. One of the men from across the lake must have gone. Tonight? I don't think any of the women would make the drive."

"So, if I want a shower in the morning, I have to drive all the way out to Woodbine."

"Pretty much, but you don't have to go. I can do it, you get some sleep."

"No, we'll go together."

It occurred to him that she didn't trust him with her car, but he let that negativity go.

"Okay, but I want to stop and check on Lucy when we swing around that way," he said.

"What about Mrs. Mulvane?"

"I don't trust her."

CHAPTER TEN

No lights were showing at the Dee cottage, no candles or lamps flickering. Mitch gave the ornamental knocker a few knocks. "Lucy!"

Kelly pounded on the door with her fist. "Mrs. Dee, this is Deputy Mackinaw. Are you okay?"

"Lucy, it's Mitch."

No answer. "Mulvane must have left, maybe took Mrs. Dee with her," Kelly said.

Mitch tried the door, and it came open. "Lucy. Lucy, it's Mitch."

Their flashlights played over the living room floor like helicopter searchlights surveying earthquake rubble. "I'll check upstairs," he said.

He followed his flashlight beam up the tight, spiral staircase. The short, second-floor hallway smelled like Lucy—gin and flowery perfume. The door to her bedroom was wide open.

"Fuck!" he shouted.

A man with a flashlight was standing on the far side of the room. An instant later he realized that it was his own reflection bouncing back at him from the wall-to-wall mirrored doors of her closet. Looking up, he saw himself weirdly reflected by the big mirror on the ceiling above the empty bed.

He'd put Lucy in that bed, had propped her up on a bunch of pillows and talked to her until she'd started to sober up. Then Mrs. Mulvane had come marching in like she owned the place and kicked him out.

No sign of either woman now. The bed was turned down and rumpled as if Lucy had slept in it. He couldn't tell if there was anything else different about the room. The wind rattled at the windows like it was trying to get in and blow the place to hell.

"Mitch!" Kelly shouted.

He bumped into the doorframe on the way out and almost tripped coming down the stairs. Lucy was lying face down on the kitchen floor; the lightweight, pink nightgown he'd dressed her in was open and bunched up around her waist. She wasn't moving. She wasn't making a sound.

"Did you try...?" He went down on his knees, took Lucy by the shoulders so he could flip her over.

"She's dead, Mitch, don't touch her," Kelly cautioned. Her voice was sharp.

He took one of Lucy's narrow, blue-veined wrists and checked her pulse. It was a dead arm, cold and still. Lying flat on his stomach, he took a close look at the half of her face pressed against the floor. She looked ghastly; her eyes were closed, half covered by her wild, rust colored hair. Her lips were puffy and blue. There was spit on them and in a small pool on the floor. He reached out and lifted an eyelid.

"Mitch!"

He knew she was dead. Her flaccid body held no spirit. "OD?" he said.

"That's for the coroner to decide. Get back, Mitch, this could be a crime scene."

"A crime scene?"

Mitch sat back on his heels. He ran the flashlight beam along Lucy's body. One arm was folded under her, there were bruises on the other one, and on the wrist he had held. Bruises on her thighs. There had been bruises before. Were there more now?

Leaning over, he took the hem of her gown in his fingers and worked it down to mid-thigh.

"Mitch, stop that," Kelly said. He did it anyway.

Kelly put a firm hand on his shoulder and helped him to stand. He let his flashlight droop, lighting the floor at his feet. He had met her for the first time this afternoon, and now she was dead. When he'd arrived, she'd been high, laughing one minute and ranting the next. Coming on to him, showing him things.

He hardly knew her, but he had a feeling that she wasn't going anywhere. He looked up at the ceiling. "What the fuck, Lucy. Now what am I supposed to do?" he said.

Kelly gave his shoulder a shake. She spoke to him

slowly and firmly. "You have to call your dad and tell him what happened," she said.

Mitch didn't mind making the drive, but he hated the idea of leaving Lucy; she'd be in bad shape right now. He took a deep breath and shivered, short hairs prickling up all over his body.

"Lucy?" She was there, alright. She was bouncing off the walls, scattered, unformed.

"Mitch. Mitch, you have to drive to Woodbine and call the station."

"Shouldn't you report it? You're the cop."

"I need to protect the scene, make sure it's not disturbed."

Would someone want to disturb the scene? He thought about the pictures, the ones he'd found in the bunkhouse, and the ones that Lucy had shown him. A big, fat envelope full of nasty Polaroids.

"I can protect the scene," he said.

"You don't have the authority."

"Fuck that."

"Mitch..."

"Can't you make me a deputy or something?"

"Mitch, I can't leave you here. You're a suspect."

"A suspect? Seriously, man? Come on."

"Nothing personal, Mitch. It's probably just an OD, right? But if we screw around, then something simple becomes a big problem."

"I shouldn't have left her," Mitch said, squatting down again.

"Her husband shouldn't have left her," Kelly

replied, her voice sharp and angry. "Mulvane shouldn't have left her."

Maybe. And maybe, Mr. Dan Dee shouldn't have passed his wife around like a joint at a party.

"Mitch, the sooner you get going, the better."

"Right. You sure you're going to be okay?"

"I'm good, just got to stay awake is all. So, after you make the call, come right back."

She really didn't understand the unseen world pulsating all around her. He stood. "Okay, I'm going." He felt like giving her a hug, but he didn't want to blow her mind.

He wondered if Kelly would do some poking around on her own. Would *she* respect the crime scene? He wondered where the big fat envelope was now.

"If you go upstairs, watch out for the mirrors. They're all over the place up there, especially in Lucy's room."

"Thanks, good to know."

"Okay, hang in there, Lucy," he said to the ceiling. He cocked a thumb at Kelly. "Don't hurt her, she's on our side."

"Jesus, Mitch. Try not to wreck my car, okay?"

CHAPTER
ELEVEN

TUESDAY

As soon as Mitch left, Kelly locked the back door, stood still and listened.

Mrs. Mulvane didn't strike her as the kind of person who went around leaving doors unlocked, so there was a possibility that someone else had entered the cottage and was still there. The cottage creaked, the wind whistled and sobbed around its sharp modernistic angles. The large glass windows rattled, but she heard no voices or furtive footsteps.

Reasonably confident that she was alone, she began checking the ground floor. There was stuff all over—empty bottles, shoes, wine corks, and other party debris.

The cottage was cold even though it was warm and blustery outside. Probably the AC had been running full blast right up until the power went out. The patio doors and all the windows were closed and locked. The stink of stale nicotine and weed hung in the air, overpowering every other smell. Kelly didn't open any drawers, and she was careful when touching things. She left the body alone.

There was a full bathroom on the ground floor. It looked and smelled like it had been puked in and half-assed cleaned up at least a couple of times. The window was open, and the curtains pulled back, but the screen looked secure. The glass medicine cabinet was empty—no drugs, prescription or otherwise.

A woman was dead. The most likely explanation was that a rich, unhappy housewife had OD'd on prescription drugs. It happened all the time these days.

Kelly returned to the kitchen and had a closer look around the body. There was nothing of interest on the hardwood floor. Just old stains, scattered crumbs, and dust bunnies.

The living room was a mess. Pillows and couch cushions were scattered on the shag carpet along with women's shoes and random articles of men's and women's clothing. On the floor next to the big-knobbed Akai sound system, there were several piles of albums. A dime bag of weed and a pack of rolling papers lay on top of the plastic turntable cover. The end tables were crammed with empty glasses and ashtrays filled with cigarette butts and a few roaches. A couple of Chianti bottles, with candles melted into their necks, stood upright on the otherwise clear coffee table.

It was difficult to put together a full picture of the scene with just a flashlight. Everything she saw was in snapshots, but as far as she could tell, there were no obvious signs of a struggle. No weapons, nothing broken. However, she wondered if the place had been tossed. The end table drawers were half open; all of the cushions had been removed from the chairs and the couch.

She was about to go upstairs when she heard the sound of a car outside. Faint squares of light, bracketed by window-frame shadows, floated across the walls. She looked at her watch; one o'clock. There was no way Mitch could have made it to Woodbine, called his dad, and come back again already.

A car door slammed. Kelly took a couple of steps up the staircase, out of the line of sight of the entranceway, then turned and stood with her flashlight pointed at the floor. She expected a knock. Instead, she heard a key turning in the lock.

"Hey, Lucy! Lucy, you awake? Don't worry, it's me, Miles."

Mrs. Dee's husband's name was Dan. Kelly didn't know anyone named Miles.

"Is the power out again?"

Kelly waited. She heard the light switch being flicked on and off.

"Lucy?"

"Who's there?" Kelly called out.

"Holly? It's Miles, what's going on?"

Holly. Mrs. Mulvane's name was Holly.

A flashlight came on; a big man emerged from the entrance hallway.

One hand on the butt of her revolver, Kelly said, "I am Deputy Mackinaw, County Sheriff's Department. Sir, you need to stop moving right now and identify yourself."

"Mackinaw. The new girl?" The man's flashlight beam sought her out.

"*Deputy* Mackinaw. Get your flashlight out of my face." She poked her light towards him, looking for his face. She stopped when it flashed on the silver star on his chest. "Who are you?" she asked.

"*Deputy* Crogan. What the hell are you doing here, Mackinaw?"

Crogan was one of the night shift guys. They hadn't met. She dialed back the tone of her voice. "What are *you* doing here? You a close friend of the Dees?"

"A close friend? Uhh, hell, I'm a friend..."

"You have a key to their cottage."

"They keep it... What the fuck is going on?"

"You always drop in on them in the middle of the night?" Kelly asked, trying to keep her voice flat.

"Hey, fuck you, Mackinaw. What's going on? Where's Lucy?"

"Mrs. Dee is dead. Don't move. This is a potential crime scene and there's shit all over the place."

"Fuck off, she's dead. Where is she?"

"Her body's in the kitchen. You shouldn't go in there..."

Crogan ignored her and went into the kitchen. She heard something crunch under one of his boots.

"Don't touch the body," she shouted and hurried after him.

Crogan stood over Mrs. Dee's body, arms at his sides, flashlight lowered. "Man, what happened? She fall?"

"I don't know. The sheriff is on his way. We need to back off until he gets here."

"Jesus, man, Lucy?" He sounded shocked.

"You really knew her, eh?" Kelly asked, putting as much sympathy into her voice as she could muster.

"Sure. I mean... I knew the Dees. Shit, does Dan know? Somebody's gotta tell him."

"The sheriff will take care of that."

"Fuck, Lucy's dead?" Crogan pushed back his hat and rubbed his forehead.

Kelly was quiet, observing him as well as she could in the darkness. She felt no inclination to touch him or comfort him. She waited to see what else he had to say.

Crogan was silent. If it hadn't been for the flashlight in his hand, Kelly might have thought there was no one there at all. Crogan had a key to the cottage, or he knew where they kept one. He must have known that Mr. Dee had gone back to the city. Kelly couldn't think of any good reason for an on-duty deputy to be way out here at one o'clock in the morning. Lost Lake was far from the center of the county's population, at the end of a long, slow-going road.

"Has anyone told the neighbors?" Crogan asked.

"Not yet. Do you think they might have had something to do with this?"

"Like what? Jesus, somebody should tell them." His voice was low, dispirited.

Crogan was guilty of something, maybe just of fooling around with another man's wife. She was pretty sure he had nothing to do with Lucy's death.

"I heard the Dees were really nice people," she said.

"Sure. Dan's a great guy, and Lucy, man..."

"You come up here often?"

"Not a lot, no. So, you think it was an OD or something?"

"Maybe."

"Lucy... Mrs. Dee, she liked to drink. I warned her about mixing booze with her prescription drugs, you know. Son-of-a-bitch."

"Mrs. Dee ever complain that her husband beat her up or anything like that?"

"Dan? No way."

"Looks like she has a few bruises on her."

"Fuck off." Crogan ran his flashlight tentatively along the body. There weren't a lot of bruises evident, especially after Mitch had rearranged her nightgown. "No, I never saw anything like that. She never said anything."

Kelly could imagine him biting his lip, tears welling in his eyes. Maybe.

When his light reached Mrs. Dee's feet, he let it fall away. "Lucy liked to drink a bit..."

Kelly waited, but Crogan remained silent. She teased her light slowly up Mrs. Dee's body.

"You get a look around the place?" he asked.

"No, I'm waiting for the sheriff."

He cleared his throat. "I can do that; you should go get some sleep. Hell, I'm the one on duty." A bit of anger had returned to his voice.

"No, I'll wait." Kelly looked at her watch; one-thirty.

"Yeah, well, if you're gonna stay, I'll head back." He turned abruptly and started walking towards her, coming right at her, like he was going to walk right through her.

There was plenty of room for him to get by her and out of the kitchen. Kelly didn't want to retreat from him, but he was over six feet tall and two hundred pounds, at least. Reluctantly, she took a half-step to the side, ready to use her flashlight as a club if he tried to touch her.

"Mrs. Dee ever complain to you about Bobby Margin?" she asked, raising her voice.

Crogan stopped. "Bobby Margin?" He sounded surprised. "Why would Mrs. Dee complain about Bobby? He's like her puppy dog, run and fetch for her."

"Just something the sheriff said."

"Bobby Margin. What's with you, Mackinaw?"

"If you're going, you should give me the key. The one you used to get in."

Crogan took another step towards her. His flashlight came up. Kelly brought hers up too. They both stopped high on each other's chest, just short of each other's faces. He looked sinister, lit from below like that. He had the bland, slab-like, Momma's Boy face of a strangler.

"Fuck you. You don't know shit, Mackinaw. Who do you think you are anyway?"

"I'm securing the scene."

"Jesus, you've been with the department, what, *two* fucking days? And you're giving *me* orders. I know what's going on with you. Everybody does."

Kelly stayed cool. She knew there was going to be shit like that. Rumors she was sleeping with the sheriff, or worse, sleeping with Gail Harmon.

"The sheriff will need that key," she said, her voice flat.

"Fuck you," he said.

Kelly held her ground. Crogan went around her and headed for the door. She stayed well back from him and helped light his way with her flashlight. She gave him some space before she followed him to the door. He didn't look back or say goodbye. From the doorway, she watched him bend down and slip the key under the lawn jockey on the right side of the door.

She stood on the steps and watched the taillights of Crogan's cruiser as they looped around the big parking area and headed out to Shangri-La Lane. They turned left towards the Cross Cottage instead of right, towards Cooperage Road.

The son of a bitch was off to tell the neighbors.

CHAPTER
TWELVE

The wind was blowing hard enough to keep the bugs down, but not enough to keep the lake from slowly filling with fog. Above the waving treetops, the predawn sky was alive with ragged clouds fleeing to the east.

"All right," Sheriff Herkemer said, dusting crumbs from his fingers. "I'll get Mitch's statement first, then yours, Kelly."

Kelly lowered the plastic thermos cup from her lips. There were just the three of them on the front patio of the Dee cottage. "You want me to go back inside?"

"No need for that. You can tell me if Mitch is lying."

Kelly shrugged. "Sure thing, Sheriff."

Obviously, Sheriff Herkemer had decided that she and Mitch had nothing to hide. Fair enough, that was his call. One of the things about being a sheriff, one of the reasons Kelly wanted to *be* a sheriff, was that you didn't have to get wrapped up in bullshit paperwork or time-wasting procedure if you didn't think it was called for.

As soon as he had arrived, the sheriff had sent Mitch to the lumber camp to get coffee and make something to eat. After a careful survey of the ground floor, he and Kelly had searched the upstairs together. They'd found nothing unexpected. The guest rooms were a mess, the Dees' master bedroom, with its mirrored cabinets and ceiling, was a mess. There was no obvious sign of a struggle.

"Do you think the place was searched?" Kelly asked.

Sheriff Herkemer made a noncommittal grunt.

They found an empty prescription bottle lying on its side on the bedside table. Valium, prescribed to Mrs. Lucy Dee, by a Dr. De Voss in Syracuse, 6/10/73, quantity: 60.

"That would do it," Sheriff Herkemer said, with a sigh.

They did not find a suicide note.

Kelly listened to Mitch give his statement. He was telling it straight, as far as she could tell. When he mentioned smoking a joint with Mrs. Dee, Sheriff Herkemer interrupted him. "The marijuana didn't do this to her, right?"

"No way."

"Then there's no need to bring it up. Did you give her any other drugs?"

"No, I wouldn't do that, not the way she was."

"The coroner's gonna know all the stuff she had in her system," the sheriff said, a definite warning in his tone.

"If there's anything else, she didn't get it from me."

"Even prescription?"

"Hell no, that shit's poison."

Her back turned to them, Kelly smiled.

In her statement, Kelly mentioned the smell of marijuana in the house, the roaches in the ashtrays, and the dime bag on the stereo. She hadn't witnessed Mitch smoking a joint with Mrs. Dee, so she didn't bring it up. When she described her encounter with Crogan, the sheriff shook his head.

"That idiot almost hit me head-on at the top of Cooperage. We're gonna have a long talk tonight." The sheriff looked at his watch. "I'm gonna interview the neighbors. If you're up to it, I'd like you to come along."

"Absolutely, Sheriff."

"Couple of hours until Thompson gets here." He raised his voice, "Mitch, can you watch the place?"

Mitch was staring at the upper-floor windows of the Dee cottage. He turned to face them. "What?" He looked spaced. Kelly wondered if he'd smoked a joint while she was upstairs with the sheriff.

"Keep an eye on the place. Stay outside. Make sure

nobody goes in until we get back or Thompson gets here. Okay? Can you do that?"

"Yeah, sure," Mitch said.

"Thanks for the coffee. Come on, Kelly. Might as well go now, I don't think we'll be rousting anybody out of bed."

Dawn was breaking as they made their way along the shore; the dripping forest on their left, the fog-bound lake on their right. The narrow, twisting path was knee-deep in mist. Overhead, the sky was clearing fast.

Kelly took off her hat and wiped her brow as they climbed the zigzagging, stone steps up to the Cross cottage.

"I'll do the talking," the sheriff said.

"Want me to take notes?"

"Not unless I say so."

When they reached the top of the stairs, Mrs. Cross was placing a cushion on one of the white metal chairs arranged around an oval table, while Mrs. Mulvane wiped the condensation from its glass surface.

Mrs. Mulvane straightened and stood with one hand cocked on her hip, the other holding the wet rag. In crisply pleated, red shorts, a white top, and red heels, she looked poised and relaxed. "We've been expecting you," she said.

"Deputy Crogan?"

"Yes, he gave us the news."

"So sad," Mrs. Cross said. She sounded like she meant it.

"We thought it would be better to talk out here. It's still quite dark inside," Mrs. Mulvane said. "Please, come and sit."

"Outside's good," the sheriff replied.

"What happened to her?" Mrs. Cross asked. No one answered her question.

"I can't offer you any coffee, I'm sorry. Would you like some orange juice? It's still cold?" Mrs. Mulvane asked, playing the hostess in Mrs. Cross's home.

"No, thank you. Mitch made us a batch of coffee and brought it over to the Dees."

Kelly wondered if he was giving the ladies a heads up that he'd already spoken to Mitch.

Mrs. Cross said something barely audible, turned, and went back into the cottage. Mrs. Mulvane tossed the rag onto a planter, pulled a pack of Virginia Slims out of her pocket, and sat down at the far end of the oval.

The sheriff took the seat at the other end of the table. Kelly hesitated.

Mrs. Mulvane lit her cigarette with a silver lighter and smiled up at her. "How nice to see your eyes for a change, Deputy Mackinaw," she said.

Kelly touched the aviators in her breast pocket and swore under her breath. Cold and hostile yesterday afternoon, bitchy-friendly this morning. She was developing a serious dislike for Mrs. Mulvane.

"Oh, I hope I didn't keep everyone waiting," Mrs. Cross said, coming back through the sliding door with a small, glass ashtray and a large, plastic tumbler.

Kelly watched her move carefully across the patio stones in silver slippers tied with ribbons that wound halfway up her calves. She wore a cute little outfit: shorts, bikini top, and a short cover-up in a jungle foliage pattern, looking like she was about to go on safari in a Hollywood comedy. She set the tumbler in front of Mrs. Mulvane, the ashtray between them, and sat down with her back to the cottage.

Kelly sat down across from Mrs. Cross, who gave her a smile. Kelly couldn't tell if the woman was sleepy, dopey, or outright stoned. She smelled freshly scrubbed, with just a hint of perfume. All of her tight little curls were neatly in place. The light make-up dusted across her cherubic face didn't completely conceal the effects of a wakeful night.

Looking at Kelly with her wet, brown eyes, she said, "You found her, Lucy... the body?"

"That's correct," Kelly replied.

"That must have been so hard for you," she said, reaching her hands along the tabletop towards Kelly.

"I've seen dead bodies before."

"Oh," Mrs. Cross replied, withdrawing her hands and putting them in her lap.

Kelly wasn't keeping count. There had been bodies and parts of bodies on the streets of Saigon, torn apart by random mortar rounds or carefully tossed grenades. There had been a boy on a snowbank in Buffalo, looking like he was asleep, except for the blue of his lips and the waxy color of his skin, darker than the snow. There were others, not all memorable. There was a woman with her head blown off by a shotgun blast, blood and brains splattered all over her Gardenville bedroom wall. That shit could get to you. Mrs. Dee was easy.

Mrs. Mulvane was staring at her. So was the sheriff.

"What?" she said.

"Yes, it's a terrible thing…" the sheriff started to say.

"Did she?" Mrs. Cross interrupted softly.

"We don't know," Sheriff Herkemer replied. He turned to Mrs. Mulvane, "Mitch said you were with Mrs. Dee when he left. How was she?"

"She seemed fine to me, under the circumstances. I'm not a doctor, of course, but she was not in any kind of distress that I could see." She inhaled and blew smoke upwards. "After your son left, she dozed fitfully. At one point, she woke up and asked me for some gin. I gave her a glass of water instead. After that she fell asleep."

"This was in her bedroom?"

"Yes, I sat with her for an hour or so. She was sleeping one off, not something unusual for her. Her breathing was fine." Leaning forward, she stubbed out her cigarette. "In fact, she was snoring quite heavily."

"What was she wearing?"

"A pink nightgown, well, negligee really."

"Did you see any pills?"

Mrs. Cross took a cigarette from Mrs. Mulvane's pack and attempted to light it with Mrs. Mulvane's lighter.

"There were none on the bedside table. I didn't go looking through her medicine cabinets." Mrs. Mulvane took the lighter from Mrs. Cross and lit her cigarette for her. Mrs. Cross smiled apologetically at all of them.

"I sat there for a while, fighting the urge to clean the place up," Mrs. Mulvane continued. "The snoring and the mess... it got to be too much. I had other things to do. When I left her, it was my intention to return and check on her in a couple of hours. But then we had the storm and the power went out."

"What time did you leave her?" the sheriff asked.

Mrs. Mulvane rested her cigarette in the ashtray and took a drink from the tumbler. "Some time around nine. I stopped by to see Denise. Around nine?" She looked at Mrs. Cross.

Mrs. Cross was staring at her cigarette burning down in the ashtray. She nodded. "Yes, about nine, I think." She looked up, first at Kelly, then the sheriff. "It was just before the power went out."

"Did you lock up when you left the Dee cottage?" Kelly asked Mrs. Mulvane.

"Yes."

"After the lights..." Mrs. Cross spoke in a hoarse whisper.

Kelly pressed on, "Do you have a key to the Dee cottage?" she asked Mrs. Mulvane.

Mrs. Cross was still talking "... it was very dark. All the flashlights..."

Kelly was about to ask Mulvane another question

when she felt Sheriff Herkemer's boot tapping hers under the table. He was looking at Mrs. Cross. Kelly shut up.

"... were dead. I keep telling Hal to replace the batteries. And the wind was... screaming. I knew something terrible was going to happen."

"Yes, I understand," Sheriff Herkemer said, raising a hand.

"I heard Sarah scratching at the window."

"We don't need to get into that right now."

Jesus Christ, here we go again.

Mrs. Cross turned to Mrs. Mulvane. "You heard her too."

Mrs. Mulvane nodded. "I saw her. Out that window, up in the trees," she thrust her chin towards the second-storey window.

"The trees were blowing all over the place last night, how could she be up in a tree?" Kelly asked. Her voice was sharp, fending off the freaky presence she'd felt yesterday when they'd started talking about Sarah.

They were all looking at her again, frowning. "She flies," Mrs. Cross said.

"Oh, I thought she just stood around and screamed at people."

The sheriff tapped her boot, hard.

Mrs. Mulvane lit another cigarette; Kelly hadn't seen her finish the last one. "Say what you like..."

"All that aside..." Sheriff Herkemer sighed.

"I saw *something* out that window. Not a person, not an animal. It scared me. There was no way I was going back outside." She looked at Kelly. "You don't understand, Deputy. Wait until you've been here a while." She sat back and took another drink.

Mrs. Cross picked up the butt of the cigarette that had burned down and fallen out of the ashtray. She put it back and stared at it.

Are they fucking with us? Kelly wondered. Are they *all* fucking with *me*?

The sheriff had turned his attention to Mrs. Cross. "You knew the Dees fairly well?"

Mrs. Cross looked up at him. "Yes, I guess, pretty well. Uh, we weren't…"

"We *thought* we knew them fairly well," Mrs. Mulvane said. "We all built here at the same time, but we didn't know each other before that."

Mrs. Cross nodded slowly, her attention back on the ashtray.

Mrs. Mulvane sat up straight. "Sure, Lucy was a bit of a flirt, but that didn't seem to bother Dan. In fact, he took pride in showing off her rather obvious charms that were forever spilling out of her clothes."

Mrs. Cross smiled. "She liked to drink, for sure. She liked to have a good time. You know, if everybody was quiet, Lucy would get things going."

"Loud. Often too loud, but Dan would let her go on, no matter how outrageous she became. It never lasted anyway. Once she got like that, she'd soon run out of steam and totter off to bed," Mrs. Mulvane said.

"Did they argue, Mr. and Mrs. Dee?" the sheriff asked.

"Sure..." Mrs. Cross replied.

"Well, argue. I mean, what couple doesn't? Lucy would get wound up and criticize Dan for this or that. Sometimes it would develop into a spat," Mrs. Mulvane said.

Kelly was unable to hold down her growing frustration. Mitch had said that Mrs. Dee had been raging when he went over to visit her. Angry at all of them. "Did any of you have an argument with Mrs. Dee?" she asked.

"Lucy was always in a snit about something. It depended on how much she'd had to drink. But her *moods* never lasted."

"When was the last time you saw Mrs. Dee?" the sheriff asked Mrs. Cross.

"Oh... Sunday? Yesterday..."

"Saturday evening, dear, remember. Mick and I dropped by just for a bit. You and Hal left the same time we did."

"You must be right."

Sheriff Herkemer stood up. "Well, thank you for your time, ladies; I know all of this must be hard on you."

The women stood up. Surprised that the interview was over so soon, Kelly stood. She forced a smile. "I *am* new here," she conceded. "Wasn't it this time last year that a woman fell off the cliff near the Dee cottage?"

"Oh." Mrs. Cross gave her a reproachful look, her eyes filling with tears.

"You knew her?" Kelly asked.

"She didn't have to know her to be sad about it," Mrs. Mulvane said, getting testy. "It's been a rough night for all of us."

Kelly knew that the sheriff was pissed off at her, but he didn't interrupt, didn't cut her off or jack her up in front of the ladies.

"Did *you* know her?" Kelly pressed on.

"No, she was a guest of the Dees, the wife of one of his franchise owners. They were introduced to us, but I really can't remember them. It was the Dees' party." She dismissed Kelly with a very slight wave of the hand and turned back to the sheriff. "I'm dying for a coffee. Do you know when the power will be back on?" she asked.

"I lit a fire under Ma Bell and Con Ed, three, four hours ago. Might be back up by noon. If you go on up to Garnett's to get some coffee, be careful; Cooperage will be busy."

This time they all shook hands before they left. Everybody much friendlier today. Kelly had the feeling that Mrs. Cross even wanted to give her a hug. Strange people.

She tried to stay quiet as they walked down the path back to the Dee cottage, knowing she'd crossed the line by interrupting the sheriff's interview. But she couldn't contain herself.

"So, Sheriff, what do you think?"

They walked on in silence to the point where she thought he wasn't going to answer her at all. "Most likely an accidental overdose," he said. "Nothing we saw in the cottage and nothing we just heard changes that, as far as I'm concerned."

"Come on, Sheriff, didn't you think they were acting strangely?"

"Everybody reacts differently to death."

"Mitch said they were all having a big argument..."

"Mitch said? Jesus, Kelly." He gave his head a disappointed shake.

"Right." She swore under her breath.

"We wait for the coroner's report. If he turns up anything unusual, we'll look into it."

"The bruises on her body..."

Sheriff Herkimer stopped abruptly, turned and looked at her. "I'm sure the coroner will have a good look at them, too." He held up his hand to stop her from saying anything more, just like he'd done to dippy Mrs. Cross. "Take a breath, Kelly."

She bit her lip. "Got it, Sheriff. Watch and learn."

He nodded. "Consider that maybe the rest of us know what the hell we're doing."

Kelly nodded.

"I got one problem child already. I need help around here, not more trouble."

Kelly nodded. She would think twice before she spoke again. But how much trouble was she going to be? That really wasn't up to her.

CHAPTER
THIRTEEN

After Kelly and his dad went to interview the swingers, Mitch had slipped back into the Dee cottage and sat cross-legged just inside the patio door. He'd tried to latch on to Lucy's spirit, but it was tricky, like trying to tune in a distant radio station in a sea of static.

He'd snuck out when Undersheriff Thompson arrived, had a few words with the man, and then set off for the lumber camp, walking along the trail that wound tightly around Deadhead Bay. Looking for company, he'd stopped at the Anderson cottage. It was far too early for Patricia to be awake, so he'd curled up in a lawn chair and dozed until he heard the sharp metallic grating of the patio door sliding open behind him.

"Hey you!"

He rolled up into a sitting position, pushing his

damp hair out of his eyes. Patricia Anderson stood on the broad, wrap-around porch of her cottage, hands on her narrow hips. "Did you blow up the power grid again?" she asked, amused.

"No, it wasn't me this time."

"What's going on?"

"Lucy Dee died last night."

"Son of a bitch. Well, come on inside and tell me all about it, dear. I've got breakfast ready."

Mrs. Anderson's place didn't look like the other new cottages across the lake. Built on the only flat piece of land on Lost Lake, it reminded Mitch of one of the farmhouses he'd seen in Blue Grass Country. Two stories, white with green trim, normal rectangular windows, simple lines. Very symmetrical, with a long lanai running off the Deadhead Bay side, facing the lake.

They sat there, side by side in big, fat-cushioned wicker chairs. Breakfast was a pitcher of Screwdrivers. "So, what happened? Did she fall off Steep Rock? Drive her car into a tree?" Patricia was curious, but not at all surprised or sad.

"Probably an OD. Coroner is on his way," Mitch replied.

"Who found her?"

"I did."

"Last night? Damn it, Mitch, were you with Lucy Dee last night?"

"Yeah, for a while."

"After I warned you about those people? Honestly, you're as bad as Bobby."

"I went over to borrow some ginger."

"Ginger. Really, Mitch, you're so transparent."

"What?"

"*Ginger.* Pale skin, freckles, red hair. Did the carpet match the drapes?" she demanded, teasing but maybe a little upset.

"Jesus, Patricia, it wasn't like that. I wanted to make a stir-fry and..."

"You thought *Lucy Dee* would have ginger? I'm sure garlic salt is the most exotic spice in her pantry. You needed ginger, and you thought of *her* first, with me right next door?"

"You must have gone to town, or something. Anyway, come on, the woman has just died."

He had gone because of the pictures, the ones of Sarah Punk, and the ones of Lucy alone, surrounded by a pack of hairy-assed jerks. "How well do you know those people, anyway?" he asked.

"Well enough to stay away from them. I told you they were bad news."

"You weren't very specific."

"We were here first, you know, by a whole year. When those people moved in, Chet and I were invited over to the other side of the lake several times."

Chet was Patricia's most recent husband, her third, Mitch thought, although there might have been more. He had died last winter. A boating accident in Italy; Patricia was vague about the details.

"It was obvious what was happening over there. Why do you think their children are never around?

They have these nice cottages, and their children are all off at camp? There was a lot of nudity and several, not very subtle, suggestions. Chet and I simply stopped responding to their invitations."

"So, you guys never..."

"*Please*," she said. "I have more respect for myself than that."

"Were they all into it, over there?"

"Well, they were certainly all involved in the inviting. But as I said, I didn't actually witness the rutting. They were a gang, a *scene*. All very chummy."

"Lucy was mad at all of them. Really pissed off about something. You ever see them fighting, arguing?" he asked.

"That sort of lifestyle unravels very quickly. I'm sure there were plenty of bruised egos and simmering jealousies. Swingers, very hip, very liberated. Nudity and drugs and orgies. Pretty juvenile when it comes down to it. All great fun until someone falls off a cliff."

"Or takes a shitload of pills."

As they started in on the second pitcher of Screwdrivers, Patricia said, "I've been thinking about LSD."

Mitch chuckled. "I didn't think that was your bag."

"I was thinking it might figure prominently in my latest novel."

From what she'd told him, Patricia was fabulously rich. At different times, she'd mentioned houses on Long Island and at Palm Springs, a ski lodge in the Alps, a little place on Santorini. But she loved her hideaway on Lost Lake the best of all, she said, because *absolutely* no one knew where she was.

She came for the peace and quiet that allowed her to pursue her favorite hobby. Patricia wrote novels for fun and thought it amusing that they made her a lot of money that she didn't really need. She called them bodice rippers. There was a row of them in the bookcase in the living room with titles like *Fatal Princess* and *Captive Queen of the Desert*. One of the things that Mitch liked about Patricia was that she had never asked him to read any of them.

"What's this one called?" he asked. He did like her titles.

"The Hasty Virgin of Versailles."

"So, that's like, 1700s?"

"Yes, it's about an overly adventurous, French noblewoman who gets abducted by pirates and carried off to Morocco."

"They didn't have LSD back then. Hell, it's only been around, what? Ten, fifteen years."

"Minor detail. I'll have some vizier whip up something *like* LSD to force on my unfortunate heroine."

"You never tripped?"

"It was not around in my youth," she said with a thin smile.

Mitch kept forgetting how old Patricia was—not

that she'd ever told him, exactly. From her stories, she had to be in her late forties. "So, you want to know if I have any?" he asked.

"Or might know where..."

"I don't sell drugs or make connections."

"I didn't mean to suggest..."

"I can share some blotter with you, if we do it together. If it's not handled right, that shit can shred your gray matter like a fucking Claymore."

"That would be wonderful."

"And no guns." Patricia had a very impressive gun collection.

"They will all be safely locked away," she promised.

"Then sure, when the time feels right."

"I've been wondering what visions are locked up in here," she tapped her temple with a finely manicured fingernail.

"Speaking of visions."

A kayak had emerged from the thinning mist. Mrs. Ratsmueller, Gisela, maneuvered the craft deftly to shore next to Patricia's dock, clambered out into the knee-deep water and pulled the sleek craft up onto the bank.

"Bet she did the whole lake and back," Mitch said. Gisela coached women's athletics at Syracuse; rowing, field hockey, basketball.

She walked towards them, holding the double-bladed paddle upright. "Like a Wagnerian spear chucker," Patricia mused.

From a distance, with her blond hair braided and

hidden behind her back, Gisela might have been mistaken for a man. Her tall body was a T formed by broad shoulders, narrow hips, and muscular thighs. It was only when she got closer that her streamlined, one-piece bathing suit dispelled any such confusion. Her breasts were modest but unmistakable, and the suit's high-cut, skin-tight crotch left no place for a man's package to hide.

The Ratsmuellers owned the only other cottage on the south side of the lake; it was on the other side of the lumber camp, just past the Margin shack. They'd been there for years. Mr. Ratsmueller, who had died while Mitch was in Nam, had been a nice guy—some kind of scientist with Dow or Corning. Their son, Walter, was athletic like his mother. Mitch didn't know him very well; he'd never hung out with the other kids on the lake.

"She never went over to the other side, did she?"

"Of course not."

They kept talking about Gisela, even as she came within earshot. "God, I wish I could tan like that," Patricia said. "It simply is not fair for a blond to tan so well."

"Man, it looks like it goes right down to the bone."

Gisela set her paddle against the wall and entered the lanai. "So, we are having booze for breakfast," she said, looking down at them. Mitch and Patricia smiled up at her.

She had a straight, flat nose, squared off perfectly with her eyes, like she was wearing a Crusader's helmet.

Up close, it was surprising to see that her face looked so much older than her body. Her eyebrows were white, and the years in the sun had left a mass of wrinkles around her eyes and mouth.

"Breakfast of Champions. You must be thirsty, come and sit," Patricia said.

Gisela shook her head. She had a powerful smile; her teeth weren't perfect, but they were brilliantly white, matching the little mask of lighter skin around her eyes.

"Some water first, I think," she said.

They watched her butt as she left the lanai. Patricia whacked Mitch on the shoulder.

"Man, I know, I know," he said, squirming in the chair.

Patricia laughed. She was always flirting with him, but she flirted with his dad too, *and* Gisela, so he didn't take it seriously.

The stories Patricia told him about her past were often about sex. In them, she was always monogamous, at least temporarily, sometimes with a man, sometimes with a woman. He didn't know if they were true, and he didn't care. They were always entertaining.

The stories that Gisela told him were different. They didn't contain a lot of detail, but he had no doubt that they were true. There were some about the war—more about the end than the beginning. About fleeing the Russians across a devastated country, about leaving her mother and brother behind, shot up and bleeding out on the wire between East and West Germany.

Gisela came back with a tall glass of ice water and a thick roast beef sandwich. They told her about Lucy Dee. She didn't have a lot to say about it.

When Patricia went to the washroom, Gisela said, "So, Bobby is back. You saw him, ya?" She had lived in Northern New York for twenty-five years, but she hadn't lost her accent.

"Yeah, I saw him a couple of days ago, over at Mrs. Parker's. Long hair, lean, all grown up. Pretty cool guy."

"And the other places, you see him around there?"

"No, but I haven't been over there much."

She wiped some mustard from her mouth with the back of her hand and looked at him with one eye closed.

"Well, except for Lucy."

She leaned forward, forearms resting on her thighs. "He promised me he wouldn't come back. Last summer, there was trouble over there, with Bobby. Not just the woman who fell from the rock."

"What trouble?"

"He was sleeping with one of those women. The husband caught them and beat them good."

"Which one?"

"He wouldn't tell me. I told him, 'Help Mrs. Anderson, she pays good, stay on this side of the lake. You're a man now, you can get yourself killed.'"

They were silent for a while. Mitch thought about

how things were when he was a kid, wondering about things that he'd never noticed at the time. How Gisela was kind of like a mother to Bobby. "Bobby used to hang around your place a lot," he said.

"Well, naturally. Mostly, those Margins, they stopped coming up in the last years. Except Bobby, and his brother, sometimes," she replied.

"Bobby ever give you any trouble?"

Gisela looked at him. "Bobby was a good boy before those people came. He would sleep at our cottage many times. From the time he was nine or ten. We would find him lying on our steps, up against the door like a dog. He had this mosquito netting, and he would put it over himself. We had to check to see if he was there, Bobby wouldn't knock."

"Why didn't he stay at the shack?" As soon as he said it, Mitch knew it was a stupid question.

"Bobby was afraid of Sarah. His father and his uncles told him that she was after them, after all the Margins, ya? Bobby didn't want to stay where she could find him in the night."

CHAPTER
FOURTEEN

Around noon, the coroner had taken Mrs. Dee's body to the morgue in Trapper Lake. The Syracuse PD was talking to Mr. Dee. Until those reports were done, there was nothing more for the Wanakena Sheriff's Department to do on the case.

In the afternoon, Sheriff Herkemer took Kelly to Shallow Rock, looking for a local hood named Hack Weechum. The very same guy, it turned out, that she'd seen at the Key Stone station yesterday evening. She'd been right, thinking he was a con. Weechum had been convicted on sexual assault and weapons charges. He had done less than a year at Auburn Correctional before getting parole.

Monday night, Weechum had beaten up a couple of guys at the Mud Road Tavern near Lake Placid. He'd been back in the county for only a couple of weeks and had already violated.

Sheriff Herkemer was eager to pick him up. "He's a violent son of a bitch, always has been. It's only a matter of time before he kills somebody. Better all-round if he's behind bars when he does it," he said.

Shallow Rock was a jumble of sagging shacks that straggled down a hill to a few lopsided docks on Little Lost Lake. It was hard to tell how many of the buildings were occupied; wood smoke from scattered, cinderblock chimneys drifted over the whole tangled mess of sheds, junkyards, and gap-toothed fences. A single line of tilted utility poles ran down the muddy main street. Con Ed line only; no phones in the whole place.

Walking around with the sheriff, Kelly felt like she was passing through a "pacified" village in Nam. The people had the same flat, suspicious expressions of bred-in-the-bone hostility. They were civil to Sheriff Herkemer, but no one had seen Weechum. No one knew where he was staying. No one could remember the last time they'd seen him.

"Come on, I'll show you what all the Sarah Punk fuss is about," Sheriff Herkemer said after they'd spoken to all the locals they could find.

They walked to the top of an almost treeless hill where they had a good view of the surrounding countryside. Compared to the dull skid stain of the village, Shaker's Bog was a vibrant, Kodachrome poster unrolling into the misty west. The sheriff pointed out a rusted, tin roof on the far side of a thin stand of drowned pine a few hundred yards out from the shore.

"That's the Hell Hole. Kids around here have been

using it as a kind of clubhouse for years. I don't know if they still do. The bog keeps getting bigger and thicker. I don't think you can even get to it anymore."

The shack looked like it was being sucked down into the swamp. "They say that Sarah and her son are buried in the muck under that thing. No sheriff ever felt inclined to check it out, yours truly included," he said.

Kelly tried to imagine what it would be like to go rooting around in the stinking mud under that rotting shack. Yeah, if she were ever Sheriff of Wanakena County, she wouldn't feel inclined to check it out either.

"The sooner it all goes under, the better. Maybe that'll put Sarah to rest," the sheriff said.

Kelly agreed. Even at a distance, the place made her feel queasy. "You don't believe in all this ghost stuff, right, Sheriff?"

"Except for a little vacation in Europe during the Big One, I've been in Wanakena County my whole life. I've heard screams and other strange noises, seen shapes in the fog, but I've never encountered Sarah Punk. I've spoken to people, reasonable people, who swear they have. It's embarrassing to listen to, but then I remember that I killed more than my fair share of phantom Krauts over in France."

"You see what you want to see," Kelly said.

"Maybe. I think most of the time your mind shows you what it thinks you *need* to see. If it can't figure out what the hell it's looking at, it picks the worst-case scenario and tells you to run like hell." He chuckled. "Or burn off a belt of ammo into the dark."

There was a big oak at the summit of the hill, and on the back slope lay the remains of an old graveyard. An overgrown plot of humped ground containing a few dozen crude, tilted headstones. There were no crosses.

"Sarah and Moses are probably buried here," Sheriff Herkemer said. "The locals were using this place up until the end of the war, when the county forced them to start depositing their dead in the cemetery at Woodbine. Wouldn't be surprised if there were more than a few bodies buried here even after that."

If Sarah was there, she was lost to time. Any of the headstones that had not been split and thrown down by the buckthorn and hogweed bore nothing more than shallow grooves where names had once been.

CHAPTER
FIFTEEN

A scream filled the darkness.
Kelly woke up with her feet on the floor, revolver in hand. It took her a moment, staring into the darkness, to realize that she was in her room in the bunkhouse, alone.

She heard footsteps. A beam of wavering light appeared under the door to Mitch's room. "Kelly? Did you hear that?"

"The scream—you heard that?"

"Yeah, it came from across the lake. I saw something falling down Steep Rock."

"What?" she said, opening the door.

"Like a shadow falling down the face of the rock into the water. I think I saw two of them..."

"You definitely heard a scream?" In her dream, the scream had been distant but clear, and it had sounded like the one she'd heard Saturday night.

"Sarah," Mitch said. "She might have scared someone over the edge again, like last summer. I'm gonna go check."

"Okay, hang on, I'm coming. Grab me something to drink, will you?"

"Coke?"

"Beer."

It was an unusual night. The sky was clear; the moon was so bright that they didn't need their flashlights as they hustled down to the dock. Mitch untied the canoe and held it while Kelly chugged a Red Cap. Looking across the lake, she swished the last of the beer around her mouth and spat it out. Moonlight illuminated the face of Steep Rock. "It's like a spotlight," she said.

There was very little mist on the land, none on the water. At the summit of Steep Rock, she thought she saw movement. "Are there people over there?"

"I heard voices before the scream, couldn't make them out."

"Let's go." Kelly tossed the empty beer bottle up onto the bank and clambered into the front of the canoe.

They moved quickly over the still water. She was sure there were shadows moving around the top of the cliff, but the sound of their paddling made it impossible to hear if they were talking. Mitch steered them directly to the bottom of Steep Rock.

It was dark in the shadow of the cliff. Kelly felt forward with her paddle, touched rock just below the surface and brought them to a halt. Small ripples revealed the position of more rocks, their rounded heads just above the surface.

Mitch maneuvered the canoe broadside to the cliff. "Hello?" he called out. He began moving the canoe slowly along the face of the rock until they reached the point where the bank was broken and overgrown.

"There's nothing," Kelly said. "You imagined it."

"Hello?" Mitch called out again. He brought them around, facing back the way they'd come, and halted the canoe. There was nothing there—no body, no swimmer, not even any garbage.

"There's nothing here, Mitch. Back us out so we can see the top."

Mitch backed them away from the shore.

A woman shrieked. Not a scream, more of a squeal. Mitch held the canoe still. They could hear laughter, male and female, coming from down the lake. There was a loud splash.

"Oh, fuck, that's cold!" a harsh male voice declared, followed by more laughter.

"What the hell?" Kelly snapped off her flashlight. "Turn around, get us over there."

Mitch swung the canoe about and headed east, angling out into the lake. They passed Dee's dock, the crime scene above it dark and silent. The next cottage over, bodies were moving around like pale ghosts in the moonlight.

A man dove off the end of the dock as they approached. Another man was in the water speaking to a woman on the dock. "Come on, Denny, you candy ass."

"It's too cold." Denise Cross, her girlish voice unmistakable.

"It's fine once you get in."

"You *always* say that."

Mitch jammed in his paddle and started to backwater.

"What're you doing?" Kelly turned, keeping her voice down.

"We shouldn't be here," he said.

"What?"

"Jesus, Kelly, look."

She looked back towards the dock. Except for bathing caps on the women, everyone was naked. Mrs. Mulvane stood casually at the end of the dock, lighting up a cigarette. Farther down, Mrs. Cross was hugging herself around the shoulders.

"Well, hello there, neighbors. Is that you, Deputy Mackinaw? And Mitch Herkemer?" Mrs. Mulvane called out.

"Oh!" Mrs. Cross squealed and dove into the lake.

The man who had just dived in returned to the dock with a few powerful strokes. He climbed up the ladder and turned to face them, hands on his hips. "Are you going to join us, or are you just going to watch?" he demanded. His tone and stance were aggressive, not welcoming.

"Hi." Mitch waved. "Sorry, didn't mean to disturb you guys."

"Mitch, it's about time we met. And Deputy Mackinaw, I'm sure you're dying to meet the boys. Why don't you two come ashore and get naked with us?" Mrs. Mulvane said.

"No, we're fucking not, Mitch," Kelly hissed.

"Then this is just uncool," he replied.

CHAPTER
SIXTEEN

Mitch didn't mind getting naked. Nudity was cool, but he felt like he'd seen way too much of these people in the raw already. Lucy was dead, and they were having a party? He wanted to get back to the bottom of Steep Rock and do another search.

"Just hold us here a minute," Kelly said.

Mrs. Mulvane draped an arm around the shoulder of the man on the dock. "This is my husband, Mick. The shy man in the water is Hal."

Mick didn't say hello. He turned and looked down the dock towards the shore. "Steve, you gonna get those drinks or what?" he said.

Mitch hadn't noticed the third man. He was dressed in dark clothes, with only his round, white face visible.

"That's okay, I'll go," Mrs. Cross said, quickly

mounting the ladder and heading for the end of the dock.

"Steve who?" Kelly shouted at the man at the far end of the dock.

"Take your clothes off, and I'll tell you," he replied.

"Were any of you diving off Steep Rock just now?" Kelly asked.

"No," Mrs. Mulvane said.

"Do you have any other guests?"

"It's none of your fucking business," Mr. Mulvane said, the guy giving off some seriously disturbed vibes.

"Did anyone hear a scream?" Kelly asked, flicking on her flashlight and pointing it at the guy at the end of the dock. He brought an arm up to shield his face.

"Hey, fuck off," he said.

"You need to get the fuck away from here." Mr. Mulvane waved like he was swatting a bug.

"Did you bring Sylvia along?"

"Sylvia?" Steve sounded surprised.

"The hitchhiker you picked up yesterday afternoon."

"Alright, that's enough of this shit. Hal, go call the sheriff," Mr. Mulvane said. "You need to get off my property," he added to Kelly.

"Where did you drop her off?" Kelly kept the flashlight on Steve, following him as he tried to shift his face away from the light.

"Get that fucking thing out of my face, or I'll shove it up your ass."

"Or is she at some other party?"

Mitch sat up straight, holding the canoe steady, taking in all the angry vibes. It was impossible to get a read on anybody's aura with all the blaring, red negativity being broadcast. Anger, surprise, and fear—all way out of proportion to having a skinny-dipping party interrupted.

Mr. Cross hustled up the ladder and down the dock without looking back, leaving only Mr. and Mrs. Mulvane on the dock. Mrs. Mulvane flicked her cigarette into the water, away from the canoe. "Can we all stop acting like children for a moment," she said.

"I asked a question," Kelly said.

"Enough. He doesn't have to answer your questions. Steve, go on up to the cottage." Mr. Mulvane pointed his finger at the canoe. "You listen to me, you fucking, little country-ass shit. You're way outta line here. I'll be talking to Sheriff Herkemer and the AG, first thing tomorrow morning. Now get the fuck out of here."

It took a special kind of arrogance to stand naked like that, your dick all shrivelled up, and crap on people. Sociopath-level arrogance, man.

Mitch could feel Kelly vibrating in the front of the canoe, like she was getting ready to leap onto the dock. "That fucker's on something," she said.

"Yeah, that doesn't really help the situation here, man."

"There's something going on." Kelly was staring at the couple on the dock, her voice low.

"I agree. You sure it's any of our business? You're

dealing with three fair-sized men here. It would be ugly."

"I've got a gun."

He tried to laugh it off. "Yeah, but then we'd have to kill them all. You know, witnesses, man."

"I could do them all with a bullet to spare," she replied immediately.

She'd done the math. "We're joking, right?" he said, keeping his voice light and free of negativity.

"Yeah, I guess," Kelly sighed. She looked over her shoulder at him. "Let's go check out the Dee place."

"Evening, folks, hope we can have a better chat next time. Clothes, no clothes, I'm cool either way," Mitch called out as he turned the canoe away. He thought that might get a laugh. Mrs. Mulvane smiled; that was it.

"They don't own the fucking lake," Kelly growled as she began to paddle. "And they're guilty of public indecency."

They're guilty of spiritual indecency, Mitch thought, but kept it to himself. "Who is Steve?" he asked.

"I don't know, some jerk I saw picking up hitchhikers yesterday. I'm sure he's a local. You recognize him?"

"No, but I've been gone six years, man."

Mitch saw no sign of Lucy as they tied up at her dock. Probably she was lying low, gathering the strands of her spirit into a coherent whole. He wondered what she was going to do to her old playmates once she'd gotten her otherworldly shit together.

"I want to check the tape," Kelly said, as they went up the steps.

Mitch wanted to do another sweep of the water below Steep Rock, but he didn't want to leave Kelly alone in case she had another run-in with the swingers. "I wonder why Sarah screamed," he said, as he followed Kelly up the flagstone steps.

"She needs a reason?" Kelly replied, without looking over her shoulder.

Using her flashlight, she carefully examined the police tape stretched across the patio door. It looked okay. She tried the door; it was locked. Mitch followed her as she did a circuit of the cottage, checking the tape over the ground-floor windows.

"I always thought they sounded like warnings," Mitch said.

"Mitch, she's a fucking fairy tale."

"You heard the scream tonight."

"I was half asleep. I thought it was a person. If I'd thought it was a ghost, I wouldn't have dragged my ass out of bed."

"Who then?"

"One of those idiots. Or maybe it was an animal."

Talking to Kelly was pointless.

The back door was locked, and the tape was in place. "Come on; let's go check the top of Steep Rock," she said.

The narrow path along the edge of the lake was deep in shadow. They used their flashlights as they hurried along, harassed by mosquitoes. "Who found the body of the woman who fell last year?" Kelly asked over her shoulder.

"Some of the people from the party, I guess."

"They found her right at the bottom on the rocks?"

"That's what I heard. I wasn't here. My dad said they were running around with Polaroid cameras, trying to get pictures of Sarah Punk."

The path narrowed as it began to climb, becoming an uneven stairway of natural rock.

Someone was at the summit. "Can we *not* be shoving lights in each other's faces," Mrs. Mulvane said, rising up from a crouch, flashlight pointed at the ground.

"She got here fast," Kelly muttered.

Up at the top of Steep Rock the moon still shone. Mitch turned off his flashlight. He spoke quickly, using his friendliest voice. "That would be really cool, man. Mitch Herkemer, nice to finally meet you," he said, extending his hand.

Mrs. Mulvane pulled off a gardening glove and shook his hand. "Holly Mulvane, pleased to meet you." She had a firm grip, soft hands. Lots of hooded energy. Kelly and Mrs. Mulvane exchanged subdued greetings.

"Hey, everybody's pretty fucked up tonight, right?" Mitch said. He practically had to step between them to unlock their horns.

"More than we realized, I'm afraid," Mrs. Mulvane said, shifting to a cool, thoughtful voice. She looked unruffled in dark slacks, a long-sleeved shirt and sneakers.

Kelly kept her flashlight down and spoke in a restrained voice. "What's going on?" she asked.

Mitch blurted out the obvious. "Lucy's dead, it's fucking everybody up."

"Yes, that's what's going on, Deputy Mackinaw. It has hit us all very hard. Hal and Mick rushed back from the city to be with us. Be here in case Dan came back, I guess? We all got a little drunk and left a bit of a mess. I came back to clean up." She was holding a green plastic garbage bag in her left hand.

"So, you *were* up here?"

"Yes, Lucy liked it up here. We had a kind of memorial, or a wake, I guess."

"You didn't seem that broke up about her this morning."

Mrs. Mulvane sighed. "We were putting on a brave face. Denny, well, she had some prescription help. She's very fragile."

"Did anyone dive off the rock?"

"Good Lord, no! Can you imagine, at night?"

"There was a scream," Mitch said.

"Oh, that was Denny. She thought she saw Sarah Punk. We all got a little rattled, that's why we left in such a hurry and didn't clean up."

Mitch smiled at her. She was lying. There was no way Mrs. Cross could make that sound.

"So, you all went skinny dipping," Kelly said.

"Does that offend you so much, Deputy?"

"Then you felt a real urgent need to tidy up," Kelly went on. She didn't do sarcasm very well. Mrs. Mulvane ignored it.

"Yes, I think it's rude to litter. You put quite a damper on our attempts to lighten up, now everyone wants to go to bed. I couldn't sleep knowing the mess we'd left up here. It's just the way I am."

Mitch heard something moving back in the bush. He turned away from the women, and listening carefully, walked slowly towards what sounded like a small animal creeping through the woods. There was something on the ground at the edge of the heavy growth. White antler, dull steel. It was there for a second and then it was gone.

"Son of a bitch," he said. He turned to look at the women. "Did you guys see that?"

They weren't listening, didn't even turn to look at him. He stood a moment staring into the darkness under the trees, waiting for his body to decide what to do. It decided to breathe and walk away.

"Did you have any guests?" he heard Kelly say as he returned to the women.

"Just Steve, who you saw down on the dock."

"Steve who?"

Mrs. Mulvane chuckled. "Steve *Faber*. Ex-Deputy Steve Faber, the man you replaced."

"Oh."

"He doesn't like you very much. He says he was

fired on false charges so Gail Harmon could bring a woman into the department."

"He was fired for discharging his weapon while drunk on duty."

"Honestly, that wouldn't surprise me."

"He's a friend of yours?" Kelly asked.

"Not really. More Hal's friend. They go hunting together sometimes. I guess Hal ran into him on the way up and invited him."

"No girl with him?"

"No, he was definitely alone. Now, if you don't mind, Deputy, I'd like to get home before the bugs eat me alive."

Kelly didn't reply.

"I'll talk to Sheriff Herkemer in the morning, try to smooth things over a little," Mrs. Mulvane said, walking past her.

"Don't bother," Kelly growled.

"Oh, it's no bother. I hate for there to be all this discord on our little lake. We should all be friends, right, Mitch? Like you and Lucy were."

"Yeah, everybody should be cool, man," he replied, distracted, still trying to make sense of what he'd just seen.

The knife had looked a lot like the one Bobby Margin wore, but before he could bend down to pick it up, it had been snatched into the darkness by a little, white hand.

CHAPTER
SEVENTEEN

WEDNESDAY

Mrs. Parker's dock was lost in the clouds, riding the mist like a magic carpet. Mitch stood very still as he watched the dawn creep over the swamp.

In his dream, Sarah had risen up at the edge of Shaker's Bog, distinguishable from the surrounding mist only by the black stones of her eyes. She had looked right at him for a moment, then turned her back and disappeared.

"What do you want?" he'd shouted at her, but she didn't look back.

Now, in the real dawn, Mitch waited for her, but she did not rise—or at least he didn't have the eyes to see her.

Mrs. Parker's screen door was unlatched. He hesitated before it, sweating in the cool morning air. In his dream, he'd wandered through her cottage looking for her body, with an overwhelming conviction that she was dead.

Then he heard the deep rise and fall of her snoring. Sagging against the doorframe, he let out a long sigh of relief.

Mrs. Parker must have really tied one on last night. She didn't wake to the creak of the door spring or the sound of his footfalls as he gingerly picked his way through her dark, dishevelled kitchen to the door of her bedroom. She lay on her stomach near the edge of her bed, entwined in a sheet, one naked haunch exposed. He didn't see her revolver, but her shotgun lay on the floor beside her, close at hand.

Mrs. Parker was okay. He padded carefully back across the kitchen and quietly pushed at the half-open door of the second bedroom, looking for Bobby.

Bobby wasn't there, but he had been. In the thin light, Mitch could see his sleeping bag lying open on a bare, stained mattress. His green mosquito netting was rolled up near the head of the bed like a pillow. His scent was in the room; humid, male sweat and the coppery tang of blood. His jeans hung from the end of the metal bed frame, a small pool of water beneath them. A jersey hung over the back of a simple wooden chair beside the bed. Nothing else; Bobby Margin travelled light.

One other thing. On the seat of the chair, there was a Polaroid.

Mitch crouched down next to the chair. He recognized the jersey; it was the one Bobby was wearing on Sunday, the one without a name or number. It was torn at the collar, and there were dark stains on the front that looked like blood. Mitch felt the sleeve; it was damp.

The Polaroid looked like it was wet too—its surface a dark, liquid glare. He picked it up carefully, holding it by the edges, twisting it this way and that until he could make it out.

Interior shot, the subject illuminated by the brutal light of the camera's flash. It looked like a barn or a shed, wooden slat walls, bare wood floor. It was a picture of a naked girl, standing with her hands tied above her head, ropes leading out the top of the picture. Hard to tell her age. She was small-breasted but had a dark pubic triangle. Her head was bowed, long hair hanging down covering her face.

Mitch put the picture back the way he'd found it and left the room. For a while, he stood in the kitchen, eyes closed, trying to steady the universe. Sarah? But there were no Polaroids in Sarah's day. And now? Did Bobby have the power to catch and bind a ghost?

Or was it another girl, a living girl? What the fuck, Bobby?

He wasn't sure how long he'd been standing there —it could have been five minutes or five days—before the creak of the screen door snapped his mind back into his skull. Bobby Margin entered the room, walking slowly, crookedly. He had a limp on his right side, and his arm pressed against his ribs on the left. He wore a faded, gray T-shirt tucked into a pair of jean shorts held up by a wide leather belt. The Bowie sheath was no longer strapped to his leg.

"Mitch," he said flatly, not surprised. Bobby didn't smile. His lips were thick and split in at least three places. Both his eyes were blackened, one cheek was raw.

"Jesus, Bobby. Man, what happened to you?"

"I'm okay." Bobby sat down at the kitchen table. He took a worn leather tobacco pouch from his back pocket. With a slight groan, he leaned forward and opened it, preparing to roll a cigarette.

"You want to smoke up?" Mitch asked.

Bobby shrugged. "Sure."

The skin on his face was pale and blanched against the angry red of his lips and the dark purple around his drooping eyelids. Mitch selected a joint from his pocket, blazed it up with his Zippo and offered it to Bobby, leaning in close to get a better look at him.

"What happened, man?" he asked.

Bobby drew delicately on the joint, letting the smoke drift up into his nostrils. He closed his eyes. "I got jumped," he said.

"By who?"

"Doesn't matter. Have a seat, man." He waited for Mitch to sit down before handing him back the joint. His knuckles were bruised and scraped. "That's good shit," he said, his speech slurred by the thickness of his lips.

Mitch sat at the scuffed oval table, drawing his straight-backed chair close to Bobby's. "Guerrero Gold, I like it in the morning..."

He was interrupted by loud coughing coming from Mrs. Parker's bedroom. "Bobby, where'd you get that Mary Jane?" Mrs. Parker asked, then started hacking again.

"From me, Mrs. Parker," Mitch called out.

"Mitch?"

"Yes, ma'am."

"Shoulda known."

After another round of coughing followed by loud spitting, Mrs. Parker walked into the room wearing a flowery patterned nightgown loosely tied with blue cotton belt. Bobby started to rise.

"I'll get it," she said, crossing to the counter in bare feet. She pumped a glass of water, which she swished around in her mouth and spat out into the sink. The curtains over the sink were drawn, but she didn't open them. Leaning her hips against the counter, she folded her arms and looked at Mitch.

Mitch slowly exhaled a little cloud of dope. "Morning, Mrs. Parker," he said.

Her hair was a loose, uneven tangle around her face. She looked tired but uninjured.

"Would you like a hit?" he asked, offering her the joint.

She shook her head. She crouched down next to Bobby, took his face in one hand and looked him over. "Well, your nose ain't broken. You lose any teeth?"

"Nah, they punched like pussies."

She pointed her chin at Mitch. "You let him in?"

"No, but I was watching him. I was out in the shitter."

Mrs. Parker stood up, leaning heavily on Bobby's shoulder, and looked down at Mitch. "You just waltzed into my house?"

"I'm sorry, Mrs. Parker, I had a dream..."

She laughed. "Oh, a dream. I can imagine what kind."

Chuckling, Bobby took the joint from Mitch and took another slow hit.

"Didn't even knock, did you?" Mrs. Parker said.

Mitch gave her a sheepish grin.

"Fuck sakes, I almost blew your head off last time. Didn't you learn a damn thing from that?" She took a beach towel from the back of one of the other chairs, turned, and headed for the door. "Sleepwalking around here can get you killed," she said.

The screen door slammed, followed a moment later by a splash.

"Come on, Bobby, who'd you have the scrap with?"

Bobby shook his head. He finished off the joint and dropped the roach into an ashtray. "Thanks, man," he said. Hunched over the table, he went back to rolling a cigarette.

Mitch sat back and unfocused his eyes, looking beyond Bobby to see him whole. The boy had a large, rippling aura, light blue and flashing with lightning, not at all like his calm physical presence. Mitch tried to touch the shimmering surface of Bobby's essence, feeling for answers, but Bobby's aura was mute, as impenetrable as sunlight.

"Got a light, man?"

"Sure, man." Mitch shook himself, leaned across the table, and lit Bobby's cigarette. "So, what happened?"

Bobby inhaled and shrugged.

Mitch had seen a lot of beat-up faces. They were always ugly distortions of humanity, carrying swollen pockets of violation and fear. But Bobby didn't look afraid or angry; he looked like he'd taken a head-butt from reality and had come up heavy with enlightenment.

"It was in Shallow Rock. Just old bullshit, man, going way back."

"You hung out there a lot when you were a kid, huh?"

"Dad was shacked up with a woman from there for a few years. He used to drop us there when he visited her folks. Merle had his girl and a few friends; they'd take off somewhere, left me with the other kids. I ain't been back for a long time."

"You didn't like it there?"

Bobby squinted through the thin stream of smoke drifting up from the cigarette held gently between his lips. "Hack had his gang. He picked on all the younger kids, had his hands on everybody, doing all kinds of fucked-up shit. I spent most of my time hiding from him. Me and Mary Ann."

Mitch smiled. "You had a Shallow Rock girlfriend."

"Girlfriend? We were like ten, eleven years old, man. We were pals. Hell, she hardly even spoke. What I liked about her, she knew how to be quiet and watch. She knew all the best places to hide, out on Goat Island and all over the bog. Saved my ass lots of times."

"So, that's why you went back, to see your old pal?"

"Nah, man, I had some other shit to take care of. I don't even know if she's around anymore."

"You writing a book?" Mrs. Parker let the screen door slam loudly behind her as she came in from the deck. Her voice was low and mocking.

Her wet-dark hair was pulled back from her face and lay over one shoulder, wetting the right breast of her open robe. He ran his eyes swiftly up her body to her drawn mouth and challenging eyes.

He stood up, surprised by a sudden sense of danger. He smiled and looked her in the eye. "No, hey man, I'm just talkin," he said.

Mrs. Parker walked past him and put a hand on Bobby's shoulder. "How's your ribs?"

"Okay, just sore."

"Good, we'll go for a swim later, get you all cleaned up."

She went back into her room, leaving the door

half-open. Mitch heard the flare of a wooden match followed by more coughing.

Bobby pushed his chair from the table and tilted it back carefully. "You doin a lot of work on the old camp?" he asked. The tempo of his words had slowed.

Mitch turned from trying to see into Mrs. Parker's room. Then he felt the rush, felt the Guerrero *descend* on him, and he realized that everything was cool. Bobby, Mrs. Parker, the weird Polaroid; everything was cool. What should be known would be known when it was time to be known.

He smiled and took a moment to remember the thread of their conversation. "Yeah, my dad wants to fix it all up. It's gonna take some time. I don't work too hard, since Nam."

"Nam," Bobby said. "I hope I get to go to Nam."

Mitch sat down. "It's over now, Bobby. For us anyway."

"You think?"

"Yeah, we're out."

"But we'll get another war, right?"

"Oh yeah." Mitch closed his eyes and leaned back. "Give us a few years, and we're gonna need to kick somebody's ass, just to prove we can."

Bobby let out a sigh. "I'm glad you made it back, man. I was worried about you."

"Worried about me?" Mitch opened one eye to look at him.

Bobby had a stoner's grin. "Well, you know, you were always getting killed all the time when we played

Guns. I can't even count how many times I shot you in the back."

Mrs. Parker came into the kitchen, went to the sink, and leaned against the counter, smoking.

Mitch smiled and shook his head. "Nam, man, it wasn't like when we used to play Guns."

"You kill anybody over there?" Bobby asked.

"Hard to say. You know, smoke and darkness, people shooting in every fucking direction. Not much *clarity*, man, you know?"

"Sure. Clarity, man, that's cool."

"I hope you never have to kill anybody, Bobby. It really fucks with your karma."

"Alright, enough of this hippie shit. Bobby needs to lay down and get some rest," Mrs. Parker said. Her aura was smaller than Bobby's—small, dark, and tight.

"Sure, cool." Realizing that he was being given the bum's rush, Mitch stood up with great care and dignity.

Mrs. Parker and Bobby followed him out onto the dock. "Thanks for the dope, man," Bobby said.

"Anytime, man. You should drop by the camp, we can rap."

Mrs. Parker helped steady the canoe with one broad, bare foot while Mitch climbed in. "Next time you come down this way, make sure you're wide awake," she said.

"Sure, sorry about coming into your place like that..."

"Don't press your luck, pretty boy." She untied his canoe and gave it a shove.

"I hear you, Mrs. Parker."

Paddling down the lake, every time he looked over his shoulder, he saw them standing on the dock, Mrs. Parker with her hands on her hips, Bobby leaning against the cottage wall, watching him until they were swallowed up by the mist.

CHAPTER
EIGHTEEN

"I got a call from the state AG this morning."

Kelly stood at attention in front of the Chair of the Board of Supervisors' desk, hat tucked under her left arm.

Gail Harmon stood up. She raised her hand about two feet above her desk, palm facing down. "We have a stack of complaints against the Sheriff's Department this high, going back years, and I have never gotten a call from the state AG, about anything. You've been here three days, and already you've put Wanakena on the radar down in Albany."

Gail was the first female Chair elected in Wanakena County, but she was no feminist hippie. Her parents owned a small marina with a general store on Silver Lake, which had been started by her grandparents. Only ten years older than Kelly, she owned a motel and bar in Trapper Lake. On the wall to the left of her desk were pictures of her with prominent New York State politicians in hunting gear, standing over big, dead animals or holding up big fish. Mounted above the pictures was the head of a twelve-point Adirondack buck that she'd killed when she was fifteen.

Kelly bit back her protests. Gail Harmon was also the head of the Police Board. She had hired her, and she could fire her.

"Yes, Ma'am," Kelly replied, stone-faced.

Gail stood for a moment, hands on her hips, letting Kelly steam. "I believe this department needs a female deputy, at least one. I had to fight like hell to get you hire. If you screw this up, there won't be another one for twenty years."

"Yes, Ma'am."

"Now sit down."

Kelly placed her hat on the edge of Gail's desk and sat in one of the chairs facing her. Gail sat down and leaned back in her chair. "Alright, give me your side of the story. And it's still Gail, I'm not that pissed off at you."

Kelly told her about her encounter with the cottagers; from the time she and Mitch had heard the scream until Mrs. Mulvane left them at the top of Steep Rock. She didn't mention that she'd been sleeping when she heard the scream.

"So, you heard a scream, and you went to investigate."

"I couldn't just ignore it, ma'am, even as a civilian. Someone may have been hurt."

"And the scream turned out to be flaky Denise Cross, frightened by a ghost."

"That's what they said."

"And you couldn't leave it at that?"

"They weren't being cooperative."

"You interrupted their skinny-dipping party, what did you expect?"

"Steve Faber was with them."

"Yes, the sheriff mentioned that. It doesn't excuse your rudeness."

"Did you know that Faber was friends with them?" she asked.

"No, he doesn't seem their type," Gail replied.

"He was on graveyard for the last couple of years, right? When most of the complaints were coming in. With Crogan, who also has some kind of friendship with these people?"

"It's odd, yeah. And worth looking into. Quietly."

When Gail had interviewed Kelly for the job, she'd told her about the high number of accusations of assault that had been made against the Wanakena department by hitchhikers in the past few years. There had been no corresponding increase in complaints made by local citizens.

"I saw Faber hustling some hitchhiker chicks two days ago. I drove one of them to Gouverneur, she had her shit together. She said Faber gave her the creeps…"

"You're picking up hitchhikers?"

"I was off duty. That's the way we need to talk to them. On their own ground, not at the station."

"You're from Saranac Lake, you know what people are like. Now everybody in the county figures you got a thing for hippie chicks."

"I'm doing my job, like you asked me to."

Gail held up her hand. "Slow down, Kelly, you don't even have your feet on the ground yet. You don't know this county. People don't know you. You're an outsider, everybody's going to resent you at first. You know that."

"I can handle it."

Gail frowned. "I don't want you to handle it. I want you to be accepted, and that's going to take time. I want your ear to the ground on the hitchhikers, sure, but I also want you here for the long run. I want you to be an influence on the Department, to start to change some attitudes."

Kelly knew Gail was right. "Yes, okay, I don't want to fuck this up. I'll get a grip. Am I gonna need to apologize?"

"We'll see. Sheriff Herkemer said Mrs. Mulvane called him this morning, saying everybody was a little overwrought last night. She said that your behavior wasn't all that bad."

"She was up early."

"She did you a favor. Still, the sheriff suggested that you spend some time at the duty desk, and I agreed."

"How long?"

"A few days, maybe a week. You can help out Betty, get a feel for the place."

"A week?"

"Less, if this cools down. If *you* cool down. It'll give you a chance to do a proper read-in of all the files." Gail pulled a thin file folder out of a drawer and handed it across the desk. "You can start with this. Not a lot of people have seen it yet, so read it here, now. Take your time. I'm not expecting any visitors."

Inside the folder was a report submitted by Sheriff Herkemer in November '72 with the findings of his investigation into the complaints against the Wanakena Sheriff's Department, and their possible links to missing hitchhikers over the past three years.

Kelly was aware of the staggering national statistics. The FBI had reported that 200,000 runaways had been picked up by law enforcement in 1972. They speculated that as many as a million kids had gone missing that year. Most of them had returned home; they didn't know how many, because in most cases there was no follow up. The numbers bothered her. Figure 95 percent went home, that meant there would still be something like 50,000 unaccounted for kids.

It was very possible that some of them had come to Wanakena county and never left.

Coming back from Mrs. Parker's, Mitch took his time paddling down the lake, hugging the north bank, slowly coming down from the Guerreo he'd smoked with Bobby. Nine o'clock in the morning and the surface of the lake was eight feet deep in wispy, drifting cloud, visibility about a hundred yards. He could hear the chugging of a small outboard, but it was hard to tell which direction it was coming from. It sounded too far away to be a threat.

The Mulvane dock was quiet, no one running around, naked or otherwise. Their bright red, four-seater inboard was tied up to the dock. At the Cross's dock, their big, turquoise pleasure craft was also secure, but their aluminium fishing boat was gone.

Mitch tied up at the Dee Dock. "Hang in there, Lucy," he said. "I just need to check something, then I'll be right back, and we can rap."

Up on Steep Rock, the sun had burned off most of the ground mist until it was only about an inch deep. With the warming sun on his back, he covered the ground in a low crouch, sometimes going down on his hands and knees. There was no sign of a party. No bottles or cans, no crumbs or cigarette butts, no fresh ash in the fire pit.

At the inland edge of the rock, the spot where he'd seen Bobby's Bowie knife, the lichen was scraped from the limestone, the undergrowth was bent and broken. There had definitely been people up here last night, but it didn't look like they had much fun.

The sound of the outboard motor had been getting louder, now it was very close.

"Shit, watch it!" someone shouted.

The engine cut, there was a brief silence followed by the screech of aluminium grinding over rock.

"The rocks!"

"No shit. Push us off."

"I can't reach."

"Use the fucking paddle."

Mitch sat down, cross-legged, and tried to picture the scene at the base of Steep Rock. Two men, grunting and bitching.

"You think we put a hole in her?" Mr. Cross in the bow, shoving them back off the rocks.

"Don't be stupid. Relax." Mr. Mulvane, for sure, in the back running the motor.

It was quiet for a few seconds. "That's it, he's fucking gone," Mr. Cross said.

"We need to take a better look at the bay. He could be snagged up on a dead-head."

"We've done it twice."

"The light's better now."

"I'm telling you, he got away. Him and whatever the fuck was with him."

"Don't start that shit."

"I saw it. We all saw it." Mr. Cross sounded scared.

"It was a raccoon or a fucking squirrel. Everybody was stoned."

"I wasn't that stoned. You ever see a squirrel take a chunk out of a guy's neck?"

"Bobby cut him. Just shut the fuck up, we're going to check the bay. We need to know for sure, one way or the other."

He heard Mr. Mulvane grunting, and after a few pulls, the engine caught.

Mitch stood up slowly, enlightenment descending

on him from the heavens. Bobby didn't get beaten up in Shallow Rock, it had happened here. And Bobby didn't cut anybody; Mitch was certain that the Bowie had been spotless before it had been snatched away.

"Sarah bites," he said.

That explained the streaks of blood on the scuffed rock all around his feet.

Sarah bites. And she must have been right on Bobby Margin's ass, just like the story said.

CHAPTER
NINETEEN

"Are you for real?"

Mitch had to blink a couple of times before Mrs. Cross' face came into focus.

"Am I for real? Hey man, don't pull that shit on me," he said. "You think I'm lying here with the answer to *that* on the tip of my tongue?"

She was bending over him with her face very close to his. Her big, brown eyes were so sincere, it almost freaked him out.

"Mitch Herkemer, what a surprise."

The damp, vinyl cushions of the lounger squeaked as Mitch straightened himself up. Mrs. Mulvane was standing behind Mrs. Cross, smiling. Mrs. Cross sat down on the side of the chair across from him. Her wide eyes had tiny, pinprick pupils and were shadowed with sleeplessness. Her naturally plump lips were slightly parted, but there was no sign of bruising. As far as he could tell, there wasn't a mark on her, no sign that she'd been close to the flying fists last night.

"You want to smoke up?" he asked.

Mrs. Cross looked up at Mrs. Mulvane, who shrugged. "Sure, why not," she said.

Mitch selected a special joint for the ladies, a mellow Thai blend, tightly rolled and dipped in liquid opium. Mrs. Mulvane came around and sat beside him, her mostly bare thigh pressing up against the worn denim of his jeans. They made a cozy little threesome, their knees touching. Mitch lit the joint and got it started. When he offered it to Mrs. Mulvane, she shook her head.

"It's very good shit," Mitch said.

"I'm sure it is," she replied, amused.

"Go ahead," Mitch said, offering it to Mrs. Cross.

Mrs. Cross took the joint and inhaled. "Oh, very nice," she sighed, as she slowly exhaled.

Mitch put a hand on her bare knee and leaned forward to take the joint. He could feel Mrs. Mulvane watching him. He offered her the joint again, and with a shrug and a smile, she accepted it. While she took a tentative haul on the joint, it occurred to him that Mrs. Cross was sitting on the recliner that Lucy had been using the afternoon they got stoned together.

"Hey, man, there's room for everybody over here," he said.

The ladies were already pretty loose. Giggling and shuffling, Mitch arranged them so they were all sitting side by side on the edge of the recliner facing the Dee cottage. He winked at Lucy, watching from her bedroom window, then turned and hugged Mrs. Cross. She wrapped her arms around him and rested her curly head on his chest.

Mitch bent his lips to her ear. "None of us is real, man," he whispered. "Be cool, it's all a dream."

Mrs. Cross squeezed him tightly and went off on a quiet, little jag of sobbing and giggling. When she straightened up to look at him, she was smiling. She dabbed at her eyes with the sleeve of her chambray shirt. "You're so cool, man," she said, and looked past him to smile at Mrs. Mulvane.

Mrs. Mulvane snaked an arm around Mitch's shoulder. "This *is* really good shit," she said, and they all started laughing because she'd smoked the joint down to the end. "You got a clip?" she asked.

"Nah, just toss it."

After a moment Mrs. Mulvane sighed and shivered. "Wow," she said. "Oh wow."

The humidity that had been creeping up all morning took hold of the day. The outside air conditioning unit came alive with a loud whirring rattle, but none of them twitched a muscle.

Mrs. Cross surprised Mitch by hooking her leg over his and practically climbing into his lap. She was wearing yellow shorts that rode up to her crotch, exposing a tanned thigh glistening with bug juice and sweat. He felt her hand on the back of his neck.

"So... Mitch, what the hell *are* you doing here, anyway?" Mrs. Mulvane asked. They all thought the question was funny.

"I've been sitting here trying to talk to Lucy."

Mrs. Mulvane looked at him, forcing a serious expression onto her face. "How's that been going?"

"Pretty good."

Mrs. Mulvane wiped tears of laughter from her eyes, sucked in her breath, and slowly brushed back her hair. She also looked unmarked, face and hands. "Wow. Wow, what the hell *is* that stuff?"

"Just some high-grade Thai."

"Wow, Denny, we've been smoking *shit*," Mrs. Mulvane said.

"Hmmmm," Mrs. Cross sighed, swinging her leg at the knee like a restless child. She walked her pale pink fingernails slowly across Mitch's chest like a spider until she reached his shirt pocket. "Oh, oh," she said when she felt the two remaining joints.

Mitch gently took her hand from his chest and placed it on his thigh. "I could really use a drink," he said. "You guys got anything?"

"No, we don't have anything," Mrs. Cross said.

"Maybe we could go to your place?"

"If you carry me."

"I can do that," Mitch said.

"I bet Lucy has something in the fridge," Mrs. Mulvane said.

"Yeah." Mitch tried to picture the inside of Lucy's fridge, but all he saw was Lucy lying on the kitchen floor.

"Maybe you could slip inside?" Mrs. Mulvane said, lightly stroking his forearm.

"Not without breaking the tape. The place is locked up tight."

"You've checked?"

"Couple of times."

"What... about... the... second... story... windows?" Mrs. Mulvane realized how slowly she was talking, laughed, and pressed her fingers to her lips. Mrs. Cross brushed back the floppy brim of Mitch's hat and started nibbling on his ear.

Mrs. Mulvane was wearing a sea-grey, nautically patterned shirt over top of a matching halter. Looking up at the cottage, Mitch slid his fingers past the shirt's big, stiff collar and stroked her bare shoulder. The Dee cottage had a complicated roof, lots of steeply pitched A-frames over the big glass expanses of the main hall and the bedroom windows.

"Maybe, if I could fly," he said.

They all laughed. Mrs. Cross stopped fooling with his ear and returned her head to his chest, tickling his throat with her tight, hairspray-tainted curls.

"I bet you can fly, Mitch," Mrs. Mulvane said.

Mitch turned to look at her. Calmly, he watched as her hazel eyes, pert nose, and flushed cheeks smoothly re-arranged themselves into a hundred different variations of themselves and then back again.

"You want another joint?" he asked.

Mrs. Mulvane paused, listening. The drone of the outboard seemed very far away.

"Yes... I would... man," she said, her pronunciation slow and precise.

Mitch released them in order to prepare another round. He had a decent buzz on. He could maintain, man. The ladies, on the other hand, were about to enter a whole new world, where everything was cool, and truth was as free as oxygen.

He took another A-bomb out of his pocket with a flourish. "I wanna take you *high-er*," he sang.

It didn't take long to find out what they were really after. They wondered if Lucy had shown him any pictures, the sort of pictures that might cause a lot of embarrassment to certain people if they fell into the wrong hands.

They were relieved when Mitch told them that Kelly and his dad hadn't found any pictures. They made it clear that if he could get them inside the cottage without breaking the tape, they would be very grateful.

"I saw them," a little girl's voice whispered down the phone line.

"Speak up... dear, I can hardly hear you," Kelly replied gently, working hard to be on her best behavior.

"They put her in the swamp." Her voice as thin and wispy as a ghost's.

Kelly felt a cold flush, like someone had injected ice

water into her spine. Clammy fingers pawed at her scalp. "Why are you whispering? Is someone with you?"

"No."

"Speak up. What's your name?"

"They killed her and put her body in Shaker's Bog."

"Killed who?" Kelly couldn't keep her voice from rising.

"Pretty little hitchhiker chick. Always wore a baby-blue halter top and a big floppy hat. Long red hair, creamy skin, all freckles."

Kelly ground the phone against her ear; eyes screwed shut, trying to hear, trying to picture the speaker. What she saw was weedy hair floating in mucky water.

"Who put her in the swamp?"

"Better go soon. She's lying there shallow, pretty soon her spirit's gonna tear loose and rise."

"When? When did they put her in the swamp?"

"Last summer. Susan Collins, she ain't pretty no more."

"Who did it?"

No answer.

"Hello? Who are you?"

Static hissed, taunting her.

"Who are you?" Kelly shouted.

Betty, the department's secretary and day dispatcher, took the phone from Kelly and placed it to her ear. She shook her head.

Kelly wiped the sweat from her face with both hands. "Can we get it traced?"

"Sure, I'll call..."

Kelly went into the back room and started pulling thick files from one of the four-drawer cabinets. The Wanakena Sheriff's Department received nearly two hundred reports of missing children every week. They kept them in stacks, filed by month, two-hole punched and fastened at the bottom of the page. Kelly threw July and August '72 onto the desk and started flipping through the July reports.

"Prank call," she said out loud.

Sweat dripped from her nose and stained the papers as she thumbed through a parade of girls' and boys' names. No Susan Collins in July. She pushed the July file aside so hard it fell to the floor with a thump.

"Fucking with me."

Nothing in August. She went back to the cabinet, pulled out June '72, and began thumbing through it, more slowly now, breathing easier.

The name jumped out at her. "Fuck! Got it, got it," she shouted, ripping the page from the Acco fastener. She scanned the form; long red hair, floppy hat.

Betty was standing in the doorway.

"Did they trace it?" Kelly asked.

"Sure, it was easy. The phone was left off the hook, didn't even bother to hang up."

"Where?"

Betty handed her a small slip of paper.

"One, Shangri-La Lane?" Kelly said.

"The Dee cottage."

"Somebody broke in."

"I haven't been able to raise the sheriff. He's out towards Stark, probably away from his car."

"When you get him, tell him I'm on my way with the keys." From Sheriff Herkemer's top desk drawer, Kelly pulled one of the spare sets of keys to the Dee cottage.

"Joe is in Oxwood, and Gene is over at Beaver Lake."

"I know, way the hell on the wrong side of the county."

"There's no cruiser for you."

"I'm taking my car."

"You don't have a radio…"

Kelly was on the street before Betty could finish.

CHAPTER
TWENTY

Sheriff Herkemer was waiting for Kelly at the end of Dee's dock. "Betty said you got a call from a little girl? How little?"

"Maybe eight, twelve. Not a woman, not a teenager."

"You could tell that on the phone?"

"Yes."

"You sure it wasn't Denise Cross? You know her voice?"

"I thought about that, Sheriff. I can hear her talking like a little girl, kinda cutesy. But it wasn't like that. This kid was quiet, I don't know... solemn. She wasn't fooling around."

"She said there was a body in Shaker's Bog?"

"A girl, a hitchhiker named Susan Collins. We have a sheet on her; she's from Columbia, Maryland." Kelly handed the sheet to the sheriff. "The caller knew the details. Her name, the clothes she was wearing. The date works out," Kelly said.

He handed the sheet back to her. "Did you check with the sheriff in Columbia, see if she'd gotten back home?"

"No, I came right out."

He shook his head. "Somebody's screwing around. You're sure it wasn't Mitch, goofing off?"

"No, it wasn't him."

The sheriff frowned. "I stopped to talk to Mrs. Anderson and Mrs. Ratsmueller on the way in and asked them if they'd seen any strangers on the lake. They didn't see anybody. Said there was a small boat out early this morning."

"What about Mitch?"

"He was sleeping one off over at Mrs. Anderson's," the sheriff said, disgusted.

Kelly didn't know what to make of that; Mitch had been gone when she'd woken up this morning. The sheriff looked abruptly down the lake. The shadow of a man appeared, striding down the dock in front of the Cross cottage. He bent down next to the rope lines of a turquoise bow rider, looked over his shoulder at them and stood up.

"Mulvane," the sheriff said, with about as much disgust as he'd said "Mitch." "I told him not to go out on the water, the shape he's in."

"Drunk?"

"I went over there to ask if they'd seen anybody moving around this afternoon. The women were all dopey, the men were half-cut, drunk and lit up on something else."

"Cocaine?"

"Maybe. Could be prescription. There's so many pills out there these days, how are we supposed to keep track? They said they were out fishing early this morning. I warned them not to drive anything until they sobered up."

Mulvane stood at the end of the dock, lit a cigarette, paced, chucked the cigarette into the water, and then returned down the dock without looking at them.

"You think they had something to do with this?"

"They're stupid enough, and they probably still have a key. I did a quick walk around, but I waited, because I want you to take a good look at the tape before we go inside."

After the coroner had taken away Mrs. Dee's body, Kelly had locked up and secured the location. They had found one set of keys in the cottage and taken them to the station along with the one from under the lawn jockey by the back door.

Kelly had tied the handles of the patio doors together with police tape. On the side door, she'd wrapped tape around the doorknob and tied off both ends to nearby trees. At the rear door, she'd looped the tape around the knob and tied it off to the iron railing of the steps. She'd tied everything tightly, using double granny knots that would be impossible to undo without damaging the tape.

"Was there anybody else over at the Cross place?" she asked, as they moved around the outside of the cottage looking for any other signs of attempted entry.

"The four of them were there, but I didn't see anyone else. No strange vehicles."

The tape remained in place at each location. She checked her handiwork and was confident that the tape had not been disturbed or replaced.

"It's solid, Sheriff, nobody got in through the ground floor."

It was a relief to be inside the cottage. The air was stale, but cool. They removed their hats and sunglasses, mopped their sweaty foreheads with their handkerchiefs, then followed the annoying, rapid, beep-beep-beep of a telephone off the hook, into the kitchen.

Everything looked the same as when Kelly had locked up, except for the handset of the wall phone lying on the floor at the end of its long cord. Kelly crouched down to look at it. Grasping the cord, she lifted it off the floor to examine the bridge between the transmitter and the receiver. Like everything else in the kitchen, it was covered by a thin film of grease and dust.

"It looks like part of a palm where she held the phone. It's pretty small," Kelly said. "Maybe they might raise a print?"

The counter creaked as the sheriff leaned against it. "The boys at the crime lab are gonna love this. A ghostly call from inside a dead woman's house. Unless we find a body in the swamp, they won't come out here. Come on, let's have a look around, and pull the plug on that damn thing."

They opened all the curtains so they could check the doors and windows from the inside. Everything was secure; nothing appeared to have been touched.

"Why would someone do it?" Kelly asked. "If they wanted to report a dead body, why do it from here?"

"Kids screwing around. We had a problem with Shallow Rock kids breaking into the new cottages, especially in the off-season. They replaced a lot of the windows and doors, that's why these places lock up so well. I caught a few of them, and Rae Parker put out the word that I'd taken up permanent residence on the lake. I figured that had put a stop to it."

There was no basement. They checked the mudroom and the side door. They went up the spiral staircase. Kelly had a feeling of déjà vu. They'd searched the place twice yesterday. Nothing had changed. All of the upstairs windows were locked and showed no sign that they'd been opened in days.

"You think the caller wanted us to come back here, to make another search?" Kelly asked.

"They want us to sweat our asses off searching the swamp. Somebody's idea of a joke."

They went back downstairs and stood with their backs to the patio door, surveying the airy living room.

"How did they do it?" Kelly said. "No way they came through any of the doors. If they got in a window, how the hell could they lock it after they left?"

The simple explanation was that she hadn't secured the place properly; left a window unlocked or did a shoddy job of taping.

She stared up at the high ceiling, looking past the slowly turning fans at the end of their long shafts. It was shadowy at the apex of the A, but there was light coming in up there. "The skylights?"

There was a row of narrow, rectangular skylights running along the length of the ceiling.

"Very steep pitch up there," the sheriff said, following her gaze.

Kelly remembered Mrs. Mulvane saying something about Sarah Punk up in the trees during the storm. "Easy enough to get up there with all the trees."

"Very narrow," the sheriff said.

"Not for a little girl."

The sheriff turned slowly to look at her, his face sagging with weariness. He raised one eyebrow a fraction of an inch, then looked back at the ceiling, arms folded over his chest. "It's a thirty-foot drop, at least."

There was a narrow landing on the second floor with a couple of chairs and a small table behind a waist-high railing, like a balcony overlooking the living room. The sheriff looked up at the last skylight which was centered above the landing. "I guess you could hang down and drop from there. Eight feet or so." They both shifted, craning their necks upwards. The skylights were not windows. "They don't open," the sheriff said.

"Can they be pulled off?"

"I doubt that."

"A rope? Attached to a tree, if you had a helper."

The sheriff shook his head, swore, and rubbed the back of his neck. "This happened a few hours ago, in daylight."

"What else could it be? I could get a ladder, go up there and check," Kelly said.

The sheriff groaned. "Waste of time. The answer's not here, it's in Shaker's Bog. Did the caller say who put the body in the swamp?"

"No, only that she was murdered."

"She say where?"

"Near Shallow Rock, was all."

"Well, we're going to have to take a look," he said with a deep, bitter sigh.

"She could be telling the truth."

"Goddamnit, you ever search a swamp?"

"No."

"Well, before we do anything else, I'm gonna check with Columbia. For all we know Susan Collins is back home, lying on the couch watching TV."

CHAPTER
TWENTY-ONE

Kelly stood at the cash register, looking out the window at the parking lot of Garnett's Diner. There were two hitchhikers: older teenage boys, sitting on the cement footing of the tall streetlight by the highway. The sun was at the treetops, and there was still plenty of light, but she knew that once it got dark, that little pool of light would feel like an island of safety in the middle of the big dark woods.

Garnett's closed at eleven. "What do you do if they're still there when you close up?"

"I tell 'em, 'jump in the back of my truck and I'll take you down to the rest stop at Sebey Junction, lot more comfortable there than sleeping on concrete and gravel.'"

"What if they don't want to go?"

"Most nights, Deputy Crogan comes out here just before closing, has some pie and coffee. They don't argue with him standing there. If he ain't around, I tell 'em, 'come with me or I'm calling the sheriff.' That gets 'em moving every time."

"You ever have to call the station on them?"

"Nah, the law in Wanakena County's got a lot of respect with these kids."

"You ever see any of the deputies pick them up?"

"Not from here."

"Anywhere?"

"No, I never seen that."

Kelly came out of Garnett's carrying her big Stanley thermos full of black coffee. It was a beautiful evening; the sunset sky was bands of soft orange and red squeezed between the clouds and the trees. It was cool and dry at high elevation, but all that would change as soon as she began the long, winding descent to Lost Lake, four hundred feet below.

She looked over at the hitchhikers. Blue jeans, jean jackets, bright blue nylon backpacks. Middle-class kids. She thought about offering them a ride to Cranston Lake, pump them for information along the way, but she was too tired. It had been a long day after a restless night; she needed to get home and get some sleep.

Settling into the seat of her Duster with her patrol belt and hat on the passenger seat, she turned on the engine and turned off the radio. Most of the time she listened to WVSL out of Saranac Lake, but the reception went to shit once you started down towards Lost Lake. Silence was better than static, and anyways, she had plenty to think about tonight.

Earlier, back at the station, Sheriff Herkemer had spoken briefly with one of the deputies down in Columbia. The man didn't know much about Susan Collins, so he'd arranged for his boss to call Wanakena in the morning. With that, the sheriff had headed down the street to have supper. Betty had already gone home, and Undersheriff Thompson was out on patrol, leaving Kelly to hold the fort.

As soon as Sheriff Herkemer had left, she'd taken the keys from his desk and slipped into the records room. Leaving the door half open, she'd unlocked the cabinet containing confidential information and removed the complaints files.

There had been thirty-two complaints filed against the Wanakena County Sheriff's Department between the summer of 1970 and the beginning of June 1973. She quickly sorted through them, pulling out the nineteen that alleged sexual assault. She stacked the thin folders on the small desk and started leafing through them.

Sheriff Herkemer's report that she'd read in Gail's office was only a summary, with few details and no names. She quickly scanned the reports, looking for any mention of Susan Collins, but her name wasn't there. After that, she began a more thorough review, starting with the most recent accusation, filed three weeks ago, and working her way back.

All of the complaints had been made anonymously, over the phone or in unsigned letters. They had been made by girls who'd been hitchhiking through the county. They all claimed to have been picked up off the highway at night and taken to a place where they were raped. Some said by one cop, most by two or more cops—some in uniform, some in plainclothes. Afterwards, they were driven for an hour or more before being dropped off on the side of the road in one of the neighboring counties.

A few alleged that they'd been taken down a dirt road and assaulted in and around the cruiser, but most of them claimed to have been taken to an abandoned cabin deep in the woods, where they had been raped on an old bed with a stained mattress and rusty, creaking bed springs. They all remembered the screeching of the bedsprings. All in all, the claims made by nineteen different girls over a three-year span were very consistent.

But there were also problems with their accounts. All of the descriptions of the offending deputies were either hopelessly vague or rang false. Cops with long hair. Cops with the wrong accents. Officers in dark blue uniforms with blue ties, wearing forage caps with large silver badges; Southern California TV cops, right out of *Adam-12* or *The Rookies*. The Wanakena department's uniform shirts were light blue, and they wore the distinctive Smokey hats with very large six-point stars on them.

Sheriff Herkemer had been unable to find any corroborating witnesses. Other than the hitchhikers themselves, no one had seen the police picking up, dropping off, or assaulting anyone. No one in the department had been able to locate the sinister cabin with its rusty bed. Kelly wanted to believe that Sheriff Herkemer was a straight shooter, and from what she'd seen so far, there was nothing in any of the complaints that justified taking any kind of action. But she felt that he could have dug deeper, especially into the activities of the graveyard shift deputies, Faber and Crogan.

Keeping a close eye on the time, she was back out at the main desk, keys returned, before the sheriff got back from the diner down the street.

As she drove down towards Lost Lake, the world got darker, and the mist began to rise. It wasn't as bad as her first night; still she was forced to take it slow. Thinking about hitchhikers, she remembered the long conversation she'd had with Debbie Ruggles. One of the problems with the complaints was that most of the hitchhikers couldn't properly describe a Wanakena patrol car. Some claimed to have been picked up by a ghost car. Wanakena didn't have any ghost cars.

Ghost cars, ghost stories. At the time, she thought they'd drifted way off topic; except a ghost had shown up in the abuse complaints. Six of the girls said that they'd seen a ghost peering in the window at them while they were being raped in the secret cabin with the screeching bedsprings.

Screeching bedsprings and peeping ghosts; pure folktale.

The thing was, once heard, those stories took up residence in your head and stayed with you. Driving into the mist-shrouded dips at the lower end of

Cooperage, Kelly found herself looking out for Sarah Punk, convinced a couple of times that she actually saw her standing by the side of the road.

Too much coffee, too little sleep, she told herself.

She kept expecting the lumber camp to be around the next curve, down the next dip, but it wasn't there. Every goddamned bridge looked the same, every tight curve and stinking swamp looked the same. The bridges; she knew for a fact that the bridges were near the end of the road. She slowed to a crawl, slower than walking speed, afraid that she'd drive into the lake.

Where was the cookhouse light?

She was on a downslope, just packed earth leading to a solid bank of fog. She stopped, and as soon as she got out of the car, she realized that the wall of darkness to her right was the cookhouse. The light over the door was out.

"Mitch?"

Carefully, she opened the cookhouse door and flipped the light switch. The lights came on. The cookhouse was empty, the woodstove cold. Her stomach grumbled as she realized that there would be no leftovers for her tonight.

Leaving the lights on, she returned to her car, put her patrol belt on, and followed the flagstone path to the bunkhouse. The air was cool and humid, she could smell wood smoke, but it was coming from down the lake. She gently eased the screen door open and found the inner door unlocked. She pushed it open, but stayed on the threshold, screen door resting against her back, listening.

She turned on her flashlight. "Mitch?"

Mitch wasn't in his bed, or under it. There was no sign that he'd been around at all since last night. There was no light coming from under the door to her room. She unlocked it and gave it a shove so that it swung all the way open. From the threshold, she probed the room with her flashlight. Nothing.

"Too much coffee, not enough sleep."

Setting the flashlight on top of the woodstove, she tossed her hat onto the bed and turned towards the dresser with its big, oval mirror. She started working her ponytail loose.

A hideous noise broke the silence. Kelly froze, heart racing, every muscle suddenly taut. It came from outside. It wasn't loud, but it spoke directly to the most primal part of her brain. It was part scream, part strangled bellow, like an animal in pain. Three, four times it gave out a wheezing, tortured moan, and then stopped.

Motionless, one hand on the butt of her revolver, Kelly waited. Staring into the dark mirror, she listened, waiting for the cry to start up again. Suddenly, just for an instant, the antique mirror lit up, revealing a pale, empty-eyed woman. All around her startled face, thin, spiky arms clutched at her.

"Fuck!" Kelly shouted and dropped down into a crouch.

Before she could catch her breath, the mirror lit up

again, just for a second. Looking up, she saw the spiky shadows, but the creature in the mirror was gone.

Darkness. She looked over her shoulder. Nothing.

The mirror came to life again, on and off. Looking around, she noticed that her bedroom window also lit up each time. Light from outside was illuminating the mirror. She sat heavily on the floor, pushing the air out of her chest in big huffs. She had no idea what was going on, but the brief flash of supernatural dread that she'd felt was gone.

The noise again, a weird, grating sound. She'd never heard anything like it before. But there was no question, something was dying out there.

The awful noise stopped, and the light began to flicker again. It was one or the other, light or sound. She crawled over to the window and rose up to look outside. The strange commotion was coming from the west, off towards Deadhead Bay. After a few moments, she realized that it was the light passing through the branches of the trees that created the spiky arms crawling across the mirror. The frightened face had been her own.

The strangled squawking came again. Kelly stood up and straightened her belt.

"Somebody's got to put that fucking thing out of its misery," she said, and went back through Mitch's room and out the door. Prodded by swarming mosquitoes, she moved quickly down the side of the cookhouse.

Revolver in hand, she rounded the front of the

cookhouse and walked carefully down the path. Pausing at the tree line, she saw lights go on and off at the Anderson cottage, followed by another assault on her ears by the sickly, animal call. Each time it was exactly the same, the call and then the flashing light, precise, almost ritualistic.

There was no increase in tempo, no note of alarm or urgency. Four flashes, followed by four annoying squawks; with a growing sense of relief, Kelly watched as the bizarre pattern was repeated one more time. Then the lights of the cottage came on and stayed on.

CHAPTER
TWENTY-TWO

The thing was, Victor Charles *always* made you pay, man, even when he wasn't at home. Sometimes, the little bastard would have the entrance to his tunnels *underwater.* Mitch remembered rising up through the stinking rice paddy into the sump, sight blurred by the filthy water dripping down his face, feeling his way towards the narrow, muddy entrance of the gook tunnel. Going in, forcing his broad shoulders through the narrow entrance.

Then hearing the muffled screams of the point man, gored by some primitive booby trap. The guy's combat boots kicking him in the face as the poor son of a bitch frantically tried to back out.

Mitch stuck there, blocking the way, the guy screaming and kicking him in the face...

So, he knew that getting his body through the

narrow skylight on the roof above him was going to be an *emotional* problem of *serious* proportions.

He needed to be mellow, and the joint he'd smoked before leaving Patricia's wasn't going to do it. Reluctantly, he took a K4 from his shirt pocket, popped it, and curled in on himself to wait. He knew it wouldn't take long.

About fifteen minutes later, the first powerful jolt of euphoria surged through his body. He waited for it to pass, waited until the feelings of well-being and invincibility evened out. Then, as smooth and silent as the fog, he was up the big maple and onto the roof of the Dee cottage. He flowed upwards, over a rear window gable and up the steep pitch to the summit of the central A-frame.

He drew a bayonet from his boot to cut through the grout around the Plexiglas cover, but he didn't need to use it. The job was already done. The bubble lifted easily out of the wooden frame.

The slit before him looked as wide as a bay window. Chuckling at his earlier fear, he didn't even hear the scraping of the cover as it slid down the roof and into the branches of the tree below.

The combination of Zoomers, Dilaudid, and Guerrero Gold *transported* him, man. One minute he was lying on the roof, and the next thing he knew, he was standing on the orange shag carpet in the middle of the Dees' living room.

It was dark inside, the cool air rank and musty.

They'd taken Lucy's body away, but no one had washed the dishes or picked up the scattered remains of her last night on earth.

"Lucy?"

She'd been dead for about forty-eight hours. At dusk, he'd seen her from across the lake, staring out the window, staring at him.

He looked towards the spiral staircase, expecting to see her wafting down the stairs, glowing with inner illumination, but there was nothing but darkness.

"Lucy, hey, I'm sorry I left you, man. I didn't leave you to *die*, you know that, right?"

He pushed his thick hair back from his forehead. The AC iced his sweat.

The smell of the place was making him dizzy. He crossed the room, pulled back the blinds and slid open the windows over the sound system. Then the chemical backwash hit him. Head spinning, he barely made it to the couch before he passed out.

The weird noise had stopped, but now, almost as creepy, Kelly heard Mrs. Anderson's high-pitched, lilting voice. As she stepped across the close-cropped lawn, she started to make out the words, not that they made any sense.

"Oh, Saginaw, Oh, Saginaw," Mrs. Anderson sang out.

It reminded Kelly of the time she'd gone to the

Preakness, some glee club singing "Maryland, My Maryland."

"What the fuck?"

"Hellllooowwww Saginaw, *Deputy* Saginaw."

"Jesus." Kelly holstered her revolver. "It's _Mack_inaw," she called out sharply.

There was a pause. "Of course, it is, dear," Mrs. Anderson replied from the open window. "I saw the light go on at your place. Come, come, Archie wants you to give him a call."

"Archie?"

"Sheriff Herkemer, dear, you know, your boss."

Kelly wondered about that as she came up the back stairs. Had the sheriff found out she'd been going through the files behind his back?

Mrs. Anderson stood in the kitchen wearing a pale blue, sleeveless dress that flounced down to her ankles. She had a highball glass in one hand, and in the other, something Kelly recognized but didn't expect.

"You were making that noise?"

"Yes, dear," Mrs. Anderson replied, casually swinging an ornate leather moose call by its whip-like thong.

"And flicking the lights off and on."

"Of course, dear, to get your attention. Whatever did you think it was?"

"That was the worst moose call I've ever heard in my life. I thought something was dying."

"Well, I'm not a hunter, or a moose for that matter," she replied with an easy smile.

"You couldn't have just honked your car horn, or walked over?"

"After dark, with all these bugs? Besides, this *was* quite effective, don't you think?" She leaned back against the kitchen counter and indicated the phone on the wall with a wave of her empty glass. "If you take your boots off, you can use the phone in here," she said, and then watched as Kelly took her boots off and crossed the tiled floor in her stocking feet.

Kelly picked up the phone and dialed. Looking back towards the door, she resisted the urge to lean her weary head against the refrigerator door. A dark shape loomed on the doorstep, giving her frayed nerves a jolt. Before she could get her free hand to the butt of her gun, Gisela Ratsmueller came through the door.

She gave Kelly a friendly nod; they had met briefly a couple of days ago. Mrs. Anderson went to her and kissed her on both cheeks, European style.

"Wanakena County Sheriff," a voice came on the line, loud and clear.

"This is Deputy Mackinaw. The sheriff wanted to talk to me?"

"Hi, Kelly? This is Tom. Hang on."

Gisela had placed her big hands on Mrs. Anderson's evenly tanned shoulders and slipped by her, going deeper into the kitchen towards Kelly. It was a familiar act, almost an embrace. Mrs. Anderson returned to leaning against the counter.

Kelly closed her eyes with a deep sigh.

"Kelly? You're at the Andersons'?" Undersheriff Thompson said.

"Yes."

"Okay, sheriff's just talking to someone right now. We're sorting things out. He wants to talk to you himself. Just wait there…"

"Sorting what out?"

"Just stay there, okay. Gotta go, we need the line." Thompson hung up.

"Goddamnit," Kelly growled, opening her eyes.

Mrs. Anderson stood very close to her, close enough to tease her nose with the scent of Chanel. She was looking at Kelly with a concerned expression, her bottom lip trapped between her teeth.

"What?" Kelly demanded.

"I was just wondering, dear, what *is it*…exactly, that you are trying to do with your hair?"

Kelly hung up the phone. "It was…" she said, tugging at her ponytail and finishing the job of loosening it, "…a regulation ponytail, that I was taking down, when I was interrupted by your imitation of a dying moose."

Mrs. Anderson shook her head. "It doesn't really work for you, dear, not with your cheekbones; maybe a nice perm?"

"I'll think about it," Kelly replied, vigorously trying to work her tangled hair into some kind of shape with her fingers.

Gisela chuckled as she poured vodka into a tumbler.

"The sheriff is going to call me back. Okay if I have a drink?" Kelly asked.

"Of course, dear. There's a phone in the den. We can all huddle there and have a nice chat. And please, call me Patricia."

"Sure, uh, call me Kelly." It was better than "dear" at least.

"You want some of this?" Mrs. Ratsmueller asked, holding up a quart bottle of vodka.

Kelly ran her hands through her hair. "I could really use a beer, if you have one."

"I'm sure I have something in the fridge. Help yourself," Patricia put a hand lightly on Kelly's shoulder and offered her a welcoming smile.

"Thanks, Patricia."

Patricia waited while Kelly took a bottle of Löwenbräu from the fridge and popped the cap.

"Would you like a glass, dear?"

"No, I'm good," Kelly replied, and took a slug of the cold beer.

Patricia's smile broadened. "Come along then, it'll be much cozier in the den."

Sweating bottle in hand, Kelly followed Gisela down a short hallway. She stopped abruptly in the doorway to the den. "Son of a bitch!" she said.

Laid out on the coffee table were six handguns and a cleaning kit. "You expecting trouble, Patricia?" she asked.

"Oh, no. Wednesday night is the night I clean my guns," she replied, with a deep-throated laugh.

For a while Mitch drifted, wondering if Lucy would appear like a vision in the slowly swirling darkness behind his eyes. She did not. He wasn't sure what she wanted from him, but it had to have something to do with the Polaroids. She'd shown them to him soon after he'd dropped by on Monday, but it wasn't his thing and he'd only glanced at them. Disappointed, she'd put them back into a big manila envelope and taken them away. He had no idea where she'd put the envelope.

He wanted to take a closer look at those pictures, for Lucy, and for the nameless girl he'd seen in the Polaroid at Mrs. Parker's. The girl hanging in the shack.

The way Mrs. Cross and Mrs. Mulvane came on to him this morning had convinced him that the pictures were more than just an embarrassment to them. The negotiations had gotten pretty hazy. He'd been more wasted than he thought he was, and even stoned, the women were cagey.

Mrs. Mulvane had admitted that she'd been looking for the pictures the night Lucy died. Not that she knew something bad was going to happen, but because she was afraid that Lucy might be showing them around. Or worse, that the little sneak thief, Bobby Margin, would steal them. She'd always thought that Lucy had kept them in her room, and when she didn't find them there, she'd become a little frantic.

After a while Mitch lifted his head and opened his

eyes. "Come on, Lucy. Work with me here." They could be hidden anywhere. "Where are the pictures?"

Silence, except for the whir of the AC.

"Fine, be like that," he said and curled up on the couch.

CHAPTER
TWENTY-THREE

Patricia sat down on the couch. "Come, I'll introduce you to my boys," she said, patting the cushion beside her. "This one was my first. Of course, it's more of an accessory than a real 'gat', but very reliable." She handed a small, snub-nosed automatic to Kelly. "I was living in Italy at the time, early sixties. A charming place where one was expected to be both well dressed *and* well heeled."

"Beretta 950, right? And is this..."

"Yes, dear, ten-karat gold plating, Corinthian leather grip. It was designed by Bijan Pakzad, a dear friend. Eight-round magazine, fits easily into a purse or even a clutch."

Kelly had never owned a clutch. The lightweight piece fit easily in the palm of her hand.

".22 Short, so really just a stinger," Patricia said. "*This* one has more of a bite."

Kelly put down the little Beretta and hefted the serviceable-looking automatic Patricia handed her. "A Browning. I've seen these around. Sure, you could take this to a firefight."

Patricia slid up against Kelly and rested a hand on her shoulder. "This is the .40-calibre model, used by the SOG in Cambodia, quite rare, actually."

Kelly liked the feel of the weapon. "Sure, this would cut right through the undergrowth."

"Drop a man at sixty yards," Patricia chuckled.

Kelly turned to look at the older woman, her face right there next to hers. Hazel eyes, dark blue eyeshadow, red lipstick, long dark eyelashes. She tried to imagine Patricia blazing away with a Browning in the jungle. As she handed the pistol back, she noticed that although Patricia's fingernails were flawlessly shaped and polished, they weren't much longer than her own chipped and naked ones.

Gisela brought them fresh drinks. No beer for Kelly this time, but a tumbler of bourbon and ice. Kelly took a long swallow and sat back on the couch, thinking maybe she should get good and pissed. One-handed, she opened the top two buttons of her uniform shirt and became aware of the smell of her sweat mingling in the warm room with Patricia's delicate perfume and the oddly arousing mixture of gun oil and hairspray.

Gisela stood near the fireplace, drink in hand. Tall, athletic; hair parted in the middle of her forehead, falling to her shoulders in a single wave on either side of her face, she regarded them with quiet amusement.

Patricia snuggled up to Kelly as she explained the many custom modifications that had been made to her Colt 1911, competition automatic. Something about the sights, the grips. Kelly was having trouble concentrating. The air conditioning was on, but it was very warm in the den. Gisela brought them all fresh drinks.

Patricia continued to describe her Colt in a throaty tone that was unquestionably obscene. She was hitting on her. Kelly's sluggish mind considered it. Patricia was sleek, attractive, and smelled wonderful. No doubt she had a very nice bedroom. It would be a treat not to have to go back to the bunkhouse and get woken up when Mitch came stumbling in.

But what about Gisela? Whatever kind of relationship she had with Patricia, she seemed okay with her coming on to Kelly right in front of her.

Patricia caressed the fat barrel of a .44 Magnum, "the most powerful handgun in the world" recently made famous in *Dirty Harry*. Kelly took a deep breath, and with deliberate slowness, sat upright. She was careful not to offend, not necessarily wanting to burn any bridges. This had all been very interesting, but there was only so much new shit a person could take in one night.

She made a point of surveying the room. "Ahh, shotguns too," she said. Placing a hand firmly, but gently, on Patricia's shoulder, she stood up.

There were four polished shotguns standing at attention in a display cabinet on the far wall. Kelly bumped her shins into the coffee table on her way over to admire them.

"Wow, Patricia, very nice," she said, swinging open the glass front of the cabinet.

"My third husband, Chet, fancied himself a hunter," she said with an indulgent smile. "He wasn't."

Gisela made a sudden snort of tipsy laughter.

"He did like the accoutrements though," Patricia added, smiling at her friend.

Kelly reached out for the tempting Remington 3200 with the sexy, blond stock, missed it, and thought better of handling firearms for the rest of the night.

"Hence, the six-hundred-dollar moose call that was so effective in luring you here." Patricia winked at Gisela, who left the fireplace and went to sit beside her on the couch. Gisela draped an arm over the top of the couch and Patricia snuggled under it. They smiled at Kelly. No hard feelings. They weren't burning any bridges either.

CHAPTER
TWENTY-FOUR

THURSDAY

Mitch woke up on the floor with a wet spot next to his head and a mouth that tasted like dirty wool. After a moment's reflection, he realized that he'd been gnawing on Lucy's gritty, orange carpet. With a clear sense of urgency, he stood up and went into the kitchen to get a drink.

By his third glass of water, his mouth and head felt much cleaner. It was still dark outside, but without a watch, he had no idea how long he'd been passed out. Long enough for the bennies to have run down, long enough for the opioid high to bottom out, long enough for his Oaxacan perception to fade.

Stuck in the material world, he took a better look at the things around him. A litter of glasses, ashtrays, and scummy plates fused to the marble countertop.

Dust on the bevelled surfaces of the oak cabinets. Crusty splotches on the brushed steel handles of the drawers.

A wisp of icy breath on the back of his neck sent a shiver down his spine.

"No way."

He began opening drawers. Cutlery... cutlery... tea towels... junk.

"Son of a bitch."

He lifted the envelope out of a clutter of odds and ends. Sure, the way Lucy had been feeling, that's where the pictures belonged, with the rest of the cast-off junk. She must have chucked them in there and died before putting them back where they normally belonged.

That's why Mrs. Mulvane couldn't find them during her frantic search. Frantic, because the power had gone out. Frantic, because she must have known that there would be cops poking around in the morning. She didn't get to the kitchen, the last place she would have looked, before she was interrupted when he and Kelly had arrived.

Returning to the living room, he lit the two Chianti-bottle candles and emptied the contents of the manila envelope onto the coffee table. There were at least fifty loose Polaroids, and a small photo store envelope. The envelope was very thin, but it gave off a strong, toxic vibe. Mitch set it aside at the far end of the rectangular table.

He began sorting through the pictures, arranging

them by location. There were pictures from inside three different cottages and some taken outside. Mostly, the participants were naked, except for a few costume parties, where the women were dressed as sexy nurses, harem girls, or playboy bunnies. The men were cowboys, firemen, and cops.

There were a lot of Lucy doing everybody, but she wasn't the only one. Mrs. Cross and Mrs. Mulvane were getting their fair share of action too. The whole gang had been photographed having sex with each other in lots of weird and wonderful ways. There were other women too, five or six of them altogether. These were just weekend warriors; the three "Ladies of the Lake" were definitely the stars of this scene.

Bobby must have stolen some of these pictures, or maybe Lucy had let him take what he wanted, to make up his stash hidden in the bunkhouse. From what Mitch could remember, there were no pictures of the casual visitors in Bobby's stash.

Unlike the ones in Bobby's stash, he could see the faces of the men in many of these pictures. Mostly, Mr. Cross and Mr. Mulvane; Mr. Dee was there too, but never getting as much. There were other men as well, men Mitch didn't recognize, except for one guy in a couple of shots that he might have seen around.

One thing for sure, the picture that Mitch had found on Bobby Margin's chair didn't belong here. There were no pictures of anyone who looked at all like the girl in the shack. There were no pictures of minors. No pictures of anyone tied up. In one picture, a big guy, the one Mitch thought he'd seen around, was holding up a pair of handcuffs, but everyone was laughing.

The curtains next to the open window rustled impatiently.

"Okay, so this isn't about *her*," he said.

One at a time, he looked very carefully at each of the pictures. "What am I looking for, Lucy?"

He took a joint from his shirt pocket, placed it between his lips, and went into the kitchen in search of an ashtray and something to drink. "Feel free to rearrange those," he called back into the living room, as he hunted for a reasonably clean glass.

When he returned, the pictures were laid out exactly as he'd left them. He sat down, blazed up the joint, and started going through them again.

When the ladies had stopped laughing, Kelly asked, "So, you... guys never had anything to do with the stuff going on across the lake, did you?"

"Oh, Gott, no. Such children, always running around, playing dress-up and so."

"Holly Mulvane has a trim little figure and Denise Cross is darling," Patricia said. "But their men are ghastly."

"Always with the cops and robbers, cowboys and Indians, bang-bang-bang." Gisela removed her arm from Patricia's shoulders and fired her fingers at Kelly.

Kelly heard a pinging sound in her brain, like the imaginary bullets were bouncing off a steel plate in her head.

"Fuck. Wait. They like to dress up like cops?"

"Cops, firemen, saloon dancing whores, ya, all like this," Gisela said, sitting back again.

"We would sit in the lanai and watch them romping around at the Dee place." Patricia pointed her chin at the Zeiss field glasses hanging next to the shotgun cabinet. "They never drew their curtains. Shameless exhibitionists, especially poor Lucy Dee. God rest her soul."

Kelly held up her hand, trying to get them to stop talking. "Cops..."

The phone rang, startling them all, setting off a new round of laughter from the two older women. While the ladies laughed, Kelly took slow steps to the end table where the princess phone sat. She ran her hands through her hair before she picked up the receiver.

"Deputy Mackinaw," she said carefully.

"Kelly? Tom."

"Yes?"

"Sheriff says don't bother coming in tomorrow."

"What? Can I talk..."

"We're doing a search of Shaker's Bog in the morning. He says you should meet us there, no need to drive all the way into town."

"Oh, okay."

"You got hip waders, civvies, you should wear them."

"Okay. Is something else going on?"

"Be down at the docks at eleven. See you then." The undersheriff hung up.

"Everything alright, dear?" Patricia asked.

"Sure. We're gonna search Shaker's Bog tomorrow."

"How nasty. Would you like another drink?"

Kelly squinted at her watch. Two a.m.

"Sure, what the hell, I guess I'm sleeping in tomorrow," she said.

"You were pissed off at everybody, and... you were worried about Bobby. Did they do something to Bobby?"

But Lucy had wandered off again. Probably pissed at him. "I know, I know, I should have listened to you when you were alive," Mitch said.

Grudgingly, he attempted to think methodically. What did he *not* see?

There were no pictures of Bobby Margin. No pictures of Mrs. Parker, Mrs. Anderson, or Mrs. Ratsmueller. Also, thankfully, no pictures of his dad. Lucy looked pretty wasted in some of the pictures, but mostly she looked like she was having a good time.

He took in another lungful of smoke and set the

roach to burn out in the ashtray. The photo store envelope fell on the floor.

"Okay. Okay." He pushed aside the pile of dirty pictures and laid out the contents of the smaller envelope in the centercentre of the table. Four pictures of Sarah Punk, and one that wasn't.

Two Sarah shots taken indoors and two taken in the bush at night. He had seen similar pictures in Bobby's stash.

One of the indoor shots showed a bunch of the swingers tangled together in a heap on a living room floor. In the background, someone had circled a corner of the window where the curtain had been pushed aside. Something was out there. There were just a few points of light against the pitch black of the night, but unmistakably a face. In the other indoor shot, the party looked like it was just getting started. Again, closer and clearer this time, a small, smudged, hollow-eyed face was peeking in the corner of a window. Each of the outdoor shots had also snatched a glimpse of a ghostly face, stark white in the flash. Never close, always back in the trees, the face unconnected to the ground.

There was one more night picture, the one carrying the heavy karma. Two lovers, clothed, in a passionate embrace, surprised by the sudden flash of the camera, their terrified faces easily identified. Mrs. Cross up against the side of a cottage clutching Bobby Margin.

"Bobby and Mrs. Cross," Mitch said. It didn't

come as a complete surprise, but still, seeing them exposed like that in a burst of merciless light, made him feel unclean.

All the "dirty" pictures of the frolicking swingers had a plastic feel to them. It was like the participants had been dipped in a glossy protective coating, sealing in any real emotions. Those pictures were phony, mechanical, selfish.

This picture was real. This picture carried *freight*, man.

"Okay, so, Mr. Cross gets jealous. Not just because his wife is fucking behind his back, but because Bobby actually means something to her."

He laid out the four pictures of Sarah in a row with the picture of Bobby and Mrs. Cross at the end. "I get it. They all figured that Sarah Punk was just creepy, little Bobby Margin sneaking around, peeping on their fun. Even after the beating last year, even after they'd warned him, he kept coming around, so they decided to kill him.

But Bobby is Victor Charles in his own backyard, he's not going to get caught a second time. Unless... you have a Judas. Someone he trusts who will betray him."

Now he saw Mrs. Cross standing on the windswept summit of Steep Rock, Bobby rushing into her arms. Men appearing out of the darkness, catching Bobby, beating him. Planning to beat him senseless and then throw him onto the rocks below. Make it look like he had committed suicide.

"But Bobby didn't die." Hot and cold snakes wriggled up Mitch's spine.

"They took him by surprise, got his knife away from him. Bobby fought like mad, but he's up against at least three big men. They had him."

Then the scream he'd heard last night. Mitch grinned at the vision. Sarah, dropping out of the trees and taking a bite out of one of them in the shoulder.

"Bobby knew exactly where the rocks were and how to hit the deep water. He broke free and *jumped* off of Steep Rock. That's what I saw falling down the front of the moonlit cliff last night. Then Sarah went over after him.

Still, it's pretty fucking extreme, right, to kill a guy because he's a peeping Tom, even if he is fucking around with one of your wives? They weren't just mad at Bobby, right? They were afraid of him. They believed he'd seen more than just a little decadent partying."

He shuddered as the icy breath—the spooky, sexy breath—ran up his neck to the base of his skull.

"When you heard the plan, you blew up. You threatened to talk if they went through with it."

He began sifting through the pile of Polaroids. He selected a picture and placed it at the center of the table below the pictures of Sarah. In the picture, Lucy, wearing nothing but a pair of harem pants and one of those funky, round hats, posed with her arms raised over her head, palms together.

He selected pictures of Mrs. Cross and Mrs. Mulvane and placed them on Lucy's left. On her right, he put her husband, Dandy Dan Dee, then Mr. Cross and Mr. Mulvane. After a moment's hesitation, he added the guy with the handcuffs. Then he sat back with his hands behind his head, closed his eyes, and tried to empty his mind.

"Who killed you, Lucy?"

Breathing deeply, letting the calming power of the weed take hold, he slowly shut himself down. After a while, he reached the still place of silence.

The AC unit clunked loudly to a halt. Mitch sat up and saw the table whole.

He reached out, took the picture of Mrs. Mulvane and laid it crosswise over the harem girl.

CHAPTER
TWENTY-FIVE

There was a girl standing in the deep shadow of the trees; dull blond hair, pale skin, a shapeless white dress. Her eyes were hollow and black. She was less than twenty yards away, close enough to see, too far to grab. She was absolutely still, knee-deep in the mist-shrouded undergrowth. Sarah Punk.

"No fucking way," Kelly said. It was nine o'clock in the morning. What kind of ghost is hanging around at nine o'clock in the morning?

She'd stopped by the Dee cottage to make sure it was still secure, before heading out to Shallow Rock. She'd suspected that the swingers might try to get back into the cottage. She didn't expect this.

"Hey kid, what are you doing here?"

The girl stood there, her face flat and featureless, her dark eyes giving nothing away. Kelly felt herself begin to sweat, felt her heart start to race. The girl wasn't moving, but somehow, she was fading into the undergrowth, just like the other night in the swamp.

"Hey kid, who are you?" Kelly shouted.

Something went whizzing past her forehead and smacked into the wall of the Dee cottage. Kelly drew her revolver and turned in the direction of the shooter. She scanned the tree line the way she'd been taught in basic, looking for human shapes, shining eyes, odd colors. If anyone was there, they were very good at hiding. She took a chance and swung her head back around. The girl was gone.

"Son of a bitch!" she shouted.

Staying low, she methodically observed the woods where the girl had been, then scanned out towards the road, across the narrow asphalt lane, and back to the woods on the other side of the parking area. There had been a slap of something hitting the side of the cottage, but no gunshot. She eased up on the trigger. Not a shooter. Some kid throwing stones at her.

As her gaze came full circle to the cottage, something moved past a second story window. Kids. Probably the same kids that got in and made the prank phone call.

The back door to the Dee place was locked, the police tape still in place. Kelly dashed to the path that led around the side of the house to the lake. As she reached the patio, she saw movement out of the corner of her eye. Someone running down the path towards the Cross cottage. Red shorts, blue top, tanned legs, a female running away.

"Stop!" she shouted.

The police tape was down; the patio door was wide open. Kelly looked into the dark living room. No one there or on the stairs, but they could easily be hiding elsewhere in the house, lying low.

She looked over her shoulder at the empty path. Go poking around in a dark, smelly house, or give chase? She holstered her revolver and took off down the zig-zagging steps toward the lakeshore. Pounding down the narrow path, she cursed herself for not keeping in better shape.

By the time she'd reached the stairs leading up to the Cross cottage, she had to stop to catch her breath. There was no sign of her quarry on the stairs or on the path. She took off her battered field cap and doubled over, spitting bile, trying not to throw up. Her eyeballs felt like a couple of hot marbles lodged in grit. She should have gone right home last night after Undersheriff Thompson called, instead of letting Patricia talk her into having another drink, and another.

A distinct, sharp crash, like someone had tossed a beer bottle, knifed through the drumming in her head. She looked up at the Cross cottage. A car door slammed shut. Struggling up the steep steps, she reached the parking area just as a yellow Corvette was driving away.

"Stop! Police!" she shouted, then stood helplessly with her hands on her thighs, gasping for breath.

The car accelerated very slowly and drove, unswerving, right into a stand of birch trees thirty yards away. There was a grinding squeal followed by a long, steady groan from the car's horn.

The horn went silent as Kelly reached the car. The engine cut off, the long door swung half-way open, and Mrs. Cross, wearing a pink, strapless jumpsuit, tumbled out onto the ground.

Kelly helped her to her feet. Mrs. Cross, lopsided with one high-heeled shoe on and one off, twisted and toppled into her arms. "Thanks you," she said, with a slurred sigh and flopped back against the car.

Kelly pinned her against the car with both hands on her shoulders. She was wasted, but showed no sign of injuries. Her head lolled; eyes closed.

Kelly took several deep breaths. "Mrs. Cross?"

Her long eyelashes fluttered open, her large, brown eyes focused briefly and then closed again. "S'alright, my husband is a lawyer," she said.

Kelly pulled her face back from the wave of boozy breath and gave her a shake. "Mrs. Cross."

Mrs. Cross's tight, wet-looking curls bounced. Her eyes came open again, faster this time. She gave Kelly a droopy-eyed smile.

"Just stand there." Kelly attempted to brace her, but Mrs. Cross started to slide. "Okay, better just sit down."

"Okkeeee Dokeeee."

Kelly eased her down until she was sitting with her back to the car. "Are you going to take me home?" Mrs. Cross asked.

Kelly opened the driver's door, leaned in, and took

the keys from the ignition. Mrs. Cross's large purse lay open on the passenger seat. Kelly made a quick check of its contents. No weapons, no drugs, no wads of cash. Closing the door, she looped the purse over Mrs. Cross's neck and helped her to her feet.

"Let's go," she said.

Mrs. Cross kicked off her other shoe, tucked herself under Kelly's arm, and let Kelly lead her across the asphalt. The door to the cottage was slightly ajar, a smashed vodka bottle off to one side.

"Is there someone here with you?" Kelly asked.

Mrs. Cross's eyes opened, widened. She squirmed free. "Not *here*. I want to go home. I don't want to stay here." She weaved, and before Kelly could catch her, fell to her knees. "I hate this fucking lake!"

Kelly crouched down, took her by the chin, and held it firmly.

Tears smudged her mascara. "I want to go home." She started crying, clutching at Kelly's forearms.

"What are you on?"

"Sheree Axe and Mommydream."

Kelly didn't recognize the names but figured they must be prescription. She doubted that Mrs. Cross had to get her drugs on the street. The crying jag ended suddenly. Grinning, Mrs. Cross reached out and slid a hand along Kelly's thigh, searching for her crotch.

"Stop that."

"Now will you take me away from here?"

"Where's your husband?"

"Working?"

She could charge her with a DWI and take her to the station, but that would get others involved. Much better to stay here and have a little talk. "You need to take it easy. We'll see about getting someone to take you home in a little while," she said.

Mrs. Cross squirmed petulantly as Kelly tried to get her through the door. Finally, she picked her up and carried her over the threshold. Mrs. Cross laughed and kicked her feet.

"Where's your bedroom?"

"Call me Denny."

The eye-watering mixture of alcohol and perfume coming off her irritated Kelly's hungover stomach. The sickly-sweet smell of weed clung to the surprisingly neat living room.

"Okay, Denny."

"What's your name?"

"Kelly."

Denny pointed with a nylon-covered foot. "Okay, Kelly, it's this way."

Kelly carried her to the bedroom. As soon as they entered, Denny started kicking, her voice losing all its girlishness. "Put me down, put me down. I'm gonna be sick."

Kelly put her down. Denny stumbled into the en-suite and immediately started retching.

Kelly went to the mirrored closet that spanned one wall. Sliding back the first two doors revealed women's clothing. Behind the third door were men's suits and casual wear. The fourth was more of the same, the hangers packed tightly together.

She went to the end of the rack and started shoving clothes aside so she could get a better look at them. There was a leather vest and what looked like cowboy chaps. A silk blouse with a puffy front, a police uniform.

Mitch spat into the open end of his cam stick and worked the crumbling face paint with his finger. It had been almost a year since the last time he'd used it. He grinned at himself in the mirror as he ran a strip of the dark green loam down the bridge of his nose.

It had been late morning when the nightmare had roused him from his bed.

In the nightmare, he was sitting at the open door of a Huey, feet on the skid, feeling the rush of the wind as the chopper weaved sinuously down a winding river valley. It was beautiful, man. Then the whine of the engine became a scream, and the scream drew him to a cabin in the swamp, the one in Bobby Margin's Polaroid where Sarah Punk was bound.

He made broad strokes along his jawline, straight strokes down his neck. He worked some of the paint over the tips of his ears, the backs of his hands, and down his long fingers; a precisely followed ritual that made sure he covered every inch of his telltale, white skin.

Sarah had sent him the nightmare, just as she'd sent him the dream the night before that had brought him to Mrs. Parker's so he could see the Polaroid. He'd seen it, seen the proof that she was a prisoner, but Bobby had fooled him with his fake aura and his easy manner, convincing him that all was well with the universe. Then Mrs. Parker had scared him off, and he'd turned his attention to Lucy.

Sarah Punk was hanging from the rafters somewhere, and he'd turned his back on her to flirt with the new ghost on the lake. No wonder she was so pissed off. He had fucked up and had to make it right.

He made bold slashes across his forehead and drew a straight line under his nose. He blackened his high cheekbones, and with a smile, gave himself raccoon eyes. He capped one end of the stick and opened the other.

It was clear to him now, what had happened. Bobby had been haunted all his life, Sarah Punk stalking him, trying to get inside his head, waiting for the moment to strike. Any normal person would have stayed away from Lost Lake, but when he was younger, Bobby had no choice, and when he got older, he couldn't resist the lure of the "Ladies of the Lake," especially Mrs. Cross.

Bobby had never been normal, and then, just in recent days, he'd become fey. Probably Mrs. Parker had been teaching him for years, nurturing his special powers until the moment came when he could turn on his tormentor. Bobby had ambushed a *ghost*, man, and took her prisoner.

Using the light green, he filled in all the spaces not covered by the loam. Satisfied with his workmanship, he buttoned his wrinkled fatigue shirt up to his neck and down at his wrists.

He didn't like the idea of going up against Bobby Margin, but he had been summoned. Sarah Punk's scream still echoed in his head, and he knew it wouldn't stop until he'd set her free.

He placed a tab of acid under his tongue and tasted metal as it dissolved. On a mission like this, he needed to be able to *see*. The powerful Frisco Freak would give him insight into the spirit world. The cabin must be the Hell Hole in Shallow Rock, but he didn't know how to get there. No problem, if he could ascend to Sarah's plane, she would guide him.

Peyote would have been better, but he didn't have any. Cool. The Frisco blotter would carry him for a good ten hours at least. He tucked the envelope with the Polaroids from the Dee cottage under the dust cover of his bed, keeping the picture of the guy with the handcuffs.

Energy, perception, balance. Check. Weapons…

Mitch didn't own a gun, hadn't even touched one since Mesa Verde. In the desert, he'd carried a sawed-off shotgun with him everywhere he went. The images in his head from that time were bleached and grainy. He couldn't remember if he'd killed anyone back then, back before his enlightenment.

His dad had always kept a shotgun in the back corner of the closet on his side of the room, but when Mitch went to look for it, it was gone. He fastened the bug net to his boonie hat and went to the cookhouse. The rack where his dad had always kept his old M1 was empty too.

"Hunh," he said.

He knew it had been there when he'd moved in two weeks ago, but he couldn't remember when it had stopped being there. Moving around the cookhouse, he discovered that there were no longer any guns at all in the lumber camp. Also, no really big knives. Outside, there was an axe embedded in the chopping block, but it was too long and unwieldy for the kind of close-quarters fighting he had in mind.

He was about to leave the porch when he noticed that there was a note on the table. It was written on narrow police notebook paper and held down by Kelly's coffee mug.

Couldn't wake you up. Searching Shakers today. Working late tonight.

The acid was just starting to take hold. Mitch stood looking down at the note, wondering why Kelly had left him a haiku. That wasn't like her. He sat down to compose one of his own on the other side of the page.

Mulvane killed Lucy
Rescuing Sarah Punk
Do you know this guy?

He placed the Polaroid of the guy with the cuffs under the note and put the coffee mug on top.

From the woodpile next to the woodstove, he took a hatchet, and from the toolbox in the shed, he took a screwdriver with an eight-inch shaft. He settled into his dad's canoe with the hatchet on his left side and the screwdriver on his right, tucked into his belt. Under the lowering clouds, he pushed off from the dock.

CHAPTER
TWENTY-SIX

Kelly shoved hard at the clothes, knocking some hangers down. It was a standard blue, Hollywood-cop shirt, with captain's bars. On the left pocket was a silver badge that said "Police" in bold black letters.

"What are you doing?"

Kelly jerked around.

It was Mrs. Mulvane. "You have no right to be here. Where's Denise?" she demanded.

Gritting her teeth, Kelly sucked air sharply through her nose. Fixing Mrs. Mulvane with a stone-faced glare, she counted slowly, silently, to ten. Mrs. Mulvane was wearing a white top and a short, baby blue skirt; not the red shorts and blue top Kelly had seen running down the path. A matching headband held her brunette locks off her face. She looked like she'd just stepped out of a country club change room, no sweat, not out of breath.

"What are you doing here? This isn't your house," Kelly said.

"'S'all right, Holly. I had an accident." Mrs. Cross stood in the bathroom doorway in a tiny pair of panties and knee-high nylon stockings.

"Get back in there and put your clothes on," Mrs. Mulvane snapped.

"You're not giving orders around here," Kelly said.

Mrs. Mulvane gave her a look of annoyed disgust. "Did you undress her?"

"You need to calm down," Kelly replied, trying hard to keep her voice low.

"Get out of here, now."

"You are interfering with an officer of the law." Kelly's left hand went behind her back and rested on her cuffs.

Mrs. Mulvane gave her the finger and strode over to the phone beside the bed. Without hesitation, she punched in some numbers. "Hello, Betty. Get me Sheriff Herkemer. Oh. Is Tom there? Good, put him on, please. Yes, it's urgent."

Kelly knew she was way out on a limb. She took her hand off her cuffs and crossed her arms over her chest. In the bathroom, Denny was loudly throwing up again.

"Tom? Holly Mulvane. Fine, thanks. Tom, this new deputy of yours, Macdaw, is illegally inside the Cross cottage. I have just arrived, and there is something very questionable going on here. When I have the full details, Mick will give you a call. But right now, I want her out."

She offered the phone with a vicious half-smile. Kelly took it from her and thought about beating her over the head with it.

"Mackinaw, what the hell are you doing?"

"Tom, look, there's—"

"Why are you at Lost Lake? You're supposed to be at Shallow Rock."

"I'm only a few minutes away."

"The others are probably waiting for you. We're wasting enough time on this foolishness as it is without you holding things up." Undersheriff Thompson was generally a pretty laid-back guy. Not this morning.

"Where's the sheriff? I've got a situation here," Kelly said.

"You're damn right you've got a situation. Get the hell out of that woman's house and get over to Shallow Rock, right now."

"Can I talk to the sheriff?"

"He's on his way to Plattsburg to talk to the State Troopers. One of the guys Hack Weechum beat up in Placid died last night, so the search for him just ramped up a notch. I don't know what the hell you're up to out there, but unless you're ready to arrest somebody for a serious crime, get your ass over to Shallow Rock, right now."

"Yes, sir." Kelly slammed down the phone.

Mrs. Mulvane had moved away from the bed and was standing by the bathroom door.

Kelly walked towards the bathroom. "Mrs. Cross?"

Mrs. Mulvane closed the door and stood in front of it. Kelly came up to her, using her height, getting in her space. "Stand aside," she said.

Mrs. Mulvane stood her ground. "You're drunk, Deputy Jakdaw."

"You want to find out what happens when I have to put my hands on you?"

Mrs. Mulvane stepped aside. Kelly opened the bathroom door and stood in the doorway. Denny was on her knees at the toilet.

"Denny."

She looked up, teary-eyed, slobbery.

"Do you want to come with me to the station?" Kelly said, trying to sound firm but gentle.

"Her husband is on his way. He will be here shortly," Mrs. Mulvane said.

Denny hesitated, then shook her head.

"Are you sure? I don't mind taking you. We can find a way to get you home."

"No, I'd better wait for Hal."

"Okay, but I'm going to call you. We're gonna have a talk, okay, Denny?"

Denny nodded and returned her head to the toilet bowl.

Kelly stepped back, rolled her shoulders slowly, and stared at Mrs. Mulvane. "It's Mackinaw," she said.

"I'll be sure to get it right on the complaint," Mrs.

Mulvane replied. "You might want to brush your teeth before going to work," she added, stepping back and waving a hand in front of her face.

Fuming, Kelly hustled back to the Dee cottage. She did a very quick search of the place, saw that nothing had changed, and then closed the patio doors. She re-tied the tape, although she wasn't sure what the point was; the damned place was like Grand Central Station.

She paused a moment on the Dee patio, wiping sweat from her forehead with a handkerchief. She considered going back and seizing the police costume from Cross cottage, but she knew it wouldn't do any good, not in court, not against these people.

It made sense, some of the swingers teaming up with a couple of bored night shift cops like Crogan and Faber. There was the opportunity, the arrogance.

Kidnapping and rape; sooner or later it is bound to end in murder. Probably an accident. They panic and hide the body in Shaker's Bog. Sarah Punk sees it and doesn't like it. She makes a call.

Sarah Punk.

Staring out at the lake, she wondered if there was a rusty old bed at the Hell Hole.

The lake tilted and Mitch slid down its asphalt plane right into Back Bay.

Mrs. Parker stood on her dock, arms outstretched

towards him. "Where are you going, Mitch? Come and have a drink."

The nose of his canoe swung slowly towards her, like the needle of a compass. Mitch had a memory vision: Bobby popping out from behind a tree, taking him by surprise. Silent, letting the stuttering rata-tat-tat of his plastic Tommy gun do the talking for him.

"Not this time, Bobby," Mitch shouted across the water.

"I'm not Bobby. Jesus, Mitch, you're stoned."

He turned sharply away from her and shot towards the swamp. The reeds and lily pads parted. He was riding again, swooping, falling. Then all was still. A huge silver snake came rushing at him through the vegetation. It circled him twice, then turned back the way it came. He dug hard with his paddle, fighting against the stubborn grasp of the reeds, to go after it.

By the time he broke free, the snake was gone. He followed the quicksilver slick it had left in its wake. Lilies as bright as beacons, like fires lining a runway carved out of the jungle floor, marked his passage. As he came to the Hell Hole, the scream became softer. His heartbeat began to slow.

"Easy, man. Easy, easy."

Bugs swarmed angrily around his head and hands. His body was soaked with sweat.

"What do you see?"

A crooked, weathered building with a splintered, tilted dock. Pitched roof, story and a half high, winding away into the black sky. One small window and a black rectangle opening in the wall. Silently, he slithered up onto the tattered planks and lay still. He listened for Bobby, but all was quiet, even the scream had stopped. He lay and breathed, lay and breathed, pulling his watery limbs together. He eased his weapons from his belt.

He didn't want to go in. Giant drops of rain fell in sticks and began exploding all around him. Arc Light flashed.

"Move, move, move."

He jumped to his feet. Hatchet in his left hand, screwdriver in his right, he charged through the open doorway. It was a single large room, dim, uncrowded. Something moved off to his left. He pivoted and threw the screwdriver. It stuck into the rotting wall with a serious thud.

Nobody there.

Nobody anywhere. He whirled around and around until he lost his balance and collapsed onto the floor. Panting, he crawled on his belly into a corner and pulled himself up so he could sit with his back against the wall. From here, he could keep an eye on the door and the window at the same time. Thunder rolled and the ground shook as the B 52's returned and started tearing up the hills.

With trembling hands, he pushed up his bug net, snapped open his Zippo, and fired up a joint. He was in the right place. He could see the ropes dangling from the rafters and beneath them, a dark stain.

The reek of the Northern Lights held the bugs at

bay. As he calmed down and fitted back into his skin, he tried to decipher the runes closest to his head. The peeling, moldy wallpaper was thick with messages, primarily about who sucks cock. An impressive list of names accompanied by fanciful drawings of dicks. There was litter in all of the corners, as if blown there by a whirlwind in the center of the room.

"Huh."

His bones dissolved.

"Oh, fuck," he said, as his jellied body slid down the wall, dripped through the cracks in the floor and fell like a big, fat raindrop into the emptiness below.

CHAPTER
TWENTY-SEVEN

Kelly drove slowly down the main street of Shallow Rock, doing her best to avoid the washouts and scattered brown puddles made treacherous by the most recent downpour. She drove with her windows open and the windshield wipers going. Steam rose like smoke from the sagging porches and rotting steps that lined the road. There were no people outside, but beneath the dripping eaves, every grimy window held a watching face.

MacLean and Boodrow were leaning against one of the patrol cars on the narrow, flat space between the last rambling shack and the village dock. They couldn't have been waiting long; the two department canoes were still in the trailer behind the car. They watched her pull up and get out of her car. She'd only met them briefly during her first few days on the job.

MacLean straightened up. "Morning, Kelly, glad you could join us," he said.

Boodrow continued to lounge against the patrol car. A few years older than her, he was a good-looking man; tall, with a square jaw and brown eyes. He looked casually stylish, his solid frame fitting snugly into a faded WWII flyer's jumpsuit. A battered boonie hat sat low over his eyes. His only striking defect was a thick Burt Reynolds .

He smiled. "Hell of a morning, huh," he said.

He'd been smiling and friendly when they were introduced on Saturday. "Jimmy Boodrow," he'd said, sticking out his hand. "Everybody calls me Boo."

MacLean was a decade or so older, a raw-boned, red-headed man who looked like he should be up on a billboard wearing a cowboy hat and smoking a Marlboro. At her swearing-in, he'd adopted the same kind of paternal forbearance towards her as Sheriff Herkemer.

The third deputy, Waverly, was wearing his uniform. He stood apart, his back turned to them, looking out towards Shaker's Bog.

"All of you get over here," he said, without turning around. Waverly was the oldest deputy on the force, a man in his mid-fifties. He was also the longest-serving; he'd run twice for sheriff in '68 and '72, losing both times to Archie Herkemer.

They moved up beside him, MacLean on one side, Kelly and Boodrow on the other. Shaker's Bog appeared as a straight line of green about three hundred yards away, and beyond that, as a flat, ragged mat stretching off into the haze.

Waverly looked at Kelly. "This little girl caller, did she say *where* in the swamp the body was supposed to be?"

Waverly had made it clear that he thought having a female deputy was not only an embarrassment to the department, but downright dangerous.

"No."

He shook his head. "The goddamned thing is a good square mile at least, maybe two. We should be looking for Weechum, not wasting our time on some stupid prank."

"The only way to do this is from the air, come in low in a bush plane. If anything's stirred up, it'll show. But from ground level..." MacLean shook his head, staring out at the bog.

"I don't know what the hell Archie thinks we're supposed to do. We need fifty men and a drag line. Three, four days at least," Waverly said.

"The caller said something about the body coming loose." Kelly stared out towards the bog like the rest of them, happy not to be blowing her hungover breath in their faces.

"Did she say when the body was supposed to be put in the swamp?"

"Last summer. Probably at the time of the murder. Did the sheriff get to talk to Columbia?"

"Not when I left. Far as we know, Susan Collins

isn't even missing. Nobody around here remembers a damn thing about her. Never heard of her."

Kelly was sure that they were all pissed off at her for making too much of the call. They figured that it was just kids screwing around; kids who got into the Dee cottage because she hadn't secured it properly.

After leaving the Cross cottage, she'd tried to reach Gail using Patricia's phone, but she wasn't at home or in her office. Kelly was convinced that Mrs. Mulvane was gathering up all of the police costumes right now and would soon be sending them to the bottom of the lake.

"If it's anywhere, it's most likely there." Boodrow waved his hand off to the right where the bog curled around into the bay and closed in on the shore. "That's the easiest place to dump it."

"Makes sense. You want to hide it quick and make it stay down, tuck it under the shack," MacLean said.

Kelly could just make out a stand of drowned trees, the rusty roof of the Hell Hole beyond it.

"Underneath, right alongside Sarah Punk and her baby boy, huh?" Boodrow said, joking.

MacLean removed his hat and scratched at his thick red hair. "Makes a hell of a lot more sense than going out in a canoe."

"How would you get out there?" Kelly asked.

"You take the Boardwalk, baby," Boodrow said, giving her shoulder a playful shove. Rock solid on her feet, Kelly gave him a narrow-eyed stare. His broad, white smile remained in place, even as he made a show of backing off. "Seriously, there's a path through the swamp on boards. The kids around here use it all the time. I say we check it out first, if the body ain't there, I don't know how we're gonna find it anywhere else. Hell, I'll go."

"I'll go with you," Kelly said. "I'd like to see the place."

"There ain't much to see."

"Christ, look at this," said, looking back over his shoulder.

A few men had come quietly down the street and were hanging around the last of the buildings. Dirty, unshaven faces, baggy pants held up by suspenders, heavy limp shirts over top of torn t-shirts, even in this heat—people straight out of a Dorothea Lange photo from the Thirties.

"Why don't we ask them?" Boodrow said.

"Sure, we can get them to tell us where Weechum is while we're at it?"

A small mob of kids had appeared out of nowhere. They were bolder than their parents, coming away from the buildings, standing closer to the deputies, but staying well out of reach. The kids, at least, looked like they actually belonged in the twentieth century. They were mostly barefoot, but their shorts, t-shirts, and halter tops were the same as any of the hitchhikers passing through the county.

Kelly looked for the girl she'd seen outside the Dee cottage, but she wasn't there. She looked up at the hill where Sarah Punk was supposed to be buried. For a second, she felt every droplet of sweat on her body quiver. The voice on the phone whispered in her ear, "Her spirit's gonna rise…"

"There's your damned culprits," Waverly said, making Kelly start. "There's no goddamned body in the swamp. Least not one that's been put down in the last thirty years. Little bastards are just screwing with us."

Grumbling, the deputies turned back to look out at the swamp. No one made a move to unload the canoes. Kelly stood with her hands resting on her patrol belt. The stifling heat was building up again, already begging for another cloudburst to come and break it up. She was aware of the big stains forming under her arms and down the back of her shirt. Deep-throated thunder rolled around the valley.

"Twenty minutes and we're gonna get hit by another downpour. We'll drown out there," MacLean said.

Waverly threw up his hands. "Okay, enough of this bullshit. Archie wanted us to put on some kind of a damn show; well, they got their damn show. Joe, you take the canoes back to the marina. Mackinaw, go get your uniform on and report back to the station."

"I'll do a quick check of the Hole, just in case," Boodrow suggested.

"Alright, but be quick about it."

"I want to go," Kelly said.

Waverly took off his hat and wiped away the sweat

filling the puffy red creases on his forehead. "Okay, but don't take all day."

While Waverly and Maclean headed back up the road into Shallow Rock, Kelly followed Boodrow's truck on a narrow, muddy track along the shoreline. After passing the last few buildings, they turned inland and followed a faint, brownish smear that ran alongside a thick stand of trees. A quarter of a mile on, the track turned sharply towards the water, entering a narrow tunnel of tightly packed, black spruce, small maples, and witch hobble. Boodrow stopped abruptly and got out of his truck.

Door scraping against the dense brush, Kelly eased herself out of her Duster as fat drops of rain began smacking against the hood of her car.

"This is it," Boodrow said. "We go on foot from here."

Reluctantly, Kelly squirmed into her slicker. Even with the snaps undone, she felt her body temperature jump up another ten degrees. Boodrow was around the front of his vehicle, crouched down, examining the mushy ground at the edge of the bog. The air was rank with the smell of decay.

"Some footprints, maybe, but it doesn't look like any vehicles have been down here for a while," he said.

A few feet into the swamp, an old walkway sat two feet above water level; gray, weathered, four-foot-wide boards resting on big log piles driven deep into the muck.

"That looks pretty serious," Kelly said.

"Yeah, might even have had railings at one time." Boodrow stood up, swatting at the gnats and mosquitoes that had swarmed out of the thick undergrowth. "It breaks down further along."

Boodrow took a big step up onto the boardwalk. Kelly grasped his extended hand and allowed him to take her weight. For a moment, as she came up beside him, their faces were close. Close enough for her to see the stubble of his night-shift beard, to see the twitch at the corner of his lips. He had splashed on some strong cologne, but other than that, he smelled honestly of coffee and late-night nicotine.

He raised an eyebrow. "Man, you tied one on last night, didn't you? That's hilarious."

"Because of Faber?"

"Yeah, they kicked him out for being drunk."

"And discharging a firearm."

"Ahh, shit happens. Who were you drinking with? I heard something about an orgy out there at the lake. You into that?"

"Fuck you," Kelly replied, not putting much into it.

"You gonna be able to make it, Mackinaw? Maybe you want to go back and lie down for a while?"

"We gonna stand around here talkin' all day?"

Chuckling, Boodrow turned and started down the boardwalk. The rain, slow and sporadic, rapped against the brim of her hat. "You've been here before?"

"A few times. Been a while, a year at least."

"You think the body could be out there?"

"Maybe. What I'm really thinking is that Weechum might be holed up out there. It's a long shot, but if he is, I want to be the one to bring him in. We need to look sharp; maybe we'll get lucky."

The solid section didn't last more than a hundred yards before it curved sharply to the right and ended abruptly. A new section, only an inch above the water, lay ahead. It was fairly straight, but the boards looked weaker.

"The good boardwalk used to go all the way out to the Hole, but at some point, most of it was torn down. Like they wanted to cut the place off," Boodrow said.

"Because of the ghost? Because of Sarah Punk?"

"You know about her?"

"I heard some stories."

"I've never seen her. But man, I'm sure *something* bad happened out there and probably more than once."

CHAPTER
TWENTY-EIGHT

The bog closed in around them as Kelly and Boodrow moved slowly along the slippery boards, the tangle of peat and sedge up to their knees on either side. Steam rising from the swamp fused with the steady drizzle, making everything blurry and close.

Boodrow was being cautious, keeping his head up and watching the fog in front of them. Up ahead, there was some solid ground, places where stunted larch and tough bushes grew out of the spongy, tangled mat. The water on either side of them was shallow, and beneath its agitated surface, small, sickly-looking fish darted around in the murk. A fat frog leapt past Kelly's feet and splashed into the water, setting her teeth on edge. It was a malevolent place—Sarah Punk's backyard.

The thunder grew louder, much closer now.

The path zig-zagged forward on short lengths of board following the slightly higher ground. Off to the right, between the lumps of weathered rock, there were patches of open water studded with gruesome, slimy deadheads that looked like the snouts of huge, petrified turtles or the rotting skulls of giant snakes, lying in wait.

Visibility continued to drop as the mist collected and thickened around the bushes and trees. The boardwalk changed to long sections of widely spaced, narrow planks nailed to split logs. A few feet further on, the boards disappeared under the water.

Boodrow stopped and turned back towards Kelly. His face was flushed and bloated, dripping with sweat and rainwater. He took off his hat and scratched at his thick, limp hair. "The path goes on just under the surface. Water's high right now, but we should still be able to make it," he said.

Kelly slapped at the bugs that clung to her hot skin. "Let's keep moving."

He took a step onto the first board, and it sank out of sight below the surface. Kelly grabbed him by the shoulder and steadied him.

"Thanks," he said. He tested the board again while she held him. "Yeah, it's just a few inches. Tricky..." he shrugged, giving her a chance to back out. "You okay?"

Kelly felt like a boiled lobster. "I'm good," she said. "How much farther?"

"There's a little island, maybe a hundred yards ahead. After that, it's easy going. We just need to get through this." He took off his slicker and draped it over a bush. "We're gonna need some help." He pulled a large hunting knife from his belt and began hacking at a spindly limb of a larch.

Kelly took off her hat and sluiced sweat from her forehead. They were both breathing heavily, sucking in the thick air. She took off her slicker and set it aside, heedless of the rain. "If Weechum's out there, he's probably gone to ground at least," she said.

"That's what I'm hoping," Boodrow replied, pausing between whacks.

Kelly attacked a limb on the other side of the boardwalk, quickly lost her footing, and nearly toppled over. Boodrow caught her by the back of the belt with one hand and steadied her until she straightened up. She nodded her thanks. "Who told you there was an orgy at Lost Lake last night?" she asked.

"Did I say orgy?" he replied with a grin. "What I heard was you had some trouble with your neighbors. They were drunk and skinny dipping, which is pretty interesting in itself, now if it was an orgy..."

"Night before last. They were skinny dipping like a bunch of kids. Do you know those people?"

"I've seen them around. When the new cottages were built, we all went out and looked at them. Must be nice to have that kind of money."

"How does Crogan end up with friends like that?"

"Miles caught Mrs. Dee speeding, must have been the first summer they were up. Let her off with a warning. She invited him over for a BBQ, or something, and all of a sudden, he figures he's part of the scene."

"Just the new people being friendly with the local cops?"

"Sounds to me like Miles is making a fool of himself, being a nuisance out there."

In the end, all she could manage was a four-foot staff, no thicker than her wrist. She paused, catching her breath before sheathing her knife. "You and Crogan are working graveyard together?"

"Couple of weeks now, since Steve got fired. I was on swing before."

"You must know him pretty well?"

"Not really. On graveyard, one guy's out on the road and the other is at the station. We don't get to talk much. A lot of county work is done alone; not like you big city cops, with your partners sitting in a squad car drinking coffee all night, eating donuts."

"What about Faber?"

"Steve's an okay guy. He got a raw deal. Sure, he screwed up, but who doesn't? Harmon came down on him too hard."

"Because she wanted me, right? A female."

"Everybody knows that. And everybody thinks Archie threw Steve under the bus. Hell, it's not your fault. You got offered a good job, of course you're gonna take it. Still, it bugs the guys, you know."

Kelly remained silent, wondering if he'd say something about the hitchhikers, about her snooping around.

"Sure, times gotta change," he went on. "Still, they could've waited until Waverly retired in a couple of years and then brought in a female."

He was humoring her, probably hitting on her. "Is Faber friends with that bunch out at Lost Lake, too?"

"Maybe. If he is, he doesn't brag about it like Miles. And he's not dumb enough to think those people are his friends just because they invite him up for a beer now and again."

Kelly handed him her staff while she slipped into her slicker.

"Hey, I know those rich assholes can rub you the wrong way," he said. "But if you're trying to make a name for yourself, going after them isn't a great idea. They're not from around here, but they still got pull."

Kelly took both staves while Boodrow put on his slicker. "I ain't trying to make a name, I'm just trying to do my job," she said.

"Well, I *do* want to make a name for myself. That's how you get yourself elected. You ready?"

"Yeah, let's go."

It was slow going. With every step, the boards sank a couple of inches into the mushy bottom and held—sort of. They took it one section at a time, Boodrow still in the lead, Kelly waiting for him to complete a section and let the board rise back up before she followed.

The steady thunder that had faded into the background of her consciousness suddenly broke overhead and started pounding them furiously. The ground shook. It was like someone had called down an artillery barrage on Shaker's Bog.

"Jesus Christ!" Boodrow shouted.

The rain came hammering down. "Fuck!" Kelly shouted.

Big drops hit the water and jumped back up, boot-top high. Heads deep in their slicker collars, they hurried to the slightly higher ground ahead. Slipping and sliding, they groped their way through a line of trees and huddled together, asses in the peat mush. Thunder and lightning broke right on top of them, in sync, shivering the trees. Rain washed over them like a river coming out of the sky, threatening to yank them loose and roll them down into the rising waters of the swamp.

They clung to each other, winded and sweating. Boodrow put his face close to hers, shouting above the roaring rain. "This'll pass."

Kelly nodded; no question of going forward right now.

They shifted, settling themselves more firmly, Kelly putting a bit of space between them. Boodrow took a cigarette from under his slicker, tried to shelter and light it, but had to toss it away in disgust. The suddenly chilly air reeked of ozone.

"You bring a flask?" he asked.

"If I'd known I'd be doing this..." she replied, pretty sure that he hadn't meant it as a dig.

He grinned and produced one from inside his

slicker. "I always have one in this rig." He wiped the top and offered it to her. "Bourbon," he said.

The thunder was still thumping the skies around them. Sheet lightning flashed and died, leaving them in midnight darkness. She took a grateful pull. "Good stuff. Thanks," she said, handing it back.

Boodrow nodded and took a drink. Kelly had herself solidly lodged now, heels dug into the tangled roots and moss, hunched in on herself, sideways to Boodrow. She looked back down the trail through the slit between her upturned collar and the lowered brim of her hat. She could only see a few feet through the heavy curtain of rain. Weechum could be out there; hell, Sarah Punk could be out there, but she was too tired to care.

The rain kept coming down, slanted by gusts of wind from the direction of the Hell Hole. Heat steamed up from Kelly's collar, yet her back felt chilled, giving her rolling waves of full-body shivers.

Nothing to do but wait.

Mitch floated in a warm sea filled with wobbling balloons of neon light.

Then there was a foot with its big toe poking out of a tear in a dirty canvas shoe, the toe's jagged nail just inches from his nose. The top of the foot was as dirty as the shoe, the skin of the slender ankle and thin, muscled calf above it, waxy-white and splotched with bug bites.

He felt himself being rolled. On his back, he could see more of the leg, right up past a muddy knee, up under the ragged, faded hem of a dress. His attention was drawn by the rawhide thong that fixed a sheath to the leg's pale thigh. In the sheath was a Bowie knife.

"Fuck sakes, Mitch, what are you on?" The leg moved back. Bobby looked down at him, eyes blue and battered, mouth still swollen. "What are you doing here?"

Mitch blinked slowly. He could see the owner of the leg now, and it made him feel as if someone had taken him by the temples, squeezed, and started stretching him out like a Gumby.

Sarah Punk.

He began to shout a warning, then stopped. Warn who? He had come to fight Bobby and save Sarah. Sarah was free, standing behind Bobby.

"I'm trippin', man," he said.

Mitch thought he heard Sarah giggle. That was really weird. A quiet little sound. He heard Bobby laugh; much louder, suddenly sinister, echoing off the walls. He tried to stand. Lightning burst outside. In the starkly illuminated doorway, Sarah floated in the air, wild hair covering her face, shroud flapping in the wind.

"Friendly, friendly!" he shouted, falling back against the wall.

"Everything's cool, Mitch. It's just a storm, man, it'll pass. Come on, you can't stay here," Bobby said.

"We should smoke up," he replied.

Bobby ignored him, and he was borne out of the rune-filled space, out into the spongy air, and poured into his canoe.

Bobby was in the back, face hidden under his bush hat. Sarah was in the front, looking over her shoulder at him. She wore a thorny crown of bugs. Behind the curtain of her lank hair, one black eye watched him while the other one looked away.

She smiled at him.

Mitch subsided into the bottom of the canoe, three inches deep in water.

Yeah, still trippin'.

CHAPTER
TWENTY-NINE

Kelly felt a firm hand on her back, up near the base of her neck. Looking over her shoulder, she saw Boodrow's smirking face and realized that she'd dozed off.

"Jesus," she growled.

"Shhh, come look at this."

Her mouth tasted like cat shit marinated in bourbon. She took a drink of warm water from her canteen, swished it around in her mouth, and spat it out. Boodrow, crouched at the top of the small rise, waved her forward, signalling for her to stay low. She slithered up beside him. The darkness had lifted, and the cooling rain had beaten down the mist. Foggy-headed, she looked out into the drizzle.

Beyond their little lump of semi-solid land was a stretch of open water. The boardwalk ahead of them was solid-looking, raised a couple of feet above the water. At the end of the boardwalk was a wooden shack, its weathered clapboards black with rain, its roof the color of dried blood. There were gaps in the wall; long, thin tears like the rifle slits of a bunker.

It sat low in the water, butted up against a small island, resting on log pilings that had been haphazardly braced over the years. The whole building listed a few degrees forward into the bog like a ship that had been abandoned just before it was about to be launched.

"The door is on the other side," Boodrow said, in a low voice.

Kelly rubbed at her wet eyes, pressing hard against her aching eyeballs.

Boodrow tensed beside her. "Shit," he hissed.

A canoe appeared from the far side of the shack, gliding silently along the edge of the open water, ghostly in the mist and rain. There was something in the front of the canoe, small and pale in the milky twilight, maybe a dog or a girl. There was a man in the back of the canoe wearing a floppy bush hat like Mitch's. The canoe pivoted away from them and disappeared into the surrounding swamp grass.

"Kids. That wasn't Weechum," Boodrow said. "Maybe he's inside, maybe they were bringing him supplies or something."

They watched, tense and impatient, as the bugs gathered around them. There was no sign of movement, no wisps of smoke coming from the stove pipe. As the sound of the rain lessened, the bullfrogs began to croak loudly all around them, and the mosquitos' whine became louder. The cabin remained silent.

Boodrow stood up. "Come on," he said, drawing his pistol from beneath his slicker.

They crossed the last stretch to the Hell Hole, Boodrow going first, Kelly following fifteen feet behind, revolver drawn. She shivered and looked behind her; nothing there, just the cold mist fingering the back of her neck.

There were heaps of garbage in the water on either side of the boardwalk, the older stuff further away from the cabin. Piles of scrap wood and brush rose like dead volcanoes above the water. Some nasty-looking stuff, jagged old tools, useless pieces of sheet metal, and angle iron. Closer to the shack, beer cans, candy wrappers, and cigarette packs floated in the green scum.

The boardwalk became a deck wrapped around the cabin. Boodrow paused by the corner of the building to let Kelly catch up. Revolver raised, he nodded to her and took a peek through a large gap in the boards.

He shook his head. "Clear," he said, his voice hoarse.

Kelly straightened out of the half-crouch she was in, feeling the tension drop away.

Boodrow cleared his throat, spat loudly into the water. "Too bad," he said.

Around the other side of the cabin, there was a doorway without a door. Boodrow went in first, Kelly close behind.

The shack's single room was dim, with deep

shadows in the corners. They paused just inside the doorway; Kelly gave the place a slow scan. No Weechum, no bodies. One window, one door. An old wood stove at the far end of the room.

The heavy pall of swamp rot and human-animal stink was spiced by the faint, unmistakable smell of weed. "I guess we know what they were up to," Boodrow said.

At the end of the room opposite the stove, a length of yellow nylon rope dangled from the rafters.

"What the fuck is this?" Kelly walked over to take a better look, avoiding the stain on the floor beneath it. The rope terminated six inches above her head in two loops separated by an elaborate knot. "Rope handcuffs," she said.

"That's new. Fucking little freaks," Boodrow said, coming up beside her.

Kelly immediately flashed on B-movie scenes of prisoners with their hands tied above their heads, being whipped. "Is that blood on the floor?"

Boodrow knelt down and took a better look. "Don't think so." He dabbed at it with his finger. "Whatever it is, it's long dry. More likely piss."

Kelly went up on her tiptoes to examine the inside of the cuffs, looking for blood.

Boodrow stood up beside her, grabbed the rope in his left hand, and whipped out his knife.

"Wait," Kelly said.

"Fuck that." He cut the rope a few inches above the cuffs and tossed them at her. "This place is contaminated. I'm not leaving that here for those little sickos to use again. Here, take a good look."

Kelly caught the cuffs before they hit her in the chest.

Boodrow was angry. "You want evidence of a crime; where would you begin in this fucking place?" He walked over to the open window, opened his slicker, and took out his flask.

It looked like there was dried blood on the cuffs. Kelly wished she had an evidence bag or even a backpack. They really hadn't thought this through. She stuffed the cuffs into the pocket of her slicker, stepped back, and gave the room another look.

There were stains all over the floor; some newer, some very old. Near the window, there was a rectangular outline where something had lain for a long time. Four by six, about the size of a double bed.

"Somebody has cleaned up," she said.

Boodrow returned the flask to his pocket without offering her a drink. "You think?"

It was too dark to read the tightly packed graffiti scrawled over every inch of the walls, but it didn't take much imagination to figure out its dominant theme. The walls she'd expected; the floor surprised her. There was some garbage and dirt in the corners, but the main part of the room looked like it had been swept. The warped, gapped floorboards were stained, but there was no dirt.

"Something happened here," she said. "Something serious enough to make these slobs clean up. Where's the furniture? There was a bed over there, for sure. What was here the last time you came?"

"They had a few wooden chairs, a dirty old mattress. Must've gotten too ratty even for them, and they dumped it in the swamp."

"Look at this." There was a long-shafted screwdriver embedded in the wall.

"Any blood on it?" Boodrow asked, half mocking.

She pulled it out of the wall; a heavy-duty, 1/8th flathead with an eight-inch, nickel-plated shaft. Clean, no rust or blood. "No," she said.

"Serious tool. Pretty good shank."

"Yeah." Three inches of green plastic handle smudged with white paint, just like the one she'd seen in the toolbox at the lumber camp. She stuck it in her belt.

"You need a screwdriver?"

If this was any kind of crime scene, it was already hopelessly contaminated. She didn't know if the screwdriver meant anything, but she wanted to make sure it didn't disappear. The person in the bush hat in the back of the canoe could easily have been Mitch.

"Never know when you might need a serious tool," she said.

"Or a shank? Man, I am really starting to like you," he laughed.

She spotted something on the floor near the wall and squatted down to take a look. "Roaches," she said.

The floor was mostly dry. She could make out a few faint, wet footprints. "These are fresh," she said.

"Man-sized boots. A running shoe." And small smudges. She gritted her teeth and let a wave of superstitious funk pass over her. "Maybe another set of runners, worn sole, a kid." A little girl. She could see the little girl.

"I'm surprised they're not all barefoot," Boodrow said.

Kelly took off her hat and pressed her palm down on the top of her head, pushing against the shivers running up her body. She took a deep breath, eyes closed, trying to concentrate. "Three. Did you see three in the canoe?"

"No, just a guy, and maybe a dog." Boodrow came over and crouched down. "Boots for sure, maybe something else. If there were others, they could have left before, or maybe headed the other way, towards Shallow Rock."

"Weechum?"

"No cigarette butts, no beer cans or empty bottles. He hasn't been here."

Kelly surveyed the room again, went over to the stove, and looked inside—damp ash. She took another deep breath. "No Weechum; maybe we get lucky with the body."

CHAPTER
THIRTY

They shared another hit from Boodrow's flask as they surveyed the surrounding area. The rain had turned to a misty drizzle, visibility a hundred yards or so. The heat was ramping up again, fast.

Kelly did a thorough visual search, flank to flank, foreground to background. The frogs had settled down, leaving the whine of mosquitoes and the patter of the dripping eaves to fill the thick silence all around them. Even the distant, retreating thunder had stopped.

"I don't see a body, or any sign that anything has been stirred up," Boodrow said.

Garbage, lots of garbage. Twenty yards or so out, a piece of angle iron sticking a foot above the water caught her eye. "Did you say there was a bed in here?" she asked.

Boodrow was leaning back against the wall with his eyes closed. "Huh? No, just a mattress lying on the floor. You think these lazy bastards would drag a bed all the way out here?" He stretched out his neck. "Nothing here, Kelly, complete washout. We should get back."

"What about under?"

"Really?"

"We came all this way."

"I ain't goin' under there. And you look like you're about to pass out. You okay?"

"I'm okay, just need to get this done and get out of the heat for a while. You don't look so shit hot yourself," she said.

"You're right, I feel like crap. Come on, we struck out, give it up."

Kelly shook her head and lowered herself down onto her hands and knees to peer into the water. Scum-covered pilings surrounded by bloated moss; everything below the surface of the water distorted and gross, thin green stalks reached up towards her. Her stomach did a slow, oily flip.

The mist drifted up and invaded her brain through her burning eyes. Everywhere she looked she saw bits of white flesh snagged in the slimy, tangled vegetation, shreds of ragged dresses stirring unnaturally in the thick, underwater moss. Sweat ran into her eyes. Her head started spinning. She felt herself being drawn forward, being sucked right off the deck and down into the blackness where Sarah and her baby were waiting for her.

"Kelly, are you going to barf?"

"Fuck, don't say..." She vomited painfully into the water.

Boodrow's hand cupped her forehead, holding it up. After the fourth heave, he pulled her back from the edge, sat her against the wall and got her to put her head between her knees.

"Drank too much last night," she said, spitting onto the dock.

He offered her his canteen. "Drink. This heat is terrible; we should have turned back an hour ago."

She refused his canteen and took a drink from her own, sloshing it around in her mouth and spitting it out. Drank again, spat and spat again, then leaned her head back against the wall and groaned.

They sat together for a few moments. Boodrow felt her forehead. "Breathe, you'll be okay," he said.

Kelly breathed and groaned and spat.

Boodrow looked at his watch. "Fuck, it's almost noon, Thompson's gonna have a shit fit. You okay to start back?"

"What you said still makes sense," she said.

"What?"

"Chuck the body under, weigh it down." She started to get up.

It also made sense that Sarah Punk would be pissed off about some stranger dumping bodies under her shack. She'd have to make the call.

"Man, you're one stubborn son of a bitch. For Christ's sake, don't move. I'll look."

Boodrow took her staff, lay flat on the deck, and started poking around the pilings. "Water's got to be about five feet deep here." He leaned further over the edge, probing. "There's bottom. This is pointless." He shifted his weight, leaned further out, and poked around near the closest piling.

"Son of a bitch!" It was closer to a scream than a shout. He recoiled, stumbled to his feet, and crashed back against the wall. "A fucking head, a fucking head!"

Kelly scrambled forward on her hands and knees. She gagged at the sight of the white thing bobbing in the middle of the stinking, black blooms of mud. Bone white and slimy. A skull, a little skull, too small to be a teenager. A baby's head.

"Moses!" she shouted. Panting, she grabbed the staff and poked at it, trying to bring it closer. The head did a slow roll, its black eyes slid open and shut.

"Fuck! Fuck, fuck! Son of a bitch!"

Boodrow was kneeling beside her. "Oh, those shithead little bastards," he said.

Kelly was still trying to get her mind around it. Was this a prank, or had they uncovered a doll buried years ago with its owner? She trembled, feeling naked and icy slick.

"Maybe it's been down there all this time and you dislodged it. Maybe Moses was just a doll. The kid was nuts, right?"

"What?"

"Sarah Punk, maybe her fucking baby was a doll,"

she pointed at the thing.

"No way." Boodrow was trying to sound sensible, but his voice had an edge. "Sarah Punk?"

Kelly felt the pull again, like something was trying to drag her off the dock and into the filthy water.

"No, no," Boodrow was saying. "Hey, don't go squirrelly on me, Kelly. It's plastic, right? They didn't have plastic back then."

Kelly slowed her panting, took a better look at the head bobbing just out of reach. Boodrow threw his staff at it. The head rolled again, exposing the neckring tied with yellow rope. He whacked her on the shoulder. "Come on, before you puke again. You'll get me going."

Kelly crawled back from the edge. "If I get my hands on those little fuckers."

"Fucking bastards," Boodrow settled back against the wall. "Probably been there for years, they pull it out every time a new person comes along."

Kelly sat back against the wall beside him, feeling the spinning in her head start to slow. She sagged, relief washing over her like a drug. She'd freaked out over a doll's head. "This fucking place," she said.

"You just couldn't give it up, huh, couldn't leave it be," he said.

"Sure scared the shit out of you."

"Oh yeah? You should have heard yourself, 'Moses, Moses!' Man, I thought you'd flipped."

"You screamed like a little girl."

Boodrow started a quiet, hoarse laugh. "Let's get

the fuck out of here," he said and stood up. He looked down at her, offering his sweaty hand. He was pretty pale too, the skin beneath his eyes sagged and his Burt Reynolds mustache drooped. Leaning on him heavily, Kelly got to her feet with another groan.

He held on to her forearm tightly and looked her straight in the eye, dead serious. "Man, *this* never happened. We found nothing. Nothing, right?"

"Right on," Kelly replied. "This *never* gets out. You screaming," she smiled. "Me screaming."

"Nobody found nothing, partner."

"Not a fucking thing." They shook on it.

The trip out was easier. There was no rain, and they were no longer worried about getting ambushed. They worked together, helping each other over the rough spots.

Boodrow had ribbed her again about interrupting the skinny-dipping party, and she'd told him what really happened Tuesday night. And then, after some hesitation, about the shit she'd seen this morning. Not the little girl in the mist, but about how fucked up Mrs. Cross was, and how sinister Mrs. Mulvane was.

He listened, letting her talk.

When they got back to the shore, Kelly peeled off her slicker. "I've got to check on Mrs. Cross, I don't want another person dying on Lost Lake."

"I can see how that would bug you, but, no shit, you should stay away from them." Boodrow opened all the doors of his truck and threw his slicker into the back.

"If you came with me…"

He turned and looked at her with a raised eyebrow. "Wow, I guess our first date went really well. Usually, when the girl pukes…"

"Fuck off. Those people are up to something."

"What? What are they up to, besides being drug fiends and moral degenerates?"

Kelly unlocked her car and opened the doors. "I've been talking to a lot of hitchhikers lately. You know the reputation this county has; abuse, disappearances…"

"That old shit, man…"

"Yeah, I know, everybody's heard about it. So, it's on my mind when I get here, you know, wondering what the hell I've signed up for."

Boodrow leaned on the hood of her Duster. "You're checking up on us?"

"Come on, of course I'm asking around. I'm a cop."

Boodrow shook his head and started back to his truck.

"Wait, listen, I'm hearing stories, but they're all out to lunch, right? Mostly they've got the uniforms all wrong, and I'm thinking, maybe we got imposters operating around here."

Boodrow turned to look at her. "Yeah, we've thought of that. Could be, or maybe it's all just hippie bullshit."

"Then I hear from my neighbor that the gang across the lake have these costume parties, the men like to dress up like cops."

He looked sceptical but let her go on.

"This morning, when I was putting Mrs. Cross to bed, I noticed a cop costume in her closet."

"You just said they like to dress up like cops."

"I'm telling you there is something seriously fucked up about those people. They're hiding something. Have you ever talked to Mrs. Mulvane?"

"Man, they've really gotten under your skin."

She took a step towards him. "Come on, man, wouldn't you like it to be them? You want to make a name for yourself? Then nail the fuckers who are doing this shit and giving our department a bad rep."

She could see the wheels turning, him thinking; did she just suggest that we frame these people?

He smiled. "Man, you really shouldn't go anywhere near those people right now. Okay? Let me handle this, you really need to back off."

She knew he was at least partly right. She nodded.

"I'll take care of it. I'll go check on Mrs. Cross, look around, see if there's anything going on. Where are their husbands, anyway? You said they were there last night and not this morning?"

"Mulvane wouldn't say. Cross didn't have a clue. So, what? You're just going to drop in on them?"

"They've seen me around. They know I'm a deputy. Hell, I'll tell them I'm looking for Miles. We were supposed to go fishing or something."

Boodrow followed her out Shallow Rock Road and then down Cooperage onto Shangri-La. She slowed down and watched in her rear-view mirror as he turned into the driveway at the Cross place.

CHAPTER
THIRTY-ONE

Kelly was so wrung out by the time she pulled up next to the bunkhouse that the sound of gunfire barely made her flinch. She got out of the car with a yawn.

At the small range behind her cottage, Patricia, dressed in tight olive-green trousers and a matching shirt, leaned intently into a two-handed shooting stance. Kelly approached as close as she dared, stuck her fingers in her ears and watched as Patricia tore apart the head of a target with her .44 Magnum.

Wincing at each boom, Kelly waited until the weapon was empty and the shooter was turning to the folding table beside her before stepping closer and shouting, "Patricia!"

Patricia lay down the big revolver and lifted the mosquito netting attached to her round, flat-brimmed cap. Smiling, she took orange earplugs out of her ears. "Dear, you look *awful*," she exclaimed.

Her tight shirt was split between her breasts by a gleaming Sam Browne. Other polished leather straps crisscrossed her back and came over her shoulders to a second holster tucked under her left arm. Small pouches were attached to a garrison belt around her waist that sported a red star on the brass face of its buckle.

Patricia placed a hand lightly on Kelly's arm. "Did you find something nasty in the swamp?"

"No. We didn't get to do a proper search, the weather... Look, can I use your phone?"

"Of course, dear. Is something wrong?"

"No, I just need to check in with the station."

"Okay, are you sure you wouldn't like to take a shower first," she wrinkled her nose, "or at least a jump in the lake?"

"I'm kinda in a hurry."

Kelly dialed the station and waited while it rang. Patricia began making drinks.

"Wanakena County Sheriff's Department."

"Hi, Betty, it's Kelly. Is the sheriff there?"

"Yeah, hang on a moment, you just caught him."

Patricia handed Kelly a large glass of orange juice. Kelly sniffed it, ignoring Patricia's frown, found it alcohol-free, and downed it. Patricia refilled the glass.

"Kelly? The Hell Hole was a washout?"

"Yes, sir. Couldn't see anything to indicate that the

ground had been disturbed. But visibility was terrible, so..."

"Understood. We need to take a look from the air. We've had a couple of sightings of Weechum around Snowshoe Lake, so I'm heading down there. We've had to shuffle people around. I need you to take the swing shift tonight, maybe hang around late if things start hopping."

Patricia was holding a tequila bottle poised over the second glass of orange juice. Kelly shook her head.

"No problem, Sheriff."

"Good."

"Sheriff, did you talk to Columbia?"

"Yeah, Susan Collins is still missing, no one has heard from her since last summer."

"Shit."

"Yeah. Okay, I'll talk to you later." He hung up.

Kelly drank the second glass of orange juice. She thought about calling Gail, but what did she really have to tell her? She looked at her watch. "Damn."

"Don't tell me you have to go back to work."

"Yeah, in about two hours. I gotta go."

"Well, here, take these with you." Patricia placed a blister pack of six Dexedrine in Kelly's hand.

"Oh, no, I couldn't..."

"Don't worry, I have tons."

"I mean... Yeah, I mean thanks, Patricia."

"Don't mention it. Now, you really *must* keep your appointment with that hot shower," she said.

Kelly paused. "Is Mitch around?"

"I haven't seen him in *ages*, not since yesterday morning."

"You think he's okay?"

"I'm miffed that he hasn't been by, but I'm not worried about him. He's like Wile E. Coyote, dear, he's foolish, but indestructible."

Mulvane killed Lucy
Rescuing Sarah Punk
Do you know this guy?

Kelly stared at the precise block letters printed on the back of the note she'd left for Mitch. She shook her head and put it down.

She picked up the Polaroid that was with it. Some kind of a party, Crogan in uniform; hat off, shirt unbuttoned, holding up his handcuffs like he was saying, "Who wants 'em?" It didn't look like anyone was paying attention to him. There was another cop, with stylish, coiffed hair, back turned to the camera, talking to Mrs. Dee, who was wearing nothing but blue eyeshadow.

Okay, Crogan partying with the swingers. Not really new information to her, but it might be a revelation to the sheriff. Where the hell did Mitch get the picture?

She'd showered and changed, and with the help of one of Patricia's pills, felt fully refreshed. No sign of

Mitch. She tucked the picture into her shirt pocket and locked up.

Boodrow was waiting for her on Cooperage just after the Shangri-La turn-off. He got out of his car and came up to her window when she pulled over.

"You look much better," he said.

"So do you."

He grinned. "They let me take a shower, ran my clothes through the wash, and plied me with coffee."

It smelled to her like the coffee had been fortified. "Really?"

"Hey, everybody kept their clothes on. Except in the shower, but that was just me...alone," he gave her a boyish grin. "Mrs. Cross was a little out of it, but you know...mellow."

They'd snowed him, or worse, he knew the swingers better than he was letting on.

"No kidding," he said, reacting to her scowl. "Hal and Mick were there too, all sitting around trying to decide if they can get out of here before the big storm hits."

"*Before* it hits? Maybe you remember almost drowning... thunder, lightning..."

"That? Partner, that was just the opening round. I don't know what it's like over in Essex County, but when we have a storm around here, we go all out."

"Where were they this morning?"

"Who?"

"The husbands."

"Fishing over at Big Moose, went out early."

"Fishing."

"Hey, right now they're stoned, having some fun in the privacy of their own homes. They're jerks, okay, but there's no way these people are killers."

"You see the costumes?"

"No, I didn't ask."

Kelly shook her head. "Okay, I gotta go."

"You doing swing?"

"Yeah."

"I'll see you when I come on tonight." He reached in and gave her shoulder a squeeze. "Later, partner," he said.

CHAPTER
THIRTY-TWO

Mitch couldn't remember a time when it wasn't raining. He couldn't remember a time when it wasn't night.

"Mitch, are you still high?"

He opened his eyes and tried to focus on the distant red glow that had spoken to him. He had been trying to make an important point but couldn't remember what it was.

"Mitch, you said you were alright. Christ, it's been hours."

The red glow was attached to a deep, warm shadow nestled in an Adirondack chair. The shadow had a raspy, enticing voice, though annoyed.

"I'm okay," he said.

"Mitch?"

The thing about Frisco Freak was that it could fool you. Make you think it had faded from your system, and then leap out of your toasted brain cells and make you do the funky chicken.

"Oh fuck," he said, as his muscles began to twitch and his bones turned to mush.

"Mitch!"

The water was as warm as the air, but it was heavier. When he hit it, to his surprise, he did not dissolve and become one with it. He sank like a stone. Lights began popping off in his brain. This was no trip. This was *the* trip, man. He was dying.

He flailed his useless limbs, jerking and twisting his torso, corkscrewing himself downwards towards the mud and the weeds. Strong fingers grabbed his hair and tugged him upwards. Fingernails scratched his shoulders, hands under his arms, heaving. He broke the surface, gasping.

"Goddamnit, Mitch. You're more trouble than you're worth," Mrs. Parker sputtered, beside him.

She guided his hands to the edge of the dock and hung there beside him while he coughed and wheezed. When he stopped heaving, she nudged him down the dock towards the shore until his feet touched rock. He tried to pull himself up, but his arms had no strength.

"Get your skinny ass up there."

With the help of her broad hands on his butt, he managed to slide up onto the dock. He lay there, chest heaving, head pounding. He was weak, but his mind felt white-cold clear, as if the frantic burst of adrenaline had scoured the last of the acid out of his system.

Mrs. Parker stood over him, low clouds scudding

above her under the heavy lid of the night. "Get up," she said.

He reached out to her. She squatted down, grasped him by the biceps and pulled him up until she could get her shoulder into his belly and hoist him into a standing position. He staggered to his feet and leaned heavily against her, realizing that she was naked too. They shuffled down the dock. When they got to the door, she slammed him against the door jamb and slapped him hard across the face. She placed one hand on each side of his head and squeezed.

"Are you a moron? That shit can kill you."

"I get that."

She slapped him again.

"I get it," he repeated with more sincerity.

Mrs. Parker stopped hitting him and helped him into the kitchen. Once she was sure he could stand on his own, she tossed him a damp beach towel. She stood close to him while she bound up her hair in a towel.

"Drugs make you stupid and helpless," she said.

"I know."

"Get your shit together, Mitch." She sounded impatient, like she didn't believe he was getting the message.

He thought she was going to throw him out, but instead, she took him to her bedroom. The windows were open; rain, sometimes coming in gusts, dotted the screen and flicked onto her queen-sized bed. She made him lie on the inside, the hotter side, up against the wall. She lay on the outside within easy reach of her shotgun on the floor.

"Now lay quiet," she said.

They lay, barely touching in the sticky heat. Mitch thought about her son Brian who had OD'd in Philly and realized what a shitty thing it was to be there, stoned stupid in front of her.

CHAPTER
THIRTY-THREE

FRIDAY

The sound of car doors slamming jerked Kelly up out of a deep sleep.

Horrified, she realized that she was sitting at the duty desk. Stumbling to her feet, she sent the desk chair rolling backwards across the hardwood floor. She looked around frantically to make sure the place hadn't been ransacked while she was out of it.

She heard Boodrow and Waverly laughing as they came up the steps. Manly laughter, but not at her, they couldn't have seen her. She straightened her uniform and rubbed her eyes.

She looked at her watch. One a.m.; they had been gone for over an hour and she'd been asleep the whole time.

They came through the door, Waverly still chuckling over something Boodrow had said. Around eleven-thirty, there had been some kind of domestic situation down at Otter Lake. Waverly, who should have gone home for the night, had decided to answer it since he knew the people involved. He'd taken Boodrow with him, for comic relief, by the look of it.

Boodrow gave her a knowing wink as he went by the desk. He had to be getting some kind of chemical boost. His face was sagging, his eyes red-rimmed, but there was a bounce in his step.

Sheriff Herkemer had called in around ten, saying that he was staying down on Snowshoe Lake with his uncle so he could take a plane from there first thing in the morning. If he was going to squeeze in a flight to check Shaker's Bog before the storm hit, he'd have to leave at the crack of dawn.

When Waverly looked at Kelly, his smile faded. "Anything happening?" he asked, stifling a yawn.

"Nothing," she replied.

"Where's Crogan?"

"Haven't seen him, haven't heard from him."

"He's gotta be on his way," Boodrow said.

Crogan had called in about nine o'clock, saying he'd be late, something about trouble with his truck, off someplace fishing. Kelly didn't hear the details; Waverly took the call.

"He said he'd be here by midnight, at the latest," Waverly said.

"It's okay, Kelly doesn't mind covering for him. Do you, partner?"

Kelly should have been off three hours ago.

"Try his house," Waverly growled. "If he's there, I want to talk to him."

Boodrow, on the phone, shook his head.

"Let it ring, the son of a bitch probably got home and fell asleep."

"No answer. I'm sure he's on his way."

"If he's been drinking, probably passed out." Waverly stood by the door, not going anywhere.

"I can go to his place and check," Boodrow offered. "You don't have to hang around. Kelly's got the desk."

Waverly shook his head. "No, Mackinaw should go, she's been sitting around on her ass all night." Angry, like she'd asked to be sitting around on her goddamned ass.

"Fine by me," Kelly said.

"She doesn't know where he lives. It'll take her forever in this weather. I can do it."

Waverly gave Boodrow a withering look. "She's not getting any special treatment around here. She needs to learn where the hell things are in this county."

"He's not gonna be there, it's a waste of time," Boodrow said, pushing it.

Kelly had already strapped on her patrol belt.

"We are *not* going to start this shit," Waverly said. "This is just what I was afraid of, having a girl in the department."

Kelly snatched the car keys from the desk in front of Boodrow. "Give me the address."

Boodrow wrote it out on a piece of paper. "It's tricky..."

"If I need help, I'll call in." She grabbed her slicker from the coat rack. "Night, Gene," she said, pushing through the doors without waiting for a reply.

Mitch lay awake, attempting to become conscious of his present reality. He was in Mrs. Parker's hothouse bedroom, lying on her bed with a thin, damp sheet between him and her spongy mattress. It was dark, except for an occasional, very dim flash of lightning at the window. Rain was drumming steadily on the roof, nearly drowning out the sound of her soft breathing beside him.

This present reality must have emerged out of his recent past, but it was difficult to remember anything from the moment he'd left the bunkhouse yesterday morning, until he'd been standing on her deck, singing in the rain. They had been naked, catching the breezes that kicked up unexpectedly now and again from the east. He'd sung "Sad Eyed Lady of the Lowlands" to her.

Mrs. Parker had not been impressed. "Mitch, if you don't stop singing, so help me, I'll tie a cinder block around your ankles and throw you into the fucking lake," she'd said.

Before that, or maybe afterward; other memories, less clear.

Sitting in the kitchen, Mrs. Parker was drinking whiskey in the chair close beside him and across from them, welded together in the darkness like a two-headed sideshow monster, were Bobby Margin and Sarah Punk.

Mitch closed his eyes and pressed hard on his eyelids, but that was still what he saw: Bobby, with the pale face of the girl-ghost resting on his shoulder, her eyes drifting in different directions.

Mrs. Parker complaining, talking to Bobby and Sarah, like Mitch wasn't even there, saying, "Give me a drunk any day. At least they pass out eventually."

Sarah Punk laughing at him.

He'd gone for a piss out back of the cottage, and when he came back, Mrs. Parker made him sleep on the floor, trading places with her shotgun. Fair enough. He needed to be reacquainted with solid ground. Sleep was slow in coming. Several times, he heard Mrs. Parker snore and then wake.

Sometime later, Bobby and a pale, long-haired girl appeared in the doorway. Mrs. Parker sat up in bed, and they talked in soft, quiet voices.

Mitch was sure that wasn't a dream.

It was supposed to be less than forty miles to Crogan's place, an hour's drive at best. Two hours after leaving Trapper Lake, Kelly was parked in front of a closed gas station in the hamlet of Wilton.

"Dispatch, this is Mackinaw, over."

The radio crackled with static. Boodrow had been coming up on the radio every ten minutes or so and harassing her with snatches of song. He'd done "Chantilly Lace," "Ring of Fire," and "Pretty Woman," among others.

"Dispatch, this is Mackinaw, over."

She listened to the hiss of the storm-tossed airwaves rise and fall, damned if she was going to say it a third time.

"Boodrow here, c'mon."

Everybody in the department ribbed Kelly for using proper military voice procedure on the radio. The sheriff's department was much more informal.

"Confirm that Crogan's place is on the west side of Casquette Mine Road, heading northwest from Wilton," she said.

Kelly had been up and down the three-mile stretch of Casquette Mine Road from Wilton to Buck Lake Road, twice, without seeing Crogan's place. There were no street numbers, just mailboxes.

"Ahhh, negatory..." Boodrow's voice was overwhelmed by a rush of static.

"Say again?"

There was another long pause. Kelly could picture him, sitting back in his chair, with his feet up on the desk. She regretted ever confiding in the guy.

"That's negatory, good buddy. North from Wilton, Crogan should be on the right. Name's on the mailbox. Can't miss it, c'mon."

"Roger, out."

Using the interior light, she read the paper Boodrow had given her. It said that Crogan's place was on the left.

A mile and a half back towards Buck Lake Road, she pulled into a dirt lane where she'd spotted a standard country mailbox on a wooden post. Lightning flickered deep within the low clouds as she got out of the cruiser with her flashlight. She had to put her face right up to the metal before she could confirm that it said Crogan.

The entrance was a narrow, single-lane notch in the trees. Kelly drove a good fifty yards before the bush backed off and revealed an open space. She stopped and put the cruiser in park.

"Down in the West Texas town of El Paso, I fell in love with a Saranac girl..."

Kelly turned off the radio, opened a bottle of coke, and used it to wash down her second dexie of the night. Looking out past the slow sweep of the wipers, she surveyed the ground. The cruiser's headlight beams revealed a single story, brick bungalow about fifty yards down the lane. It was dark except for some light around the back. Across the lane from the brick house were the charred remains of an old farmhouse. The lane went past the houses for another twenty yards and disappeared into a cluster of old wooden buildings. Back there, a single bulb high on a pole shone weakly. The place felt more desolate than Lost Lake. She sat still for a while.

Waverly had sent her out here, to an unfamiliar part of the county, on a shitty night, because he thought she wasn't pulling her weight. Boodrow had really wanted to do it for her. Misplaced chivalry, or was there something more complicated going on? Boodrow had also wanted to go to the Hell Hole alone. That turned out to be nothing.

"Fucking paranoia," she said, putting the cruiser in gear and rolling the rest of the way to the bungalow.

She parked in the lane and got out of the car. Flashlight in hand, she walked around the house. The light over the back porch was on, no lights inside. No truck out back. She went up the back stairs, pressed the doorbell, and heard it buzz. She was reluctant to shout. She leaned on the buzzer again. No answer. Silence, except for the rain beating on the plastic cover of her hat. Turning around, she played the flashlight over the backyard. A gas barbecue, lawn furniture, and a trash can overflowing with beer cans. Further back, there was a large plywood shed.

She opened the screen door. The main door gave way when she tried the knob. Slowly, she pulled it shut again and took her hand off the knob. Out in the country, people didn't usually leave their houses unlocked.

If Crogan was inside sleeping one off, where was his truck? If he was inside, did she really want to go through the whole scene of rousing him? Better to do a whole extra shift than go through that. On the other hand, if he wasn't home, this would be a good opportunity to poke around inside the creepy bastard's house.

Maybe that was the setup. Crogan was hiding inside, waiting to jump out and embarrass the hell out of her. Reinforce the lesson that she shouldn't be going into other people's houses uninvited. Kelly gave the doorbell another long push.

A gust of wind picked up a beer can and sent it scraping across the patio stones. Kelly jerked at the sound.

"Fuck off," she said.

The assholes were up to something. Was it a coincidence that she was way the hell out here, all by herself?

There was still no light or movement inside. She turned her back on the house and went to check the shed. It was locked with a heavy padlock. She stared at the dark outbuildings below the single wobbling light on the pole. Sweeping her flashlight beam over what looked like a small, low barn and a roofless shed, she stopped when it flashed on a patch of polished metal.

She walked carefully across the slick grass to the muddy lane. As she approached, it became clear that there was a pickup truck backed into a high wooden stall next to the barn. She poked the watery beam of her flashlight into places where the darkness was deepest, revealing nothing. Across from the stall, there were heaps of scrap wood in front of another low building. The light came back to her, reflected by the dirty glass of windows barred with wooden slats.

"Crogan?"

She coughed, pissed off by the weakness in her voice. Louder and more firmly this time, she shouted, "Crogan, it's Mackinaw."

She walked over to take a closer look at the truck. It was a black Chevy with New York plates. Crogan had a Chevy, but it was red. She ran her light down the side of the truck towards the back of the stall; nothing but blank, worn wood back there. She went into the narrow space between the truck and the wall and tried the truck's door. It was locked. Climbing up on the side step just behind the cab, she peered in the window.

Movement behind her reflected in the window. She threw herself to the right towards the open space. Metal clanged against glass. She landed hard on her side, trapped between the truck and the wall. She rolled onto her belly and scrambled out on all fours. As she got clear and started to rise, a boot slammed into her side, low on her ribs. The kick rolled her over onto her back.

Gasping, she drew up her knees, desperately trying to catch her breath. A muddy boot descended slowly towards her face. Blind, she felt her patrol belt being pawed at. Awkwardly, she reached for her holster. It was empty. The pressure of the boot on her face increased and shifted to cover her mouth and her nose. The world behind her eyes lit up, searing white, and then went black

CHAPTER
THIRTY-FOUR

Pain brought her out of the darkness. New pain. It felt like her hair was being pulled out of her scalp. The ground was moving under her. She realized she was on her back, being dragged like some Stone Age woman in a cartoon.

She dug her heels into the mud. Slipping and grunting, she got enough purchase to thrust up her pelvis and get her butt off the ground. She twisted hard to the side, yanking her slick hair free of his grasp. She rolled and rose to face him. His fist came at her face out of the darkness. She took the blow on her forearm and stumbled back. She gained her balance and looked up.

The man stood with his arms extended towards her, holding her revolver in a two-handed grip. His shoulders were hunched forward as he leaned solidly into his stance, the deadly end of the barrel no more than a foot from her head. He was a big man, taller and heavier than her. His face was blurry and deep in shadow.

"On your fucking knees, bitch!" he shouted, cocking back the hammer.

She'd heard the voice before. She couldn't place it. Local; definitely not Crogan.

She leapt forward, crashing into him, grabbing for the gun, shoving it upwards. It went off, exploding beside her face; a high, wild shot. Pressed together, they grappled for the weapon. She slammed a knee at his groin. He twisted and blocked it with his thigh. She raked his hands with her nails. He dropped the gun.

Sour, boozy breath washed over her. "Cunt," he said.

He caught her with a solid blow to the gut that doubled her over. Helplessly, she threw up the remains of her stomach onto the ground. He shoved her from behind, pushing her down into the mud and vomit. Landing on her hands and knees, she held herself up, heaving painfully, again and again.

Head spinning, she felt him grabbing at her from behind. She dropped onto her stomach. He tore off her service belt. A hard knee between her shoulder blades crushed her into the muck. Cold steel snapped around her left wrist. She was hauled halfway to her feet by her manacled arm. Another blow slammed into her bruised gut. Her knees gave way, and she was dragged by the arm across the lane.

On the other side, she was thrown down on her ass, her left arm cuffed to something above her head.

She dangled awkwardly, knees barely brushing the ground, gasping, flopping against the rough wood of a building. Looking up, she saw that she was cuffed to a wooden strut nailed across a window. She pulled at it, but there was no strength in her extended arm.

She kicked and twisted, swinging wildly with her free arm. The attacker got behind her and slammed her face into the wall. He reached around her waist, tore open her belt and zipper. In a single motion, he yanked her pants and underwear down to her knees. Then again, working them down to her ankles.

"Touch me and I'll fucking kill you!" she shouted, her voice rasping painfully out of her throat.

"You wish, bitch."

A cold, muddy boot kicked her in the butt. She tried to turn herself around, striking blindly, but there was nothing there. For a moment, she hung, catching her breath.

The truck engine roared. Harsh, white light seared her eyes as she twisted. "Fuck you!" she shouted.

The light veered off. "Stupid dyke!" the driver shouted at her as the truck headed up the lane towards the road.

The truck stopped next to the patrol car. Yanking at the cuff, she watched him get out of his truck and open the cruiser door. He was going for the keys, either to take them with him or throw them away. A moment later, he drove off. She watched him go, noting that he turned left, heading south.

The key to her cuffs was in her pants pocket, out

of reach. The keys to the cruiser had been in the ignition, where they were supposed to be. The bastard knew that. He had to be a cop.

She hung her head and concentrated on getting her breathing under control. Her ribs and stomach ached. Hard to tell how much damage had been done there. Her nose wasn't broken. She could breathe. She was alive.

Once she'd caught her breath, she crouched down and started springing upwards, slamming her shoulder into the bottom of the wooden bar. It cracked. She pulled the cuff to the middle of the strut where it had started to give way, wrapped her free hand around the imprisoned wrist and pulled. It gave a little more. She jammed her boots against the wall, walking herself up as far as she could and threw herself backwards. The strut parted, and she slammed hard into the mud.

Knees up, she wheezed and groaned, staring up at the cloud-heavy sky. Warm rain fell on her hot skin. Parting her swollen lips, she took some into the flannel pit of her mouth. Once her head stopped spinning, she let out a low painful growl, raised her hips, and pulled up her pants.

She stood slowly, tentatively, cuff dangling from her left hand, her right pressed against her ribs. They ached, but there was no sudden, searing jab, no nauseating click of fractured bone.

The beam of her flashlight, lying on the ground, made a small white circle on the wall of the stall. She crossed the lane and stood above it, hesitating. Fearing another attack out of nowhere, she looked all around before squatting down to pick it up.

Her hat was at the front of the stall, next to a long-handled spade. She remembered the clash of steel on glass. The bastard had tried to hit her with a shovel.

She spent a long time searching for her revolver, slipping and stumbling in the rain, trying to recreate the fight. The thought of losing her sidearm was as humiliating as being left bare-assed hanging by her own cuffs. When she couldn't find it, she became desperate. She got down on all fours, angrily rooting around where she thought it should be.

"Fuck! Fuck! Fuck!" she shouted at the ground. Her arms and legs gave way, and she collapsed face first into the mud. Exhausted, she rolled over onto her back, her arms flung out at her sides. Her right hand touched metal. Kelly smiled.

Revolver firmly in hand, she stood up. She was going to find the son of a bitch who did this to her and drink his fucking blood.

Moving slowly, she retrieved her belt, fastened it around her waist and holstered her revolver. She took the cuff off her wrist and returned it to its pouch. What she needed now was a drink; a gallon of water to wash out her mouth and soothe her throat, and then something much stronger.

She followed the lane back to her cruiser and confirmed that the keys were gone. If he'd tossed them, there wasn't a hope in hell she could find them in the dark. Without the battery, her car radio was useless. She would have to use the phone in Crogan's house.

There was a light switch near the back door. She turned it on and tracked her muddy boots across the kitchen floor to the wall phone. She stood a moment, listening. The house was quiet.

She didn't want to call the station. The thought of speaking to Boodrow right now was revolting. She didn't think that this had been a practical joke; it had been too violent for that. She didn't know who was responsible. Maybe it had nothing to do with the sheriff's department, but there was no one she was willing to trust there at the moment, not even Sheriff Herkemer.

She dug out her notebook and looked up a number. The clock on the wall said four a.m. Time to find out if there was anyone she could trust at all.

After she'd made the call, Kelly drank several glasses of water, then dug around in the messy kitchen until she'd found a bottle of Jack and poured herself a generous four fingers. She'd put her hat on the kitchen table and pushed a chair into the corner. Then she'd turned out the lights and settled down in the dark, revolver in her lap, watching both entrances to the room.

After a while, she undid her pants, took off her tie and unbuttoned her blouse. She drank the Jack slowly, feeling it burn her swollen lips. The house was warm and musty, smelling of men, sour milk, and burnt coffee. Also, nicotine and weed. Either there had been a party here or Crogan shared the place with a couple of slobs; one man couldn't make such a mess all on his own. Dirty dishes were piled in the sink and stacked on the counter; the garbage can was overflowing with beer cans and booze bottles.

Before long, her eyes became too heavy to keep open. Her weary body sagged in the uncomfortable chair. She tried to sit up straight, but soon her head drooped onto her chest and she dozed off.

The phone rang. She jerked forward, groaning at the sudden jolt of pain in her ribs. Her eyes darted around the room. Nothing. She stared at the phone hanging on the wall. After the fifth ring, she went over and picked up the receiver, holding it to her ear without speaking.

"Hello, Miles?" It was a woman's voice.

Kelly remained silent.

"Miles, what the hell is going on? Miles? Who is this?"

The woman hung up. Kelly replaced the receiver. It was hard to be certain, but the sharp, arrogant tone of the caller reminded her of Mrs. Mulvane.

A half-hour later, the phone rang again. Kelly picked it up and waited.

"Hello? Kelly, is that you?"

It was Boodrow.

There was a long pause. "Kelly, don't fuck around,

partner. It's Boo. I've been trying to raise you on the radio. What the hell is going on?"

Kelly let the silence play out a little longer.

"Kelly? Why aren't you on the radio? What happened?"

"Mackinaw here," she said at last.

"Jesus, you had me worried. What happened? What the fuck are you doing?"

"Crogan's not here. I'm waiting for him to show up," Kelly said.

"You should have called in."

She let that pass.

"You're just sitting around Crogan's house? Quit doggin' it and get back here."

"I'm gonna wait until it gets light out, then I'm gonna have another look around."

"What for?" There was another pause while he waited for her to answer. "Did something happen? For fuck's sake, Kelly, get your ass back here."

She hung up, waited for a couple of minutes to see if he would call back, then returned to her chair and Crogan's Jack.

The sky had lightened, but the sun was not yet up when she heard a car coming down the lane towards the house. She pulled up her zipper and buckled her belt. Cursing, she stood up and walked stiffly across to the kitchen window.

A Ford station wagon rolled to a stop beside the house. It was Gail.

CHAPTER
THIRTY-FIVE

"It's a beautiful morning..."

Rae gave Mitch a warning look. He stopped singing.

"Here." She handed him her Remington twelve-gauge. "Take a seat and wait your turn."

Mitch took the gun and settled back in the chair, easing his naked butt onto the cool, wet wood.

He smiled as he watched her dive off the dock. She split the still water with hardly a ripple and disappeared under the surface. She came up and headed away from the dock with long, purposeful strokes.

"It's a beautiful morning..."

An hour or so ago, Rae had invited him up off the floor and into her bed. It had all been very easy and natural. No words spoken at all. Very cool. After that, she was no longer Mrs. Parker; she was Rae.

The rain had finally stopped. A gentle breeze,

enough to cool the skin but not ruffle the waters, blew in off the lake. The clouds were higher and less oppressive. Long fingers of mist rose up from the swamp towards a ragged patch of blue sky. A few loons called, impatient for the rising sun.

"Think I'll go outside for a while…"

Rae disappeared under the water again, then emerged, stroking steadily back towards the cottage. She went straight to the shallows near the end of the dock and stood with the water just above her waist. She gathered her thick hair and swept it back over her shoulder.

"The water is perfect," she said, giving him a smile.

She picked up the soap from the dock and started scrubbing her face. Mitch watched her duck her head under the water, then come up and start lathering her arms and heavy breasts.

Shifting uncomfortably in the chair, he complained, "You're killing me, man."

Rae laughed and crouched down in the water.

"What the hell am I supposed to be watching out for?" he asked, forcing his gaze back out over the lake.

"Hack, mostly."

"You figure he's coming here today?"

"Perfect place to lay low for a while. Once the state troopers get involved, they'll be all over Shallow Rock. He's gonna need to eat, gather up some scratch."

"What are you talking about?"

"Jesus, Mitch, how long have you been out of it?

Hack broke parole; beat the hell out of a guy, might have killed him." She began brushing her teeth.

Mitch stood up, shotgun at the port, and stared towards the swamp. "What're you gonna do?"

"Be ready for him, and when he shows, blow his fucking brains out." She spat into the water. "Maybe even get a bounty."

Mitch leaned the shotgun against the wall and watched as she came down the dock towards him, her taut skin shedding droplets of water. Rae came right into his arms, her cool, slick skin giving him shivers. She wound her arms around his neck and kissed him.

Mitch put his lips next to her ear. "It's a beautiful morning," he sang softly.

She stepped free and gave him a playful push. "You stink, get in the water," she said.

He hesitated, reaching out to stroke her shoulders. "Go on." She turned him around and slapped his butt.

Mitch took a few steps down the dock and dove. The water was warm by Lost Lake standards, but cool enough to be bracing. He dove deep and then shot back up to the surface. It felt good to have full command of his limbs again.

"Why did Bobby bring me here?" he asked, looking up.

Rae stood on the dock, hands on her hips. She looked down at him with a frown. "Bobby didn't bring you here, Mitch. You brought yourself here. You paddled right up to the dock and jumped out of your canoe."

"Shit." Rae's canoe was tied up on the other side of the dock, his was nowhere in sight. "I didn't tie up?"

"Nope," she replied. "From the wind we had last night, it's probably back at the edge of the bog somewhere. When the weather clears, we can go look for it."

Mitch swam away from the dock. He stroked hard, pushing himself, testing his muscles and his coordination. Not bad. He returned to the dock at a slower pace. Standing in the shallows, he picked up the soap and started washing. "But Bobby was here, right?"

"Bobby was here last night, like always." She had her hair in a rope over one shoulder and was wringing it out onto the dock.

"There was a girl with him?"

She nodded. "Mary Ann."

"Really, no shit? His pal from Shallow Rock?"

"Girlfriend now. He finally took notice of her."

"Huh, right on. So that's Mary Ann Weechum, Hack's cousin. How old is she?"

"Sixteen, almost seventeen. She always was tiny, skinny as a rake."

All soaped up, Mitch made a shallow dive back into the deeper water, wriggling and doing somersaults to rinse off. Thinking of Bobby and Mary Ann together made him happy. He came up near the dock. "She's got a lazy eye?"

Rae sat in the chair with the shotgun resting across the arms. "That eye makes her look simple, but she's a clever girl. I swear she can see perfectly in two directions at the same time. And she can pick her way through the swamp like she's walking on water."

Or flying, Mitch thought.

He climbed up on the dock and went and stood in front of Rae. He pushed the hair out of his eyes and spread his arms wide. "There, clean as a whistle," he said.

She smiled at him. "Not bad, all you need now is a haircut."

Mitch kneeled in front of her. She set the shotgun against the wall beside her and parted her knees so he could get closer.

"I saw Mary Ann in a picture. A fucked-up picture," Mitch said.

"You saw that?"

"Yeah, here, the other day. What the hell was that?"

Rae slid up on the chair until her thighs trapped Mitch's ribcage. She leaned forward and took his face in her hands. "I thought you didn't believe in messing with other people's lives."

"Is Bobby into weird shit?"

Rae gave him a quick, soft kiss and withdrew, shaking her head. "You know, Mitch, you'd be damned near perfect if you didn't talk so much."

He smiled. "Did Bobby take that picture?"

She sighed. "Hack took that picture, maybe a year ago. He had one of his rats deliver it here to Bobby."

"Why?"

"So Bobby'd go try to save her and he could jump him. Bobby didn't know the picture was a year old. Bobby figured it for a trap, but he went anyway."

"Why'd Hack want to jump him?"

"Old shit going way back. None of your business."

It was difficult to think clearly with her so close. He ran his hands along her thighs. There was something enchanting about her weary, washed-out eyes, even the sag and hollows beneath them. He wanted to kiss her again.

"So, what happened?"

"Hack and a couple of his boys jumped him." Rae pushed him back and stood up.

He placed his hands on her hips and stood up.

"Mary Ann helped him," Rae said. "They fought their way free. Otherwise Hack and his goons might have killed him."

That couldn't be right. Mitch figured that the swingers had beaten Bobby, tried to throw him off Steep Rock and kill him. Lucy had shown him. He closed his eyes and let out a long sigh. He'd been stoned out of his mind. Figured it all out with the help of a ghost. Jesus.

"Hack always had an unhealthy interest in Mary Ann. He hated the way she and Bobby got on, the way they helped each other out."

"So, after Bobby... rescued her, Mary Ann took a serious shine to him?"

"Hell no. Mary Ann's been in love with Bobby all her life. He just didn't see it. She followed him everywhere."

"Man...all that time, Bobby thought he was being haunted, it was her. Why didn't she just tell him?"

"Bobby was being an idiot. Mooning over those rich bitches, being their little servant boy."

Mitch thought about the Polaroids of Sarah Punk out in the woods, peeking in windows.

"So, they saw things. All the shit that was going on around here, right? Both of them, out there wandering around in the dark. Mary Ann saw everything Bobby saw."

"Leave it alone, Mitch." Rae slid past him and picked up her shotgun. "Come on," she said, opening the screen door. "Let's take advantage of the cool air while it lasts. There's a monster storm coming on."

CHAPTER
THIRTY-SIX

Kelly took off her shirt and threw it onto the toilet seat next to her patrol belt. Her revolver lay on top of the toilet tank. She reached back to unfasten her bra but was brought up short by the pain.

"Can you help me with this?"

"You should go to the hospital," Gail said, coming into Crogan's small, cluttered bathroom.

Kelly bent forward, leaning heavily on the stained sink. "It's not that bad," she said.

"Then why did you call me?" Gail asked, unhooking Kelly's bra.

Kelly straightened up, eased out of the straps, and let it fall to the floor. "I need somebody to watch my back."

She turned to the side and stood up on tip-toe, trying to see the large area of pain centered on her right ribs. There were two, palm-sized patches of brownish purple low on her ribs, and two larger ones low on her stomach. Not pretty to look at, but there wasn't a lot of swelling.

"It's not bad," she said, sucking air slowly through her nose. "I can breathe okay."

Gail picked up Kelly's bra and put it on the toilet. "May I?" she asked, then proceeded to probe Kelly's bruised side.

Suppressing a grunt, Kelly leaned forward over the sink again.

"It looks like shit," Gail said.

In the naked light of the unshaded bulb, Kelly started washing the dried mud off her face. There was an arc of rust-colored, lacerated skin running from her cheekbone to her forehead around her right eye. Her lower lip on that side was puffy and cracked.

"It's the light," Kelly said. "It makes everything look worse than it is."

Gail stepped back and looked over Kelly's shoulder. Their eyes met in the mirror. "Well, there's no bones sticking out. Still, you need to go to the hospital to get checked out."

"There's no time for that."

Kelly looked steadily at Gail, aware of the older woman's discomfort. She had given Gail a fairly complete account of what had happened, leaving out the part about having her pants pulled down to her ankles. She knew Gail suspected that there was more to the story.

"Just watch my back, okay?" Kelly said.

So far, her trust in Gail had been well-founded. The married, mother of three had asked only a few quick questions before rushing out of her house at four-thirty in the morning to come to Kelly's aid.

Gail had called the station and told Boodrow that everything was okay, no need to send anyone. There was still no word from Crogan. Nothing new from Sheriff Herkemer. Gail went back to the doorway and regarded Kelly sternly. "You need..."

"I just need a shower. I really need a fucking shower, okay? Then I'll be fine."

Gail tapped the butt of the Smith & Wesson automatic tucked into her belt. "Okay, I'll watch your back," she said, and went out into the hallway, leaving the door open.

Kelly took a dexie from her pants pocket and downed it dry.

Her feeling of being soiled and cold overcame her disgust with what might be on the bottom of Crogan's tub. She left the shower curtain pulled back. The hot water reminded her of how chilled she'd become and gave her a stinging body map of her injuries. She didn't linger.

The only clean towel Gail could find was about the size of a bathmat. While Kelly did her best to dry off, Gail stood by the open door, looking down the hallway.

"You didn't recognize the attacker?" she asked.

"No. I couldn't see him clearly. I heard his voice."

"So, why are you so sure that the attack had something to do with the department?"

"Waverly sent me out here, just to give me a hard time. Boodrow wanted to do it; I mean, he really wanted to. Then after that, I'm sure he was fucking with me, trying to slow me down or make me give up on the whole thing," Kelly said.

"Maybe he was just being a jerk. How would he know what was going on out here? You said he called and got no answer."

"Yeah, that's why he wanted to get out here himself, to check. Yesterday morning it was the same thing with the Hell Hole. He was determined to get out there and take a look, and he wanted to go alone."

"What was he looking for?"

"The body, Susan Collins. See if it had come loose somehow, so that it could be seen by the caller. Or... fuck, to see if the girl had done something, cut it loose."

"The little ghost girl?"

Kelly growled.

"And you didn't find the body."

"Maybe we could have looked harder. I wonder if we had found it, maybe Boo would have hit me with a shovel."

"I don't see how that explains what happened here."

"I interrupted something. That's why we need to go out there and have a good look."

"After that you have to go to the hospital and get checked out."

Kelly shivered as she dressed in her clammy clothes.

"Your ribs could be cracked. You took a couple of shots to the head, you might have a concussion."

Kelly left her wet hair down and her blouse unbuttoned in the steamy heat. She folded her tie and put it in her breast pocket. "He didn't rape me," she said.

Gail sighed. "Good."

"I'll make a report when I know what the hell is going on."

Gail called the station again and talked to Boodrow, who was still there by himself. She shut down all of his questions and asked a few of her own. There was still no word from Crogan. Sheriff Herkemer hadn't called in, so his plan to take a flight probably hadn't changed. She told Boodrow to call Undersheriff Thompson and get him into the station; she'd be calling back.

It was much cooler outside. Gail looked off to the west. "I hope he gets off first thing. This weather isn't going to hold."

"Look over here." At the far end of the low building where she had been handcuffed, fresh-looking tire tracks cut into the grass. They followed them around the side of the building to a tarp-covered car.

Gail pulled off the tarp. "Nice car," she said. "No way it's Crogan's."

It was an orange Mustang with white racing stripes

down the hood. "I've seen that car," Kelly said. "Couple of days ago. The driver talked to me."

"Who?"

"Hack Weechum. He was watching Faber try to pick up some hitchhikers. I didn't know who he was at the time."

"Weechum hiding out here? Do you think he attacked you?"

Kelly shook her head. "This guy was bigger than Weechum." She was becoming convinced that the voice she'd heard was Faber's. "Weechum hanging out with Crogan and Faber?"

Gail left the tarp on the ground, and they returned to the track.

Kelly unflinchingly retraced the course of the fight. The truck was gone, but its tracks were clear enough. The scattered, washed-out remains of her stomach contents provided useful signposts.

"Son of a bitch," Gail said, when she looked at the strut where Kelly had broken free.

Kelly picked up the shovel. The smooth wooden handle was at least four feet long; the wide, pointed metal blade was pitted with rust and had some dark earth stuck on it near the point.

"Not a great weapon for close quarters," Kelly said. "What the hell was the bastard doing with a shovel? Back here in the rain, in the dark?"

At the opposite end of the barn, a sagging door hung partially open. Kelly went in first, revolver in hand. She cursed as something went scurrying away in the shadows. The weak morning light slanting through the ill-fitting wall made faint lines across the dirt and sawdust floor, leaving the corners in deep shadow. The barn was nearly empty and looked unused. Along the right side, there were three shoulder-high stalls. The first two were empty except for some crusty manure and brittle fodder. In front of the last stall, Kelly found a dead flashlight.

Inside that stall was a freshly dug hole, the dark earth stark against the dusty, faded straw around it.

"Digging something up?" Gail suggested.

The hole was about five feet long, three feet wide, and two feet deep. "Getting ready to bury something," Kelly said.

"Jesus, not you."

"No. I don't think he was expecting me. Maybe it was for something that was to be delivered."

"It's too shallow for a grave," Gail said.

Kelly walked around the hole. "I interrupted him." She tested the strength of the stall and then leaned against it. She could feel Gail staring at her. Weechum's car was here, but Weechum wasn't. Faber and Crogan were the swinger's playmates. Weechum... Weechum was Shallow Rock.

"Fuck," she said. "I know what happened to Crogan."

"What?"

"Sarah Punk got him. Come on."

CHAPTER
THIRTY-SEVEN

There was a pickup truck facing them, taking up the full width of the humped track.

"Red Chevy," Gail said, as she got out of the car.

Kelly got out much more slowly, unwinding her cramped and aching body. She looked at her watch. Seven-thirty. It had taken them an hour and a half to get here from Crogan's. Non-stop, they had rolled through Trapper Lake without checking in at the station.

She leaned on the hood of the station wagon, trying to stretch out her back without ripping apart her ribs. "Crogan's?"

"I think so." Gail felt the hood of the truck with her hand. "Cold," she said. She tried the driver's side door. "Locked."

Kelly tried the passenger door; it was locked too.

She took a quick look around before looking in the window. Nothing special: wrappers and several beer cans on the floor, a hula girl stuck to the dashboard, an overflowing ashtray.

"Two types of cigarettes," she said. There was a crumpled Marlboro pack on the floor, brown and white filtered butts in the tray.

She caught sight of her face in the side mirror, stark and ugly, distorted by drops of condensation. Her right eye looked like it was filled with blood, the skin around it several shades of purple and yellow. She cocked her head and touched her lopsided, fat lower lip.

"No lipstick on the filters," Gail said.

Kelly stepped away from the mirror and edged towards the back of the truck. "A three-man job," she said. "Two men to pull the body from its hiding place under the Hell Hole and lug it all the way back here. A third man back at base digging a temporary grave."

The mosquitoes emerged from the bushes and descended on them. Gail turned up the collar of her long-sleeved denim shirt.

The truck was backed up to the edge of the swamp. The bed was empty except for a coil of blue nylon rope and a heavy tarp folded up near the cab. There was water between the ribbing, but no dirt. Leaning on the truck, keeping her feet out of the swamp, Kelly read a sticker on the back bumper.

"Honk if you think I'm sexy."

Gail sighed and swatted at the bugs. "Crogan, for sure."

Kelly crouched down for a better look at the ground. There were two sets of footprints in the mud, one on each side of the truck. "Two going in, none coming out," she said. Then her heart did a fluttering little two-step, and the ground began to sway. She was at the mid-point of her latest amphetamine rush, alert, but paying for it.

"Kelly, are you okay?"

"I'm okay, just give me a sec."

Gail stared into the bog. "This is starting to look like a very bad idea, we should get some back-up," she said.

Kelly looked up at the sky. "Sheriff should be here any minute, and Maclean is supposed to meet him when he lands."

"If he got off in time."

Kelly took several deep breaths, and then let Gail help her stand. "We need to see the scene before someone messes it up. Things could go missing." She thought of the long-shafted screwdriver sitting on the passenger seat of her car and the rope handcuffs that had fallen out of the pocket of her slicker somewhere back along the trail.

"All right," Gail said. Nervous excitement in her voice.

They hurried back to the station wagon. "Better bring your rifle," Kelly said.

"I have my sidearm."

"There are some open stretches. Last time I went down that path, I was wishing I had a rifle."

Gail fought a smile that was pulling at the corners of her mouth. She opened the swing gate of the station wagon and drew her scoped Remington from its padded case. From the side pocket, she took a handful of long rounds and slipped them into the front pocket of her loose jeans.

She took a faded, green canvas pack and shrugged into it. "I always take this when I go hunting," she said in response to Kelly's look.

Kelly buttoned her uniform shirt up to the neck, turned up the collar, and drenched her forearms with Gail's bug juice. She could feel the weather building towards another storm: pressure dropping, cold air rising, gusts of warm wind rattling the trees.

Gail loaded a round into her Remington and drove it home with a solid, confident click.

At the edge of the bog, they hesitated again. Leaning on Gail, Kelly took a step into the mud and then up onto the boardwalk. "You ever been out there?" she asked as she helped Gail up behind her.

"No."

"Then you're in for a real treat."

"What makes you so sure they're dead out there?"

"Sarah Punk."

"What the hell does she have to do with it?"

"She's the one who got us out here in the first place. She's the one who made the call." Kelly started off, moving quickly on the firm boards.

"Then what? She ate them up?" Gail asked, standing, giving her some distance.

"She *fucked* them up, that's what she does," Kelly replied, looking back over her shoulder.

"I thought you didn't believe in ghosts."

Kelly kept moving, eyes front now, watching the misty length of the walk ahead of her. She made a frustrated, grunting sound. "I'm starting to believe in Sarah Punk," she said.

"Oww, whatcha got to do that now, for?"

"Hush, I'm looking for spider nests."

Mitch opened one eye at a time, cautiously assessing his present reality. Ceiling above him, floor beneath him, room stable. It was very quiet.

"Owww, I'm tryin' to keep watch."

"You keep watchin' and hold still."

The voices of a woman and a girl slipped in through the screened window on the other side of the room. He smiled. The voices were *not* inside his head. In fact, his head felt pretty good. His whole body felt pretty good, except for his hands. He lifted them to his face. There were faint streaks of cam paint down the back of his fingers and seven or eight angry, red mosquito bites on each one.

"If you'd put it in a ponytail, it wouldn't get so messed up."

"Then all them bugs would be in my face 'stead of my hair."

Mitch scratched at the back of his hands, otherwise keeping still. He was relieved to realize that he knew who the speakers were. He smiled, closed his eyes, and drifted until the quiet conversation tugged at his ears again.

"Music never stopped all night. Every light on, place all lit up. Like watchin' the drive-in movie."

"How many cars?"

"The 'Cuda, the Beemer, the red Chevy and the little green Jeep. Just the 'Vette with the busted front end at the Cross place. Dee, still just the big 'Carlo."

"Only the Jeep and the Chevy could make it."

"You figure they come by road."

"Too lazy to walk."

"When?"

"Night."

"It'll be dark soon, anyhow," Mary Ann said.

"We'll see what Bobby says."

Their voices were low, with a cold edge of underlying tension. Mitch was naked, and suddenly he *felt* naked. His underwear lay on the floor, over towards the window. As quietly as possible, he crawled across to them and stood up.

"He's up," Mary Ann said.

He pulled up his lightweight, khaki boxers and looked out the window. There, looking back at him, all checkered by the screen, were a pair of black eyes that made his palms start to sweat. He wasn't thinking ghost so much anymore. *Possession* came to mind.

Rae's voice made him jump. "Get your clothes on and get out here, Mitch."

"Yes, ma'am," he replied.

"I already seen everything last night," Sarah...Mary Ann laughed, making him very uneasy.

"Uhh, where are my clothes?"

"In the kitchen."

His fatigue pants were hanging over one chair, garrison belt still attached, and his shirt was hanging over the back of another. His socks were on the fender of the woodstove, his boots by the door. He pulled on his stiff, dry pants, and hurried outside barefoot.

"Gotta take a leak," he said.

He headed for the outhouse, then stopped at the first convenient tree and let out a long sigh. The trees swished and hissed at him, the wind starting to come in strong from the west.

He found a mug and filled it with strong-smelling coffee. No milk in the icebox; he considered whiskey then decided against it, remembering that he was getting his shit together. He grabbed a handful of saltines from the cluttered table and headed outside.

Mary Ann was perched on the arm of the Adirondack chair at the end of the deck, looking his way. Rae was standing behind her with a brush going at the girl's long, tangled hair. Hair so blond it was almost white, not very thick, the color and texture of wood smoke and mist. Rae not so much brushing it, as combing it out, like the fur of an animal too long in the bush. There was a small pile of dead bugs and debris at Mary Ann's feet.

Her thin lips were smiling at him, until they turned into a grimace which revealed stained, crooked teeth, too large for her mouth; solid looking, sharp, carnivorous. "Owww," she said.

Rae grunted an apology.

Mary Ann wore the same dress he'd seen in his nightmares and his dreams. Shapeless, mid-calf length, not white, faded to just no color at all. It was hiked up high on one leg, which she was swinging, pale and provocative, strapped with the antler-handled Bowie in its sheath. Blue canvas shoes on large feet, the big toe sticking out of each one. Mitch looked up to her face; he tried to look into her eyes, but they were hard to capture, always slowly moving, one drifting after the other. He nodded and smiled, forcing a shiver back down his spine.

She had a small, delicately pug nose, the kind some girls would pay a fortune for. It looked out of place in the middle of her long face.

He widened his smile as he slipped past her. She had bug-bite splotches on her face and neck, small and precise. Mary Ann was not a scratcher.

Rae offered him her cheek as she continued to tug at Mary Ann's hair. He kissed her and took a couple steps out to the end of the deck.

He looked to the west and watched a black cloud-avalanche roll down the mountainside into the valley, filling the lake. It looked like a biblical sea advancing to swallow the world. He'd seen it before, most summers, this time of year. Thunder in the sky, lightning in its depths and a shit-locker full of rain. It would come on in waves for the next twenty-four hours or so, raging and letting up, and raging again.

"Nuff," Mary Ann said.

"All right, all right." Rae straightened up and bent backwards, hand to her back. "Least we got some of it."

Mary Ann shook her head and her hair fell around her face like stage curtains three-quarters drawn.

Mitch's head was much clearer this morning, but that didn't mean that everything made sense. He had a very clear memory of a foot in a blue shoe, toe right in his face. He cocked his head at Mary Ann. "You sure you and Bobby didn't pull me out of the bog yesterday?"

Rae answered for her. "I told you, you come up to the dock on your own steam. High as a kite," she said, lighting up a cigarette. "Bobby and Mary Ann helped you onto the dock; otherwise, you would have hit your head and drowned."

Was that how it happened? There was an airstrike coming in, B52's... Okay, he'd been seriously tripping. He'd have to take her word for it.

"You flopped around like a fish," Mary Ann said.

It seemed so strange that she could talk. He kept expecting her to scream.

"Then after, you were out here in your birthday

suit singing 'bout Arabian bums." Mary Ann laughed, her drooping shoulders shaking; laughing with her lips only, her eyes always moving.

"Arabian *drums*." Mitch winced. "Sad Eyed Lady of the Lowlands."

"All that damned singing and the snoring. You kept us all up all goddamn night. Nobody got any damn sleep, 'cept you," Rae growled and started to cough.

"Fuck, I'm sorry."

Mary Ann was staring at him. Mitch felt himself blush. He noticed her scraped knees and knuckles; her long, ragged fingernails. She was sixteen. He remembered the picture of her strung up like a piece of meat in the Hell Hole. He remembered what Rae had said about Hack having "unnatural" desires for her. The kid had seen more shit in seventeen years that he'd seen in his whole life, including Nam, and he was embarrassed to say "fuck" in front of her?

"Where's Bobby?" he asked.

"Keeping watch," Rae replied.

"He'll be back soon," Mary Ann said.

Mary Ann with the big Bowie strapped to her leg. Mary Ann with the purple recoil bruise on her right shoulder. Mary Ann who smelled like mud, nicotine, and cordite.

CHAPTER
THIRTY-EIGHT

"Fuck," Gail whispered.

"Yeah." Now that she saw it, Kelly felt no elation at being right, she felt sick.

It had taken over half an hour to make it to the soggy little island where she had waited out the downpour with Boodrow less than twenty-four hours ago. They had approached it warily, crawling up and settling in just below the brow like a couple of hunters in a blind.

She was sweating heavily, soaked to the skin by the humid mist that snaked around the tortured trees and smoked along the length of the boardwalk all the way to the Hell Hole. The light was weak, but visibility was good enough to make out a black, restless cloud of insects swarming around a crumpled, gray bundle on the shack's tilted deck.

Gail had her rifle up to her eye, using the scope. "Susan Collins?"

"Yeah, must be."

Kelly could see well enough with the naked eye. Besides the frantic whirl of insects, the water around the shack's piles twitched with the movement of fish and God knows what else. A black bird swooped in low over the water and came to rest on the peak of the tin roof.

Lying there, watching for human movement, she felt a fierce sadness. "They probably didn't mean to kill her," she said. "You rape enough people, sooner or later, shit happens. They panicked and ditched the body quickly, intending to move it later."

"But they didn't get around to it. A shitty job," said Gail.

"Any sign of them?"

"No."

"In the water?"

"Can't tell from this angle."

Kelly had travelled the last stretch, slipping and stumbling on the submerged boards. Now, anger and horror released fresh gouts of adrenaline racing through her body.

The sickening whine of mosquitoes was in her ear. The yipping cry of an osprey high above them made her clutch the mud. She heaved herself up. "Cover me," she said.

"We should wait a little longer. They could be in the shack. Wait..."

"Cover me," she repeated and struggled down the slight embankment to the last, stable stretch of boardwalk. She drew her revolver and paced carefully down the remaining fifty yards to the shack.

Rae was wearing an ankle-length, faded denim dress, cinched at the waist with a wide leather belt which held her Colt six-shooter. Next to her twelve-gauge up against the wall, was an army surplus small pack with the butt of a revolver sticking out from under its flap.

She flicked the butt of her cigarette into the lake, took the coffee mug from Mitch's hand and pushed him up against the wall. She pressed her body against his, thigh between his legs, and ran her fingers roughly through his hair on either side of his head.

"You look good, Mitch," she said. "Your eyes are clear, and you can speak without sounding like an idiot."

"Thanks…"

"Now there's a man worth having around, I could even get used to the hair."

Mary Ann sniggered.

Rae rose up a little and gave him a firm kiss. He held her around the waist, ignoring the butt of her .45 jabbing him just above the crotch. She tilted his head down and held it. "You keep off that shit, and you can come by and visit me anytime you like."

"Yeah, Rae thanks for setting me straight, man. I..."

"I want you to answer me a question, and I want you to tell the truth," she interrupted him, her voice as intense as her pale green eyes.

"Ah, sure."

"Those pictures you took from the Dee cottage, did you show them to anyone?"

There was no point denying he had them. "No," he said.

"You get 'em all?"

"Pretty sure, 'cept the ones Bobby already had."

She eased back a little. "Where are they?"

"In the bunkhouse, hidden."

"Good. I want you to go back there and burn them. I don't care about the dirty ones, you can do what you want with them; keep 'em, or give 'em to your dad, but the ones of Bobby and Mary Ann, you know the ones I'm talking about, I want you to burn those."

He nodded. The pictures he'd thought were of Sarah Punk, which the swingers had thought were of Sarah Punk, until they decided it was Bobby Margin hiding in the bush, peeking in their windows.

"There's no need for the kids to get caught up in all the shit those people caused," Rae said.

He could relate. "Right on. Yeah, I can do that."

"Bobby and Mary Ann never saw nothing, ever," she said.

"Cool," he replied, nodding again.

She kissed him, hard and quick, then stepped back and took him by the arm. "Let's get you dressed and on your way."

"Right now?"

"I got a feeling all hell's about to break loose. Best you do it right away."

"But it's gonna start pouring like crazy."

"That's good," she said, pushing open the screen door. "It'll cover you. Steer clear of the Mulvane place, move off the path when you get there, go right through the bush."

She sat him down and fetched his socks from the stove. Mary Ann stayed outside, keeping watch.

"At least tell me what's going on," he said.

She gave him his socks and stayed close, a hand on the back of his neck as he pulled them on. "The kids spotted Hack last night, he's holed up with the Mulvanes."

"He's here on the lake? With them?"

"He's their drug dealer. I figure it was Mulvane who got him early release." She chuckled. "Like it or not, they're all big pals now."

"Does my dad know?"

"No, else he'd be here with a fucking army. You can tell him. Call him from Blondie's phone. *After,* you burn the pictures."

Rae got his boots and stood over him while he put them on. He looked up at her. "You're expecting Hack to come here, to come after Bobby and Mary Ann, because of all the things they saw?"

"They never saw nothing."

"Right, he'll have help, you know. Mulvane and Cross already tried to kill Bobby once," he said.

She didn't correct him. "We can take care of ourselves against Hack and some whacked-out city slickers."

He laced up his second boot and stood up. "I know how to fight, Rae. For Christ's sake, I was in Nam!"

Resting her hands on his bare chest, her smile softened. "I told you what you had to do. You got a problem following orders, soldier?"

He knew she was right. Rae, Bobby, and Mary Ann on their own turf; he'd just be in the way. He shrugged into his fatigue shirt. "Okay," he said. "But then I'm coming right back here."

He tried to pull her in for a kiss, but she slipped away from him, grabbed his hat, stuck it on his head and hustled him out the door.

Mary Ann was out on the deck pointing a big, shiny revolver down the lake towards the Mulvane cottage and making soft explosion sounds. She held it with both hands, leaning back to carry the weight. It was a Colt Python .357, nickel plated, the flashy favorite of "The King" and other celebrities. Very expensive. Where did she get something like that?

He wrapped Rae in his arms and gave her a long kiss, reluctant to go.

"There's Bobby," Mary Ann said.

Rae twisted in his arms and turned to the west. On the

far side of Back Bay, a couple of hundred yards as the crow flies, the lakeside path came up on some bald rocks. Bobby stood there with a rifle in one hand. He was lit by a strange, intense ray of sunlight slanting in from the east, his figure sharp and dramatic against the storm-wall backdrop.

"Man, there is some *heavy* karma coming down the pipe, I can feel it." Mitch said.

Bobby waved and then disappeared down the path moving with an uncomfortable lopsided lope. It would be a toss-up whether he or the storm got to them first. "Best you wait and hear what he has to say," Rae said.

Mary Ann was farther down the deck, the Python dangling in her hand, tilting her slight frame to the right. She looked tense, but very happy, her face turning slowly this way and that, watching, sniffing the wind. Her scanning gaze came to rest on Mitch, one eye at a time. He took the look as an invitation and asked the question uppermost in his mind.

"All the time you spent in the bog; you ever see Sarah Punk?"

"Sometimes when the light's just right and I look down in the water," she teased him.

"Jesus, Mitch, you still going on about that?" Rae grumbled.

"It's been bugging me since I was a kid. I saw the plane crash in fifty-two."

"You told me. I saw it too. Joe Margin was a stupid man, and a drunk. He never should have taken off in that weather. It was an accident."

"But I saw…"

"She was my nanna," Mary Ann said.

"What?"

"Sarah Punk was my nanna."

How could that be possible? "Sarah had a baby before Moses?"

Rae spoke up. "She had a baby after Moses, two or three." She touched his cheek. "Mitch, that whole story was made up to throw off the law when they came pokin around after the Margin Brothers got killed."

Mitch looked at her without comprehension.

"Sarah Mosby, Mary Ann's granny, was a Siren; you know what that is?"

"Sure," he replied. Shallow Rock Sirens, like the ones immortalized in cast iron on the woodstove in his room, were women hired by the Moose River Cooperage Company as cooks and washerwomen who provided additional services on their own time. They were fondly remembered by the old lumberjacks he'd interviewed when he was a teenager.

"She was fifteen when she signed up, already had baby Moses before that. Lots of the sirens had kids. They used to bring 'em in from Shallow Rock on Sundays in the summer to go on outings. One day there was a boating accident. The Margin Brothers, drunk as skunks, rammed into Sarah's canoe. Baby Moses was drowned."

"Not shot?"

"No, he drowned. Sarah went home to Shallow Rock, had him buried in the little cemetery up there."

"And she didn't kill herself?"

"Course not, why would she do a thing like that?"

"She set up shop at her cabin, right there on Bitch Creek," Mary Ann said.

"The whole reason the company hired those women in the first place was to keep the men from running off to Shallow Rock all the time, getting drunk, missing work," Rae said. "Her place on Bitch Creek attracted a lot of men. One man in particular went by the name of Joe Stilwell."

Mitch knew that name. Joe Stilwell was the third hunter, the one that got away.

When she got within the last few yards of the shack, Kelly noticed a change in the water. Her eyes followed a Coca Cola colored plume to a couple of torn up, half-submerged bodies close to the deck. The stink of decay increased and sharpened. The ancient swamp stink had a new layer of shit.

She looked away and peered through a torn slat into the cabin. There was no movement inside. At a glance it appeared unchanged from yesterday. She turned and waved to Gail, then watched her come, not wanting to look at the stinking mess beside her. Gail walked carefully along the boardwalk, rifle at the port.

She stopped once and looked over her shoulder for a few seconds, then came up to Kelly.

"Jesus," she said, pulling her shirt up over her nose.

Kelly did the same. The misshapen heap under the gray tarp lay at the end of the wrap-around dock, near the far corner of the cabin. They stopped beside it, just outside the bug cloud. Kelly felt no desire to look under the tarp; she knew it was Susan Collins. She looked down. There were two bodies floating in the twitching, filthy water—one on its back, propped up by a small patch of thick, slimy lily pads, the other snagged up on the nearest piling.

Two men with their heads ripped open, faces blown away as if they'd been looking up. The rest of their bodies were mostly underwater, so it was impossible to say if there were other wounds. The body against the piling sat higher in the water. The grisly cavity where its face used to be was now gray mush, black with insects.

Gail stood beside her, touching her shoulder with one hand, pointing down into the water with the other. "What the fuck is that?" She sounded close to freaking out.

Next to the body at the piling, a little white face stared up at them with lifeless eyes. Kelly pointed out how the rope around its neck was attached to the lashings that bound the bundle on the deck.

"It's a doll. Looks like those assholes used it as a marker, had it tucked in under the deck."

Boodrow had poked it loose yesterday, she'd been

too sick to follow the rope, too eager to agree with him that it was just some kind of prank. Is that what he really believed, or did he know that it led to the body weighed down in the mud under the shack?

"Jesus, what happened here?" Gail said.

"Shotgun, close range." Kelly started to gag. She coughed and spat away from the bodies then wiped her mouth with the back of her cold hand.

"Dead for a few hours," Gail said, pushing the words out in a short burst.

"Yeah, I'd say this happened last night for sure."

"Who are they?"

Kelly forced herself to look more closely at the body near the piling. She didn't recognize it at all, beyond the fact that it looked like a big man.

"I think that one's Crogan," she said, breathing through her mouth as she spoke. She was convinced that one of them had to be Crogan.

"The other guy?"

"Too long dead to be Faber. Boodrow is still at the station." Fucking Boodrow, was he in on this or not? "One of the swingers maybe, or somebody we don't know about."

"Fast shooting to get them both," Gail said.

"They went into the water, mucked out the body and heaved it up on the deck. Somebody must have been up here waiting, an accomplice, maybe. They're in the water, floundering in the dark..."

"Fish in a barrel," Gail said without sympathy. "Who's the shooter?"

"Someone who wanted to get rid of his accomplices?"

"But we find the bodies, we can connect the dots right back to them."

Kelly tasted sweat on her lips, blood on her tongue. "Maybe it wasn't planned. An argument—they freaked out on each other..."

She heard Mitch's voice from her first night on Lost Lake. "Suddenly she rises up out of the murky water, right between the two brothers. They freak out and blast away at her. Bam! Bam! They shoot right through her and blow each other away..."

Kelly felt her knees start to tremble. She had a feeling that what little air was left in her lungs was being sucked out by the gross stink all around her. Gail started to gag. They stumbled together away from the bodies, back to the far end of the deck. Gail bent over and vomited into the water behind the shack.

Kelly leaned on her—half to comfort, half for support—and endured more body-wracking heaves. Eyes blurred with tears, she looked down the boardwalk where movement had caught her eye.

"Oh fuck," she gasped, fumbling for her holster.

CHAPTER
THIRTY-NINE

The man on the boardwalk appeared to be floating towards them.

"What the fuck?"

"It's Weechum," Gail said, backing away, keeping low.

Kelly straightened up and drew her revolver. Her brain did a dizzy swoop and she stumbled forward, almost going over the side. Regaining her balance, she blinked slowly, clearing tears from her eyes.

She recognized him from the parking lot of the Key Stone station: Hack Weechum, lean and loose-limbed, smiling at them, right hand raised in greeting, almost a benediction. A dangerous, redneck Jesus, walking on black water.

"Wait," Gail hissed. Kelly heard her fumbling around behind her, picking up the rifle she'd dropped when she'd started to vomit. Weechum kept coming.

Kelly held her revolver at her side, afraid that if she raised it her arm would shake.

"Got it."

Kelly took a deep breath and stepped forward. "Halt," she said.

"Are you folks okay?" Weechum called out without breaking his stride.

Kelly levelled her revolver at him, willing her arm to be still.

"All right, that's enough, Hack," Gail's voice, coming from behind her, was firm.

Weechum raised both his hands to shoulder height, the left a couple of inches lower than the right. "Mrs Harmon, I thought I recognized your Woody back there. You're a long way from your office this morning," he said, his voice nice and calm.

"Felt like doing a little hunting. I said stop."

Weechum, about halfway between the shack and the little island, stopped. He raised his hands a few inches higher, becoming a bit more lopsided, palms towards them, fingers spread wide.

"There's no need to get all excited. I'm not looking for trouble," he said.

"You're wanted for murder," Gail replied.

"That's bullshit. I didn't mean to kill that guy."

"What are you doing here, Hack?"

"I heard something nasty was going on out here, so I came to see what the fuck it was."

As they were speaking, Kelly advanced up the boardwalk until she was ten feet away from Weechum, close enough to be sure of her shot if Gail missed, but still giving him lots of room. He looked fast; had the manner of a sociopath who wouldn't betray a whisker of emotion before striking. She wondered, uneasily, how long he had been sitting back there on the little rise, watching them, making plans, coming up with lies.

He was wearing a lightweight, long-sleeved shirt, unbuttoned, collar turned up. The untucked T-shirt underneath it was dark with sweat. He wore a faded, camouflage-pattern ball cap that shaded his eyes in total darkness. His big smile was on display: friendly, mildly surprised. The hair sticking out the sides of his cap was stiff and dirty.

"I want you to take out your gun and lay it down, real slow," Kelly said.

"Look, I'm cooperating here. I want you to know I ain't got nothing to do with whatever the fuck that mess is behind you." He leaned to his right, trying to look past Kelly.

"Your gun, Weechum," Kelly said.

He frowned at her like she was being impolite. "Okay, take it easy. I know the drill." Left hand still in the air, he reached slowly around behind his back with his right hand, wincing slightly. "Look, two fingers."

He brought the gun around, holding it by the butt with two fingers. It was a revolver, a Colt Python.

"Put it down," Kelly said.

"You sure?"

"Put it down."

"Okay." He leaned forward, bending at the knee. His hand disappeared into the mist on the boardwalk. He grinned at her as he straightened up, showing her his empty hand.

Kelly swore under her breath. "Take a step back," she said.

He took a step back.

"What happened here, Hack?" Gail said.

"You tell me, ma'am, I just got here."

Kelly was annoyed that Gail had interrupted her before she was finished disarming him. She couldn't hold this position forever; already she was sagging to the right where her ribs were weak. There was a painful throbbing behind her right eye.

"You came looking for something," Gail said. She sounded like she had a grip on herself. She was on speaking terms with Weechum, not surprising in a place like Wanakena County.

"All of a sudden there's talk. People sayin', 'Hack Weechum's gone crazy, slaughtered a bunch of people out in Shaker's Bog.' You know, the kind of talk that gets a man shot *on sight*."

"Who's saying that?"

"Talk's all over town since last night. I tell you, some son of a bitch is tryin' to set me up. Come on; let me see what the hell's going on." He took a step forward.

"Stop!" Kelly barked.

"Maybe I can help you?" He wasn't looking at her; he was looking at Gail.

"I'll drop you right there," Kelly said, taking a step forward.

Weechum stopped and looked at her. He was sweating, but his features were placid. Closer up, she could see the edge of a white gauze dressing poking above his T-shirt, looking as if it was covering a wound on his shoulder. His left eye had a shiner and there were a couple of deep scratches on his cheek. She glared at him, anger making her stand straight and hold steady. He was looking at *her* injuries, judging his chances.

"You're a hard-ass bitch, aren't you," he said, the way he said it more of a compliment than an insult.

"Where's your other gun?"

"Only got the one."

"Bullshit."

"Guess you got to come and frisk me." He put his hands behind his head.

Kelly hesitated. He was too slick, too confident. "Get down on your knees," she said.

"I got nothing to hide," Weechum replied loudly. He settled down on his knees. "You want me on my knees..."

Alarm bells started going off inside Kelly's already noisy head. Her brain was jumpy and jangled, short-circuited, missing connections.

"I got you, Kelly," Gail called out from behind.

"Hell!" Weechum shouted. "I'll get right down on my belly!"

"Shit!" Kelly shouted.

Weechum dove flat onto the boards, clearing the line of sight between her and the little rise. A ragged white star lit up the dark shadows beneath the stunted trees. The air around her head buzzed with lead insects. She heard the sharp slap of bullets hitting the shack and the unmistakable rattling of an M16.

She dropped into a crouch as the shooter emptied his mag in one long burst. Behind her, Gail let out a cry of shock and pain.

There was no time to turn around. She could see Weechum, lying flat on the boards in front of her, the barrel of the Python rising above the mist aimed at her chest. She squeezed off a couple of rounds and threw herself out of the line of fire.

For about half a second, she was falling, confused, helpless, until she hit the muddy water. She went under, twisted painfully, and shoved her head back above the surface, feet frantically searching for the bottom.

The M16 was still stuttering. Grounding on the mushy bottom, she stood upright, water at her breast, eyes at the upper level of the mist. Weechum was crouched on the boardwalk above her, less than ten yards away. The Python swung towards her, seeking her out. A big, white flash, tinged with yellow and red, bloomed from its mouth. A cone of water erupted off to her left.

She fired before she was set, wasting two more rounds far to his right.

The water danced towards her. She went under and swam painfully through the nightmarish slime away from the boardwalk. She surfaced for a swift breath, and without looking back, went under again, stroking towards the dark shadow of a garbage pile.

A submerged branch slashed her forehead, dangerously close to her eye. She back-watered and surfaced, trying to stand on the slope of discarded brush and junk. Most of it was underwater, but some plywood, two-by-fours, and odd bits of metal poked above the surface. Grasping the curve of the scabby brown tube, she was able to get her feet underneath her and gain some balance.

The gunfire had stopped. Keeping low, heart hammering dangerously in her chest, she wiped the filth and blood off her face and tried to get her bearings. The garbage pile shielded her from the shooter on the island thirty or so yards off to her left. The end of the boardwalk and the shack were in front of her. Looking up through the mist, she saw Weechum's blurry form, crouched down, creeping towards the Hell Hole.

"Gail, look out!" she shouted. Digging in with her right foot, she raised herself up to shoulder height above the water and fired at him twice before drawing down on an empty chamber.

The top of the garbage pile started jumping, ripped apart by a fresh mag-load of M16 rounds. Swearing, she slid back down the angle of the pile, flicked open her revolver and dumped the empty shells. With a cold, shaking hand, she took a snub-nosed bullet from her belt. Full-body shivers overtook her, forcing her to pause, costing her precious seconds as she painstakingly fitted each of her six spare rounds into the cylinder.

The M16 stopped, and in the short silence that followed, she heard the deeper buck of a .303. A single, sharp shot. Weechum swore. Gail was still alive and kicking.

"The shack, asshole," Weechum shouted.

"I can't see her," a man's voice, thin and nervous, replied.

Gail must have made it inside and fired through one of the slits in the wall.

"Just tear the fucking place apart!" Weechum shouted back.

The M16 opened up again, bullets ripping into the cabin. Kelly could hear the rotten boards splintering. As she scrambled up to the top of the pile to get a shot at the island, her right foot got tangled. She stomped at it and the ground gave way, her leg punching down into a prickly mass that grabbed her calf and held. Steadied, she rose up above the mist, awkward and lopsided, and fired three rounds at the M16's muzzle flash.

A heavy round thumped into a piece of plywood, showering her with dirt and thin little darts of wood. A second one pinged off a scrap of iron inches from her fingers and went screaming past her ear.

She was exposed to both shooters now, but when she tried to shift position, her foot wouldn't budge. Flattening herself on the pile, she fired, more or less blindly, in the direction of the Python. The trash she was lying on gave way beneath her; she screamed as her upper body slid halfway down, pulling at her ribs. Foot stuck, head hanging down below the surface of the mist, she fought to take in a lungful of the foul, steaming air.

As far as she could tell, she hadn't hit either one of the shooters. The .303 was silent.

"Gail!" she shouted.

Four shots snapped into the brush and water next to her entangled leg.

"Fuck!" she wailed, and began to thrash, arms flailing, trying to work her leg free. She felt a slashing burn along her left arm. Looking over her shoulder through half-drowned eyes, she saw that a long piece of angle iron had gashed her bicep and gone up into her shirt, hooking her. She was pinned in place, right leg trapped, left arm snagged, right hand holding a nearly empty gun.

The .303 had fired only once.

Another Python round smacked the water, close enough that she felt the half-spent round hit her boot. She lowered her head, fighting terror, fighting despair. Gail was probably wounded or already dead and she was caught like an animal in a trap, waiting for the hunters to come and finish her off.

CHAPTER FORTY

Rae faced the approaching storm, shotgun resting easily on her shoulder.

"Everyone on the Moose River crew knew that the Margin Brothers were assholes, so when Joe came out of Shaker's Bog and told his crazy story about them freaking out over a ghost girl, they all figured it was some kind of sick joke. It was several days before they even bothered to look for them. By the time the bodies were found, Joe Stillwell was long gone."

She spoke like someone reminiscing about the good old days.

"The sheriff had heard about the accident that killed Baby Moses, and naturally, he had his suspicions about the mother. 'Course, when he went to Shallow Rock, he got told the same story."

Mitch, standing close beside her, ventured a

doubtful look at Rae's tranquil face. "They told him that the mother had killed herself months ago, and now her ghost was haunting Shaker's Bog?"

Rae chuckled. "Sheriff Ryerson didn't believe in the supernatural, but he was up against it anyhow. Sarah had signed on with Moose River as Peewee Shaker; her signature was an X. There was no record of the birth of Peewee Shaker. Or Sarah Mosby, or Baby Moses, or Sarah Punk, for that matter. She was a ghost, just like everybody else in Shallow Rock."

Mitch turned to Mary Ann for confirmation. A moment ago, she'd been putting her Python back in her small pack, now she and the small pack were gone.

The cool air on the leading edge of the storm made him shiver. "So, everybody was in on it, everybody told the same story?"

"Those that mattered; everybody else was smart enough to keep their mouths shut." A few big drops splattered on the deck; a long shadow rushed over the choppy water. "Come on, we'd better get under cover," Rae said.

There was a moment when the sky was a dull brown, then the storm-night engulfed them. They just beat the rain inside. Rae set her shotgun against the wall and stood to one side of the window. Outside, it was only slightly brighter than night, thunder grumbled in the far west. The wind ebbed and moaned, sending spray through the screen.

Mitch sat in his usual chair, reached for a joint, and

found his shirt pocket empty. He started talking to fill the silence. "So, the plane crash..."

Rae sighed. "I told you. That was an accident. There was no curse on the Margins. All that shit was stuff they made up over the years. It made them feel important."

"But Bobby didn't know that. He thought he was being haunted."

"Till a couple of nights ago. He finally figured out that the thing dogging his ass was more guardian angel than ghost." Rae turned from the window, and he saw the white flash of her smile. Bobby came through the door with Mary Ann right behind him.

"Speak of the devil," Rae said.

Bobby moved easily in the darkness. "Hey Mitch," he said.

He set the hunting rifle down on the table, took off his hat and shook it. "Son of a bitch, it's coming down out there." He sat heavily in the chair next to Mitch, wiped his hands on a towel, took out his tobacco pouch and started rolling. Mary Ann slipped into the spare bedroom, the one with the window that looked inland, towards the road.

Rae waited for him to speak. Once Bobby had fired up and taken a drag, he gave his report. "Hack and Mulvane lit out in Faber's truck about two hours ago. I waited a bit to see what the others would do. They sat tight, so I came back."

"Who's there now?"

"Just the two ladies and Faber."

Rae turned from the window, looked at Mitch, and then at Bobby. She was about to speak when Mary Ann slipped into the room holding a finger to her lips. "Shush," she whispered.

Bobby and Rae became still, listening. Mitch strained to hear. There was something, a sound neither wind nor water, a mechanical sound. A muted snickering.

"That ain't thunder," Bobby said.

Mitch knew that sound at any range. "M-16," he said.

"Shallow Rock," Mary Ann said. In an instant, she was out the door with Bobby and Rae behind her.

Mitch joined them at the end of the dock, staring out through the rain in the direction of the shooting. The black wall of the storm had reached the edge of Shaker's Bog. He heard a few quick shots, then the long ripping snore of automatic fire.

"Sheriff caught up with them in Shallow Rock?" Rae suggested.

"Caught up with who?" Mitch said.

"Maybe some state troopers got lucky?" Bobby said.

"*Hack* got lucky," Mary Ann replied with disgust.

With a furious pull, Kelly ripped her shirt loose and slid down the slope of garbage, coming to rest with her right leg still trapped and her head half underwater.

She lay there panting, with just her mouth and nose above the slime. She didn't hear the bush plane until it roared overhead, its pontoons nearly scraping the roof of the Hell Hole. She felt a surge of hope; Sheriff Herkemer must have made it up from Snowshoe Lake.

Grunting, she pulled herself into a half-sitting position and used both hands to explore down into the rubbish holding her foot. At the knee, she encountered a rough maze of metal coils. Bedsprings. She took hold of the laces in the front of her boot and the top of her sock at the back and began working her foot up and down, side to side, forcing back the tangled metal.

She heard Weechum shouting but couldn't make out the words above her own tortured breathing. The sound of the aircraft engine faded into the distance.

Slowly, the metal grip started to give.

She realized that even if the sheriff did manage to land, he couldn't get any closer to the bog than the dock at Shallow Rock. If Maclean was already waiting for him, it would still take them at least an hour to get to her, plenty of time for Weechum to finish her off. She straightened up and began kicking, driving her boot up and down. Her pant leg came up, the springs chewed at her calf like a horde of fire ants.

With a last, angry cry, she pulled her leg free and fell back into the water. Head spinning, she righted herself and stumbled away from the junk pile until she found solid footing on the swamp bottom. She wiped the blood and rain from her eyes, drew her revolver with its last desperate round, and made for the blurry shadow of the shack.

The world took a brownish, sepia tinge, as if she was already long dead and entombed in a faded, forgotten photograph. Slugged by a wave of dizziness, she stumbled, then stood with her hands pressed against her clammy forehead, fighting to stay upright. She pictured herself floating face down in the filth next to the other bodies. No fucking way.

Wind whipped the waters, shredding the mist. She could see the boardwalk only a few feet away at neck level. There was no sign of Weechum. The corner of the cabin facing the boardwalk looked like it had been chewed by a giant beaver.

She reached the edge of the boardwalk, got her elbows up on the boards, and tried to heave herself up. Her arms quivered like they were made of Jell-O. Cursing hoarsely, she fell back into the water. Weeping with frustration, she edged along the boardwalk, away from the bodies, searching for higher ground. Beyond the hissing wind, she thought she heard the bush plane running in for a landing.

A tidal wave of rain fell on her from the sky, making her stumble again. She found her balance and stood with her head lowered, panting. The goddamned swamp was trying to kill her.

"Fuck you," she croaked. Turning her hot, unfocused eyes to the sky, she opened her mouth and let the cascading rain pour in.

A few yards farther along, she found a spot where

she could wedge a foot into the crook of a piling and hoist herself up onto the streaming boards. She rolled onto her back and lay still, as heavy as a clod of mud. She laid her hands flat on the boards and felt the slashing rain cleanse the burning furrows made by the diseased metal of the bedsprings.

The world went from brown to black. She struggled to her hands and knees. "Gail!" she shouted.

Forty yards away, the Hell Hole was invisible, swallowed by the storm. She crawled, then stood and walked carefully down the slippery boards. "Gail!"

At the corner of the shack, there was a dark, slug trail of blood that began next to the tarped body. Without even a glance at the bodies in the water, she followed it around the far corner of the deck to the open door of the Hell Hole.

CHAPTER
FORTY-ONE

Mitch shifted uneasily as the distant firing continued. "Can we get over there?"

"Not in this weather," Bobby said.

Rae turned to him, her hair plastered to the side of her wet face. "Mitch, you need to get back to the camp."

"Yeah, cool," he replied.

Mary Ann came out of the cottage carrying a rubber-handled hatchet. "You dropped this on the dock," she said, a little smile on her face, one black, merciless eye staring directly at him.

He waited until the second one drifted in. "Thanks," he said.

"Might need it on the way back." They both knew she wasn't talking about cutting firewood. Her aura was like mist rising from red-hot pavement just after a rain shower. Mist shot through with flickering snakes of electric blue light.

"Be careful going past the Mulvane place. And burn those pictures as soon as you get back," Rae said.

"That's cool. I'll take care of it." He tucked the hatchet into his belt.

A new sound coming from the direction of Shallow Rock drew their eyes skyward. A bush plane dropped out of the low clouds over the village, headed for Shaker's Bog, flying straight towards the approaching storm wall.

"Gutsy bastard," Rae said.

Mitch stood, mesmerized, remembering standing on another dock years ago, watching as a bush plane was ripped out of the sky by an unseen hand.

Rae gave him a hard shove. "Go on, get. There's nothing you can do here."

Reluctantly, Mitch turned his back on Shallow Rock and jogged into the swaying trees.

Gail sat propped up against the wall, pointing her revolver at the doorway.

"Kelly?" Her voice was weak and frightened. The gun, held in both hands, swayed in a small arc left and right.

"It's me, Gail. Thank God, I thought you were dead."

"Help me, Kelly. Help me, I'm blind," she wailed, lowering the gun.

The contents of Gail's first aid kit were strewn about her on the bloody floor. Kelly knelt beside her, took the pistol from her icy hands and held them in hers. She leaned in close, keeping her head back from Gail's bloody face.

Struggling to keep the horror out of her voice, she said, "Did you hear the plane? That had to be the sheriff, I'm sure he saw us."

"They got me in the leg and then this." Gail pulled her hands loose and fluttered them around her eyes. "I'm afraid to touch anything. It feels bad, Kelly. Jesus, how bad does it look?"

"You're gonna be okay," Kelly replied.

Gail's face was a mass of battered, purple flesh, scored with shallow slash marks and pierced by slim, ragged splinters of different sizes. One thin, blond sliver was lodged deep in the swollen flesh of her left eyelid. It was impossible to tell if it was in the eyeball, or just above it.

"Be still, okay. Don't move your eyes," Kelly said softly. "It's gonna be okay." She took Gail's hands and gently put them down on her thighs. "It's not that bad, just don't touch it."

"I don't fucking believe this," Gail said in an angry whisper.

Kelly had her own problems. She was weak and stiff, all her movements tentative and foreshortened by her aching ribs. Blood dribbled into her eyes from the cuts on her forehead. A red rivulet coursed down her left arm and dripped off her elbow. The deep scratches on her leg and the backs of her hands burned like hell. She found a gauze pad and lashed it to her arm with medical tape.

"Kelly?"

"I'm right here, Gail. I'm gonna take care of you." The sight of Gail's face made her sick. "Mostly, it's just caked blood and swelling. I want to look at your leg first."

Gail had done a good job of patching herself up. "It was the M-16," she said. "It went right through the muscle, nice and clean."

She had cut off her pant leg below the knee, stuffed the entry and exit wounds with gauze, wrapped it with a triangular bandage and secured it with her belt. The belt was still tight; the bandages were wet and red, but not soaked through.

"I had to take care of my leg first, Kelly. I didn't know how bad it was. I could hear you outside shooting..."

Kelly could see what had happened. Gail was hit out on the deck, crawled inside, bound her wound, and then went to the corner to fire from one of the slits. The brittle shack wall had proved worse than useless as cover.

"You scared the shit out of Weechum, might even have winged him," Kelly said.

She found Gail's canteen, still half full, and helped her drink. Her lips were starting to take on a bluish tinge. Kelly took a short swallow and then made Gail drink again.

"It's a good thing you brought that pack. Girl Scout training?"

"Brothers." Gail started shivering badly. "M-m-orons, couldn't last five minutes in the bush without breaking something or slicing something off. How are you, K-Kelly?"

"I'm okay. A few scratches and I think I tore my ribs. I didn't get hit. Neither one of us is gonna die any time soon."

At least they weren't going to bleed to death.

Her watch had been lost somewhere in the bog. How long had it been since the plane was overhead? Fifteen minutes, thirty? She pictured the sheriff and Maclean edging along the drowned boardwalk, worried about an ambush. If they bumped into Weechum...

"Kelly, I don't want to go blind," Gail said. She was holding her head still, looking straight ahead.

Going by the book, she shouldn't be messing with an eye wound at all, but Gail needed to feel that something was being done. "It doesn't look that bad. I'll clean you up a bit, okay? Just hold still," she said.

She wet some gauze and dabbed at the caked blood, concentrating on Gail's right eye, which didn't look as bad. The scratches oozed a little, but they didn't bleed. It was a slow process, interrupted every time Gail's body was wracked by a wave of shivers.

Exhaustion weighed down Kelly's limbs. "I gotta stop this for a bit, Gail. Just be cool."

Slumped against the wall, Gail didn't answer.

Kelly straightened her up and got her to drink again. "They'll be here soon," she said as she rummaged through Gail's pack. She wanted to keep Gail talking. "What was Weechum up to?"

"I don't know, he did-dn't know what was behind us. He didn't shoot those guys."

Kelly sat on her heels with her eyes closed. There were things that needed to be done. Gail should be flat on the ground, wounded leg elevated, but there was nothing to work with in the stripped-down cabin.

"He saw your Woody; he had to know he would run into you." Kelly unrolled Gail's canvas survival kit. There were matches in a metal tube and fire starter cubes. She should get a fire going, boil some water.

She unfolded a thin, silver space blanket, wrapped it around Gail's shoulders like a cape, and sat heavily beside her. The rain beat steadily on the tin roof. It was a nice sound; it reminded her of childhood, of being in a tent, warm and comfy in a sleeping bag.

CHAPTER
FORTY-TWO

Mitch settled easily into the Airborne shuffle, just the right speed to match the ten or so feet of visible path unwinding ahead of him. He settled into the familiar trance; forebrain shut down, animal instincts reaching out in all dimensions. The hatchet didn't sit comfortably in his belt, so he carried it in his right hand like a Hollywood Indian on the warpath.

The Mulvane cottage appeared like a lighthouse perched high on a rock, white light strobing through the rhythmically waving tree branches. It invaded his peace of mind, slowed his shuffle, and brought him to a halt. Light was pouring out of the gaps in a dozen half-closed curtains. The outdoor lights were on too, illuminating the glistening patio furniture and the flagstone path down to the lake.

Sweet giggles weaved their way through the falling raindrops to tickle his ears.

On a broad landing just a few steps down from the patio, a dark-haired woman danced in the rain, her thin, white nightgown soaked and transparent. Denny Cross, stoned out of her mind again.

Pretty, scented Lady of the Lake. Her aura was large, diffuse, and complicated—part lily-white lamb, part blood-red Judas. He had no intention of getting his fingers entangled in her karmic pie. He'd keep to the shadows and slide on by.

"Hey, dipshit. Get your ass back in here!" A male voice banging into the night. A big shadow, backlit by the light from the patio doors. Denny swaying with her face upturned to the rain, oblivious.

"Get me all wet, you stupid, little slut!" The man shouted, bounding down the stairs, his arm swinging in a wide arc. There was a loud, wet slap as his big paw made contact with Denny's butt. She howled in surprise and pain.

Shit.

Mitch dashed up the stairs. When he reached the landing, the guy had Denny over his shoulder like a sack of potatoes and was heading back towards the cottage. Denny was squirming and beating his back with her fists. "Let me go, Steve, let me go!"

There was another sharp smack. "You like that, baby?"

Denny screamed, her head jerked up, and her eyes flew open. "Bobby!" she shrieked and started kicking.

Faber was barefoot, wearing some stupid, Hugh Hefner-type, shiny robe that came down to his knees, slick with rain. She slid off his shoulder and landed neatly on the flagstones in a crouch.

"Cocksucker!" Faber shouted, starting to turn.

Denny leapt into Mitch's chest, wrapping her arms around his neck, legs gripping his waist. "Bobby!" she cried.

Mitch caught her and stumbled back, trying to regain his balance while she tried to kiss him. "I'm not Bobby," he snapped, moving his face to avoid her lips. He let her go, but she didn't fall.

"Bobby? You son of a bitch," Faber shouted, charging towards them.

Mitch could have felled him with a swing of his hatchet, but he wasn't ready for that kind of escalation, just yet. He took a firm stance and let Faber crash into him, squishing Denny between them.

Faber fell back. Denny screamed and fell to the ground.

"I'm not Bobby!" Mitch shouted.

Moving like a bobcat on speed, Denny darted behind Mitch and was up on his back in a flash, arms tight around his neck, howling in his ear. "Get him, Bobby, kill the asshole!" Bucking like a child, she pushed his bush hat down over his eyes.

"Stop that!" Mitch shouted, shoving it back up.

Faber was right there in front of him, robe hanging open, showing off his tight, black mesh briefs. They looked ridiculous; the automatic he held inches from Mitch's forehead didn't look silly at all.

"Drop the hatchet, shithead!" he shouted, hurling boozy spit in Mitch's face. The twitching finger on the trigger looked eager, his meat-slab face looked hungry and irrational.

"Fuck you, Steve," Denny snarled.

Mitch knew that people doing coke at nine-thirty in the morning were not amenable to negotiation. He dropped the hatchet. "I'm not Bobby," he said.

"I don't give a fuck who you are."

Denny stuck her face out past Mitch's shoulder. "Fuck you, Steve!" she shouted again.

Faber flicked the tip of his gun from Mitch's forehead and gave her nose a vicious crack. "Shut up, bitch," he said.

Denny howled and fell to the ground. Mitch started to move, but Faber had the gun back on him very fast.

"Oh yeah, motherfucker? Go ahead, make my fucking day," he said, shoving the gun hard into Mitch's forehead.

"For fuck's sakes, man. Make my day?" Mitch sighed. "Motherfucker?"

Mrs. Mulvane appeared on the step above them, emerging suddenly out of the glare, holding a big gun in the palm of her hand. She smashed it against the side of Faber's head.

"Fuuuuck!" Faber wailed, his free hand coming up to his face as he staggered. Mitch caught his arm and wrenched the automatic from his hand. Mrs. Mulvane backed up a step so she could cover them both with her shiny revolver.

Another Python. Mitch froze, standing straight with the automatic down at his side.

Mrs. Mulvane's voice slashed through the rain. "Back off, you idiot. That's Mitch Herkemer, the sheriff's son. Go on, get in the house. You too, Denny."

Hand to her bloody nose, Denny flashed Mitch a wounded look and hurried up the stairs.

Faber wasn't going so easily. "You fucking bi…"

"Steve, I'll blow your balls off," she interrupted him. The Python hammer made a loud click as she cocked it.

Faber straightened up. He gave Mitch a baleful look. "Give me my gun, asshole."

Mitch shook his head. He was tired of being the only one around here who didn't have a gun.

"Go get a drink," Mrs. Mulvane said to Faber in a quieter tone. "I'll take care of him."

Mitch didn't like the sound of that. He felt the side of the automatic to make sure the safety was off.

Faber spat. "I'm fucking bleeding," he muttered as he shuffled up the stairs.

Mrs. Mulvane eased the hammer down on the Python. "Come on, Mitch," she said. "We need to talk."

Mitch hesitated at the open patio door while Mrs. Mulvane dealt with her party guests. It was more than just monkey-brain curiosity that kept him from slipping back into the dark and heading for home. Things might have changed since Bobby had left. It was worth a little risk to find out if Hack had returned.

Faber was sitting on the flat arm of a leather couch in the far corner of the living room. Mrs. Mulvane stood back from him, holding Denny by the wrist with one hand, the Python down at her side in the other. She spoke in a quiet voice, while Faber swore loudly back at her. Denny tried to drift towards Mitch, but Mrs. Mulvane yanked her back without taking her eyes off Faber.

Mitch was uncomfortable with his back exposed, so he stepped inside and slid to his left until he had a curtain at his back. These people were a sniper's dream; the bright lights put everyone inside on a stage and blinded them to anything going on outside.

Denny had stopped bleeding. At Mrs. Mulvane's prompting, she slid up to the end of the couch and stroked the back of Faber's hand. He continued to glare, his bloodshot eyes shifting from Mitch to Mrs. Mulvane and back.

"Go on," Mrs. Mulvane said, her voice louder, with a suggestive, teasing note. "Why don't you two get out of those wet clothes and take a nice hot shower? The one in the master bedroom was designed for two."

Faber stood up and grabbed Denny tightly around

the waist. With his eyes on Mitch, he took hold of one thin shoulder strap of her gown and yanked it hard once, twice, ripping the whole nightie down past her boobs. He had the look of a naughty, eight-year-old ape-boy.

"Go on and have some fun," Mrs. Mulvane said. "Mitch won't be staying long. Don't worry, you won't have to share."

The mingled auras in this place were wicked and foul, they swirled around each other creating a poisonous whirlpool that threatened to drag down anyone who so much as dipped a toe inside. Mitch started edging back towards the open door.

As they headed for the master bedroom, Faber gave Denny another slap, gathered the material of her gown at her waist and pulled upwards, giving her a vicious wedgie, forcing her to hurry along on tiptoes. She cast an imploring, pitiful glance over her naked shoulder at Mitch.

Mitch concentrated on being unmoved.

He felt like putting a bullet in the back of Faber's head, or better still, beating it to a pulp with the butt of his pistol. He looked away. He didn't want to carry that karma.

Mrs. Mulvane turned her smile on him, allowing him to see some of the fear behind her eyes. "Come in, Mitch, please," she pleaded.

"Where's Hack?"

She didn't try to bluff him. "I don't know, Mitch, honestly. Hack was here yesterday, last night, but he left before dawn with Miles Crogan. I don't know where *anybody* is. Hal and Mick left a couple of hours ago to go into town and get supplies, they figured they'd be back before the storm hit. I'm left here alone with Denny and that drunken slob. I'm terrified."

She was lying about something, maybe everything. He ignored her and listened to the house. He could hear Faber moving around recklessly in the master bedroom, probably looking for more speed, or a gun. The cottage walls creaked; the acres of glass rattled in the wind. The stereo was silent. No other sounds. He had a profound sense that they were alone. No Hack, anyway.

"Mitch?"

Let it be. These people had sent their evil deeds out into the universe, and now karma was bringing it all back home. He didn't want to be here when that happened.

"Mitch, please, we need you."

There had been no outright confessions, but during their stoned discussion two days ago, the ladies had pretty much confirmed what Lucy had told him. They had lured Bobby to Steep Rock and beat him up. They were going to throw him onto the rocks, make it look like a teenage suicide.

Their plan had failed because they didn't know about the sweet spot at the bottom of Steep Rock. And they hadn't figured on Sarah Punk dropping down on them out of the trees like a rabid bearcat. That didn't make them any less guilty.

They had no right to ask him for help. Thing was, he just couldn't get Faber's ape-boy leer out of his head.

"Mitch?" Mrs. Mulvane was looking at him the way people sometimes did when he'd been thinking.

"Yeah?"

"Mitch, come in and have a drink, please."

"Yeah, sure," he said. "Maybe we could turn off some of these lights."

CHAPTER
FORTY-THREE

While Mrs. Mulvane shut down the overhead lights, Mitch went straight for the kitchen and the phone. He took up a position, leaning on the counter near the sink, where he could see the whole room.

He stared at the empty phone jack on the wall. "Where's the phone?"

"In the trash."

"Hack?"

Mrs. Mulvane nodded. "We had three phones. He smashed them all. All the ones at the other cottages as well."

"Paranoid son of a bitch."

"Terrifying son of a bitch. Don't you understand? Yesterday, last night, it wasn't a party, Mitch, we were hostages. Miles turned on us, he's with Weechum now."

"Then Hack took off, and your husbands just left?"

"I couldn't stop them. They said they were going for supplies."

It looked like there had been a party last night; booze and beer bottles, half-empty glasses and full ashtrays on the end tables and coffee table. There were dishes in the drying rack next to the sink. It was untidy, but the house was clean, not at all like Lucy's place. Nicotine and cheap weed hung in the air that smelled mostly of coffee. The AC wasn't running at the moment, but the place still had an unnatural chill.

"Useless fucking cowards," she added indignantly, standing a few feet away from him, the Python down at her side. The rain had smudged the mascara at the corners of her red-rimmed eyes, giving her a vulnerable look. Her pupils looked alright; she was running on nicotine, caffeine, and nerves—not uppers.

Their eyes locked, joining them in a mutual, hooded suspicion that had a very intimate feel. Her eyelids drooped, showing pale blue eyelids. She was neck-deep in the whirlpool, reaching out for him. He wasn't sure if she wanted to pull herself out or pull him in.

Faber's voice rumbled out of the bedroom, slurred and angry. Something whacked against a wall, followed by a faint whimpering protest from Denny.

Mitch's eyes darted to the bedroom door and then back to Mrs. Mulvane. "Are there any guns in there?"

"No."

She moved in on his right, leaning against the counter next to him, snuggling up beside him. He could feel the cold skin on the back of her hand rubbing against his gun hand.

"Any other guns in the house?" he asked, eyes returning to the bedroom door.

"Not that I know of." She was watching the bedroom too. "We had a couple of hunting rifles and a shotgun, but somebody took them, I don't know who."

Mitch crossed his arms over his chest and slid a couple of inches down the counter, breaking contact, but staying close enough that he could give her a quick elbow to the side of the head if he needed to. He looked down at the sleek, nickel-plated revolver in her hand.

"Where'd you get the Python?" he asked.

"It's Mick's, he left it here for me."

"Man, that's a heavy piece of hardware; can I have a look at it?"

She looked up at him, head cocked, eyes softening. "We're friends, right, Mitch?"

He smiled down at her. "We're cool," he replied.

"We have to trust each other."

"We're cool," he repeated. "Here, I'll trade you." He flicked the thumb lever to safe, and holding the Colt by the barrel, offered it to her. "It's easier to handle, and you get more bullets," he said.

She transferred the Python to her left hand, took

the Colt in her right, and flicked off the safety before handing him her gun. So much for trust.

Mitch hefted the Python. It was big, perfectly balanced, and heavy. By comparison, the .45 felt like a toy. This one looked like a pampered showpiece, highly polished and engraved. Along the barrel, it said The Mighty Mick, and in the space between the grip and the cylinder, there was an erect cock rising out of a shamrock.

"Jesus," he said.

Mrs. Mulvane was watching him. "The boys had them done last year right after they bought them," she said with a disdainful smile. "Dan's has a dick wearing a top hat, Dirty Dan."

Mitch gave the cylinder a spin confirming that every chamber was loaded. The smoothness of the action calmed him.

"Hal's cock is on a cross," Mrs. Mulvane added. "He's 'The Omega Man.'"

"Omega Man?"

"Because he's always the last man standing," she replied dryly.

Assholes.

There was a sharp, grating sound from beyond the bedroom wall, metal on glass.

"He's in the bathroom. Medicine cabinet," Mrs. Mulvane said.

Mitch pointed the Python towards the bedroom door, very gently stroking the trigger. The Python action was said to be as smooth as silk.

"I always imagined your parties would be more about, you know... sex, not so much about... guns," he said.

"It started out that way, the parties. It was just a lark, a way of making all those pompous suits look ridiculous. It was never as much fun as I thought it would be, and now I'm sick of it, Mitch. So damned sick of it all."

She sounded sincere. The way things were turning out, she was probably telling the truth. A steady banging started coming from the bedroom. It was rhythmic, sounding just like a headboard being slammed into a wall.

"Let me go. Let me go. *Fucking*, let me go!" Denny shouted.

Mitch felt mentally fractured, his attention running along several cracks at the same time. He was listening to the house, to the night outside; he was thinking over options, but mostly he was interested in the Pythons.

"Did Mr. Cross take his with him?" he asked.

Mrs. Mulvane put the .45 on the counter and took a pack of Virginia Slims out of the pocket of her tunic. "Yeah, he had the gun belt and everything."

"Did Dan take his with him back to Syracuse?"

She frowned. "Probably, they all love those guns."

"Does Hack have one?"

"One of those?" She lit her cigarette with a gold lighter, hauled deep and exhaled. "No, there was just the three. They made a big deal about it."

Mitch wished that he'd taken a better look at the gun Mary Ann had been playing with. He hadn't noticed any engraving, hadn't been close enough to see. He could easily imagine Mary Ann sneaking into one of the cottages and snatching such a treasure. But if none of them had been stolen?

"Let me go, you pig, let me go, let me go!" Denny shouted in time with the banging.

This was a hateful place. "You got keys to the Jeep out back?" Mitch snapped, making Mrs. Mulvane jump.

"Yes."

"Okay. We get Denny, jump in the Jeep, and get the fuck out of here. We go right through to Trapper Lake. I'll drop you at the station, I'll keep the Jeep."

Mrs. Mulvane still had a cigarette going. "Can we make it? The roads..." She moved to him, almost touching. Her eyes chased his down. The way she looked at him, she had a different plan in mind. The reason she'd invited him in here in the first place.

"I'm not packed," she added, like she was sharing an inside joke.

"You got a purse, money, credit cards. You're good."

She stubbed out her cigarette. "Why bother? The only problem here is Steve. And now *we* have all the guns."

They heard glass breaking in the bathroom, Faber shouting something, sounding angrier than ever. Mitch took a half step towards the bedroom.

"Just wait, Mitch!" Mrs. Mulvane raised the .45 halfway up, pointing in the direction of the bedroom door. "What are you doing?"

"I'm getting Denny, and getting out of here, with or without you."

Denny screamed, pure fear this time. There was a heavy thud.

"Shut the fuck up, bitch!" Faber coming through loud and clear now.

Mitch waved at Mrs. Mulvane with the Python, motioning her towards the bedroom. He was going in, and he didn't want her behind him. "Go, go!" he shouted.

Denny screamed again. Mrs. Mulvane shook her head. "I'm not going in there."

"Shit!" Mitch shouted, and ran straight at the half-open door.

No fucking around, no caution; Zen moves. He put his shoulder into the door, throwing it open. The room was smaller than he'd imagined. It was dominated by a king-sized bed with golden covers and a brass headboard. Denny was tucked in a ball up near the headboard, one wrist cuffed to the brass work. Faber was standing beside the bed, a thick pipe raised over his head ready to strike her.

Trigger action as smooth as silk, man. The Python went off as he was raising his arm, before he could draw a bead on the bastard's center of mass. The bullet buried itself in the middle of the bed.

It made a very loud bang indoors. Faber jerked

awkwardly towards the sound and fell against the wall. Mitch gripped the Python by the barrel, turning it into a club, as Faber skirted the bottom of the bed and charged towards him. Big guy, furious, coked to the gills, with a big, solid weapon in his hand.

He didn't have a chance.

Mitch was inside Faber's striking range, shoulder into the guy's chest, before he even took a swing. Mitch swung the Python, landing a solid blow with the heavy butt to the side of his head. Faber crashed against the wall and crumpled into a ball. Mitch booted him in the head, then stomped down hard on his hand, making him drop the bar. It was so fucking easy. Faber was in a ball, hands over his head; naked, whimpering, and bleeding.

It was enough. Mitch stepped back, panting.

"Let me go, let me go!" Denny shouted.

She was naked, her back turned to him as she yanked at the headboard, slamming it angrily against the wall. There was a broad bruise on her thigh, up near her butt.

She looked over her shoulder. "Get the key! The fucking key!" she shouted at him, totally freaked.

Mitch had no idea where the key was. "Stop!" he shouted. Then louder, "Stop doing that. Hold still!"

He climbed on the bed, grabbed her by the wrist and pulled it back to expose the full length of chain between the cuffs and the brass work. "Look away!"

She tucked her face beneath his armpit. He steadied her arm with his left hand, placed the mouth of the Python a fraction of an inch from the chain, and fired. The .357 slug split the chain and smashed into the wall. The blast burst a dam in his head, sending a wave of exhaustion rolling over him. He tossed aside the Python and collapsed face down on the bed. Denny hugged him around the shoulders, crying and slobbering in his ear.

It took a while to get his heartbeat down, get his head together. It was time to go, but he felt sleepy and sluggish, the way he always did after the rush of violent action. Raising his head, he could see that Faber hadn't moved. With a great, sighing effort, he sat up on the bed.

"Nice and fucking slow, Mitch." A man's voice, calm, but very hard. "Stand up, hands where we can see 'em."

He looked towards the end of the bed, sweat misting his eyes.

Three people standing there. Three guns pointing at him. One of them was a Python, one was an M-16, and the third was Faber's Colt .45 held by Mrs. Mulvane.

CHAPTER
FORTY-FOUR

Kelly looked over at the stained outline on the freshly swept floor of the Hell Hole. The spot where a bed had stood for years. She could almost hear the screeching of the rusty springs; almost see the pale face of Sarah Punk peeking in the window. The bed and the ghost that everyone had dismissed as teenage, pothead fantasy.

Kelly knew that the bed was real. Her leg and hands still burned from its embrace. If the bed was real, then so was Sarah Punk.

It was all about Sarah Punk.

Sarah had been there to greet her on her very first night at Lost Lake. She had been on Steep Rock. She had made the call from the Dee cottage that got the law poking around the Hell Hole, panicking the killers into moving the body. Sarah had been here yesterday, cleaning up the place, knowing that it would be crawling with cops after the ambush. Kelly had seen her with her own eyes, leaving in a canoe with Mitch.

It had to be Mitch; the hat, the screwdriver from the lumber camp, probably used to dismantle the bed so it could be dumped in the bog. He'd even left a note. Some crazy shit about Sarah Punk, Mulvane, and Lucy Dee. Strange note, and with it, a picture of Crogan, who was now floating in the slime just a few feet away. Ten to one, the other guy was Mulvane.

Sarah wasn't a ghost. She was a witch. She possessed some kind of primal hoodoo that gave her power over people like Mitch. Kelly was certain that Sarah had set up the ambush, had drawn the fish into the barrel, and then stood on the dock and watched as Mitch blew them away.

"Why?" she asked out loud.

Gail didn't answer. She lay tightly wrapped in the space blanket, eyes closed, her breathing slow and shallow.

Backwoods justice? Punishing the men for the things she'd seen them do? The men who had polluted her bog with the body of their victim?

Kelly's thoughts gave her no comfort. Death outside the door, the stink rising again as the rain let up. Death hovering over Gail. Maybe Sarah was more than a spectator in the whole squalid game of kidnapping, rape, and murder. Maybe she had a reason to shut up Mulvane and Crogan for good. Maybe she wasn't the only one.

Sarah, Mitch, the swingers, Hack Weechum, and at

least two deputies were mixed up in this shit one way or another. Who else?

"They have all been fucking with me," she said. "I knew it from the first day."

Everyone on the whole God-forsaken lake; Mrs. Cross and Mrs. Mulvane with their bogus complaint against Bobby Margin, the sheriff not challenging them. Mitch, Mrs. Parker, even Patricia and Gisela, all acting like Sarah was a ghost when they all knew that she was deadly and real. Boodrow, the sneaky son of a bitch, he had to be in on it too.

"Gail! Kelly!" Sheriff Herkemer's voice from the boardwalk was cautious and hopeful.

Kelly tucked Gail's hand under the blanket and stood up slowly. She felt pretty solid, all things considered. Peering out one of the slits, she saw the sheriff, with Maclean behind him, moving cautiously towards her, weapons drawn.

"Hullo! Deputy Mackinaw, Gail, are you there?"

The service revolver in her belt had one round left. She checked the mag on Gail's Smith & Wesson then tucked it into her belt behind her back. The spare mag in her back pocket.

"Hullo, it's Sheriff Herkemer, are you okay?"

Rescue had finally arrived and now she felt reluctant to reveal herself. She considered opening fire first. Why take chances?

Get a grip, girl. She wiped the sweat from her face with the palm of her hand. You've had a rough twenty-four hours. You're not thinking straight.

She took a deep breath and called out, "In here, Sheriff. Gail's been shot."

She was overly paranoid, making wild assumptions. Maybe.

Be cool, be quiet, and watch your back. Around here, if you trust the wrong people, you end up with swamp water in your brain.

Mitch let the smoke drift from his lips, doing his best to suppress a cough. "Local grown, right?" he said, in a shallow, constricted voice.

Hack Weechum took the joint from his hand. "I sell it, man, I don't smoke it myself, usually, but things are tight right now."

"You do what you gotta do, man," Mitch said in a soft, diplomatic voice, watching as Hack's rough, dirty fingers placed the joint between his thin lips and drew. The ragged fingernails reminded him of Mary Ann.

Lots of family resemblance; Hack had the same restless, black eyes as his cousin, so dark that the iris was swallowed by the pupil. But unlike Sarah's, his moved together all the time. He was much bigger than her, his hair darker and thicker, but he had the same animal leanness, the same smell of muddy water and gun smoke. Shiner around his left eye, scratches in his beard. No surprises there.

Mitch sat on the floor, back against a pine-panelled wall, knees up. Hack squatted in front of him, balanced and comfortable. He didn't appear to be armed, but Mitch suspected he had a gun tucked safely behind his back.

"I bet you've got some real good shit," Hack said, returning the joint, extending his arm almost full length so Mitch could take it.

Mitch smiled. "Man, I got Northern Lights, Thai, Acapulco Gold. You come over to the camp, I'll show you."

Hack nodded. Same misty aura as Mary Ann; a faded, white cloud shot through with electric-blue streaks, throbbing like a boss engine on idle. "I figured you were a generous guy," he said. "Sorry we had to tie you up, man."

"That's cool." Mitch brought the joint to his lips, the rope handcuffs making it awkward, but not unmanageable.

Drained and outgunned, they had taken him without a fight. His hands had been tied, and he'd been brought downstairs to an empty room. Once they had him sitting on the linoleum, Mr. Mulvane had fashioned rope shackles for his ankles, then wrapped his knees tightly with duct tape for good measure.

Hack had sent Mr. Mulvane back upstairs, but Mrs. Mulvane remained, leaning against a square pillar in the middle of the room, once again in possession of her husband's Python.

"Just till you've cooled down a little, so you and me can come to an understanding," Hack said.

"I can dig it."

Mitch worked at staying cool. He relaxed his muscles, withdrew his senses inwards, away from the contact points with the restraints. The trick was to convince your body that it was comfortable, there was nothing it wanted to do, nowhere it wanted to go. Don't fight the ropes, don't even test them. Deny their existence.

"Look, I need you to be straight with me," Hack said. "No fucking around." The harsh weed cut some of the foulness of his breath.

"Lay it on me, man. What can I do for you?" Mitch replied.

"You were at Rae Parker's last night."

"Yeah, my canoe got swamped, she took me in."

"Bobby Margin there?"

From experience, Mitch knew that lying in this kind of situation was just a waste of time. He didn't see any point in wasting time right now. "Yeah, he was around. Hanging out," he said.

"And Mary Ann."

"Yeah."

"How they all doing?"

Mitch thought about that for a second. "Armed to the teeth. Expecting trouble," he said.

"From who?"

"You, mostly."

Hack took the roach from Mitch before it burned his fingers and dropped it to the floor. He rocked on the balls of his feet. "Yeah, there's been some serious misunderstandings around here lately," he said in a regretful tone. "And now we got a situation could turn into a flat-out war. I ain't got time for that."

"No one wants that, man."

"Holly told me how you tried to help her and Denny clear out. You'd like to keep this whole thing from going south, wouldn't you, save some lives?"

Mitch couldn't see Mrs. Mulvane's face in the gloom, only her relaxed stance and the glow of her cigarette. The cottage was very quiet. No music, no voices, no headboards slamming against the wall. He hadn't seen Crogan or Mr. Cross, but he had to figure that they'd returned with Hack and were upstairs now, along with Faber, Mr. Mulvane, and Denny.

That was a lot of fucked-up people to have in the mix. Who do you back with all that A-type testosterone swirling around under pressure? It looked like Mrs. Mulvane was putting her money on the local boy with the hard body and merciless eyes.

"Absolutely, man," Mitch said.

"Good. All you gotta do is take a message to Bobby. Tell him we're even, man, no hard feelin's, no grudges. He can have Denny. She's got a car and money. They can take off, go on a road trip, go to Vegas, go to fucking Disneyland, anything he wants."

Mitch hadn't seen that one coming. He didn't doubt that Denny would want to go with Bobby, get away from this place and these people. But it couldn't be as simple as that.

"What about her husband?"

"He's not going to be any trouble, Bobby knows that. People around here have come to their senses and figured out that the best way to keep Bobby quiet is to give him what he wants."

"He wants Denny?"

"Of course, man. She's the reason he came back this summer, even though he was told it could get him killed. Man, I've never seen a guy lose it so badly over a piece of tail. After all the shit that happened last year? He still couldn't leave her alone."

Mitch remembered Mrs. Ratsmueller saying something like that. He remembered the Polaroid of Bobby and Denny up against a wall. "How's he gonna trust you after what happened at Steep Rock?"

"You tell Bobby, no more tricks from these guys. It's been tried, man, and it didn't work out, okay, you win. He gets Denny, he keeps his mouth shut, and they get the hell out of here, today, and don't ever come back."

It seemed to Mitch they were overlooking one big factor. "What about Mary Ann?"

Hack stood up, one smooth movement. He looked down at Mitch, frowning, anger in his voice. "Bobby doesn't give a shit about her, man. He's just fucking with her, takin' advantage of her big-hearted nature." He kicked Mitch's boot.

"Be cool, man, just askin'."

"He'll run off with that dippy slut in a heartbeat. I'll look after Mary Ann like I always done. All you gotta do is take the message and come back here with the answer."

Mitch thought about the picture of Mary Ann tied up in the Hell Hole. Rae said it was Hack who took that picture. Bobby knew that. Would Bobby really dump Mary Ann after all she'd done for him? Leave her to Hack?

Hack kicked him again. "What's your problem, man?" he said, sharp, almost a shout.

"No problem, man. It's just, I gotta piss like a racehorse. How am I supposed to think straight?"

A switchblade appeared in Hack's hand. Before Mitch could flinch, or even breathe, he slashed the taut duct tape around Mitch's knees with a single stroke.

Hack smiled; anger snuffed out like a warning flare hitting the water. "Hey, man, nobody can think when they gotta go." He offered Mitch his hand.

Mrs. Mulvane took a step from the pillar and aimed the Python at Mitch's head as he stood up.

"Holly can help you out, man. I got some things to deal with. I'll be back in a few minutes."

"Sure, right on, man."

Hack held out his hand to Mrs. Mulvane. "Better give me that," he said. "He tries to molest you, just shout really loud, I'll come runnin'."

Smart; never leave a prisoner alone with an armed guard, especially one with fluid loyalties. Mrs. Mulvane handed Hack the Python. She looked at Mitch, hands on her hips.

"Washroom's that way," she said, motioning with

her head. "I'll help you with your zipper, but I'm not holding your dick."

Mitch started shuffling towards the door. "No one asked you to, man," he said.

Hack's laugh, an eerie echo of Mary Ann's, bounced off the walls as he headed up the stairs.

CHAPTER
FORTY-FIVE

Mitch fumbled with the hem of his fatigue shirt, trying to get at his belt. His head was clear; Hack's local shit hadn't even given him a buzz, but with the palms of his hands tied facing each other, he was helpless.

He turned to Mrs. Mulvane, leaning on the doorframe of the small washroom. "Seriously, man, I can't do this," he said.

"I can see that," she replied, her tone friendly again. Very deftly, she undid his belt and pulled down his zipper.

"Looks like Hack came back," Mitch said.

She pulled his damp fatigue pants and boxers down past his butt. "Yes, I was as surprised as you."

"Did Crogan come with him?"

She returned to the door. "No, and Hal didn't come back either. They ran out on us."

"Who's here now?"

"Steve, Hack, Mick, and Denny. Boo Boodrow and Dan were supposed to show up, but they haven't yet."

Mitch, who had spent years in the army, had no problem going with someone watching. Mrs. Mulvane, who had seen more than her fair share of dicks, didn't look away.

"Why would they come here?" Mitch asked.

"To go after Bobby again."

He finished and shook himself as best he could. Mrs. Mulvane came in close, tucked him back into his boxers, and carefully zipped him up.

"So, we're still friends," Mitch said.

"I have the keys to the Jeep in my pocket," she replied quietly.

"Right on, untie me."

"There's no time, and it's better if Hack does it anyway."

He was surprised that Hack had left them alone; either he couldn't read auras, or he had some good reason to trust Mrs. Mulvane that Mitch didn't know about. His bush hat had fallen over his forehead; she pushed it back so she could look into his eyes.

"Once you're in the woods, I'll slip away," she whispered. "You double back, and I'll meet you on the road in front of the Dee Cottage. We'll get out of this damn place together."

"You don't think Hack's plan is going to work? Hand over Denny, stop the feud?"

"With these crazy people? Not a chance. But we

need to stay on Hack's good side until he lets you go. The others listen to him."

"What do you need me for?"

"We'll talk about that, come on."

"What about your husband?"

"Fuck him. Fuck all of them, Mitch. Fuck them for the shit they did while my back was turned."

"What shit?"

"Never mind, come on." She took him by the arm and led him back to the rec room, matching his baby steps, the rope shackles giving him only about a foot of play. "I suspect he wants to use Dan and his big Caddy to get him past the checkpoints. It doesn't matter if his plan works, as long as it gives us a chance to get away," she said.

She pointed to the far end of the room where there was a heavy, overstuffed couch, a couple of armchairs, and a big ottoman covered in gold velour. "Over there, sit down," she said as she headed for the bar.

Mitch went to the wall between the couch and the ottoman to take a good look at the windows. If he went up on tiptoe, the bottom of the window was at his eye level. It was still twilight outside. He had no idea what time it was—late morning, noon? The hard rain had turned to drizzle. There was little to see: some bushes, the ground dropping away to the lake, the flagstone steps off to the right. Thunder rumbled in the distance. Outside, the heat was rising rapidly, the storm's next furious outburst building up in the west.

"That's no good," Mrs. Mulvane said from behind the bar. "Even I couldn't squeeze through there."

It wasn't just that the windows were narrow. They had a solid frame in the middle, forming three boxes about two feet long and a foot and a half wide, double-paned and screened.

"We kept getting broken into during the off-season," she added, lighting up a cigarette.

Mitch turned away from the wall and started towards her. "Anything back there you could use to cut these ropes?"

"No, Mitch, can you settle down for one minute?"

He perched on the thin seat of a long-legged stool, resting his elbows on the bar. His hands were red and starting to swell. When Mrs. Mulvane covered them with hers, he hardly felt her touch. She leaned towards him, conspiratorial rather than seductive. She had cleaned the make-up from her face; she looked harder now, the redness in her eyes ugly to look at.

"Listen, Mitch, you have the wrong idea about me."

He looked past her. There were glass shelves behind the bar, a couple of decorative plates, and a few heavy-looking steins.

"Mitch, look at me."

He looked at her, wondering how many plans she had going on in her mind.

"I didn't kill Lucy. I may have gotten fed up with her and left before I should have, but I never fed her any pills. She was fine when I left her. Anything she took after that was by her own hand, or somebody else's. Not mine, I swear."

Mitch was having trouble reading her aura; it had retreated in the presence of the more aggressive ones in the cottage, and his perception had been weakened by his surrender to violence upstairs. There was a hint of frustration in her voice, like you hear from people who can't understand why they are not being believed.

"Think about it, Mitch. If I'd killed Lucy, do you think I would have left without the pictures?"

Fuck. The pictures. The ones he was supposed to be burning right now.

Mrs. Mulvane lifted his face by the chin. "Everybody thinks Bobby took them and has them hidden at the Parker place, but you found them, didn't you?"

Mitch let his head rest in her hand. "I didn't find them; Lucy's ghost showed me where they were. *She* believes you killed her."

Mrs. Mulvane let go of his chin. "Don't talk nonsense, Mitch, for Christ's sake. This is serious."

Nonsense? He'd been doing K-4, Zoomers, and Guerreo that night, not the best shit for communing with the dead. It was possible, under the circumstances, that there had been some miscommunication.

He kicked himself again for not grabbing some peyote before skinning out of Casa Grande. The details were fuzzy, but there must have been a reason. He'd been in a hurry. People were trying to kill him. There might have been a woman…

"Son of a bitch," Kelly swore, pushing at a soft, red blister on the side of her big toe. Her feet were as pale and gross as the fish she'd seen swimming in Shaker's Bog and stank just as badly.

"I will attend to that in just a moment, ma'am, if you will be patient," the young medic replied as he carefully dabbed at the inch-long welts on her right calf.

"I haven't got all day, Jonathan, right?"

Kelly sat on the floor of a Wanakena County Ambulance with Jonathan kneeling in front of her, bent over her outstretched leg.

"Yes, ma'am."

"Ouch," Kelly's leg jerked as the mercurochrome was firmly applied.

The Wanakena County Ambulance Corps routinely dealt with casualties in remote locations, often several hours away from the hospital in Trapper Lake. They came prepared to deal with a wide variety of injuries on the spot. Jonathan, a Quaker and conscientious objector, had attended to Kelly with Germanic efficiency and detachment.

While his partner and the crew from a second ambulance were struggling to bring Gail out of Shaker's Bog by stretcher, he had wrapped Kelly's ribs, applied ointment to her swollen lip, bandaged the cuts over her left eye, and sewn nine stitches into her arm. He had given her shots, eye drops and pills. He had even provided her with a pair of clean, dry socks.

The back doors of the ambulance were open, a mosquito net draped over the opening to keep the relentless bugs at bay. The smell of rain-washed grass, antiseptic, and cigar smoke reduced, but couldn't smother, the odor of decay that rose from her body and clothes. Radios spoke in harsh metallic bursts from the open windows of two patrol cars where Sheriff Herkemer and a State Police troop commander stood with their heads close together. When he had arrived, the troop commander had come over to Kelly and shook her hand. He told her she'd done a damn fine job, and vehemently promised that they would get the bastards who did this to her and Gail.

Blue and red flashing lights tinged the storm-twilight sky up the hill where Shallow Rock Road entered the silent village. Weechum had tried to kill one of their own, the boys were gathering up there, straining at the leash. A black Ford pickup slewed to a stop behind the State Patrol car, throwing up clods of mud and grass. Sheriff Herkemer and the major glanced towards it, then returned to their conversation. Boodrow got out of his truck and stared at the ambulance as he strapped on his patrol belt. He made a tentative wave towards Kelly, then joined the sheriff.

Kelly returned to drying her feet, rubbing them vigorously with a rough towel, digging in painfully between her toes where the rot had already set in.

Jonathan worked without comment on the scratches the demon bed had made on her calf.

When she was finished drying her feet, Kelly looked up. Boodrow was coming towards her. "That's good enough," she said to Jonathan. "Can you look at these blisters now, please," she said, pulling back her leg and rolling down her pant leg.

She raked her hair with her fingers, dragging it back into a stiff ponytail. Boodrow ducked under the bug net and sat just inside. He placed a box of .38 shells on the floor.

"From what I heard, I figured you'd need a reload," he said with a grin. His chipper attitude was a little forced.

Jonathan capped the mercurochrome bottle. "The deputy will be going to the hospital as soon as the other casualty arrives," he said.

Boodrow, looking at Kelly, raised an eyebrow. "Yeah, right," he said.

It annoyed her how much she appreciated that. She was also annoyed by his appearance. He looked pretty fresh for a man who had just come off the night shift and probably hadn't slept in twenty-four hours. Obviously, he'd had time for a quick shave at the station before he was relieved. His uniform was clean and barely wrinkled.

"How's Gail?" he asked.

Kelly shook her head. "Pretty bad, but I think she'll live."

She had come out more or less on her own steam with some help from the sheriff. It had been hard leaving Gail lying there with Maclean, but there was nothing she could do for her. If she was going to catch Weechum, she had to get out of Shaker's Bog.

On the way out of the Bog, the sheriff had filled her in on his trip to Snowshoe Lake. It turned out that Faber had been living down there at his aunt's cottage while she was away. The neighbors reported that Weechum had been staying there too, off and on, before he became a fugitive. There had been a loud party Saturday night, visitors arriving in a couple of muscle cars and a white Lincoln Continental and staying till daylight. The last time anyone had seen the two men was in the early hours of Wednesday morning.

"You look like you've been in a brawl," Boodrow said.

"A couple of them," she replied, anger and accusation in her voice.

Boodrow heard it. "What?" he said.

The feelings came from her gut, but she wasn't sure they were justified. She jerked as Jonathan lanced a blister.

Boodrow wouldn't leave it be. "You got a problem with me?" he demanded.

"Nah, no problems."

"No problems? You cut me out of everything last night. Going over my head to Gail like that makes me look like a fucking idiot. What the hell did I do to deserve that?"

"Now's not the time to get into it."

"Damn it, Kelly, I want to know what you've got against me, when all I've done since you got here is try to help you out and watch your back."

"You were screwing me around."

"*Me* screwing *you* around? You shut down the radio on me. Just like that. No explanation, left me fucking hanging."

"You gave me the wrong address."

"The hell I did. You wrote it down wrong. You were tired, remember; we both were."

"You didn't want me to go to Crogan's. Did you know what I'd find?" she demanded.

"Fuck off. Is that it; you think I'm involved with those assholes? It was a shitty night and a shitty job to lay on a rookie. Waverly was screwing you around, I was trying to do you a favor," he replied, angrily.

Jonathan, his ears turning bright red, scowled, and sliced open another blister. Kelly didn't flinch, her eyes on Boodrow. "All that shit on the radio; you were stalling me."

"Because I figured Crogan was going to drag his ass into the station any minute and put an end to the bullshit," he replied, swiping impatiently at the mosquito netting. "Why didn't you tell me that you'd been attacked?"

"You didn't want me to go to the Hell Hole either."

"And how did that turn out?"

Kelly scowled, looked down at her wrinkled feet

and watched Jonathan apply a small bandage to the little pink blotch that had appeared.

"You were too quick to get us out of there yesterday. We missed the body."

"That was my fault? Come on."

He was right. She had wanted to get out of there as much as he did. She was grasping at straws now. "Crogan and Faber..."

"They're not my buddies! I wasn't on shift with them. What, because I'm the same age? Those guys hadn't even started high school when I graduated. Jesus, cut me a little slack here."

Kelly looked up at him, her eyes narrow, jaw tight, clenching and unclenching her right hand. Last night it had been clear to her that he'd had something to do with the attack, but there was nothing concrete to back up her suspicion. That made her feel guilty and uneasy.

Boodrow threw out his arms. "What, is it my mustache?"

Kelly had to bite her lip to keep from laughing. "Yeah, it kinda is," she replied.

"Well, fuck me!"

She hated his thick, Burt Reynolds mustache. Not just the hair, but the whole macho, smart-ass attitude that it implied. Boodrow hadn't been that much of a jerk, really. He'd been pretty decent yesterday when she'd been puking her guts out.

"I am done here. You should rest now, Deputy,"

Jonathan said. "You should not be doing any vigorous activity until you've had your head examined." He backed out of the ambulance, giving Boodrow a pinched-faced look of disapproval as he pushed past him.

"Smoke 'em if you got 'em, Scooter," Boodrow said.

Just like Burt Reynolds. That didn't mean he was mixed up in rape and murder.

Jonathan took his bag and head up, walked over to the other ambulance. There was a silence between them, a slow resumption of normal breathing, a lowering of heat after confrontation. Kelly began putting her socks on. Boodrow took one of her boots and shook it out for her.

The wail of a siren announced the arrival of another State Patrol car up on the hill. "Looks like we're gonna have a hell of a party," Boodrow said. "Word is Crogan and Faber, acting on an anonymous tip, were trying to recover a body from the bog when Weechum and his partner ambushed them. You and Gail caught them in the act, you fought them, but they got away."

Kelly stopped with the second sock hooked on her toes. "That's not how it happened. Weechum interrupted *us*," she said. "He tried to kill us, but he didn't kill Crogan. And there's no way the other guy in the water is Faber. Faber was probably the guy with the M-16 who shot up Gail's face." She frowned. "The sheriff knows that."

Boodrow shrugged. "That's how he reported it. Maybe he didn't hear your story right."

"No way. He saw the scene at the Hell Hole. We talked about it, we discussed what happened. Why the fuck would he say that?"

"Sounds to me like he doesn't want to muddy the waters. Maybe he's just trying to simplify things; keep everybody focused on Weechum. We know he's a killer."

Kelly took the wet boot from Boodrow and eased it onto her foot. "Before the shooting started, Weechum said he was being framed."

Boodrow had her other boot; he loosened the laces. "If it's not Faber in the bog, then who is it?"

"Ten to one, it's Mr. Mulvane."

"You still think the swingers were that involved in all this shit?"

"With the hitchhikers, yeah." She began lacing up.

"Then who do you think killed them?"

"I have some ideas. Who do you think the sheriff's covering for?" She spoke as casually as she could, bent forward, looking down at her laces. Boodrow didn't answer. She looked up at him again. "If you want me to trust you, I've got to know what's going on. You've got to tell me all the shit that nobody's telling me."

He looked over at the sheriff, then slid closer to her. He spoke quietly. "About two months ago there was an incident down in Arizona. Some kind of drug rip-off gone bad. Couple of people were killed, a bunch of people were arrested."

"Mitch?"

He nodded. "Sheriff Herkemer flew out there and had a little father-to-father talk with the good sheriff of Pinal County. He told him about how Mitch was a war hero and all. Good, clean-cut, country boy trying to get his life together. Decent guy, no criminal record, too naïve for his own good. Might have fallen in with the wrong people without knowing it, more likely he just happened to be in the wrong place at the wrong time."

"What were the charges?"

"They were dropped, against Mitch anyways. What we heard through the grapevine was, they were serious; weapons, assault."

"Drugs?"

"Nothing about possession. The sheriff flew back; Mitch came home a few weeks later and moved into the lumber camp."

"Somebody could have fucking told me that before I moved in with him," she said.

"There was nothing to tell. We'd just be spreading rumors about the sheriff's son."

Kelly took the second boot from Boodrow. This time she looked him in the eye. "What does Mitch Herkemer have to do with the dead bodies in Shaker's Bog?"

"It's complicated."

"Give me the highlights."

Boodrow stroked his mustache. "Mitch was an odd kid..."

"No shit."
"Into the supernatural, folk tales, ghost stories."
"Sarah Punk?"
"Yeah."
Kelly closed her eyes. It was all about Sarah Punk.

CHAPTER
FORTY-SIX

"Mitch?" Mrs. Mulvane snapped her fingers in front of his half-closed eyes.

"What?"

"Did you keep them?"

"The pictures? Yeah." Man, hadn't he already had this conversation.

"I'll give you ten thousand dollars for them."

"That's why you need me, the pictures."

She was staring at him intently, like it was some kind of negotiation. "I don't have the money on me. I'll sign over the ownership of the Jeep to you as a down payment."

"What shit?"

"What?" she snapped, giving her head a frustrated shake.

"What shit were they getting into behind your back?"

She sighed. "I don't know." She took a deep drag from her Virginia Slim.

Mitch waited.

Blowing smoke to the side, she turned to look at him. "It wasn't enough for the bastards—the orgies, the costume parties, the weed. Around the time that they hooked up with Steve and Miles, they started doing harder drugs. Dan turned mean, started getting rough. That's when I backed away. The boys started going out late at night; sometimes we wouldn't see them until morning. I thought Weechum was fixing them up with young hookers."

"It had to be worse than that to want to kill Bobby."

"I didn't know. I don't want to know…"

"You set Bobby up to die, and you didn't even know why?"

"They weren't going to kill him. Just rough him up and scare him so he'd turn over the pictures. That was the plan. Then all hell broke loose."

"Mary Ann," Mitch said with a chuckle. "So, you just wanted to beat the shit out of the kid. No problem, man."

She straightened up, new lines of worry forming around her mouth.

"Why do you want them? For blackmail?" Mitch asked.

"No, I want to destroy them. They're disgusting; I don't want them ending up in the press, or… anywhere."

"What if I burn them?"

"Okay, as long as I watch you do it. I want to stir the ashes."

"You'd pay me ten thousand for that?"

"Yes."

He would have found it funny, except that he was beginning to doubt that those pictures would ever be burned. They had a karma all their own, and it was fireproof, man.

"Okay, I'm in. You and me, Holly. But first you gotta loosen me up, just in case something goes wrong."

She stubbed out her cigarette, looked towards the door into the empty room. "I don't know knots," she said.

"Give it a try."

Blue nylon rope was wound four times around each of his arms just above the wrists, the wrists forced together tightly by three more loops in between them. Mitch had never seen anything like it, the work of a professional. From his angle, there didn't appear to be any knot at all, the rope disappearing into itself like a snake eating its tail.

Mrs. Mulvane lifted his hands to look at the underside, shook her head. "My *husband* did that." She worried at the rope half-heartedly.

"Get my legs then, go on, do it," Mitch said, impatience giving an edge to his voice. He stood up, knocking over the stool as she came around from behind the bar. "Go on," he said, fighting to control himself.

She dropped down to her knees. "This looks simple enough, but if I untie you, Hack..."

Mitch twisted to get a look, resting his hand on the top of her head for balance. "Untie it, then make a loose knot. Doesn't matter, it's just for show. Come on."

She began working the knot. "You better remember I did this for you."

As soon as he felt the ropes loosen, he shoved her backwards and forced his ankles apart. Mrs. Mulvane fell on her ass with an angry grunt. "Mitch, what are you doing?"

He kicked at the ropes until they came free. "Hack's not gonna freak just because I got my legs free," he said.

Mrs. Mulvane stood up and backed away from him. "What are you going to do now?"

"I don't know," he replied, forcing himself to stand still.

She took a few more steps back, then glared at him, hands on her hips. "If you come near me, I'll scream."

"Be cool, man. We're still friends, right? Nothing's changed."

"You're taking a hell of a chance. *If* he lets you go, you better double back and meet me. I'll wait ten minutes at the Dee Cottage. If you don't show up, I'm going to go to the lumber camp. I'll burn the whole damned place to the ground."

Thunder rolled in the west, loud enough to be heard in the basement, reminding them of how quiet the cottage had become. The single light went out, the fan slowed.

"There goes the power," Mrs. Mulvane said. She looked at her watch. "Hack should have been back by now. I'd better go see what's going on."

Mitch took a step towards her. "Just fucking cut me loose, man," he said, keeping his voice low.

"Not now. Just stay here. Let me see what's happening. If we have a shot, I'll get a knife and be right back."

She didn't wait for a reply; she turned and left the room very quickly, almost at a run.

"Help me out here," Kelly said, sliding her patrol belt to the edge of the ambulance.

Boodrow threw the mosquito net up onto the top of the ambulance and gave her a hand. She stood and stretched, testing out Jonathan's tape job on her ribs. It was good to get out of the steamy confines of the ambulance. Sweat slithered about under her damp clothes.

She looked up into the murk. There was no sky; they lived inside a dark cloud slowly filling with water. She washed her face with her hands, wishing the rain wasn't so hot. Over the past forty-eight hours she had become so used to being wet, she felt like a reptile.

Putting Gail's gun down on the ambulance deck, she undid her belt, unzipped her uniform trousers and began tucking in her shirt, smoothing it out over the irritating grooves that had been dug into her skin.

Boodrow made a point of looking away.

Kelly looked over her shoulder as she zipped up; the sheriff and the major had moved apart. They looked like they were arguing, their words drowned out by the hot wind that had begun tearing at the trees. The tempo of the rain increased again, forcing them to duck back under the roof of the ambulance. They sat on the edge of the deck with the netting up, the rain beating down the bugs.

"What does Mitch's interest in Sarah Punk have to do with the three bodies in Shaker's Bog?" she asked.

"You heard about the bush plane that went down there, back in '52?"

"Yeah, belonged to the Margin brothers."

He nodded. "Mitch was on the dock of the lumber camp when that happened. He threw himself into the lake, tried to drown himself. When Archie fished him out, the kid came up babbling shit about Sarah Punk and Baby Moses. Must have been four, five years old."

"So what?" she said.

Boodrow opened the box of shells and began slipping them into the loops in her patrol belt. "So, when he got older, he kept going out to Shaker's Bog, pretty soon he wound up at Rae Parker's place. Have you met her?"

"No."

"Lotta' woman there. I mean, there's something... powerful, scary about her."

Kelly shrugged. "Okay."

"There's been stories about her for years. About how her two husbands and her son died, about how she always had a bunch of young Shallow Rock kids hanging around her place. That she had sex with them, let them drink and smoke dope. And not just fucking around, cult stuff. Earth-Mother-Goddess shit."

Kelly gave him a disgusted look. "Why didn't somebody do something about it?"

A sudden burst of radio traffic caught their attention. The major was talking into a hand mike stuck out the window of his car.

Boodrow finished with her belt and started on the empty chambers of her revolver. "It was all rumors, just crazy talk going around. Too freaky to be real. Anyway, it was only Shallow Rock kids, so who cares, right?"

"And Mitch. What about his dad?"

"Archie was a deputy at the time." Boodrow returned the loaded revolver to her holster. "I was just a kid, but I heard my uncle talking with the other deputies about it. They said he went through a rough patch after his wife died. They said he had a soft spot for Rae Parker."

"He slept with her?"

"That's another rumor. A lot of people figured that was why he bought the old camp in the middle of nowhere, to be close to her. Anyway, he didn't have a problem with Mitch hanging around with Rae."

Something was wrong there. Kelly remembered the performance Mitch had put on, telling her the Sarah Punk story. It was obvious that the point of the story was to keep Mitch and the other kids away from Shaker's Bog and Shallow Rock.

"You're telling me about things that went on twenty years ago. Ancient history," she said.

A car door slammed. They both turned and watched as the state patrol car took off. Sheriff Herkemer was coming towards them in a hurry, his feet slipping on the wet grass. Kelly stood up and strapped on her patrol belt. She felt pretty solid on her feet, the familiar belt and the wet clothes keeping her tight and upright.

Boodrow stood up, put his hands on her shoulders. "Not ancient history, Kelly, *family* history—the deadliest kind of all. Keep that in mind, okay. A lot of kids passed through there, most of them moved on, a few became very close. Mary Ann and the motherless boys, Hack, Mitch, and Bobby; they were a family."

"Mary Ann?"

The sheriff was only a few feet away. Boodrow stepped away from her and turned towards the boss. Sheriff Herkemer was red-faced and sweating heavily. Beneath the brim of his plastic-covered campaign hat, his eyes were weary and harassed.

"They're going in." He spoke loudly to be heard

over the sound of the rain beating on the roof of the ambulance.

Kelly shook her head. "He's not there."

"I know. He's probably at Lost Lake. But the major figures if he's there, he's trapped. The only way out is through Woodbine, and we've got that covered. He wants to clear Shallow Rock first, then if we have to, sweep Lost Lake. It's his show. I have to go with him. If his boys start kicking down doors in Shallow Rock, it'll be a bloodbath."

"So, he figures if Hack is at Lost Lake, he's already in the bag," Boodrow said.

"Yeah, he's in the bag, and there are a bunch of innocent people in there with him," the sheriff replied.

Not all innocent, Kelly thought. Not by a long shot.

"The phones are out. Rae Parker can look after herself, so can Mrs. Anderson and Mrs. Ratsmueller, if they're warned. No telling what's going on with those other people. They may be helping him. Maybe he's taken hostages," the sheriff said.

"I'll go," Boodrow said. "I have my CB and scanner; I can relay through Betty."

"Good, just find out what's going on. Get a fix on the bastard, but don't try to take him alone. Just give us a heads up if he runs."

"I'll go with him," Kelly said. There was no time to challenge the sheriff about his account of what happened at the Hell Hole. It didn't matter right now;

Weechum, Faber, and Mitch were at Lost Lake; that was where she needed to be.

"You're going to the hospital," the sheriff said.

"I'm okay, Sheriff."

"I could use her help," Boodrow said.

Up on the hill, someone began speaking through a bullhorn. The sheriff looked at his watch. "Hell, Gail isn't even out of there yet." For an instant he stood looking past Crogan's truck towards Shaker's Bog.

"We're going now, Sheriff," Boodrow said.

"Yes, right, get going." He turned and headed for his patrol car.

There was a loud crack of thunder to the west, sharp and stunning, like a jet breaking the sound barrier. The sheriff stopped and turned back towards them.

"See if you can find out what the hell is happening with Mitch," he shouted. "I swear that boy has a goddamned *talent* for standing directly in front of the fan whenever shit is coming down the pipe."

CHAPTER
FORTY-SEVEN

"Mitch was a war hero?" Kelly asked as she opened the passenger door of Boodrow's pickup.

"Well, around here anyways," Boodrow replied.

Kelly climbed carefully into the hot cab, shut the door, and immediately cranked down the window all the way. He had a very clean truck for a single guy. No crap on the floor, no cigarette butts in the ashtray, no rips in the shaggy seat covers. All of the dashboard surfaces were clean and shiny. The gun rack in the back window held a spotless M-1 carbine.

Boodrow settled himself behind the wheel. "He had a couple of medals, Bronze Star, I think. And a Purple Heart. He was in the local paper lots of times back in '68."

She wiped rain from her face.

"Mitch got the medal because he was captured, for

like a day, then they got bombed by our own guys, or something. He got away and brought a couple of guys out with him," Boodrow said.

"Is that when he got the Purple Heart?"

"I guess. Got some shrapnel in the side of the head, concussion," he turned the ignition. The truck fired up with a nice, even roar.

The sheriff had told her that Mitch had landed in Nam in January of '68. "Right at the beginning of Tet," she said.

Boodrow worked the long stick into reverse. Looking over his shoulder, he asked, "Tet, what was that?"

"*Big*, fucking shit storm."

Boodrow chuckled. "Well, there you go."

Wrong fucking place at the wrong fucking time.

Mitch drove his shoulder up under the long glass shelf. It flew off its brackets, skinned the top of his head, and shattered against the bar behind him. One of the decorative plates followed, breaking loudly. The second plate bounced painfully off his knee.

Swearing, he crouched down behind the bar and listened. It was hard to hear now; the wind had taken hold of the cottage and was shaking it, howling around its corners and under its eaves. Faintly, he could hear the sound of footsteps crossing the floor above him. He couldn't hear any voices.

He found a good shard, about six inches long with a sharp edge, and sat against the wall with his knees up. Holding the glass between his knees, he began sawing at the underside of the loops that held his hands together.

It was no good; he couldn't hold the shard firmly enough to make any impression on the nylon rope, and it kept slipping between his knees. He tried holding it between his boot heels, bending over it in a tight curl. He made a little progress, but it wasn't good enough.

Time had passed, fifteen or twenty minutes at least. That could only mean one thing: the deal was off. He was on his own. He tried lying down on his stomach and wedging a shorter shard into the corner of the wall just above floor level. No luck.

Plan A had been to follow Mrs. Mulvane, rush past her at the top of the stairs, and take his chances with a dash through the foyer and out into the woods. It had occurred to him too late; he'd made it only halfway up the stairs before he heard her slam and lock the door.

Plan B was to break the shelf and cut himself loose. That wasn't working either. He struggled to his feet and surveyed the room. The pool table.

Grunting and squatting, he searched through the glass until he found a longer piece; a corner piece, four inches wide, with a good seven inches of blade. He lost more time trying to pick it up with his nearly senseless fingers. He had to stop and force himself to breathe. He picked up the glass and took it over to the pool table. After several tries, he had it wedged firmly into a corner pocket with the sharp edge up. Facing the table, he crouched down and started sawing.

Rain hammered at the windows. The wind came panting down the mountainside, bending the trees to the east, then sucking back, yanking everything to the west. In the tense silence between blasts, Mitch thought he could hear Denny singing upstairs. With the power out and the AC off, the basement was starting to heat up. Sweat rolled down his forehead beneath the limp strands of hair that had fallen in his eyes.

The wind retreated again. He heard a heavy door slam shut. Loud voices from the foyer. Stamping boots. Denny had stopped singing, and now someone was talking very loudly. Aggressive, confident; a big-bellied voice.

Mrs. Mulvane was arguing with it and losing.

He started sawing faster, thighs and arms aching, fingers about to burst like boiled frankfurters. The door to the basement banged open. The stairs shuddered under the pounding steps of a heavy man. Mitch started for the door between the rec room and the empty room, trying to head them off so they wouldn't see what he'd been doing. He almost made it.

"Freeze, cocksucker, or I will blow your long-haired, psycho head right off your fucking shoulders!"

A moment of complete bewilderment. Dandy Dan Dee, the gentleman purveyor of fine automobiles throughout the North Country, the guy from the goofy commercials with the top hat and walking stick, standing there as large as life. He wore a gunslinger's belt around his thick waist, the butt of a big pistol sticking out of the holster. Daniel Dee, husband of the late Lucy Dee, filling the doorway, wearing what looked like a camouflage-patterned safari suit.

Holding an AK-47, for fuck's sake.

Mitch briefly registered that Faber and Mrs. Mulvane were standing behind Dan before the solid wooden butt of the Commie assault rifle struck him in the gut.

He doubled over with a groan. Sudden, shocking breathlessness.

Man, you just never got used to that.

CHAPTER
FORTY-EIGHT

Boodrow's Ranger rocked and rattled like a steam locomotive as he took it through a washed-out curve on Lost Lake Road.

"Shit!" Kelly shouted as they drifted past the narrow shoulder. Tree branches raked the passenger door with a hideous screech. She yanked her head away from the window, narrowly avoiding another gash on her head.

"Son of a bitch!" she shouted, hands braced against the narrow dashboard, feet instinctively scrambling to find the brakes.

Boodrow worked the stick, swiftly got the truck back on the oiled-dirt surface and up to speed. Kelly caught herself just short of shouting, "Slow down!"

She tried to look up at the sky through the frantically swishing windshield wipers. It was almost as dark as night again. They slid dangerously around the next curve and barely skinned past a large, swaying maple that beat angrily on their roof as they went by. Kelly took Gail's Smith and Wesson from behind her back, laid it on the floor, and fastened her lap belt. She didn't like seatbelts, but if they ran into anyone coming the other way, she'd be through the windshield and halfway to fucking Mars before she knew what hit her. It was very unlikely that anyone would be on this stretch of road in this weather; still, Boodrow was pushing too hard.

The CB and the police scanner, sitting together on the floor hump, were screeching and hissing at each other like a couple of wildcats trapped in a burning sack.

"Go ahead and turn that off, Christ, it's driving me crazy," Boodrow said.

Kelly flicked them off, one less sound in the symphony of drumming rain, throbbing engine, and flapping windshield wipers. Before it had started to squeal incoherently, the scanner had been alive with reports of multiple shots fired in Shallow Rock. An officer down. A wounded man in custody by the name of Weechum.

"Fat chance," Kelly had shouted.

"Half the people in Shallow Rock are named Weechum, the other half are married to them," Boodrow had replied.

Boodrow geared down to a crawl as they dropped towards one of the Moose River Company's wooden bridges. The roiling water of the unnamed creek was less than an inch below the deck. He took it easy as he started across.

"Who is Mary Ann?" Kelly asked, now that she had a chance.

"Hack's younger cousin, raggedy little thing, but kinda cute in her own way."

"Cute? About four feet tall, long hair, dark eyes?"

"A little taller than that, but yeah. You met her?" Boodrow shot her a quick glance.

"I've seen her around. The kid has a set of lungs."

"That's her. Right, like I was saying, you have Mitch and Hack fighting for momma's attention, and you got freaky little Bobby Margin with a thing for young Mary Ann, which doesn't sit well with Hack."

"How the hell do you know all this?"

Boodrow was hunched over the steering wheel, keeping his eyes on the deck. "I'll get to that, just stick with me," he replied. "Jump forward. Three years ago, the new cottages were built. Rae hated that. They were invading her territory, screwing with her privacy, luring away her children."

Kelly stared out the passenger window and let the rain cool her face. She had almost no way of knowing if anything Boodrow was telling her was true. He kept talking. "I hadn't thought about this for years, then there was the call from the Dee cottage and all that shit at the Hell Hole."

Sweat was seeping from under the bandages over her left eye and starting to sting. Kelly took off the cap that Boodrow had given her to replace her lost campaign hat and wiped her forehead with the palm of her hand. The bandages on the backs of her hands were coming loose. She felt a moment of sickness as scenes from the Hell Hole flashed behind her closed eyes; the Python rising out of the mist, the slug trail of blood leading to the cabin door.

The roar of the creek rushing beneath them was louder than the wind. Boodrow's voice was faint in her ears even though he was speaking in a half-shout. "When I talked to the cottagers yesterday and they told me what had been going on, I started putting things together."

"You didn't tell me any of this," she said without opening her eyes.

"When did I have a chance? I'm telling you now. I figure that right from the first summer, Rae sent Bobby and Mary Ann to spy on the new people, freak them out. They played up the old Sarah Punk story. Got Mary Ann to do some random screaming in the night."

The truck came to a stop. "Okay, this should be fun. I don't carry chains in the summer," he said.

Kelly opened her eyes and sat up straight with a groan. They had come to the end of the bridge. The surface of the road rising sharply in front of them was coated with a sheet of rippling rainwater. Boodrow dropped down into low-lock before going forward, very slowly. He kept talking.

"They scared the shit out of the rich kids. After the

first summer, none of them ever came back to the lake." Boodrow was trying to sound cool, but there was strain in his voice.

Kelly clutched the dashboard again. If they lost momentum and started slipping backwards, it could get tricky. She let go of the dashboard long enough to unbuckle her lap belt again.

"Last summer, Rae turned it up a notch. Had the kids start sneaking into the cottages, even when people were home, stealing little things, you know, or just moving them around."

"Creepy crawly," Kelly shouted. She had read *The Family* from cover to cover, twice.

"Yeah, like the Mansons."

"Just to scare them."

"Yeah, that's how it started out for Charlie and his girls too."

Laughing, Dan put a meaty hand on Mitch's shoulder and flung him back into the room. He landed on his side. Before he could begin to uncurl, Faber kicked him in the head. He was hauled to his feet by the hair. Faber stomped down on the top of his left foot. Mitch jerked it up and hung in Faber's grasp, one footed, head down, arms bound together in front of him as if in prayer.

"Nice fucking hat." Dan's voice boomed at him

from inside a metal echo chamber, setting off a terrible, painful reverb.

Mitch's mind overloaded as it tried to sort through the gaggle of different pains clamoring for attention. He gasped for air. A kick to the side of his knee collapsed his other leg. He fell to his knees and Faber hauled him back to his feet.

"Stop that, you idiot, you'll kill him!" Mrs. Mulvane shouted.

From deep down in the dark pit of pain, Mitch heard a very particular sound. The click of an AK's folding bayonet being snapped into place.

"I'm not going to kill him, I'm just gonna cut his balls off."

"Dan, stop. Stop, for Christ's sake, we need him."

At that moment, Mitch felt something very close to love for Mrs. Mulvane. His head was jerked up, he opened his eyes, but he couldn't see.

"Stop it!" Mrs. Mulvane shouted again. "We need him to talk to Bobby."

"Not anymore. New plan."

Mitch felt a line of fire blaze across his cheek.

"Dan!"

"I ain't gonna kill him. Where else are we going to find our very own murdering, psycho, freak?"

"*That's* the new plan?" she snapped.

"You shut the fuck up!" Faber shouted, getting his two cents in.

"Cutting off his balls might get messy. But does he

really need his tongue? This is for raping my wife," Dan said, and kicked Mitch in the balls.

Mitch fell to the ground, totally helpless, his mind screwed into his body by a one-way circuit cable of pain. He curled in on himself, trying to protect his balls from any further attention.

Gasping, he jerked convulsively as a rough, foul-tasting finger was shoved into the corner of his mouth. He could hear Dan and Faber laughing. He didn't bite; he was too desperately focused on trying to breathe. The fishhook came loose, he swallowed and gasped.

"Holly, give us a hand here. Holly?" Dan said.

"She took off," Faber said.

"Fuckin' bitch! Go after her. Tie her up if you have to. Nobody's running out on us," Dan shouted.

Mitch was perched on the knife edge of total despair. Then it happened. He didn't hear it. He felt it. Even with his eyes closed, his brain all hunkered down in the mud, he felt the bastards freeze.

The scream.

The next thing, he not only heard, he saw it clearly in the darkness of his mind. An acre of glass shattering, a million sharp, glittering pieces hanging in the air, suspended for an instant, then dropping straight down and crashing onto the floor above them.

"She couldn't do that," Faber shouted.

"They're shooting at us, asshole," Dan barked back at him.

Then again, another mighty waterfall; the other double-story window dissolving and raining down.

"*They're* attacking *us*?"

"Fuck 'em, we'll sort this shit out, right fucking now, come on."

"What about him?"

There was another crash, much smaller this time. Then a whoosh, and a whiff of gas.

"Cocksuckers are trying to burn us out! Leave him, we might still use him. Come on, go, go!"

"That's my girl," Boodrow said, patting the steering wheel. "There's a pint in the glove compartment, I think we deserve a little snort." He continued to drive slowly as they shared a couple of slugs of Jim Beam. "The road gets really bad from here on in. Two more bridges to go."

They rounded another tight corner and shuddered to a halt. "Shit. This one is going to be tricky," Boodrow said.

They were on a steep downslope. Muddy water boiled over the deck of the bridge in front of them, pinning a small island of brush against the sagging railing. The smooth white trunk of a birch stuck out of the island at a sharp angle. It had passed above the wooden railing and jammed itself against one of the braces of the truss, completely blocking the roadway.

"It's a whole damned tree, looks like it was torn out by the roots," Boodrow said, as he put the truck into park and pulled the handbrake.

"Part of the bank must have collapsed upstream," Kelly said. "You got a chainsaw?"

Boodrow leaned back in his seat, made a thoughtful face, and scratched the thick hair at the side of his head. "I guess I do," he said, then turned and gave her a wink. "All gassed up and ready to go."

She wasn't surprised. Boodrow always seemed prepared. "Go get it, I'll have a look," she said, deadpan, not wanting to encourage him.

She got out of the truck, swearing at the pain in her ribs. While Boodrow went around to the back, she leaned against the open door and tried to work out some of the stiffness in her body. The back of her left bicep felt like it was caught in the teeth of an eight-inch-long zipper, but otherwise it felt pretty good. She itched all over. She gritted her teeth and ignored the torment. She knew that if she started scratching, she'd never stop.

The bridge creaked as the water and the debris pressed against it. There was some erosion of the soil around the cement footings, but nothing serious, at least at this end. Kelly walked out onto the deck; the water streaming over it came to just above the welts of her boots.

"It looks okay," she shouted back at the headlights of the pickup.

Something had changed. It took her a moment to figure out what it was. The rain had stopped. She walked carefully along the slippery deck, holding on to the railing, until she came to the snagged-up tree trunk. She looked up to where it had lodged against the joint of a vertical beam and a strut. The old wood was creaking loudly; even in the poor light, she could see a few inches of exposed, rusted bolt.

She turned. "Better hurry," she shouted.

Boodrow was a black shape coming towards her. He didn't speak. Lightning flashed in the low sky.

"This thing isn't going to hold much longer," she shouted.

He didn't reply.

A little smile trembled and died on her lips. There was something inherently, irrationally, threatening about a man with a chainsaw. Hollywood knew that. Boodrow knew that.

"Quit fucking around, jerk," she shouted.

Silently, he stalked towards her, shoulders hunched, the chainsaw dangling confidently from his right hand. She was all alone in the middle of nowhere, tree trunk behind her, rushing water on either side and a slippery deck beneath her feet. Gail's automatic was on the floor of the truck.

"Boo, quit fucking around, I mean it."

No answer. He was close now, his face unseen under the brim of his hat.

She didn't need Gail's gun; she had her own. Six shots at close range, no problem. She froze. Drop your guard for just *one* fucking second and life could turn on a *dime*.

Boodrow had reloaded her revolver. With bullets

from a box that *he'd* brought. It had never occurred to her to check them.

"Boo!"

He was almost within swinging distance, right hand going for the pull cord.

She went for her gun. She'd had one round left when she came out of the swamp. Just blast away until she came to it. Unless, he'd changed that one too.

Fuck.

CHAPTER
FORTY-NINE

Boodrow ducked down the instant Kelly's gun came out of its holster. He looked over his shoulder, then whipped back around.

"Hey!" he shouted, coming out of the crouch towards her, chainsaw in hand.

She fired.

"Christ Almighty!" He stood there, upright, absolutely still, wide eyes staring straight at her.

A blank round makes a different sound, has a different kick than a live round. Kelly knew the instant she'd pulled the trigger that she'd fired a live round.

"Who are you shooting at?"

"Holy shit, Boo."

"You were shooting at me?"

Kelly lowered the gun to her side. "Why didn't you say something?"

"When?"

"Just now, coming at me with the chainsaw."

"I couldn't hear what the fuck you were saying."

"Okay, fuck, I'm sorry," she replied, angrily.

"*Coming at* you?" Boodrow exclaimed, his voice rising. "I was *walking* towards you. This thing isn't even on."

"Okay, okay. I missed, alright," Kelly said. The way her hand was shaking, it took her three attempts to holster her gun. Jesus, she'd almost killed the guy.

Boodrow squatted, set the chainsaw down. "Holy fuck," he said, holding his face in his hands.

Kelly stood there stupidly. Fucking paranoia. Also, fuck; he was only five feet away, and she'd missed! Her bruised ribs must have thrown her off balance. Bad judgment, itchy trigger finger, and lousy aim—great way to go into battle.

Head down, Boodrow said "Holy fuck" several more times. Then he took a few deep breaths. Kelly waited, calming herself down. It bothered her that she couldn't recall the instant that she had actually decided to shoot. She just did.

Looking upstream, she scanned the rolling muddy water, looking for more big chunks of debris. The rain had ended, but the creeks around here would keep rising for at least another couple of hours. The bridge was groaning loudly.

"Okay, okay," Boodrow said at last, looking up at her. "I know you've had a really fucking bad couple of days. You're beat. You're rattled, hey, that's natural. We've been pushing you too hard."

"Boo, it's not..."

He held out a hand towards her, palm up and started to rise. "There's all kinds of shit going on, stuff coming at you from every direction. But, man, you have *got* to get over this thing you have about me. For Christ's sake, Kelly."

"I know, I know."

"Maybe talk to me next time before you decide to blow my head off." He bent down, picked up his hat and put it on.

"I was..." she bit her lip.

He picked up the chainsaw. "Okay?"

"Okay. I'm sorry. Can we just leave it? Not tell anyone?"

"I'm not going to tell anyone, but for sure, *we're* going to talk about it again." He paused. "That and you're drinking." There was that fucking Burt Reynolds smirk.

Boodrow gave her a sidelong glance, then stepped past her to examine the tree trunk. "This looks straightforward," he said. "Why don't you bring the truck up? I'll take care of it."

"Okay."

"I'm going to fire this up, so don't be alarmed," he said.

"Oh, fuck off."

The chainsaw started on the second pull, just as she was reaching the bank.

"Kelly," Boodrow shouted.

She turned and looked at him.

"You're not going to shoot me in the back, are you?"

She gave him the finger, then started up the slope, shaking her head.

Some yogi's voice in his head. *"All we are is the result of what we have thought."*

"I don't know, man. I never thought he was going to kick me in the *fucking balls*," Mitch said.

It was dark and hot. The ground was hard. He could hear muted gunfire; M16s, AKs, small arms. Artillery in the distance. He could smell smoke. Somehow all of these things must have significance, but it was really hard to figure out, man, because of all the fucking pain.

He knew he wasn't in Nam, the smells were all wrong.

"None of this was my idea," he grumbled.

He tried to get a grip on the pain; tried pulling it all together into one, big, blazing ball, contain the ball inside of a high-walled triangle of ice. Problem was, little blobs of pain kept splitting off and jumping over the wall, head going one way, stomach another. He'd just manage to corral his knees and then his balls would take off.

He was very thirsty; his mouth dry and foul with a gross mixture of nicotine, dirt, and blood. A solid memory: Faber's fat finger poking around in his mouth. And another taste, metallic, but thinner than blood.

He knew it right away. They had slipped him some blotter. Why would they do that? Did they think it was going to turn him into some kind of moron sitting around staring at his toes?

Dicks. He could handle any shit they could get their hands on. One tab, even two tabs, bought off of some undergrad at, like, Albany or Syracuse. Shit, he could maintain, no problem. He tried to uncurl, gagged, and started puking. Not a lot came out.

He rolled to his other side, got his legs straightened out, got up on his knees, swayed dangerously, but stayed upright. He took deep breaths. His head began to clear. Lightning filled the small, bunker-slit windows. Thunder... then...

Scritch, scritch, scritch at the window, like an animal trying to claw through the screen. He stood up. Shying away from the sharp stabbing pain in his left foot, he shifted his weight to his right leg. His right knee buckled, and he fell on his butt.

Scritch, scritch, scritch.

He stood up with much greater care this time, testing out the carrying limit of his right knee before setting down his left foot. Painful but stable. Whimpering, he started towards the window with a disjointed, two-legged limp.

He stopped when the middle window exploded inward. Slack-jawed, he watched as a small, heavy object sailed into the room, hit the carpet, and bounced.

He couldn't tell what it was. At least it didn't shatter and spew out flames. He waited a few seconds. It didn't explode.

He looked at the window. Ghost face. "Get over here," it hissed.

Kelly had no problem with Boodrow's truck. She had grown up driving a stick. She matched her speed to the visibility, knowing there was one more bridge to come.

As soon as they were moving, she said, "So, the swingers discover that they've got this little Manson family living next door. Why didn't they go to the sheriff?"

"They talked to Archie lots of times, but always on the QT. They didn't want a big fuss, didn't want to draw attention to their lifestyle."

"And the sheriff didn't do anything about it?"

"Nothing I ever heard of. And with Mitch back? Look how he dealt with Mrs. Dee; an OD, and he says nothing about the suspected drug dealer living across the lake, who was fucking her when her husband was away?"

Kelly shifted uneasily. Was that really what was happening?

"Once Mitch got back, he started hanging around the new cottages, a bigger, scarier version of Bobby, carrying around a big knife, staring at people from the woods, patrolling up and down the lake in his canoe.

He hit on Lucy Dee, probably because she was the weakest link in the group," Boodrow said.

"Or he just wanted to get laid."

"The swingers decided to fight back. They got Hack on their side. Crogan and Faber started throwing their weight around. They went to the Parker place and threatened Rae. They caught Bobby sneaking around and put a beating on him. Then there's the ghost call. That had to be Mary Ann, setting them up."

"If Crogan and the swingers didn't put Susan Collins' body in the swamp in the first place, how would they know where to look? How could that be a trap for them?"

"Maybe they got a call too, or a tip from someone else. Maybe they took a shot because the Hell Hole belonged to Rae's family."

Kelly downshifted, brought the truck almost to a stop. "Rae Parker is from Shallow Rock?"

"You didn't know that? She was born Raelene Helena Weechum. Her mother, Sarah Mosby, ran a whorehouse at the Hell Hole back in the day."

"Rae Parker is Mary Ann's mother?"

"Aunt. Also, she's Hack's aunt. Course in Shallow Rock, cousin and aunt, aren't particularly precise terms. Hack and Mary Ann are both grandchildren of Sarah Mosby. They could just as easily be half brother and sister."

"Sarah Mosby have anything to do with Sarah Punk?"

"All that curse shit with the Margins? That's just a ghost story. Hell, Rae was shacked up with Frank Margin for a while. She took care of Bobby when he was like seven, eight years old, brought him into the Shallow Rock fold."

Of course, she didn't know any of this shit. She was an outsider. In a place like Wanakena County, secrets are what everybody knows, and nobody talks about.

CHAPTER FIFTY

Mitch stumbled forward, no idea what Mary Ann expected him to do. "My hands are tied," he said, holding them up towards the window.

"Get up here." The big Bowie flashed in and out of the broken window, held tightly in Mary Ann's fist.

"Oh. Yeah, that would work."

It took him several attempts to get his gimpy body standing up on the ottoman and his arms out the window.

He couldn't see what she was doing, but he had a vision of her squatting over his hands, sawing away with the sharp Bowie. The ropes snapped free. He roared like a gored bull as the blood started rushing back into his strangulated capillaries. He lost his balance and fell on his back with a hard thump.

Mary Ann's face appeared at the window. Her hair swayed as she laughed.

Mitch waved his burning hands in the air, panting, shouting. "Ah, ah, ah, fuck, fuck, fuck!"

There was a burst of automatic rifle fire. Bullets splashed against concrete, cracked through the windows, and smacked into the panelling high on the far wall. Mary Ann had disappeared without a sound.

Mitch rolled over, tried to get up on his hands and knees, and collapsed. He crawled on his belly towards the thing she'd thrown in the window. Solid metal wedge, short, rubber-coated handle. It was his hatchet. He tried to grasp it but couldn't get his fingers to bend. He had flexibility in his wrists, but his fingers were still burning themselves back to life.

The M-16 ripped off half a mag outside. A man's voice shouted, "You little bitch!"

He looked over his shoulder at the window. Mr. Mulvane's red face was looking in. "Motherfucker!" he shouted.

Mitch rolled towards the window as the room strobed with muzzle flashes. Bullets chewed into the bar. He kept rolling until he was tight against the wall and out of the line of fire.

He forced himself to lie still and be quiet, gritting his teeth, shaking his hands back to life. The shooting stopped. He could hear people moving around upstairs, then more shouting outside—Dan and Mr. Mulvane, maybe others.

A bellow of surprise rose into a pitiful wail and was

drowned out by a giant blast of thunder directly above the cottage. It sounded like an ancient tree being ripped apart. The dying thunder merged with the hard thumping of an AK. More shouts. Mr. Mulvane, screaming like a baby. Denny outside too, laughing like a lunatic.

Hack shouting, Dan shouting back.

Hack: "I got her, go, go!"

"Rae?"

"Yeah, get moving. Bobby's still out there."

"Mick got Mary Ann, winged her at least."

"If he did, I'll rip his fucking lungs out. Go get him. Go!"

Mitch stood up, limped over to the hatchet, and kicked it through the door into the empty room. Two or three more kicks brought it to the base of the steps. Enough feeling had returned to his hands that he was able to make a fist around the rubber handle. Step by step, he bumped awkwardly up the stairs, dropping the hatchet every few steps. When he reached the door, he rested, slowed his breathing, and listened. No crackling flames, no voices. He fumbled with the doorknob. Locked.

He stood, braced himself sideways against the wall, took the best grip he could on the hatchet and chopped at the wood above the knob. The hatchet flew out of his hands and went bouncing down the stairs.

A great crack of thunder rocked the Ford. Kelly shifted into second and sped up.

Boodrow sat hunched forward, watching the road. "Crogan and Faber, I don't know what stupid shit those two were up to. Maybe Steve was dealing drugs with Weechum. Maybe they were screwing with hitchhikers. Miles might have had some plan to make himself a hero by finding the body."

"Then who killed Susan Collins?"

"I don't know. Crogan's not the kind of guy to murder anyone. Bobby Margin, on the other hand, there's something sick about that kid. He's always hitchhiking. He could have been trolling the roads for years, meeting chicks, bringing them home to 'Mother'. Maybe they were doing weird, ritual shit at the Hell Hole. Remember the ropes hanging from the ceiling?"

"Fuck." Kelly didn't like the images that flashed through her mind.

"Listen."

Kelly slowed again. The windshield wipers were on intermittent, the wind had died down. It sounded like a maniac woodpecker was working over a tree in the distance.

"There," Boodrow pointed into the mist towards the lake."

"M-16. The bastard that shot Gail," Kelly said.

"Faber?"

"I'd put my money on it. He couldn't have done the killing at the Hell Hole, he was at Crogan's, but he had plenty of time after he attacked me to meet up with Weechum and get here ahead of us."

"Yeah, he could be a killer. He was always more fucked up than Miles. Do you smell smoke?"

"Yeah." Kelly worked her way up the gears, rushing the truck through the encroaching fog, holding it tight through the tree-crowded corners. "Sum up," she said. "What the hell is going on out there?"

"The swingers fucked with the wrong people. I figure Rae, Bobby, and Mitch plan to kill them all and put the blame on Weechum and Faber."

"That's a hell of a frame to pull off."

"Not if you're the only witnesses."

On the surface, it was hard to see Mitch as a killer; he didn't have that vibe. Mrs. Parker? Freaky little Mary Ann? You could easily disappear down the rabbit hole trying to guess at that shit. Some people's motives were unfathomable to a normal person's mind.

Kelly flashed on Gail's bewildered, bloody face, her frightened voice. No rabbit hole there. She chanced a quick look at Boodrow. "With Weechum and Faber," she said. "I consider this a shoot-on-sight situation."

Boodrow looked at her, dead serious. "Right on, partner," he replied.

There was one more rabbit hole he wanted to point out. "That woman who went off Steep Rock last summer. That investigation got wrapped up really quickly too."

"Okay?"

"Mrs. Mulvane said to me yesterday, the victim,

Beverly McConnell, earlier that night she'd been all over Bobby Margin."

"Mary Ann was jealous? Pushed her off?"

"Wouldn't really have to push her…"

Up another rise.

"Stop!"

Kelly hit the brakes. The wheels locked, and they slewed left then right as they slid down a low grade and came to a stop facing another swollen creek.

"I guess we're walking from here," Kelly said, as they got out of the truck.

Ten yards in front of them, the road disappeared into a swirling eddy that had eaten away the riverbank and was chewing up what remained of a crumbling cement footing. The bridge looked like a sinking ship; the wooden truss twisted, the roadway awash and listing badly. The section closest to them was already underwater.

"Walking or swimming, partner?"

The bridge was less than forty feet long, canted about ten degrees upstream, the raging current tugging it down. Kelly walked up to the edge of the water and crouched down to take a better look. "It's no more than a foot deep here." She stood up, pointing, "If we keep to the right we'll be above the current."

"The far bank looks solid, it's. It's gonna go from this end," he said.

"The railing looks like it's holding," Kelly replied, raising her voice. The rushing water and the cool air were exhilarating, blowing away the cobwebs of weariness that had clouded her mind. "Got any rope?"

"No time for that. If we're going, we gotta go now, come on."

They turned and hurried back to the truck. Kelly slipped Gail's automatic behind her back, touched the spare mag in her back pocket.

"Here, take what you can." Boodrow brought the box of .38 shells from behind the seat, took a handful, and put them in his front pocket. Kelly jammed handfuls into both her pockets.

Boodrow smiled as he tucked a spare M-1 magazine into his shirt pocket. He looked thrilled, totally confident. Like everything was going his way.

"You figure this is the end of Sheriff Herkemer, don't you?" she said.

"No matter how this plays out, he's finished. Shit like this happens in your county, you eat it," Boodrow replied.

Kelly nodded. Right or wrong, that was the nature of the job.

"Wanakena needs young blood," Boodrow declared. "Someone with deep roots in the county who can still keep up with the times."

"Bet you already got your slogan prepared," she said.

Boodrow snapped a mag into the M-1 and cocked it. "Boo Boodrow for Sheriff. *His* son won't murder you."

CHAPTER
FIFTY-ONE

The narrow stairway throbbed with electric light; the open mouth of a hungry snake lined with pine veneer teeth. Mitch dismissed the pulsing neon colors, opened his eyes and focused on the doorknob. It kept changing colors; flamingo pink, ruby rouge, cat's eye green. Every time he reached for it, it moved away.

Line of fire across his cheek. Dandy, fucking, Dan Dee. "All that time in Nam, man, and I gotta come home to be cut by an AK? In the rec room of a *cottage*?"

More shouting from beyond the door. A truck starting. Then quiet. He could smell smoke.

"Hello!" he shouted, then clamped his mouth shut. He was no longer tied, and he almost had his hands back, but he was in no shape for a fight.

A second vehicle departed. Very quiet now. He banged his head against the door. "Hey, hey!"

A big swoop forward into darkness.

He was lying down. He rolled over and felt a slap across his face.

"Mitch, are you okay? *Speak* to me, Mitch, I need you."

He opened his eyes. Staring down at him was Mrs. Mulvane.

"Hey, Holly," he croaked. He felt himself being lifted by the shoulders. "I think your house is on fire, man."

Kelly paused at the water's edge.

It looked like the bridge had tilted another couple of degrees in the last few minutes, the upstream edge dipping further beneath the churning water. The main struts squealed and cracked as they slowly parted from the old flathead bolts that had held them together for a hundred years.

"We can make it, but this thing is gone in twenty minutes," Kelly shouted.

"Then I'll go first," Boodrow shouted back, cheerfully.

M-1 slung, he held Kelly's hand and took the first tentative step, sinking to the top of his boot before he touched bottom. His grip tightened. "Tugs a little," he said, after a sharp intake of breath. He took another step, "Okay, footing's solid."

Kelly put one foot into the water. A thick, loamy smell rose from the grasping current. Alone, she would have been swept away with the rest of the bobbing debris. Three large steps together, firmly gripping each other's forearms, and Boodrow was able to grab the guardrail. He tested it then pulled her up.

They clung to the weathered one-by-six boards with both hands. "Okay?" Boodrow looked sideways at her. "It's solid."

"Okay."

They shuffled sideways, feet never leaving the slippery deck, hands never leaving the mushy, waterlogged railing, four points of contact at all times. The deck kept tilting, lifting them up as the far side was plowed further under the waves. By the time they'd reached the center of the bridge, half the roadway was submerged. Looking over her shoulder, she watched as several deck boards humped up and snapped. The whole bridge shook and shrieked as the stringers, jammed between the force of the current and the structure of the stubborn truss, started to twist like licorice sticks.

Overhead, a strut gave way with a loud crack. Kelly tensed and hunched in on herself, no time to move or even look up. A four-by-four beam swung past her shoulder and slammed into the railing. The wood shivered and cracked beneath her fingers. She waited helplessly for the railing to rip loose. The beam swung a second time, hit again, then dropped onto the deck and was borne away by the flood. The railing held.

There was a moment's stability. A brief sigh of relief. She loosened her grip enough to edge a little further along. Then the rest of the struts started to go, the air crackling like the Fourth of July.

"We're going down!" she shouted.

She had the terrible sensation of being lowered towards the water as the deck returned to an even keel. It was like sitting backwards on a teeter-totter, going down.

"We're gonna lose both ends!" Boodrow shouted. "Come on." He turned towards the bank and started slogging through the ankle-deep water.

She followed, one hand on the railing, risking a couple of high steps before the water was halfway up her calves and the current almost knocked her off her feet. The crumbling bank was less than ten feet away, a flat, narrow shelf of mud crowded on both sides with crazy, tilted saplings reaching out to her.

She shoved her feet forward along the bottom, each step harder, the distance gained shorter—making headway by the inch. Too slow. She let go of the railing and pumped with both arms, eyes fixed straight ahead. The water rose to her knees.

A Jeep skidded around the corner at the top of the hill, too far to the right, almost in the bush. It careened back across the narrow road and slammed into the trees on the left side, thirty feet away from them.

Boodrow halted and shouted something.

"Don't stop!" Kelly yelled, shoving his shoulders with both hands.

The bridge settled, rocked, and then lurched to the left, knocking her sideways. Muddy bubbles rose in front of her. She pushed past Boodrow and dove clear of the wreckage, half crawling, half swimming the last few feet.

Scrambling through the slurry, she clawed her way to solid ground. Splayed flat, she reached back, grabbed Boodrow by the collar and hauled him up beside her. They crawled on their stomachs until the saturated gravel turned to hard oil-top, then lay still, panting and spitting. Kelly craned her neck, looking up.

The Jeep driver's door swung open, a man lowered himself to the ground and staggered out into the middle of the road. He took a couple of steps towards the bridge then stopped, staring at it. He stood there, dazed; blind to Kelly and Boodrow lying on the ground a few yards away.

Sandy red hair plastered over a deathly pale forehead. Wild darting eyes, no jacket, no weapon in his hands. His shirt was torn and soaked black with water and blood. The antler handle and a few inches of broad, steel blade stuck out of his right shoulder, up near his neck.

"Mr. Mulvane?" Boodrow called out, getting up on his knees.

Kelly lay still. Mulvane? She thought he was floating near the Hell Hole with the top of his head blown off. Mr. Mulvane didn't answer or even look in their direction. He took another drunken step towards the river.

A second vehicle came to a splashing halt at the top of the hill. Kelly stood; legs braced like a sailor. She wiped the mud from her eyes and unbuttoned the flap on her holster.

A man got out of the vehicle. He was hard to make out at the top of the steep rise, mist marching up the road to meet him. A dark silhouette against the grey, uncertain sky; a big man, wearing a floppy bush hat, raised a rifle to his shoulder.

"Don't shoot!" Boodrow shouted.

The rifle spat flame and thumped out a short burst of lead that splashed up the mud around Mr. Mulvane's feet. Kelly dashed straight for the trees on the left side of the road and shouldered her way past the outer layer of the thick undergrowth.

She drew her revolver and turned. Through the broad, drooping leaves, she watched as Mr. Mulvane took several bullets in the back and fell face down into the mud.

"Can you walk?"

Mitch watched Mrs. Mulvane through half-closed eyes. She looked like a sheepdog that had gone for a swim, her curls loose and dirty. Her nose sniffed at him, her eyes encroached on his, filling his vision. She pawed at the gaping red trench on his cheek. "Christ, how bad did he get you?"

Big brown eyes, tiny little pupils, dog's breath. Her questions meaningless yips. "I'll get a cloth," she said.

"Water," Mitch croaked.

The doggie went away. Mitch laid his head back against the wall.

His nostrils twitched. He turned his face in the direction that his nose had gone. There were odd layers to the light, but he could see straight through the living room to the open patio doors. In the darkness at floor level, there were a few little red and yellow flowers blinking at him. A thin, flickering creeper clung weakly to the wooden doorframe.

Mrs. Mulvane handed him a glass of water. He easily found his lips and poured it over his tongue.

"You're high. They gave you LSD, do you know that? Can you handle it, Mitch? Mitch, can you fucking *hear* me?"

She was a long way away, a little woman with a mile-long arm reaching out to him, white rag in hand, patting his face.

"I'm cool, man. More water," he said.

"Mitch, we have to out of here. Can you walk? How did you cut yourself loose, do you have a knife?" She was twitchy, pinprick eyes darting around. The lady had found something stronger than coffee to perk her up.

"More water," he said.

With the second glass finished, he made another

effort to get his shit together. "Where is everybody?" he asked.

"Gone, but they could be back any minute, we have to go, *now*."

He was sitting on the floor; she was kneeling in front of him. Drops of water dappled her cheeks like freckles. Her thin, light-green rain jacket hung open, brushing the floor. Her head was very large. "Can you stand? Come on, get up."

There was blood on her hands, maybe his, maybe someone else's.

"Easy, easy," he said. He had to plant his legs far apart to accommodate his tender, bowling-ball-sized nuts.

"I can't carry you, Mitch."

He settled on his aching parts, leaned against her, and patted her shaggy fur. She let him go, and he found he was pretty steady. "I'm going," she said.

"Where are you going?"

"To the other side of the lake where it's safe, to the lumber camp."

"Hang on, I'll come with you," he said.

"Okay, we have to go on foot, *carefully*. I'm telling you, everybody around here has lost their minds. If they find us, they'll kill us both."

"Maybe we'll kill them," Mitch replied with a little laugh. "Do you have a weapon?"

"I have this," she held up a knife with a three-inch blade. Beneath the light raincoat, her white tunic was also splattered with blood.

"I have a hatchet," he replied proudly.

"Where is it?" she demanded, feeling him up.

"At the bottom of the stairs. I'll just go get it, and we can be on our way," he said.

"No, I'll get it. Just stand there. Stand, don't sit, Mitch—stand. I'll be right back."

She hustled off, bare feet squishing in her muddy white Adidas.

He looked around, eternal twilight. Not too much smoke. Front door closed, no light shining through the little panes of glass. Walls holding nice and steady. Spaced-out freak in the round mirror, looking at him.

"Everything is cool," he said, nodding at the freak. The freak nodding back.

Sound of a firefight in the distance. Cool. There was always a firefight in the distance. He looked out through the patio door across the room. Mist rising above the shadowy layer of light.

Oh, shit.

A monster coming through the door: a three-legged, two-headed beast. One head an eyeless scarecrow with a stitched-up mouth, the other a peg-legged pirate with an eyepatch and a bloody face.

CHAPTER
FIFTY-TWO

Kelly broke past the tree line and wove her way through the low branches until she came to the bumper of a Jeep JC jammed up against a big maple. Boodrow was crouched behind the rear wheel, forearms covering his bowed head. She threw herself flat on the ground as a new burst of gunfire ripped into the gas tank, snapped through the plastic windows, and zinged off the engine block.

Boodrow unslung the M-1 and sat with his back against the tire. "Cease firing!" he shouted.

Silence, then another burst of automatic rifle fire, heavy rounds, something heavier than an M-16, ripping into metal. Sharp odor of gasoline biting through the heavy air. On hands and knees, she crawled to the end of the Jeep and peeked past the rear bumper.

The guy was maybe forty yards away, standing beside a Jeep Commando, a big two-door hardtop with its engine running, headlights cutting weakly through the mist. A big guy in a bush hat. She couldn't tell if it was Mitch.

She rose up on one knee, took a two-handed grip on her revolver, and lined him up. A long shot, not likely to hit, but maybe it would make him move or speak. She squeezed off two quick rounds. One smacked metal. The man disappeared.

"What are you doing?" Boodrow shouted.

"What are *you* doing?" she shouted back.

"Just don't do anything, okay. Keep down. I'll show him we have some firepower too." Boodrow popped up and let fly with six or seven shots on semi-auto, taking out the headlights of the Commando. Pretty good snap shooting.

"This is Deputy Boodrow and Deputy Mackinaw of the Wanakena County Sheriff's Department. Cease firing. You are firing on officers of the law," Boodrow shouted.

Kelly crawled back behind the Jeep. Staying low, Boodrow moved to meet her.

"Cover me and I'll go for position," she said.

He shook his head vigorously.

"Put down your weapon and come out!" he shouted.

"Fuck that! I'm fighting for my life up here, buddy. The locals are on the warpath. Weechum's got Holly and Denny hostage at the Cross Cottage. I'm goin to get them. You want to join me, come on up."

"Join you? You just murdered a man," Kelly shouted.

"Self-defense, lady. He tried to kill me."

She didn't recognize the voice, not Mitch for sure.

"Put your gun down and we can talk," Boodrow shouted.

The Commando's door slammed shut. The vehicle backed down over the hill. Boodrow stood up.

"You believe any of that?" Kelly asked.

"Hack taking hostages? Yeah."

"Who was that?"

"Don't know, not a local. Mr. Cross?"

"I didn't think he was that big."

"The bastard had an AK."

"Yeah." Boodrow slung the M-1, walked out onto the road, and looked up at the crest of the hill. Kelly remained behind the Jeep. She cracked open her revolver and replaced the bullets she'd fired. Boodrow went over to the body and crouched down.

"Mulvane for sure. Dead for sure," he said.

Kelly waited a few more seconds then went out and joined him, revolver still in hand. Mulvane was laid out flat on his face, palms down, feet turned outwards. There were four small holes high on his back, not a lot of blood there. The right side of the shirt, down from the shoulder, was soaked.

"That didn't kill him, but it probably would have," Boodrow said. "You ever see a knife like that around here?"

Kelly took a closer look without touching it. Genuine elk antler handle, solid-looking. Well made, but not particularly expensive. "Lots of knives like that around," she said.

Boodrow stood up, looked back up the road. He was handling the whole thing very well, she thought, considering that this was his first firefight and dead body of the day. It had taken her a little longer to adjust.

"I thought you said Weechum and the swingers were on the same side," she said.

"Maybe they were. Maybe they still are. Come on, let's get under cover. I'm fucking tired, aren't you tired?"

"Yeah." She *was* tired. They had barely escaped with their lives back there. Just now, before even a shot was fired, they'd almost fucking drowned.

There were serious things happening on Shangri-La Lane, people's lives probably in danger, but right now, suddenly, she hardly cared. She was shaking when she sat down next to Boodrow. He took out his flask and offered it to her. She took a quick drink. It burned, but the rich bourbon smell, the act of tipping the flask, stilled her shakes.

Boodrow took a drink and tucked it away with a sigh. "Okay, we don't hardly know shit," he said.

Kelly lay on her stomach, put her nose to the shallow run of rainwater flowing past the front wheel of the Jeep, and sniffed. No gasoline. She lapped at it like a dog. Boodrow drew a plastic case from an inside pocket and delicately lit a cigarette with his wet fingers.

He inhaled and let the smoke drift slowly out of his mouth. "There's some kind of fight going on over there. Both sides are heavily armed."

Kelly sat down, shifting her soggy butt in the dirt until her ribs didn't hurt so much. "That beam almost took my head off," she said.

"I know. I thought we were goners," Boodrow replied, shaking his head.

The smell of his cigarette reminded her of hunting with her dad. It was comforting, but also made her a little dizzy. It was hard to think straight. Who was at Lost Lake right now? How many guns did they have? She wanted to go to sleep.

"You know," Boodrow said. "It might have been Dan Dee. The guy with the AK. He's a big guy."

Kelly had never met him. "Lucy Dee's husband. I thought he was in Syracuse."

"He might have come back since we were here yesterday."

"Jesus, that was yesterday?"

"Yeah, you believe that?"

"Tell me it's not like this every week around here."

Boodrow laughed. He was about to say something when a loud explosion ripped through the air followed by a big, sucking rush of wind. Kelly jumped to her feet, ran out into the road, and looked towards Shangri-La Lane. A roiling black cloud rose up beyond the crest of the hill.

"Son of a bitch," Boodrow said.

Kelly pointed to the thin trail of lighter smoke

almost directly in front of them, then to the new one. "That's Mulvane's cottage, so that must be Cross."

They stood, listening. No gunfire. "This place is fucking Looney Tunes," Boodrow said.

Kelly returned to the Jeep and made a quick inspection of its interior. There was lots of blood on the driver's seat, nothing else that jumped out at her. No weapons. Leave it for the forensics guys, whenever the hell they showed up. She closed the door.

"Which way?"

"We came for Weechum. If he's alive and has hostages, then he must be at the Dees'," Boodrow replied decisively, his energy was coming back.

She felt it too; body and mind ramping up for another go. "Okay, not on the road."

He motioned with his head. "Up through here, close enough to the edge, so we don't get lost. When we hit the junction, we slip along to the west for a hundred yards or so before we cross over."

"Sounds like a plan."

He ground out the butt of his cigarette with his boot heel. "I'll go first," he said, offering her the M-1.

She shook her head. "The way I'm shooting today?"

"I didn't want to say it," he replied, with a grin.

"Come on," Kelly sighed.

They pushed into the woods, Kelly leading. Boodrow spoke wistfully, "I wish we had more firepower."

She'd been thinking the same thing. "If it comes to that," she replied. "I know where we can get some."

"Get over here and give Bobby a hand," the pirate head demanded in a low, husky voice.

Close up, the monster revealed itself to be Rae and Bobby joined at the hip. Rae's left eye was half-closed by blood dripping from a bandana tied around her forehead. "Make yourself useful," she said, looking around the room. "Hang on to the guns."

"Hey, Mitch," Bobby said, splitting open his ragged, uneven lips. "You made it out okay." He handed him first a shotgun and then a hunting rifle. "Pretty smoky in here."

"It'll do. There, over there," Rae said, pointing at the couch in the far corner.

Bobby helped Rae hobble to the couch. Mitch followed with the guns. Outside it was twilight, inside it was night right up to the waist in most places, way over the head in the corners. "Where's Mary Ann?" he asked.

"If she ain't right on my ass, I don't know where the hell she is," Bobby replied. He didn't sound worried.

Suddenly, the night beyond the windows blazed with light. Directly across from them, the kitchen window became a glowing rectangle that spat out long red and yellow darts of light that ricocheted off the chrome appliances. To his right, through the vast, empty windows, the lake shimmered with hard-cut diamonds. The air was tangy with gasoline. Backlit trees cast shadows that swayed in the yellowish mist.

"Cross cottage," Bobby said.

"Hack's moved on. Mitch, get my belt."

He didn't know where her belt was. He studied her face for clues; all he saw were the lines of pain around her mouth and eyes.

"Mitch, put down the guns, and take off my belt. I need to lay down."

Bobby pulled the .45 from her wide, brown belt. Mitch unbuckled it.

Carefully, he and Bobby laid her out on the chocolate-brown couch. Bobby controlled her shoulders and upper body, while Mitch steadied her hips and one useless leg. The leather squeaked as they settled her head on the low, padded arms.

Mitch remembered the voices he'd heard in the Mulvane basement. "Hack shot you?"

"Grazed me, that's all," Rae replied. "Fell out of the damn tree and broke my leg, hit my head."

"Where's your hat, man?" Bobby asked him.

"Dan Dee took it."

"I'll get it back for you, with his scalp," Bobby replied, as he slipped a pillow under Rae's back.

"Just the hat would be cool, man," Mitch replied.

Bobby handed Rae the .45 and she cradled it on her stomach. Mitch tried to kiss her. His lips ended up on her chin.

"For Christ's sake, Mitch," she growled angrily, pushing him away. "Are you stoned?"

"Rae..."

"It's not his fault," a woman's voice spoke behind him.

"How the fuck did she get in here?" Bobby demanded.

Mitch whirled around. Mrs. Mulvane stood near the basement door cradling his hatchet to her chest, looking as meek and mild as a little lost lamb. "Dan Dee forced LSD on him while he was tied up," she said.

Rae's head was flat on the armrest, .45 at the end of her extended arm, pointing at Mrs. Mulvane. Bobby had the shotgun up at the shoulder.

"Wait!" Mitch shouted. He stood between them, hands up, palms out. "It's cool, it's cool; she's with me."

"Who else is here?" Rae demanded.

"Nobody?" Mitch said, staring at Mrs. Mulvane for confirmation.

Mrs. Mulvane nodded. No major shakes; eyes skidding around all over the place.

"She came back for me, she saved my life," Mitch said.

"We would have saved you," Rae said.

It was a hanging moment, auras trembling in the silence. Outside, the Cross cottage burned brightly, casting them all as shadows. Mitch held out his hand to Mrs. Mulvane. "Give me the hatchet. Come over here, we can all be friends, right?"

Bobby's shotgun tracked Mrs. Mulvane as she handed Mitch the hatchet, slipped under his shoulder, and wound an arm around his waist. Full body shakes now.

"It's okay, Bobby," Rae said. She set the pistol on the couch beside her and raised herself up on one elbow to look at Mrs. Mulvane. "You're telling me they forced drugs on him. Why the hell would they do that?"

"They were going to blame everything on Mitch, you know, drug-crazed Vietnam vet," Mrs. Mulvane replied, giving Mitch a squeeze. Her voice was pretty steady. The lady could adapt, man.

"What do you mean, everything?"

"All the killing. Bobby, you, Mary Ann."

Rae didn't seem bothered that Mrs. Mulvane was holding him so close. "Fucking idiots. How does Hack plan to get out of here?"

"I don't know. He took money from all of us. He wants Mary Ann with him."

"Did he hurt Denny?" Bobby demanded. He had the shotgun at the port, tense, like he was ready to butt-stroke her.

Mrs. Mulvane spoke carefully. "She's really stoned, really out of it."

"Did he hurt her?"

"No, not the last time I saw them. Uh, he has her

on a rope, tied by the hands. But not really tight. I couldn't do anything. He wants to make a deal..."

"We know," Rae said.

"I went with them to the Cross Cottage, but once he started pouring gas all over the place, I took off," Mrs. Mulvane said.

"I'm going," Bobby said.

"Just hang on," Rae snapped at him. "You know Hack ain't going nowhere."

Rae turned her attention to Mitch. "Did you burn the pictures?"

"The pictures. Rae..."

"Mitch, I asked you to do *one* goddamned thing..."

"I got sidetracked..." Mitch said. It was too complicated to explain.

Rae waved at him, chuckling. "How stoned are you?"

"Just a little. I can handle it."

She shifted her gaze to Mrs. Mulvane. "You want those pictures burned?"

"Yes, I do. I'll pay for them, ten..."

"Keep your money. Mitch, listen carefully. You go on back to the lumber camp, burn all the pictures of the kids." She looked at Mrs. Mulvane. "Burn all the pictures of Mrs. Mulvane, keep the rest."

Mrs. Mulvane nodded.

"Burn the pictures, then go to Blondie's and stay there, no matter what. Make sure Holly here doesn't go anywhere until I've had a chance to talk to her. Stay off the road..."

Rae stopped talking. Bobby took a step backwards. Mrs. Mulvane wrapped her hands around Mitch's chest and buried her face in his back. Mitch looked over his shoulder towards the patio door.

Mary Ann was standing hardly ten feet away, as if she'd risen up through the floor. Her wet dress hung limply off her narrow shoulders. A ragged cloth was tied around her right calf, black with blood, but not bleeding. Her small pack was strapped across her chest, hanging down at crotch level with the butt of her Python sticking out the flap.

Mitch wanted to thank her, but the words couldn't find their way to his lips.

She wasn't looking at him. Her face was in flat, ghostly mode. Featureless, except for the eyes, which had fixed themselves, one after another, on to the back of Mrs. Mulvane's head. Mitch thought about the things Mrs. Mulvane had done: setting up Mary Ann's boyfriend to be murdered, bad-mouthing him to the police. It looked like Rae was willing to let that go—Mary Ann, maybe not.

"Hack ain't at the Dee cottage no more," Mary Ann said.

CHAPTER
FIFTY-THREE

What the fuck was he up to?

Across the narrow, misty road, the big guy in the bush hat was leaning on the side of the Commando, playing with a Colt Python. He looked around casually. He was supposed to be worried about Bobby Margin and Hack Weechum. He didn't look it.

It was already night under the trees. Kelly did a three-sixty scan of her surroundings, looking for something that didn't belong. Nothing out of place besides Boodrow waiting patiently a few yards behind her. Wet leaves whispered as she withdrew from the tree line to meet up with him. They crouched with their heads close together, mist up to their waists.

Kelly wiped the sweat from her forehead. "He's just across the road," she whispered. "Just standing there like he's waiting for somebody."

"Maybe he's waiting for us." He motioned with his head. They crept back to the edge of the road.

Dee had put the Python away; now he was looking at the mag of his AK, pressing down on the bullets.

"Cover me, I'll go talk to him," Boodrow whispered, holding out the M-1.

"It's a fucking trap," she hissed.

"I don't know. You see anybody else?"

He pressed the rifle on her. Reluctantly, she holstered her .38, and took the M-1. Kneeling on one knee, she raised the rifle and lined up on Dan's big gut. Boodrow pressed against her from behind, his chest against her back. She felt his nicotine-bourbon breath as he leaned over her shoulder, cheek to cheek. "Yeah, right through there. Nice, clean shot," he whispered.

"Stay out of my line of sight."

"It's okay, I'll come at him from up the road," he replied. He had a hand on her shoulder. Jesus, did he want a kiss?

She shrugged him off impatiently and sighted again. Dan wasn't doing anything; he was so casual she almost expected him to start whistling. It was just too fucking weird. She started to lower her weapon.

Drop your guard for *one* fucking second and the world can turn on a *dime*.

She couldn't speak, she couldn't breathe. Boodrow had her in a chokehold; a very good one. A sleeper. The M-1 fell from her hands as she tried to reach around and grab at his head. Her feet flailed. His mouth was wet in her ear.

"Be cool, Kelly. This is for your own good," he said.

She reached back and grabbed for his balls and was blocked by his thigh. Darkness closed in all around her.

"I'm trying to keep you alive. Shush, shush," he whispered.

Exploding lights, nothing.

Not death. Not sleep. A loud, ragged sound, in and out. A harsh voice penetrating the gasping darkness. "Why didn't you just kill her?"

"It's better if we choose where the bodies wind up."

All her breath was coming in through her nose. Disgusting, woolly dryness filling her mouth. She was gagged.

"Man, I can't believe you're still hedging your bets."

"I'm not hedging. I'm using my head."

The ringing in her ears made it hard to tell the speakers apart. She dared not open her eyes.

"Yeah, sure, you sneaky bastard."

Swaying sickeningly. Cold steel on her wrists.

"Where's Herkemer?"

"Stashed in Mulvane's basement."

"So, we take her there. He can kill her, for starters."

"Waste of good pussy. Why not fuck her if she's gonna die anyways?" No mistaking that voice. Faber.

"Shut up, you fucking idiot. They're gonna know if she's been raped." That was Boodrow.

"So what?"

"And by who, you fucking moron. If anybody's going to fuck her tonight, it'll be Herkemer." Boodrow again.

"I don't think he'll be up to it." Faber's vile, sniggering voice. "Dan busted his nuts."

Her senses were improving. Her breathing becoming shallower and more even. Doors opening.

"No way, Boo, you ride up front with me."

"Leave her in the back with shithead?"

"Up front." She didn't know that voice. Dan Dee?

She was sitting up in a narrow back seat. Faber beside her, his hands all over her.

"Cuff her legs."

"Nah, man. We don't want to do that. *Fuck*, no." Faber's hands spreading her thighs.

"Then buckle her in." That must be Dan, running the show.

"We should blindfold her, use her shirt." Faber, hands on her buttons.

"Stop that fucking shit!" Boodrow, shouting. "You need to watch her eyes. Get your fucking hands off her."

"Fuck you."

"Quit screwing around and buckle her up." Dee, up front, probably in the driver's seat.

Faber's hands in her lap, in her crotch. Seat buckle snapping.

Sitting in the back seat of a two-door; must be the Commando. Faber all over her, pushing her up against the wheel well on her side, the guy smelling like shit, literally. Engine firing up loudly.

Faber's fingers trying to find her zipper. Gross heavy breathing. Moving now. It couldn't be far, just a couple of minutes.

"Where's Holly?" Boodrow in the seat directly in front of her.

"She's with Hack, but don't worry about her. She always goes with the winner."

Speeding up, gears shifting.

"What about the lezzies across the lake?"

"Not a peep. Plenty of time to deal with them."

"Holy shit!"

Another roar, another explosion. Even through her closed eyelids, Kelly saw the light.

"That's your place, man."

"I'm gonna kill that little cocksucker!" Dan Dee, angry.

"Look out!"

"Fuck!"

No squealing tires, no horn. Furious impact. Screeching metal drowning out everything else. Kelly was thrown forward and then snapped back like a rag doll. Engine still throbbing, a moment of bruised-air stillness.

She opened her eyes and frantically tried to make sense of the situation. She was the only one wearing a seat belt. Boodrow was slumped against the dashboard on the passenger side. Dan was jammed up on top of the steering wheel with Faber half on top of him. Big lumpy men, dazed and groaning.

Kelly pulled the latch on the lap belt, put her back against the wheel well, and started kicking.

CHAPTER
FIFTY-FOUR

The moment Mary Ann spoke, there was another loud explosion from down the lake.

"The Dee Cottage," Bobby said.

Mary Ann's eyes were still on Mrs. Mulvane, who was shaking and mumbling something that sounded like a prayer into Mitch's back. Out on Shangri-La Lane, there was a terrific crash. Metal on metal.

Bobby jerked the shotgun up. "A fucking car accident?"

Rae pointed at Mitch. "Get your ass over to the camp and burn those pictures," she said. "Stay off the road, stay clear of Steep Rock. Go on. See if you can do what you're told for once!"

Faber was draped over the back of the driver's seat. Kelly drove her boot heels into the side of his hip, forcing his body to slide backwards. His shirt snagged on the seat, exposing his pudgy, white skin. She took aim at his ribs and kicked harder.

Howling, he flopped onto the back seat, hands clutching at his ribs. Kelly scrambled upright and clubbed him on the side of the head with her cuffed hands, drawing blood. Crouching down, she drove her shoulder up under his armpit and pinned him to the wheel well.

Gasping through her gag, she dug in his pocket until her fingers closed around a large set of keys. She yanked them out. Staying low behind the seat, she found the thin handcuff key and worked it into the post on her left wrist. As soon as her hand was free, she tore open the flap of Faber's holster, grabbed his automatic, and yanked it out.

"Kelly!"

Boodrow in the front seat, pointing a revolver at her.

She kicked the back of the bucket seat. He fired, turning the hatchback window into a spider's web. Left-handed, she fired, threw a leg over the seat, and rolled over into the narrow cargo space. Boodrow's .38 banged again as she unlatched the tailgate.

She rode the tailgate as it dropped open. Eyes open all the way, she tumbled through the misty air and landed on her back with a bone-jarring thud. Above her, Boodrow was on his knees, throwing up the shattered hatch with one hand and blazing away at her with the other.

Dirt sprayed her face as bullets smacked the ground beside her head. She rolled, got up on her hands and knees, and dove for the bush. Scrambling through the undergrowth, darting between the trees, she ran in a low crouch, choking on her gag. With each step, she rose higher and moved faster, running away from the shouting and shooting back on the road.

She tripped and fell headlong into a broad dip. She tore the gag from her mouth and lay on her back, panting, Faber's automatic pointing up into the darkness. She heard a few more shots, forty, fifty yards away? She waited, breathing, listening. She waited until her chest stopped heaving.

She shifted her weight, settling down on the damp forest floor, head pounding, eyes burning, jaw aching from grinding her teeth. She sensed blood dripping from the torn stitches on her arm, but she was so wet, she had no idea if it was a little leak or a torrent. The throbbing in her ribs was so constant now that she was reminded of it only when she made a sudden move.

Wounded and alone in the dark. Enough pain to make you pass out. Enough pain to make you want to curl up in a ball and wait for the hunters to put a bullet in your head. But it wouldn't be that quick. There would be abuse, humiliation. That thought quickened her heartbeat and kicked her weary adrenaline pump back to life. Fear and anger were about all she had left, but they were enough to get her back into the fight.

The cuff key had been lost back in the truck, so she locked both cuffs to her right wrist. Her mouth was dry and disgusting. She sat up and sucked rainwater from little pools on the surface of the rock.

Priorities. They'd taken her revolver and Gail's automatic. Faber's .45 had a seven-round clip. How many times had she fired? Twice, three times? At best, she had five rounds left. For the moment, the .38 cartridges in her pockets were useless.

What happened?

The Commando had hit another vehicle. She was pretty sure she'd heard Patricia's voice out on the road. The volleys of pistol fire right after the crash bore that out. Boodrow had chased her into the woods; she was almost sure of that. Was he waiting for her out there, or had he doubled back?

There hadn't been any shooting for a while. Hard to imagine Patricia losing a gunfight with a couple of stunned bozos like Faber and Dan Dee. If Patricia was back there, Gisela would be there too.

Kelly rose slowly up out of the hole and headed in her best-guess direction back towards the crash site. Her steps became less painful and less cautious as she went along. No shouts, no shooting, no more explosions or car wrecks. A few distant ripples of thunder; Mother Nature getting ready for another kick at the can.

The forest was definitely getting lighter the way she was going. Voices. Metallic noises; bolts and mags and cocking handles clattering. She crouched down.

"There, over there!"

Off to her left, Boodrow yelling.

"I see her!" Dan shouting in a rapid, coke-fired voice. "I fucking got her, I got her, I got her!"

Thrashing and snapping of undergrowth. She turned towards the sound. Bullets plucked at the branches above her head and tore bark from the trees to her left and right. Straight ahead of her, a white muzzle-flash star.

Dan Dee, charging right at her, firing an AK from the hip.

CHAPTER
FIFTY-FIVE

Mitch stopped and sifted the night air through the fine-meshed sieve of his expanded mind. He smelled Mrs. Mulvane; Virginia Slims, clean-shaven, city sweat, and the dusty mixture of powdered makeup and dried blood. There was the smell of the woods; wet limestone, sharp pine, and smoke.

Mrs. Mulvane tugged at his arm. "Are you lost?" she hissed.

"Don't interrupt," he admonished her, gently.

"Mitch?" She sounded scared.

He touched a finger to her lips. "Be still," he whispered.

There was something else on the sluggish air. Something thicker than stone, more primeval than pine. Swamp water musk, rich decay, pure animal sweat; Mary Ann. No point in looking for her, but she was nearby.

It was hard to tell if he was still stoned, or just really fucking *aware*, man. There had been a lot of shooting out by the road. He didn't care about that. That was far away.

Mrs. Mulvane moved around in front of him and put her hands on his shoulders. "Mitch, this *is* the path, we're okay. Come on, it'll take us back behind Steep Rock and around to the bay."

He took hold of her wrists and pulled her in close. He knew the voices would come, even before they spoke.

"Come on, Bobby, I ain't got all night!" Hack calling out from higher up, off to the right.

Mitch cradled Mrs. Mulvane's head firmly against his chest.

Bobby, shouting back. "Where you gonna go on a night like this?"

"I got plans. Come on, now. Come and get this bitch, or I *will* hurt her."

Denny not singing now. "Please, Bobby, please," she cried.

Silence. Then a short yelp of pain.

"Come on, Bobby," Mitch growled. "*Come on, man.*"

Mrs. Mulvane squirmed free of his grasp. "Mitch, ignore that," she said. "We have to keep going."

"We should help Denny."

"Bobby's going to help her. *We* need to get to the lumber camp and burn the pictures."

Mitch was afraid that Bobby wasn't going to help Denny.

"Mitch, for Christ's sake, we have to go."

Suddenly, the ground disappeared from beneath his feet. His body felt like a blob of free-falling silly putty. "Oh, fuck," he said.

"Let me go, Mitch, you're scaring me."

He squatted, bringing her with him. He was still stoned. That Up-State shit was more powerful than he'd thought.

"Mitch, quit fucking around. We have to go," Mrs. Mulvane hissed at him.

Mitch wrapped an arm around her throat and backed into the bush. "We need to lie down and be quiet for a while," he said. "Then everything will make sense."

Kelly fired once towards the muzzle flash, then took off to her right. When she figured she was clear, she stopped and looked back.

Dan called out to Boodrow. "Over here, over here, over here." The man was seriously wired. She'd fired at him, and he'd just kept coming.

They were less than twenty yards behind her, right and left. She ran on, trying to get some breathing room. They came after her, driving her like wolves on a deer, away from the vehicles and towards the lake.

Only four rounds left. If she could get one of them, she could take his weapon and turn this thing into a fair fight. They were firing on the run, their shots landing closer. She was outgunned, but she was faster. She hit Shangri-La Lane without breaking stride, dashed across the broad pavement and went to ground on the other side.

For a moment there was silence, then she heard them calling out to each other on the far side of the road, their words unclear. Another heartbeat, then they attacked.

Dan had discarded the AK. He opened up on her from the tree line with a pistol. Boodrow charged across the road to her left, firing in her direction. She ignored the bullets whacking the trees above her, drew a bead on him, led him just a fraction...

She fired two rounds, and he sank below the mist. She didn't have time to see if he stayed down. Dan was shouting and charging across the road, a gun in each hand, firing as he came. She got off one shot at him before he disappeared into the bush about ten feet to her left.

She took a quick look out at the road. No sign of Boodrow.

Swearing, she retreated. One round left.

"I'll tell you a secret," Mitch whispered to Mrs. Mulvane. "If you lie very, very, still in the dark, no one can see you. Not even Victor Charles."

He was lying beside her on the ground, deep in the mist. Her face right up close to his, eyes zipping around like pinballs, breathing heavily, her lungs making a sound like tearing cloth.

"I just need a few minutes to deal with the shit that your friends gave me, Holly. Just a few minutes of peace and quiet so I can crawl out of the whirling cesspool you dragged me into."

She was quiet for a while, then whispered, her lips tickling his ear. "Where are the pictures, Mitch?"

Somewhere Denny was still pleading and crying. He wanted to help her, but before he could do anything, he had to shake off this pack of chemical monkeys clinging to his brain stem.

"You'll never make it to the camp, Mitch. You know that, not in a million years," she persisted. "Tell me where the pictures are, so I can go and burn them like we all agreed."

He didn't think she had much of a chance making it to the bunkhouse on her own. Not tonight. And if she did make it, he knew she'd do whatever the hell she wanted with the pictures, no matter what they'd agreed. He pondered the problem, and after some time, enlightenment found him.

He smiled. He wasn't Mrs. Mulvane's protector any more than he was the guardian of the Polaroids.

Let her run her karma up against theirs, the only possible outcome was the correct outcome.

"They're in my room, the middle room of the bunkhouse, under the dust cover of my bed. You can burn them in the stove right there."

"I hate to leave you like this, Mitch," she said. Her eyes had become a little less freaky, her breathing quieter. "But I can't wait any longer." Her hand subtly tried to pry his fingers from the handle of his hatchet.

"No," he said.

With a last annoyed huff, she was gone. He waited until the sound of her passing had completely died before he relaxed. That settled, he dropped down into the well of vanishing; down where all this nagging shit would devour itself into nothingness.

CHAPTER
FIFTY-SIX

Kelly had no trouble stalking Mr. Dee.

He tore through the undergrowth, swearing loudly, firing angrily into the darkness. He called out to Boodrow, but Boodrow didn't answer.

She had tucked her shiny silver star into her pocket and smeared her face with mud. Her filthy hair, armored with a layer of dead bugs and forest debris, tumbled loosely around her face. Her breathing was under control, her pains all registered and tucked away.

She tracked him from well back, fifteen yards or so. He was a big man, the white smear of his face showed clearly whenever he turned her way. She kept to his left as she followed him, figuring Boodrow was off somewhere to his right.

It felt good to be the hunter.

The flames from the Dee cottage could be seen

through the thinning trees to her right. Chain lightning slashed at the dark blue clouds but cast no light. She kept checking her six. There were other people moving around in the woods. Two men up high on her left were shouting at each other. Mr. Dee was drifting in that direction.

One bullet.

Sneak up right behind Dee, shove the .45 against the base of his skull and blow his head off; effective, but hard to explain to investigators. It would look a lot better if she took him from the front. Worth the risk.

A woman cried out, her voice thin and pathetic. Dee stopped. "Boo, did you hear that? Where are you, you little shit?"

Not a sound from Boodrow; the clever bastard happy to hang Dan's ass out there as bait for Kelly to jump at.

Her fraying nerves wouldn't let her wait any longer. Darting between the trees, she slipped past Dee, angling for a spot in front of him. He turned and fired in her direction as she passed. The rounds went high.

"Fucking bitch!" he shouted, fighting with the slide of his automatic.

The ground rose sharply as she closed the last few feet between them, becoming a treacherous maze of uneven limestone blocks. She slipped and came up against a young maple.

She could hear him huffing and spitting. She could smell him, Cuban cigars, sharp copper sweat. She slid her left foot forward, testing the footing, before she leaned out to have a look. He was less than four feet away, half turned away from her, swatting at bugs with a Python in his right fist, pushing back his broad-brimmed bush hat with his left.

Close, very close. She came out from behind the tree, extended arm braced at the elbow. Nice clear shot at his back, the bastard staring at something in the other direction. It was straight-up murder at this range. Her arm started wobbling.

Look this way, you asshole.

Very close behind her, Sarah Punk's scream shattered the breathless night. She twitched and lost her footing. Dee whirled towards the sound, and they stood face to face, stunned for a strung-out second as the scream wound down. As Kelly shifted to regain her balance, the Python barked and bit into the rock at her feet. She fired her last bullet and saw the top of Dee's head fly upwards, his body falling backwards.

She leapt on him as he went down, eager to get his gun before Boodrow came charging out of the woods. He landed on his back, arms flung over his head. She straddled his chest, threw her upper body across his shoulder, giving his head a furtive glance as she elbowed it aside, reluctant to see the bloody mess she'd made.

There wasn't one. She hadn't blown his head off, only his broad-brimmed hat.

Roaring, Mr. Dee started to rise. Kelly dropped her gun and held his wrist with both hands, bearing down on his shoulder and outstretched arm. Dee kicked and bucked. Kelly rode him, trying to get a grip on his wrist bone so she could snap it.

He grabbed her hair with his free hand and tugged her head back. With an angry, animal yell, she yielded, hands sliding down to his forearm. Firm grip in her hair, he twisted under her. Kelly let go of his arm with her right hand and jammed her manacled forearm hard into his throat. Dee squawked like a duck and let go of her hair. She leaned in harder, throwing her shoulders into the push, determined to flatten his windpipe before he could buck her off.

He punched her hard in the side of the head, rocking her. She took it. He hit her again and she lost her balance. They slid apart, Kelly rolling to her right, away from the blow, Dee to the left. As his right arm slithered beneath her, she stripped the Python from his hand.

She came up on her side facing him. Dan squatting with his back against a tree, one hand on his throat, the other reaching out for her.

The Python action was as smooth as silk. One decisive click and bang. Dan flopped backwards, slid slowly down the wet tree trunk and sat, head resting on his busted chest. Kelly lay still, pointing the Python at him as she struggled to catch her breath. Fighting off a new wave of dizziness, she scanned the mist, blurry-eyed, waiting for Boodrow to attack.

Mitch climbed up the rocky shore of Lost Lake. The roiling sky above him writhed with intricate chains of transcendental lightning. Gunfire and thunder echoed in his ears as he shed the last thin layer of Up-State, acid snakeskin. Sarah was standing at the top of the cliff with her Python down at her side. She screamed.

Mitch sat upright, clear-eyed in the darkness. Mrs. Mulvane was gone. His hatchet was still firmly in his grip. A couple of quick shots sounded off to his left.

"Let her go, Hack. We'll help you get out. Tomorrow, man, when the weather breaks. You can be halfway down Moose River before anyone shows up here."

Bobby and Hack still shouting at each other. Mitch sat cross-legged, listening.

"Trip like that, I need Mary Ann."

"You can do it on your own."

Both voices were moving. Bobby's more than Hack's.

"I ain't leaving without Mary Ann, so quit fucking around."

"Let Denny go. I don't want her anymore, man."

"Bullshit. You just don't want Mary Ann to know, you gutless little creep."

Denny pleading. "Please take me, Bobby, please. I always loved you."

Mitch spat some of the sour crap out of his mouth.

"*She* sure wants *you*, man," Hack taunted.

"Just be cool, okay. I'll talk to Mary Ann. See if we can work something out."

If this was supposed to be some kind of trap for Bobby, it had already failed. Bobby was being cautious, and Mary Ann had his back. Mitch didn't like Hack's chances. Didn't look good for Mrs. Cross either, unless Bobby did want her; then there'd be a whole different kind of ugly.

The swingers, man. What a clusterfuck; running around trying to kill each other when they should have been going after Bobby.

Mrs. Mulvane had run off on him. Why was that? Oh yeah, the pictures. Fuck.

He was just starting to rise when he heard a single shot, close enough that he could see the red and yellow muzzle flash and feel the air rumble through the mist.

It didn't look like Boodrow was going to show. Kelly eased up, found a place to sit more comfortably, and risked shutting her eyes for a minute. After a little while, the sickening revolving in her head stopped.

She flipped open the cylinder of the Python and gave it a twirl. "No shit," she said with a hoarse sigh. One round.

She crawled over to Dan's body, where a thick cloud of insects had already gathered over his chest and face. Squatting, Python at the ready, she searched his soggy clothes. No .357 rounds on his belt or in his pockets. Walther PPK, empty. Her thighs started trembling, her knees gave out and she sat down hard, shaking all over.

Male voices up the hill still shouting at each other.

When the shakes had played themselves out, she unsnapped the canteen from his belt, sniffed it: water. Keeping the canteen, she pushed herself on her butt away from the body until it was out of sight. For a while after that, the dizziness and the shakes took turns harassing her as she tried to get a handle on the situation.

Mr. Mulvane was dead, Dandy Dan Dee was dead. Crogan, and probably Mr. Cross, were floating next to the Hell Hole without their heads. Faber was probably dead. Patricia and Gisela probably alive. Mary Ann was alive; she'd just heard her.

Mrs. Cross and Mrs. Mulvane were possibly hostages of Hack Weechum, probably up on Steep Rock where all the shouting was coming from. Mitch was stashed in the basement of the Mulvane cottage. And no doubt, Bobby Margin and Rae Parker were out there, armed, bent on murder, or at least some seriously aggressive self-defense. Boodrow, that little fucker, was around too.

She drank the rest of the water and let it settle.

Okay. Check the crash site for Patricia and Gisela. Kill Weechum, take his hostages into custody. Locate Mitch Herkemer or his body. Somewhere along the line, kill Boodrow.

Piece of cake.

She heard a single shot, close enough that she knew

it was a Python. Weechum had a Python. Quietly, she unwound herself and started picking her way through the trees, watching her footing on the rocks, heading uphill towards the sound of the shot.

Ugly fucking wound, Mitch thought, as he squatted over the body.

There was a short flicker of sheet lightning, followed a few seconds later by a roll of thunder.

Insight. The body on the ground was a spiritual black hole, sucking in all the free-floating, unresolved destinies in the vicinity, including his own. Swallow them whole and sort them all the fuck out. All he had to do was wait and see who showed up. He stood up and faded back into the trees.

He heard them coming.

Be cool, man. Don't think. Let the righteous Tao guide your hand.

CHAPTER
FIFTY-SEVEN

A rock turned beneath her foot. Kelly stumbled to her knees and stayed very still. She was blown out, wrung out, nearly blind. It occurred to her that she was basically just blundering through the woods now.

Cordite, blood, a hint of perfume; she was close to where the shot was fired. Feeling like a small animal that had just stepped into a trap, she eased herself into a semi-comfortable position and waited for the hammer to come down.

She couldn't hear anything above the maddening whine of mosquitoes. Movement, back the way she'd come; a shadow, a slight swirling in the mist, nothing more. She wanted to shake her head and scream. Again, she sensed movement behind her, back towards the road. Fucking Boodrow. She had to keep going uphill.

Climbing between large rocks, she reached a flat stretch of ground covered in pine needles. The path. She didn't have the strength to hold still and listen. She stood up, glanced over her shoulder, and then set off in the direction of Dead Head Bay. Walking upright, head above the mist, she forced herself not to break into a mindless, headlong run.

She heard the insects as she rounded a tight bend. That particular, frenzied whine they made when they descended on helpless flesh. Checking her six, she squatted down to have a look at the body, curiosity stronger than fear.

A woman wearing a light raincoat lay across the path, head resting on a flat rock on one side of the trail, legs, from the knees down, out of sight on the other. There was a huge gunshot wound in the side of her head, large, ragged, and wet. The exposed side of her face was badly mutilated, but she could tell it was Mrs. Mulvane.

There was a slight scuffling just inches away. Her eyes went to the sound. Out of the darkness and fog she discerned a boot. Looking up, she made out the body of a man standing beside a tree.

Looking down through the mist, long, matted hair framing his bloody face, was Mitch, hatchet in hand and a finger to his lips. Smoke and sweat radiated off him in waves; and perfume, the same perfume that clung to the stinking body at his feet. Fucking psycho lurking over his victim.

Boodrow had been right all along.

It took four or five seconds for her sluggish mind to process what she saw, then about a second and a half for the rest of it to play out.

Mitch raising the hatchet above his head.

Rocking back on her heels, feeling for balance as she hauled up the Python in slow motion to point at his chest. One round. Wait for it.

Thunder at her back. Bullets hitting the tree, chips flying at Mitch's face as he threw the hatchet at something behind her.

Whirling and rising, bringing her gun around. New target. No second thoughts.

The shooter's head jerking away from the hatchet, his revolver pointing at her.

Wait for it. Squeeze.

Boodrow, surprised, stumbling back, blood erupting from his chest.

Turning. Mitch already gone.

He was in the wrong spot.

Watch out. You're in the wrong fucking spot. Mitch wanted to shout, but he was too winded to speak.

Hack was standing at the very edge of Steep Rock, holding Denny on a rope wound around her wrists and neck. His right arm extended, pointing a Python at Bobby.

Bobby, both arms raised above his head, no weapon. Total surrender. "Okay, okay!" he shouted.

Hack yanked on the rope, pulling Denny in tighter, his left arm across her chest. Denny limp, blubbery, pleading; not stoned anymore.

"Don't hurt her, man, just hand her over," Bobby shouted, really scared.

Mitch judged the distance. Four or five good strides and he could be on top of Hack. Then what? The fucker knew exactly where he was. Make a move towards him, he steps off and they both die. Shoot him, they both die. Grapple with him, you all go over and die.

All or nothing. Turned out Hack Weechum was a fucking Zen *master*, man.

"I wanna hear it," Hack said.

"I want Denny," Bobby shouted.

"Mary Ann, you hear that?"

"She hears me," Bobby, pleading.

"Say it. Shout it."

Mitch did a fast scan. Mary Ann nowhere in sight, which meant exactly nothing.

"I don't love you, Mary Ann. I'm sorry. I want Denny."

"Make me believe you, little Bobby boy," Hack taunted him. "Who do you love, man?"

"Denny, okay. I want to go with her. I want to get away from this fucking shithole and never come back!"

Mitch held his sweaty hair back from his eyes. Really, man? Maybe Bobby was playing him, but it sure didn't sound like it.

This had to be the path to Steep Rock. She'd been up it twice, three times before. Up near the top it became steep, natural steps of limestone.

She'd shot Boo Boodrow dead. Just like that. It had taken a minute, no more than two, to get over it and plunder his body. She took his revolver and headed towards the shouting.

She was close. She could hear Weechum and someone else shouting, back and forth. One big step and she was able to see the clearing. Weechum held Mrs. Cross in front of himself like a shield, pointing a pistol at another man. Nothing but dark sky behind him.

She cleared the last step. No time to think. She charged towards Weechum. Tackle him, get his head clear of the hostage and blow him away.

Hark fired. Denny screamed as they dropped out of sight. They were there one second, gone the next, as if a trap door had opened up beneath their feet.

Then Kelly's feet went out from under her, and she was sailing headlong, arm outstretched. Landing hard; all the abused places on her body jabbing her with knives. She felt her ribs parting as her head thumped against the stony ground.

Hack's shout kept ringing in his ears, even more than Denny's cry. It was an "Oh shit," shout. The man had lost his footing. Not very Zen after all.

Mitch thinking: maybe he'd heard something more than just surprise in Hack's voice, maybe he saw something moving like jack rabbit shadow in the mist near Hack's feet. Hard to say, man. Shadow; there and gone.

Bad place to go over the edge. Big sharp rocks down below. Mitch knew that, but he was moving anyway, angling for the proper spot to line up a jump.

More of a shuffle than a run; Bobby stopped him with a hand to the chest. "Easy, Mitch, easy," he said.

"They went over," Mitch gasped.

"Yeah, I saw, man. Off by a fucking mile." There was a little shake in Bobby's voice. No more fear.

"We gotta..."

"Not a hope in hell, Mitch. Be cool, Mary Ann's gone to take a look."

"Mrs. Mulvane is dead back on the trail," Mitch said.

"Hack must've got her on the way up here."

"Where..."

"You ought to go help your friend, man, looks like she took a hell of a fall."

"What?"

Mitch followed Bobby's nod. Not more than ten

yards away, Mrs. Ratsmueller was kneeling down next to a body on the ground. Kelly.

"Come Mitch, what good are you doing there? Come and give me a hand," Mrs. Ratsmueller said, sounding annoyed.

Mitch turned and grabbed Bobby's sleeve. "Anybody else around here that we need to worry about?"

"Maybe." He bent down and picked up his hunting rifle. "I'm gonna check on Mrs. Parker, have a look around."

Mitch hustled over and knelt down opposite Mrs. Ratsmueller who was prodding the back of Kelly's skull with her long fingers. Kelly moaned.

Back there on the trail, he'd barely recognized her. Bright, red-rimmed eyes looking up at him through a tangle of wild, dirty hair. Feral; acting on instinct, whirling and shooting. He'd decided to get the hell out of there before her instincts decided to take him out too.

She lay flat on her stomach, face turned towards Mrs. Ratsmueller, her right arm outstretched with a revolver in it. Her shirt was yanked up past her waist, showing a trim of dirty wet t-shirt. Her butt and the backs of her legs were covered in mud and pine needles. Her patrol belt was gone.

"What happened?" he asked.

"She tripped. Before that, who knows? Take the gun," Mrs. Ratsmueller replied.

It was a .38, which was odd. Back on the trail he

thought for sure she'd had a Python. As he pried her fingers from her grip, she bellowed and kicked her legs.

"Sorry, man. Sorry," he said.

There was a large, round lump up near her shoulder. Mrs. Ratsmueller was calm. She probably saw a lot of these kinds of injuries coaching at the university. "Come round here. I will take the arm. We'll roll her over, carefully," she said.

"Hack Weechum and Mrs. Cross went over Steep Rock," Mitch said.

"I saw this. Bad spot, ya?" Mrs. Ratsmueller replied without looking at him.

Kelly groaned nonstop as they rolled her over onto her back. New waves of sweat washed over Mitch's body. He'd seen a lot of wounds and injuries, but there was something about dislocations that made him dizzy.

Kelly lay on her back, eyes closed, panting.

"This is not so bad; you will be fine," Mrs. Ratsmueller said as she wiped sweat from Kelly's forehead with a handkerchief.

She looked over at Mitch. "You look like a crazy hermit man," she said.

Mitch touched his cheek. "Dan cut me with an AK, can you believe that?"

"Ya, give me your shirt."

Mitch looked down at Kelly as he stripped off his shirt. "Looks like she's been through the wringer," he said.

Her face looked like hell. It was smeared with mud. Blood and pus oozed from cuts above her left eye. Bug bites were swelling up around her right eye. Her lips were swollen and chafed. There were grimy layers of sweat on her neck and arms, her skin all raw and puffy from the humidity. Mitch smelled swamp-water shit, bourbon, and bile on her breath.

Mrs. Ratsmueller was examining a fresh bruise on the side of her head.

The top buttons of Kelly's uniform shirt had been torn off. Her hat was gone, her badge was gone. There was blood on her left sleeve. Her right sleeve was torn up to the elbow. Handcuffs were fastened to her right wrist. He had no idea what the hell that was about.

Her t-shirt was pulled up in the front. Mrs. Ratsmueller traced a blue line along her white belly. "Seatbelt," she said, as she undid Kelly's belt and unbuttoned her trousers.

Kelly's breathing had settled down. Mostly, she was moaning now, not speaking. One knee was ripped out of her trousers. There was blood on her fingers and the palms of her hands. The backs of her hands were scored with puffy ridges.

"I've seen guys come out of a tiger cage that looked better than her," Mitch said.

Kelly let out a long, grinding sigh as Mrs. Ratsmueller brought her arm down to her side. Mitch handed her his balled-up shirt and watched as she gently worked it up into Kelly's armpit.

"We will be done in just one moment and then you

can have a nice, long sleep," Mrs. Ratsmueller said as she shifted into position. "Patricia has nice pills for the pain. Everything..."

In mid-sentence, she gave a decisive pull. Kelly's howl was drowned out by a new wave of rolling thunder.

CHAPTER
FIFTY-EIGHT

SATURDAY

Mitch lifted the cast iron cover plate, set it aside, and looked down into the firebox. He had just cooked a midnight breakfast for five, so he had a nice bed of coals.

He dropped the Polaroids into the stove one at a time and watched them burst into flames. They burned quickly, bubbling and curling, giving off a slight plastic smell. One by one, he watched them turn to ash. The seven spooky pictures from Bobby's stash that seemed to show a ghost lurking in the dark forest around the swinger's cottages, and the four from the envelope Lucy had given him.

Finally, the tabloid-grade picture of Bobby and Mrs. Cross caught embracing against the wall of a cottage. He jabbed at the ashes with an iron poker.

"When we're done, we'll dump the ashes in the old shitter," Rae said.

He hung the poker on the side of the stove and turned around. Two coal oil lamps gave a yellowish glow to the near end of the cookhouse. Rae was sitting at the end of the dining table, her broken leg resting on a chair. It was splinted with lengths of padded one-by-fours and professionally bound with triangle bandages from Mrs. Ratsmueller's comprehensive first aid kit. Mrs. Ratsmueller sat beside her. Dirty plates wiped clean of eggs, bacon, and steak had been pushed aside to make room for the pile of pictures laid out between them.

Outside, the storm was in a full-throated rage. Lightning framed the small, sturdy windows. Angry thunder beat the air, the wind ebbed and sighed like the ocean, but in the cookhouse, it was quiet enough to hear the hiss of the lamps. From the screened porch, deep in the darkness at the far end of the room, he heard Mary Ann's little laugh.

The storm was bound to go on all night, and even after it passed, it would be hours before the lake was calm enough for a plane to land. Bobby and Mary Ann had been out to Moose Creek and reported that the bridge was gone. Not a stick of wood left, the water still rising. Nobody would be coming to Lost Lake by road for weeks.

Six hours had passed since Hack and Denny had gone over Steep Rock. It would be another twelve, at least, before there were any visitors from the outside world. A lot of painkillers and booze had been passed around. Everybody was cool.

Rae and Mrs. Ratsmueller had divided the remaining pictures, about fifty in all, into two piles, one twice as large as the other. Rae tapped the larger pile with her finger. "Those ones go too," she said.

Mitch placed a hand on her shoulder and leaned across her warm body to look at them. "Why these ones?" he asked, as he began to gather them up.

"You can see faces," Rae replied.

"The guests. Some important people, I think. We keep them out of it," Mrs. Ratsmueller said.

"Fewer people the police have to question, the better. No big scandals," Rae added, stroking his bare arm.

Mitch turned from the pictures to look at her. She was gorgeous in the soft light; her hair, loose and unbrushed, tumbled over her shoulders, front and back, streaked with rich veins of silver. A thin bandage pushed her right eye down in a sexy half-wink. Her revolver and belt were somewhere by the door with her hat and boots.

She was as happy as he'd ever seen her. Her mouth and eyes were smiling together for a change, the effects of Patricia's Percocet and his dad's Crown Royal. With Mary Ann's help, she had washed up in the bunkhouse using the old porcelain basin and water heated on the bunkhouse stove. Mitch was sorry he'd missed that; he'd been at Patricia's, helping put Kelly to bed, then sitting impatiently while Mrs. Ratsmueller put three stitches in his cheek.

He returned to the stove and burned the new batch of pictures as carefully as the last. One by one, matching his karma against theirs and doing just fine. Most of these pictures were black and white; a few were in color. They all burned the same.

He didn't recognize any of the guests. Middle-aged people; Denny the youngest person in any of the pictures. They all looked pretty stoned or drunk. The pictures were not flattering.

Mick's idea, Mrs. Mulvane had said; something about making people look like fools. If that was their plan, then they'd succeeded. Mitch didn't feel a lick of sympathy for any of them.

Lucy was in a lot of the pictures. Life of the party in some of them, passed out drunk in others. Denny too, dancing and laughing. Mrs. Mulvane in some of them, watchful, always aware of the camera. There was nothing arousing about them. It was a shame that so many people had to die over something so dumb.

Karma, man.

He thought he recognized the man in the last picture. "Isn't this the deputy, the guy Kelly shot?" he asked, turning around, holding up the picture.

"Boodrow, ya. Burn it," Mrs. Ratsmueller said. Rae nodded.

He wasn't going to argue with them. He opened the front of the stove and gave the coals a good stirring before returning to the table where Rae and Mrs. Ratsmueller were discussing the remaining pictures.

Mitch was struck by how alike they were. Not in appearance, but in spirit. They were about the same age, both widowed. They had built modest cottages with their husbands, back in the early '50s, when the old lumber camp and the Margin shack were the only other buildings on Lost Lake.

He waited patiently, hands on Rae's shoulders, bending close to look at the pictures, enjoying the scent of his Irish Spring on her hair. They had three small piles now. One for keepers, one for burning, and the one they were working on. Mrs. Ratsmueller would hold up a picture for Rae to look at. They would decide its fate with a few words. They always agreed.

Mitch looked at the keepers. Nice, clear shots of the three swinging couples, one with Crogan, a couple with Faber. Some of them were costume party pictures; police and cowboys, cowgirls and naughty maids, all working hard at having a good time. There were a few shots that showed angry faces glaring at each other.

Down to the last pictures. About twenty keepers, ten rejects.

"We keep this one, look at Dan," Mrs. Ratsmueller said. Dan looking pissed off while Lucy entertained three men.

"No, it burns," Mitch said. He picked up two

more pictures from the pile. "These too." They showed Lucy and several men.

Rae nodded. "Ya okay," Mrs. Ratsmueller said.

He gathered up the rest of the rejects and returned to the stove.

As he burned the pictures, he listened to Rae talking, comfortably tired and boozy. He wondered if anyone was going to sleep tonight. There had been talk about the need to go back out and make sure there were no other survivors.

At first, there were bad dreams, some more like flashbacks, which kept waking her up. Creatures gnawing at her ankles, bugs biting at her face, skin burning, bleeding, sloughing off her body. Falling past an endless rock face, slamming and banging against every outcrop on the way down. Sinking, sewn into a sack with blind, scummy fish with sharp teeth. Thrashing helplessly. No gun, no bullets, no air. Trying to scream, gagging, suffocating.

Then waking, sweat sliding off her shaking skin, polluting the hospital-white bed sheets. Relief, embarrassment, bewilderment. Shouting, not screaming.

A nurse touching her gently, not trying to hold her. Speaking softly. "It's okay, you're safe now. It was only a dream."

Dozing. Drifting. Waves washing her from a sinking ship. Bound; a chainsaw sputtering in the dark.

A man with a hatchet, a thousand ghosts rising silently from misty water, staring at her.

A nurse gently restraining her when she tried to rise. "You've had a bad fall, dear, and some other misfortunes. But don't worry, you're safe now."

Her body slowly sensing the sheer, unbelievable luxury of being clean and dry, naked between crisp sheets. All her wounds tended to. Soft wavering light, the lulling beat of rain on the roof. Discovering that her arms and legs moved at will.

A kind nurse stroking her hair, soothing her. It was like being a sick little girl again. Well, if her mother had spoken with a correct Bryn Mawr accent and smelled of **Chanel** No 5, if her childhood bed had smelled like lavender and face cream.

She remembered talking. She'd needed to talk, to sort out the nightmare from reality, to make sense of it all. The nurse was willing to listen no matter how much she rambled on; asking her in a concerned, patient voice, how she got her wounds. The sympathetic nurse with sweet gin breath and an interest in guns.

"My mother called them hell raisers, and she's one who ought to know," Rae said, in the same tone she'd used while telling the story of Joe Stilwell and Peewee Shaker.

"She said every two or three years, usually in late summer, people would start talking about raisin' hell.

Everybody feeling it coming on. 'Yes sir, time to cut loose and raise a little hell.' Not talking about just any old Saturday night booze-up.

"People would congregate out on Goat Island. That way, when the fires got out of hand the village wouldn't burn down. Women and men going wild, everything free, everybody free, drinking and fornicating. Lots of fiddling and drumming. Raisin' hell, alright, and the devil calling the tune.

"Everybody havin a ball for the first day or two. But, sooner or later, *sure as shit*, things would start to turn mean. Men and women getting jealous, old grudges and feuds bubbling back up. **It** always started with smiles and laughter, and 'Drink to your health, brother. Always ended with knives and shotguns. Bodies buried in the bog."

Mitch stood still, the willies giving him the once over.

He was hearing the voice of Sarah Punk, right here in the cookhouse where it must have been heard a hundred times before, back in the day. The place smelling just the same too; bacon grease and wood smoke, coal oil and rain.

Hey Kelly, don't tell me there's no such fucking thing as ghosts.

He turned and looked at Rae. She was talking to him, her face dimly lit.

The red end of her cigarette waved vaguely towards the lake. "That's all this was. Those people, those *swingers*. They had their expensive clothes and fancy cars and big houses. They got tired of their city life, golf and cocktail parties, and shit. They got bored. They got the itch. So, they found themselves what they thought was the perfect little place to raise a little hell.

But it doesn't matter how much money you've got. The devil *will* have his due." She had a good hacking laugh at that. "They thought they were in Shangri-La, but it turned out they were in fucking Shallow Rock."

"Karma," Mitch said.

Rae shook her head. "For Christ's sake, Mitch, I just told you in plain English what it was. Why you gotta go slapping some Jap word all over it?"

Mitch smiled. Rae had insisted that his blotter go into the fire, along with most of his other illicit substances, properly crushed up.

He had heard Rae give the same explanation of events a few hours ago when they were all together at Patricia's. The swingers were just a temporary nuisance, they were never going to last on Lost Lake. Hack was different, he was violent and stubborn, a family problem that had to be settled for good and all. They were working a plan to capture him and turn him over to the police when the damn fool swingers went off their nut, going after each other in some kind of murderous, jealous spat, getting in the way.

"I would have killed any of them that put us in danger," Rae had said. "But as it turned out, we didn't have to hurt a fly. Guess that's some of your karma thing, Mitch."

He wondered about that. He wondered about the shadow at Hack's feet on Steep Rock, wondered about the big, ugly wound in Holly's head. He wondered about the bruise he'd seen on Mary Ann's shoulder yesterday morning, and about something Denny had said a million years ago when they were stoned on the lawn chairs. About how the night that Lucy died, she'd seen Sarah Punk up in the trees.

All he knew for certain was that Kelly had killed Boodrow, and Hack and Denny had fallen off Steep Rock. Besides that, there'd been a lot of shooting and shouting and random, uncalled-for *violence*, man, going on all around him.

There was one other thing he knew for sure. Bobby and Mary Ann had saved his life.

He refilled Rae's tumbler and Mrs. Ratsmueller's mug, took a box of Oreos from the cupboard and went out to the porch. Bobby and Mary Ann were spooning on the old couch, shoes off, Bobby with his shirt off, Mary Ann easily tucked into him. Freaky; only a week ago he'd been sitting right here telling Kelly the story of Sarah Punk and the Margins.

In the faint glow coming from the cookhouse, they looked angelic. They smelled far more down to earth. Neither one of them saw any sense of washing up, not with more work still to be done tonight. Their plates were wiped clean, their mugs empty, a couple of butts in the big, Black Label ashtray. If they thought there were any survivors left on Lost Lake, they weren't afraid of them.

He looked at Mary Ann's right leg. Neat bandage close to the ankle, her leg five kinds of dirty from there on up. Naked; the Bowie knife and sheath gone.

Hunting rifle on the floor, and a Chief Special .38, that Bobby must have been carrying as a backup, was on the coffee table. Next to it was Mary Ann's small pack with the butt of her Python sticking out the flap.

Mitch put the box of cookies on the table and crouched down. There wasn't enough of the gun's body sticking out for him to see if it was engraved. His hand inched towards it.

Dan Dee's Python had been found next to Boodrow's body. He figured the "Mighty Mick" had gone off Steep Rock with Hack. That left the "Omega Man." If Mary Ann had been carrying it around since Thursday morning, when Mr Cross was laying dead in the water, well, that raised some serious questions. Then again, it might be just another nickel-plated Python.

"Watcha looking for, Mitch?" Mary Ann asked, in a soft, smoky voice.

He withdrew his hand, and still crouching, turned around. Her face was as pale as the moon, both black eyes locked in on his.

"I just wanted to say it again, man, thanks for saving my life," he said.

"You shoulda heard the way you howled when them ropes come off," she replied.

"And I was wondering if there was an inscription on your Python?"

"Not that I ever seen."

Mitch nodded. Leave it at that. Righteous trust.

"Well, thanks again," he said, standing up.

"Any time, man," Bobby said, looking up at him over Mary Ann's shoulder. "When we go out later, we'll get you your hat back, too."

CHAPTER
FIFTY-NINE

Kelly was eating breakfast in Patricia's bed. Steak cut up for her into small pieces, home fries, eggs, bacon, and toast, prepared by Mitch and brought over on a tray by Gisela. She ate left-handed, her right arm in a sling. Patricia sat perched on the bed, looking elegant in a long, emerald-green nightgown, her right arm in a chic, black sling.

Kelly was ravenous. She ate, Patricia talked.

Based on her conversations with the other survivors, Kelly's nighttime ravings, and her knowledge of her decadent neighbors, Patricia had engaged her writer's imagination and created a narrative to explain the madness that had occurred on the other side of the lake.

In Patricia's story, Dan Dee and Holly Mulvane were the villains of the piece.

"The swingers had their groovy, naughty, little

scene, and it was all fun and games for a while. But these things never last. The novelty wears off and sooner or later everyone is just going through the motions," Patricia said, in a breezy tone that suggested that she'd indulged in a little, non-prescription, morning pick-me-up.

"The men went looking for bigger thrills; they hooked up with Crogan and Faber who introduced them to the evils of abduction and rape. At first, the ladies didn't know what their husbands were up to, exactly, but over time there must have been enough hints and vague boasting to make them very uneasy.

"The orgies continued. They had made a name for themselves amongst their uptight city friends and colleagues. They had an image to maintain, bosses to impress, and politicians to grease. The wives were under a terrible strain. They became difficult, there were arguments and threats.

"Denny's complaint against Bobby was a cry for help, an excuse to get the sheriff out to the Lake to talk to her. She might have broken the whole thing open, but Holly Mulvane got a grip on her and kept the focus on Bobby.

"Lucy Dee was also on the verge of a blow-up that would have exposed them all. Holly took care of her too, helping her to ingest a little too much Valium. Her death shocked and frightened Denny, who had retreated into a Serax fog by the time you and the sheriff spoke to her on Tuesday morning.

"By the next afternoon, she'd sobered up and managed to slip away from Holly. She snuck into the Dee cottage and made the ghost call, giving the most damning, if vague, information she had. There was a body hidden in Shaker's Bog."

Kelly was listening. She didn't bother to object; she was too busy stirring runny egg yolk into her home fries and shovelling them into her mouth. She was in the mood for a little light entertainment before she had to get down to the serious business of checking bodies and taking statements.

"Yes, it's all fun and games, until someone loses a wife," Patricia said with a dramatic sigh.

"Despite his jolly demeanor," she went on, "Dan Dee, the jumped-up used car salesman, had been seething with jealousy and resentment for some time. Even in the middle of an orgy, he somehow managed to be a cuckold, his wife always getting a hell of a lot more action than he was. Worse, Crogan was screwing her when he wasn't around. Not quite the way it's supposed to work, I shouldn't think.

"When Lucy died, in his dark heart he believed that his greedy playmates had accidentally killed her with rough play, the way they'd killed Susan Collins the summer before. His drug-weakened mind snapped. Faber, his only true friend, told him about the plan to move the hitchhiker's body, so he armed himself and quietly returned from Syracuse, vowing revenge. He teamed up with Faber. They caught Crogan and Cross in the water at the Hell Hole, blew their brains out, and then hurried to Lost Lake to deal with the rest of their friends.

"Hack Weechum, if not directly involved in the murder, was aware of what was going on. He had given the swingers some advice, but he was far too clever to get involved in the messy business of moving the body. Hiding out at the Cross Cottage, he must have grown concerned when Crogan and Cross failed to return. He and Mick Mulvane went to see what had happened and ran into you and Gail. After the shootout, they returned to Lost Lake and met up with Faber and Dee.

"Hack somehow got the upper hand, probably while the swingers were fighting each other. He took Mrs. Mulvane and Mrs. Cross hostage. He couldn't control them both and was forced to shoot Mrs. Mulvane. Meanwhile, back at the cottage, Dan stabbed Mick in the neck. Mick fled, but Dan and Faber caught him at the washed-out bridge and killed him.

"Returning from the bridge, they crashed into Gisela and I, who were trying to get away from the lake. They attacked us. I don't know why—perhaps to dispose of witnesses? Gisela was bent down, picking up her gun off the floor; my right leg was pinned by the seat, my right arm hanging useless. Perhaps they thought we were easy meat. I merely took my Browning from my right shoulder holster and fired left-handed. Two shots were sufficient to deal with Faber. Dan ran away before I could draw a bead on him."

Patricia's story was entertaining but didn't come close to explaining everything.

"What makes you think it was Dee who was the resentful and jealous one, and not Mulvane or Cross?" she asked.

"It's obvious from the pictures, dear..."

"The pictures?"

"Oh. Yes, I suppose we should finish up here and go downstairs. I have a few things to show you."

The Polaroids told a sordid story. After examining them, Kelly turned to the statements that Patricia had taken last night, "while events were fresh in everyone's minds." The statements were very short.

Rae had suffered a broken leg while tying up her canoe just before the storm hit. She had spent the night in her cabin with Mary Ann, Bobby, and Mitch, until this morning, when they had braved the rough water to come to the lumber camp.

Patricia and Gisela, frightened by the fires and shooting, were attempting to flee the lake when they were hit by Mr. Dee's Jeep Commando and were attacked. Patricia killed Faber in self-defense. They didn't see Kelly or Boodrow at all.

Bobby and Mitch heard the gunfire from the far end of the lake and went on foot to investigate. They checked out the burning cottages but found no one until they discovered the bodies of Mrs. Mulvane and Deputy Boodrow together on the path, halfway up Steep Rock. At the summit, they found Hack, holding Mrs. Cross hostage. Probably thinking they were cops, Hack fired at them just before he fell over the edge, taking Mrs. Cross with him.

Kelly had a sinking feeling. All of the survivors were on the same page, literally. She placed the single sheet of foolscap down on the coffee table next to the rows of Polaroids, stood up, and went to the window.

With her left hand, she gathered the fluffy white bathrobe, which Patricia had lent her, tightly around her neck. There was something close to sunlight coming through the open curtains of the lanai. The rain had stopped, the clouds were breaking up. A wicked wind still bent the trees and tossed up big whitecaps on the lake. Tall, wavering flames licked at the Dee cottage. There were big columns of smoke coming from further down the lake.

"They're still burning," she said, without turning around. "Even after all that rain."

"They flared up a couple of hours ago. Mitch and Bobby have gone to take a look, but I doubt there is anything we can do about it now," Patricia replied.

Kelly realized that the fix was in. A narrative had been chosen and it was becoming a reality, like a wall being built, brick by brick. There were the Polaroids, there were the witness statements. There was her patrol belt sitting on the coffee table, which Mitch, Gisela, and Bobby all said she'd been wearing when they'd found her. And there was her gun, which Mitch said he had taken from her hand. Her gun, not the one she had taken from Boodrow's body. Patricia had cleaned and oiled it.

"It didn't occur to me until this morning that you might have wanted it to remain, *'as is.'* I'm sorry if that's a problem. You know I simply can't abide a dirty weapon," she'd said, her face the picture of innocence.

No doubt there were many other details that had been brought into line with Patricia's narrative. There had been plenty of time to make sure that all the loose bricks were neatly cemented in place.

Kelly's memory of what had happened last night was patchy, the images filmed with misty condensation, but she was sure that her gun and belt had been taken from her before she was loaded into the Jeep. It was possible that the gun she'd taken from Boodrow's body had been her own. It was possible that sometime during that desperate, frantic night she had recovered her belt and put it on, an instinctive action that she didn't remember.

Or there could be a much simpler explanation, one that the witness statements suggested. She had not been kidnapped at all.

She turned. Patricia sat on the edge of the couch, neat as a pin, relaxed—a mason confident of her workmanship.

"I believe that, given the physical evidence, the State Police investigators will conclude that Dan Dee, in a murderous, rage, murdered Deputy Crogan and Mr. Cross at the Hell Hole, then returned to Lost Lake, killed Mr. Mulvane at the bridge, Deputy Boodrow and Mrs. Mulvane on the path, and would have finished off the rest of us if you had not put a stop to his rampage. Meanwhile, Hack killed himself and Mrs. Cross and I killed Faber in self-defense"

Kelly took a kick at Patricia's wall. "I saw Mitch on the path; he was standing in the shadows, with a hatchet..."

"Yes," Patricia interrupted, her face scrunching up sympathetically. "You said a number of silly things like that last night, dear, about Mitch and cults and ritual sacrifice. And ghosts. After what you've been through, it's normal to have nightmares, but they are best forgotten with the morning."

"Why are you doing this?" Kelly asked.

"Doing what?"

"Smoothing things over, putting everything on a nice silver platter."

"We're doing no such thing. But honestly, dear, can you imagine how frightful a long, drawn-out investigation would be? The boorish, slavering, *national* attention our little community, and we as individuals, would be subjected to. And for what? The guilty have already been punished. There are only corpses left to arrest."

Kelly had come for Weechum and Faber. They were dead. Why muddy the waters?

Patricia patted the couch next to her. Kelly sat

down. She felt cornered but not afraid. Patricia and the others had taken care of her last night, bathed her, tended to her wounds, and watched over her sleep. Last night, she had been a victim. It was going to be very difficult to transition back into being the law.

"You know I'm very fond of you, Kelly," Patricia said, taking her left hand in hers. "So, think carefully about what I have to say. Two things; first, head injuries are very tricky."

"I..."

"*Very* tricky. If you tell a crackpot story to the investigators, like the one you told me last night, with ghosts and cults, and Mystical Mitch standing in the forest with a hatchet..."

"I didn't say that."

"Something very like it, dear. People will come to the logical conclusion that you have suffered brain damage. Your testimony will be politely ignored, and your career will be finished.

"Second, which story do you think the investigators would be inclined to believe? That Deputy Boodrow was killed in the line of duty, or that he was a bad cop who kidnapped you and tried to kill you?"

Fucking Boodrow.

"Ask yourself this: do you want to be the deputy who shot her partner under dubious circumstances, or the deputy who avenged her partner's death?"

A petulant, scuff-footed kick. "What about the truth?"

"Seriously, dear? Do you know the truth?"

She did not. Fucking Boodrow, whispering reassurances in her ear as he knocked her out. Was he such a coward that he couldn't admit what a shit he was, even to himself? Or did he have a plan, a stupid, desperate plan, to try and save them both that didn't work out?

Patricia continued, firmly, reasonably. "Either Boodrow was a bad cop who tried to kill you, and you killed him. Or, he was killed by Dan Dee, and you killed Dan Dee. Either way, they are both dead, both killed by Dan's Python."

True, and they had died less than a half an hour apart, which made it impossible to know the sequence. Fair enough. She wasn't eager to admit what had happened to her. The truth made her look foolish and weak.

"It doesn't mean that you have to stop investigating the missing hitchhikers or protect Boodrow's name if it comes up. But right now, clarity and simplicity are what we need to get us all through this nightmare," Patricia said.

"You're not doing all this just for me," Kelly said. "Who else are you trying to protect?"

"Ourselves, our *sanity*, dear. Our privacy. Honestly, you have no idea what kind of a shit storm this will become if the investigation gets bogged down in unimportant detail and gets dragged out."

Kelly took a last kick at the wall. "Mary Ann was there," she said.

"You saw her?"

"I heard her."

"No one else did. And what would it matter if she was? Don't tell me, 'It's all about Sarah Punk.'"

"I didn't say that."

"Yes, you did, over and over again while you were thrashing about in your sleep. Exactly that. 'It's all about Sarah Punk. It's all about Sarah Punk. She killed them all.'"

"She instigated it. She wanted all of those people dead, especially the women."

"A ghost wanted all those people dead?"

"Not Sarah Punk, I mean Mary Ann Weechum."

"Really, dear, is that what you're going to tell the investigators when they arrive?"

Kelly looked away. The idea had come to her in the swamp, amidst the stink and the bugs, the terror, and the blood. Visions of ghosts rising in the mist. A girl with supernatural powers over men.

She didn't want to believe it, but the idea clung to her like stinking swamp water. Sarah had been at the Hell Hole the morning before the murders. She had been "up in the trees" the night that Lucy Dee died. She had been very close to where Mrs. Mulvane was killed. She was the reason that Hack Weechum and Denny Cross were standing at the very edge of Steep Rock.

"It's possible," she said, looking at Patricia.

Patricia shrugged and limply waved her good arm towards the far side of the lake.

"All this, dear? The death of six men and three women. The fire and the fury, the *madness*. That's an awful lot to put on the slim shoulders of one shy, teenage girl, don't you think?"

CHAPTER SIXTY

ONE YEAR LATER

Looking out at the lightly-misted lake, Kelly watched as Gisela secured Patricia's new Northwest Ranger to the dock. The far shore was an impenetrable tangle of green except for the stark gray slash of Steep Rock. The once-soaring Dee cottage was nothing more than a burnt-out stump almost entirely swallowed by the surrounding forest.

"Where's Mitch?" she asked.

"Over there. He wanted to have a last look around before he left," Patricia replied.

"Is he coming out with us?"

"Rae keeps her car in Shallow Rock these days. They'll be heading out through Shaker's Bog as usual."

"I'm going to have a talk with him; won't be more than an hour at the most."

"Well, don't be too long, dear. I have to maintain a certain level of sobriety to fly that thing, and I find that really quite annoying."

Kelly went on foot, trudging along the path around Deadhead Bay.

To cut down on air travel during the investigation, the state detectives had taken over the lumber camp as their headquarters. While she was working with them, Kelly had stayed with Patricia. Later, after all the fuss had died down, she was able to rent a room of her own in Trapper Lake.

The investigation had gone more smoothly than she could have imagined. The state police detectives treated her as part of their team, not as a subject of the investigation. Faced with a sprawling, complicated crime scene, they were happy to rely on her account of what had happened. They had sought clarification on a few points, but never seriously questioned her word. No physical evidence had turned up to raise doubts about anything she had said. Praised by Gail and Sheriff Herkemer, spoken of in gushing terms by Patricia, Kelly was treated as a hero. It had embarrassed the hell out of her.

The press arrived hot on the heels of the investigators. Excited by the body count and the possibility of titillating details, they clamored for information. Kelly was staggered by their numbers and aggressiveness. At the first press conference, she'd been reduced to responding with short, surly answers. Patricia had come to her rescue, drawing the spotlight to herself with a gripping account of her shootout with Faber, and then feeding the reporters with carefully chosen, spicy gossip and authoritative speculation about her neighbors across the lake.

The investigation quickly developed along the lines she suggested; there had been an explosion of jealous rage in this backwoods Shangri-La that had consumed its inhabitants, while the locals did their best to stay clear of the madness.

The next few months passed by in a blur of activity as the case was quickly wrapped up. Sheriff Herkemer retired in November. With his endorsement, Kelly ran unopposed for his job. She was Sheriff of Wanakena County before the snow started to fall.

Mitch was waiting for her, standing with his hands on his hips, ankle-deep in mist. It was hard to remember how he'd looked a year ago. He was wearing jeans instead of shorts, boots instead of running shoes. His blond hair was thick and unruly, but confined to the top of his head, drifting no lower than the bottom of his ears. Clear blue eyes, no droop at all to his eyelids. Most surprising of all, was the full beard, thick and neatly trimmed, a couple of shades darker than the hair on his head. The scar on his cheek was hard to see if you didn't already know that it was there.

Some Yogi's words running through his head. *"Only the hand that erases can write true things."*

Mitch remembered the strange feeling of being erased. In the darkest hours of Saturday morning a year ago, he had held a flashlight while Bobby poured gasoline onto the floor where he'd been cut by Dan Dee. Before lighting the place up, they'd soaked the living room couch where Rae had lain, and placed beside it, wiped clean of prints, the shotgun and hunting rifle that Bobby had handed to him that night. It turned out that they both belonged to the Mulvanes.

They found Dan Dee's AK on the north side of Shangri-La at the edge of the tree line. Wearing a pair of Patricia's gardening gloves, Mitch had cleaned his blood off of the attached blade with an oily rag. They had taken "Dirty Dan" from where Kelly had dropped it near Boodrow's body and put it next to its dead owner.

Mary Ann found his hat near Dan's body, his old boonie hat with HERKEMER printed on the inside of the headband. While the investigation was on, he'd left it hanging on a hook in Rae's kitchen. The detectives had a good laugh when he told them how he'd put a bullet hole in the brim, almost blown his own head off, clearing a jam down in My Tho.

Over the winter he'd lived with Rae and Mary Ann in Lake Placid, where she had a small house and ran one of the ski resort's bars. Mitch put in some hours behind the bar, but most of his time was spent homeschooling Bobby and Mary Ann after the court made Rae their guardian. His dad, after turning over the house attached to the police station, moved in with

Betty, who also retired in November. They were married in May.

There was another wedding coming up in a couple of days, this one down in South Carolina after Bobby graduated from the Marine Corps Depot at Parris Island. It was going to be a quick and simple affair that would ensure that he and Mary Ann were eligible for married quarters as soon as they arrived at Camp Pendleton.

Mitch heard Kelly coming up the path long before she emerged from the woods. He'd been expecting her.

"Afternoon, Sheriff," he said with a grin, extending his hand.

"Afternoon, Mitch," she replied, shaking his hand with a firm grip.

Kelly hadn't changed that much. She had lost a bit of weight, looking very comfortable in her pressed and starched uniform, campaign hat sitting perfectly level on her head. She had a gold star now, instead of a silver one, on her shirt and hat. No sunglasses. Since she'd become sheriff, she'd ditched her old aviators. She seemed happier than when he'd first met her, but still wound pretty much as tight.

They'd seen each other several times since the investigation; Kelly always curious to hear how Bobby and Mary Ann were doing, talking about the future, never the past. He knew there was a lot of shit bothering her about what had happened, and he'd wondered how long it would be before she came looking for answers.

She stood in front of him, mirroring his pose, hands on her hips. She didn't pretend to look around, didn't bother with small talk. She got right into it.

"The call from the Dee Cottage," she said. "I know it was Mary Ann. She came through the skylight, right? You or Bobby must have helped her get back out with a rope."

The investigators had questioned Mary Ann about the call, because of the "little girl" voice. They'd ended up feeling foolish, suggesting that a superstitious little girl had entered the cottage of a dead woman like some kind of international cat burglar. The answer was obvious; Denny Cross had untied the police tape, used a spare key to get into the cottage, made the call, then slipped out and re-tied the tape. With all due respect to the heroic Deputy Mackinaw, everybody screws up now and again.

"I had nothing to do with it," Mitch replied. "At the time it happened, I was passed out with Mrs. Cross and Mrs. Mulvane. They never said so, but I figure it was Bobby and Mary Ann."

"Why did they do it?"

"So you'd catch the sons of bitches and get the body out of their bog."

"Why call from the Dee's?"

"Where else was she gonna call from?"

Kelly shrugged, accepting the point, pressing on. "Why report it then, and not before? Was it because they now had you to back them up if the swingers went after them?"

Mitch thought that was funny. "They didn't trust the cops. Then you came along. Mary Ann thought that was wild. A woman deputy, maybe she could be trusted. Think about it, man, you show up and all hell breaks loose."

He could see her thinking about that. Not happy.

The detectives had gone easy on Bobby and Mary Ann. There was no reason not to. They were just innocent local kids trying to stay clear of the shit in Shallow Rock and the freaked-out weirdness on Shangri-La Lane. There was nothing to link Bobby to the swingers except for the informal complaint made by Mrs. Mulvane and Mrs. Cross, which Sheriff Herkemer had thought was bogus at the time. It was pretty obvious that Mrs. Cross, in a moment of panic, wanted to blow the whistle on her little gang, and then regretted it. It was Mrs. Mulvane's idea to accuse the local kid who was just trying to mind his own business.

Her voice got tighter as she started to get to the heart of it. "The night of the ambush at the Hell Hole, all of you were at Rae Parker's." It was the unspoken accusation that had been hanging out there between them all along. He had given it a lot of thought himself.

"Did we put together a war party, sneak out there and kill Crogan and Cross? I can tell you flat out. I didn't kill those guys, and I know that Rae didn't either."

"What about Bobby and Mary Ann?"

"I wasn't with them the whole night, but it's a

small cottage. I didn't hear them leave. I didn't see them walking around with shotguns."

He'd had a nagging suspicion that Rae's job that night was to keep him occupied so he didn't see anything suspicious or go wandering back out to the Hell Hole in his semi-stoned state. He'd put that negativity away, and as time went by Rae proved that she had more than a one-night-stand interest in him.

He didn't mention the Python Mary Ann had been carrying the next morning. There was no point, really. When the area around the Hell Hole had been dredged, they'd found two shotguns, one belonging to Mr. Cross, the other to Mr. Dee. They also found the "Omega Man" with a bullet in every chamber. The "Mighty Mick" was found on the rocks at the bottom of Steep Rock, every chamber empty.

"They could have sneaked out, slaughtered Crogan and Cross, and slipped back in without me knowing. But I saw them early the next morning; they were cool. You can't just blow people away and not be fucked up by it. It would show."

"Not if you're a couple of sociopaths. Grew up abused, neglected, never properly socialized."

"Sure, they had a rough upbringing, but Bobby and Mary Ann were good at hiding, not fighting. They spent their time sneaking around and holed up where Hack and his little gang couldn't find them. They learned to move like ghosts. Ghosts don't kill."

"Really? That's not what you told me when I got here. What about the story, Mitch? Sarah Punk. Two men with shotguns, lost in the mist, get spooked by a ghost and blow each other away. Mary Ann didn't just know the story. She lived it. Bobby lived it too."

Mitch looked away. He was pretty sure that Bobby and Mary Ann had killed Crogan and Cross. It would have been easy for them to hide near the Hell Hole and ambush them while they were in the water. They'd probably been stashing their stolen shotguns near the Hell Hole that morning when they'd found him there, tripping.

As far as he was concerned, it was straight-up self-defense. The swingers had tried to kill Bobby once, and he had reason to believe that they were going to try to kill him again. In Shallow Rock, you don't give your enemies a second chance.

Kelly's eyes were locked in on his. "I need to know if I've made a big fucking mistake here, Mitch," she said. She wasn't trying to bullshit him. She felt the weight and was trying to deal with it in a righteous manner.

"It's possible, but it's a hell of a stretch, man."

"Do *you* think they did it?"

The swingers figured they could get away with killing Bobby, because, like the hitchhikers, he was a nobody. In their world, he was; the kid had no money, no connections, the loser didn't even own a car. Problem was, they weren't in Albany or New York City; they were on Lost Lake.

Mitch had learned a hard lesson in Vietnam; understand *where* you are and *who* you're dealing with—

before you go throwing your weight around. Of course, the swingers never went to Nam; they didn't know that there are places in the world where arrogance is a capital crime.

Kelly could understand that, but it would be easier on her if she didn't know the truth. "No," he said.

Sheriff Mackinaw laughed, tension down about fifty percent. "Then it's just a coincidence that you're moving back out to the coast?"

"I've been thinking about that ever since I got here."

"Patricia just happens to have a house in San Clemente that needs a sitter."

"She's full of surprises," Mitch said with an honest nod.

"And the bar in Oceanside that you convinced her to buy, right outside the gates of Pendleton..."

"That place is a gold mine, man."

Kelly sighed, a strange sound for her. "Rae is going to hate Southern California," she said, letting it go.

"Yeah, but she's willing to give it a shot, at least till next summer, give the kids time to settle in."

"Mary Ann is going to hate Southern California."

"Nah, most of those jarheads are from the backwoods—Arkansas, West Virginia, Tennessee. She's gonna be right at home with those crackers and they're gonna *love* her."

"And you're gonna be close at hand too, just in case."

Mitch shrugged. Mary Ann had probably pushed

Hack and Denny off Steep Rock. That was still self-defense, at least as far as Hack was concerned. Mrs. Cross was just collateral damage. He couldn't fault her for that. It was possible that Mary Ann had killed Mrs. Mulvane. That bothered him. If Mary Ann had killed her, then the motive was jealously, not self-defense. That would be murder, which put a bad spin on all of the other killings.

Mrs. Mulvane was killed by a .357, the bullet too smashed up by the point-blank passage through her skull and into the rock beneath it for forensics to determine which gun it had been fired from. It was assumed that it had to come from Dee's or Mulvane's Python. After all, the "Omega Man" had been lying in the mud beside the Hell Hole from the time Mr. Cross was killed, until it was dredged up a few weeks later.

He never saw if there was anything engraved on the gun Mary Ann carried around in her small pack. He'd passed on the chance to do that Saturday morning. He never saw the gun again.

He had a recurring vision: Sarah Punk wafting along the surface of the dark, misty bog near the Hell Hole, unnoticed by the state trooper on guard inside, her white hand underwater, releasing a Python. He could see its barrel shimmer as it sank out of sight.

Just a vision, man. Just another Sarah Punk ghost story.

The strangled cry of a dying moose made them both twitch. Patricia had appeared on the dock across the lake.

"I guess that's your boarding call," Mitch laughed.

Kelly shivered. "God, I hate that thing. Do me a favor and take it with you to California, hang it up over the bar or something."

Patricia was waving at them, shouting something. Mitch strained to hear. "Sounds like she's looking for a Sheriff Saginaw," he said.

Kelly laughed. "Did you see her book?"

"The Last Siren of Shadow Lake? I read the back cover."

"Can you believe that? She took a story of infidelity, drug abuse, murder, rape, kidnapping... and turned it into a *love story*."

"Man, it *was* a love story, don't you see that?" Mitch replied.

"A back-country deputy with a chip on her shoulder and a Vietnam vet who talks to ghosts?"

"No, not that shit. Mary Ann loved Bobby Margin. When he heard that Hack had been released from prison, he quit his job, came back here to protect her, and discovered that she had been watching his back all his life. They finally got together. They beat the odds and made it out of Shallow Rock alive. I'd say that's a love story, man, with a hell of a happy ending."

ABOUT THE AUTHOR

B.E. Smith is a veteran teenage hitchhiker of the early 70's and more recently, a thirty-year veteran of the Canadian Armed Forces. He currently lives in Kingston Ontario, writing full time, still married to his resourceful and multi-talented high school sweetheart after thirty-four eventful years.

To learn more about B.E. Smith and discover more Next Chapter authors, visit our website at www.nextchapter.pub.

Shallow Rock
ISBN: 978-4-82419-936-2
Large Print

Published by
Next Chapter
2-5-6 SANNO
SANNO BRIDGE
143-0023 Ota-Ku, Tokyo
+818035793528

17th October 2024